THE CONFESSION

THE UNBROKEN SERIES: HEAVENLY RISING

SHAYLA BLACK
JENNA JACOB

DREAM WORDS LLC

THE
CONFESSION

ONE BEAUTY. TWO FRIENDS.
SHATTERING SECRETS.

THE UNBROKEN SERIES: HEAVENLY RISING THREE

NEW YORK TIMES BESTSELLING AUTHOR
SHAYLA BLACK

USA TODAY BESTSELLING AUTHOR
JENNA JACOB

THE CONFESSION
The Unbroken Series: Heavenly Rising (Book 3)
Written by Shayla Black and Jenna Jacob

ISBN: 978-1-956445-09-1

This book is an original publication by Shayla Black and Jenna Jacob

Copyright 2022 Shelley Bradley LLC and Dream Words LLC

Cover Design by: Rachel Connolly
Edited by: Shayla Black and Amy Knupp of Blue Otter
Proofread by: Fedora Chen

AUTHORS' NOTE

THE UNBROKEN SERIES: Heavenly Rising saga is a serialized succession of novels that MUST be read in order. If you've purchased this book and have not read the others in the saga, here is the reading order

The Choice
The Chase
The Confession
The Commitment (coming July 25, 2023)

We hope you enjoy reading these stories
as much as we did writing them.

Happy Reading!

Shayla Black
Jenna Jacob

ABOUT *THE CONFESSION*

One Beauty. Two Friends. Shattering Secrets.

In the aftermath of danger and death, Seth Cooper blurts his darkest secret to Dr. Kenneth "Beck" Beckman and Heavenly Young. Fearing he's shocked them, he disguises the tragic details, but it's impossible to close the Pandora's box he opened so recklessly.

After that night, Seth wages a one-man war against his ghosts while avoiding Heavenly's well-meaning comfort and Beck's probing questions. The change in Seth's demeanor makes the other two fear that their dreams of shared tomorrows are crumbling. As weeks spill into months, the strain between Beck, who's impatient to start their future, and Seth, who's doing everything to avoid it, intensifies—leaving Heavenly squarely in the middle. If she follows her white-picket-fence dreams, will Seth's refusal to give them more than half-truths break their hearts and separate them for good? Or will he finally risk confessing all so they can embrace their forever?

** Series must be read in order **

C HAPTER
ONE

E
ight years ago, I killed my wife and son.
The words Seth Cooper had spoken moments ago echoed through the room and rattled around his head. Predictably, his girlfriend, Heavenly Young, and the man he shared her with, Dr. Kenneth Beckman, just stared at him in stunned, open-mouthed silence.

Fuck.

For months, Seth had buried this confession. Now he wished he could take it back. Since he couldn't, he cleared his throat instead. "That's it. Now you know. I'm going to go help Liam start repairing the house."

Putting the mountain lodge back to rights after their battle earlier this morning with Beck's long-lost religious fanatic "family"—who had brought an army, raided the mountain, and done their utmost to kill him in retaliation for betraying their sect and felling their leader years ago—was a shitload better than the people he loved staring at him like he was a monster.

But aren't you?

Seth started to sweat. He couldn't stand here, in the bedroom where he and Beck had made love to Heavenly like it might be their last time, and deal with his past breathing down his neck while his future gripped him by the throat. He needed air. He needed to breathe.

When he turned to leave, Beck grabbed the back of his shirt and marched him to the bed. "Sit the fuck down. What do you mean you killed your wife and son?"

Beck wanted gory details? After the morning full of gunfire, death, sorrow, and loss, Seth couldn't word-vomit all this shit. He hadn't wanted to ever talk about his nightmare again. Everything felt too raw.

"Exactly what I said. Eight years ago, I was married to Autumn. We had a son, Tristan, who was three months old. And I was a cocky asshole who made stupid-ass mistakes that killed them." He sprang to his feet. "That's all I'm going to say."

Heavenly gasped, settling a gentle hand over his. "Oh, Seth. I'm so sorry. Your wife and three-month-old? That must have been devastating. Obviously, you feel guilty, but it wasn't your fault…"

He turned to her. After what he'd just confessed, his angel still wanted to touch him? Absolve him? "Worst fucking day of my life, but it *was* my fault. Every bit. It's ancient history now. No sense digging it up."

"Except it's still wrecking you," Beck pointed out. "I know you, man. You didn't kill them yourself. What happened?"

Seth's head pinged with a thousand things he could say. The horrible truth wasn't one of them. Why couldn't these two just leave it the fuck alone? The details would only make things worse, and after watching Beck's youngest brother, Zacharias, struggle to cope with his wife's and daughter's deaths… It hit too close to home.

He stood. "I can't do this right now. I've spent the last eight years trying to move the fuck on. I changed everything about my life, and I finally found some happiness. I can't go back."

Seth knew he shouldn't, but as he prowled to the door, he glanced at Heavenly. She blinked at him. Her lips trembled as she fought tears. Her wide blue eyes said she was somewhere between dumbfounded and crushed. And he'd put that expression on her face because he was doing his damnedest to outrun his demons.

Not only are you a monster but you're an asshole, too. Good job.

Before he could escape, Beck flattened his palm on the door and dropped his voice. "I get that you're in a bad place, but you can't just leave. We need to talk this out. Help us understand."

Of course Beck wasn't thrilled with his duck-and-run. The surgeon wanted him to spill his guts and explain it all away so they could go on with their happy lives. But there was no absolving him. There never would be.

If he submitted to their inquisition, it would only reinforce the fact he was a killer.

"I've told you everything you need to know. Interpret that however you want. The rest is my past, my problem, and my bullshit. Leave it the fuck alone," he growled, then he yanked the door open. He didn't dare look back before he slammed it behind him.

After Seth left, the door rattled in its frame, echoing in the still room. His anger and anguish bled into a silent scream that choked the air from Beck's lungs.

What the fuck had just happened?

Even a blind man could see that Seth was barely keeping his shit together. Beck wasn't entirely sure what was tearing him apart. Grief? Guilt? Either way, he wanted to drag Seth back and force him to spill his torment. Purge his pain. Whatever he needed. Seth couldn't just turn his back on the love the three of them had worked so hard to grow. But if Beck pushed too hard, would Seth walk away altogether?

Christ, the blood isn't even dry from my drama before another starts slicing us open.

"Beck?" Heavenly reached a quivering hand out to him. She looked stunned. He saw his own worry reflected in her eyes. "What was that? Why did Seth say he'd killed them? We both know he isn't capable of that. He doesn't mean that literally, right?"

"Seth is a protector. Despite what he says, he didn't kill them on purpose." So why had Seth convinced himself that he had?

Wrapping his arms around her, Beck drew Heavenly close, providing her a necessary anchor as he kissed the top of her head.

"I know he didn't." A heartbeat passed, then she peered up at him. "We'll talk to him again when he's less upset. But what about you? You went through a lot this morning. How are you doing?"

Beck sighed. "Honestly, I'm feeling guilty as hell. Adam's dead, and Dean… I don't know if he's going to make it," he said of the lodge's caretaker and his police officer friend. "They'd both still be here if not for me. Their blood is on my hands."

Heavenly shook her head, her blond curls brushing her arms.

"They didn't have to come and fight. They *chose* to. We all supported and defended you because we love you."

"And I'm so fucking grateful. But I wish Jedediah and Esther had never sent Zacharias to find me. I wrote my biological family off a long time ago. Why couldn't they do the same and go on with their miserable fucking lives?" And leave Gloria out of their delusional bullshit, too.

Heavenly pressed herself against him. "Because they were horrible people. I'm so sorry your brother and his crazy followers attacked you, so sorry you had to kill your own flesh and blood…"

"To me, they were nothing but depraved zealots, hungry for power and revenge. None of those bodies outside have meant a thing to me since I left Messiah City." He tilted Heavenly's head back, cupped her cheek, and gazed into her eyes. "You and Seth are my family now."

"You're my family, too." She teared up. "I'm worried about Seth. I don't know what to say or how to help him."

Beck felt clueless, too. "Let me find him, talk to him. If I go for a few minutes, will you be okay?"

"Of course, but maybe I should go with you."

Whatever secrets Seth was keeping, was he more likely to spill them if Heavenly wasn't within earshot? "Let me approach him first, man-to-man. I don't know if he's reluctant to talk because he's ashamed. The male ego can be a fragile thing."

Reluctantly, she nodded. "Make sure he knows we love him."

"He knows, but I'll remind him." He kissed her softly. "I won't be long."

Beck caught her worried expression as he left the room. That alone made him want to punch Seth first and ask questions later. Unfortunately, if he landed the first blow, the heavy-fisted PI might knock him out, like he had Pike a few months back. And violence wasn't going to solve what was wrong between them.

Looks like it's going to be a cage match of words.

As Beck shut the door and started down the stairs, he glanced down to find Seth's pal, Liam O'Neill, ascending.

"Ah, you're just the man I wanted to see." The Irishman headed straight for him.

"I'm damn sorry about the damage your lodge sustained. I'll pay for the repairs. Tell me how we can help clean up this mess."

Liam waved his offer away. "No worries. My biggest concern isn't the lodge. If you want to help, get Seth home as fast as you can. Circumstances are taking a toll on him."

Was Liam's infamous woo-woo—the psychic ability he'd seemingly inherited from his mother—kicking in? Or had Seth opened up to his old friend? "You and Seth go way back, don't you?"

"A decade."

"So…you know about his wife and son? How they died?"

Liam reared back, clearly shocked. "He told you about them?"

Beck nodded. "He says he killed them."

"That's how he sees it."

"Why? He didn't really kill them, did he?"

"I can't answer that without breaking his confidence. All I can do is recommend that you and Heavenly pack your bags and take him home."

"All right. We can do that, but I'm worried. Heavenly is near tears. Seth won't talk to us. If you can give us an idea of what really happened to Autumn and Tristan so we can help him—"

"It's not my tale to tell. When he's ready to say more, he will."

"What's holding him back? Is he seriously worried that Heavenly and I won't look at him the same way? Or that we won't love him anymore?"

"Aye. You thought the same thing twenty-four hours ago before you told everyone about your childhood in Messiah City and how you escaped. So you should understand, mate." He clapped Beck on the shoulder. "You were just there."

"But all my worries were unfounded bullshit. I fucking sliced my biological father's throat, and not one person here turned their back on me. Seth must see that."

"It's not the same. You had a bloody good reason for killing him. The man was a monster. Autumn and Tristan were innocents. They were Seth's world."

Liam's words were a gut punch. "You still can't convince me that he intentionally killed them. I'll get him home and keep trying to open him up. When he's ready to talk, I'll listen and help put him back together, just like he did with me."

"When that day comes, you will." A ghost of a smile played at the edges of Liam's mouth. "Go now."

"Thanks, man." Beck offered Liam his hand.

The other man pulled him in for a hug instead, and Beck was glad they had finally, truly become friends.

Then they both retraced their steps, Liam descending the stairs and Beck disappearing into the bedroom once more.

Heavenly was waiting, anxiously wringing her hands. "You weren't gone long. What did he say?"

"I didn't talk to Seth. Liam stopped me on the staircase. He says it would be best for us to pack up and take Seth home now.

Understanding lit her eyes. "Liam is worried about him, too?"

"Yeah." Beck sighed as he dragged their suitcases from the back of the closet and tossed them on the bed. "That worries the hell out of me."

"Me, too. I'll help you pack everything, then we'll get on the road. Hopefully, leaving here will help calm Seth's distress. Maybe if he's less...angry? Upset?" She shrugged. "Or whatever that was, then he'll open up."

Maybe. But Beck had a suspicion they'd need a crowbar, too. Seth seemed locked up tight.

They worked in near silence as they emptied the closet, drawers, and bathroom. As Beck zipped the last suitcase shut, Heavenly picked up her tote and nibbled nervously on her lip. "Ready?"

Beck scanned the room. "I think that's everything. I'll start loading the car."

"I'll find Seth. Any idea where to start?"

"Somewhere downstairs." Beck pulled her into his arms, stroking a palm up her stiff back. "Hey, don't worry. We'll work this out, little girl. Seth moved across the country to be with you. He followed you to Vegas. He flew to Wisconsin to help you say goodbye to your dad. He's been there every time you've needed him. He won't just walk away."

The worry etched into her expression said she wasn't convinced.

"But when I upset him last Christmas, he left me and flew back to New York. I didn't hear from him for months. What if Seth doesn't want to come home with us now?"

Her fear wasn't unfounded, but Beck didn't want her assuming the worst. "He will. Let him know we're leaving. I'll be close if you need me."

"What excuse can I give him? Raine, Liam, and Hammer are staying at least until morning. Gloria and Buddy, too," she said of Beck's ex-wife and her fiancé. "What if he questions why we're suddenly eager to go?"

"Tell him I want to get back to LA and check on Dean. It's not a lie. I'm anxious to see how he's doing and how River is holding up." Since his best friend was gravely injured, Raine's brother was probably a mess.

She nodded. "He won't argue with that. But you know it's not your fault your fam—I mean, those crazy people—attacked us?"

Beck loved that she was trying to take some stress off of him. "Yeah. But I'm crazy, too."

"How?"

"Crazy about you." Beck pressed his lips to hers, kissing off her little smile. Then he hugged her tight one last time before grabbing all their luggage. "Let's go say goodbye to everyone."

Without a word, she followed him downstairs. When they reached the main level, Beck stacked the suitcases beside the front door. When he turned, he caught sight of Liam in the kitchen. The rest of the group had clustered in the living room, which overlooked the back of the house. And through the windows, leaning over the porch railing, Seth stood, gazing across the pool and staring at the breathtaking vistas of the mountains and tall pines in the distance.

He looked solitary as fuck.

Stifling a curse, Beck threaded his fingers through Heavenly's, then led her toward the others. "I hate to cut this party short since we had such a banging good time, but we're, um"—he gestured toward Seth—"heading home."

Gloria swatted his arm. "Kenneth Beckman, what an awful joke!"

"Too soon?" he quipped.

His ex-wife gazed across the porch at Seth. "Obviously."

"How long has he been out there?" Beck asked.

Liam approached, looking grim. "Since I ran into you on the stairs."

"What's wrong?" Gloria asked.

Heavenly shrugged. "We think the horrible things that happened here today were too much for him."

"The death?" Gloria sent them a dubious frown. "He was a homicide detective—in New York City. He's seen far worse."

"Maybe PTSD?" Beck offered, not that he expected his ex-wife to buy that, but if Seth didn't want to share his secrets with the people he loved, he wouldn't want them shared with everyone else. "After all, there was a reason he quit the force."

"Whatever's going on, he's really upset." Heavenly tried to hold her emotions in and failed miserably. "He's shutting us out."

"Oh, honey," Gloria cooed, dragging Heavenly into her arms. "He'll come around. Trust me. When it comes to men, I'm an expert. You just need to give him some time."

"She's right," Raine added with an encouraging best-friend smile. "Today was a lot for everyone. I'm sure he'll be fine once he has time to process."

"I hope you're right, princess." Beck squeezed her shoulder. The carnage couldn't have been easy on the woman who'd had to kill her father. They had that in common.

"I am. Time really does heal all wounds."

Heavenly took Raine's hand and squeezed. "Thanks. How long are you three planning to stay?"

"Liam will be meeting with some contractors tomorrow. We intended to stay for Adam's funeral, but Ngaire says she's flying him back home to Oregon. We'd attend, but she wants to keep her husband's service to immediate family only. So we'll probably be home Sunday morning. I'll call you. Maybe we can all get together for dinner one night next week?"

"I'd like that." Heavenly did her best to smile.

But she was probably thinking what Beck was—they'd get together if Seth was doing better by then. If not... He really didn't want to consider that. Seth closing himself off from them would tear them apart.

After hugs and goodbyes, Heavenly stepped away from Gloria and Raine, then turned her attention to Seth, still alone on the porch.

Gut tensing, Beck clapped Buddy on the shoulder, then released Liam's hand. "Thanks again, man. For everything. I owe you. Send me the bill for the repairs—"

"We'll deal with it later. You have bigger worries now." Liam's gaze followed Heavenly walking softly toward the back door.

"You going to be all right?" Hammer asked.

His old friend asked a great fucking question. "All I can do is try, man. You all take care. I'll send you updates on Dean once I've seen him."

The men nodded, then he turned to Gloria, wrapping her in a tight hug. She patted his back, then eased away with a reassuring smile.

"Heavenly, I'm going to load up the car. If Seth gives you any shit about leaving, blame it on me."

She shook her head. "Hopefully, it won't come to that."

Then she reached a shaking hand to the back door. It glided open as Beck grabbed the suitcases and hauled them out. He slid into the driver's seat and waited, hoping that a change of scenery was all Seth needed.

If not, Beck didn't know what the fuck he was going to do.

Heavenly let herself out the back door of Liam's luxurious lodge, the chilly mountain air brushing her face. Since Beck's biological family and The Chosen from Messiah City had attacked the place from the front, the damage sustained around back was almost nonexistent. Here, she saw no sign of law enforcement, bodies, or coroners. It would be tempting to pretend the deadly battle had never happened.

She wasn't surprised Seth had chosen the most peaceful place on the property to brood. Though she didn't quite understand his reaction to the fight, she understood loss and the need for solace, the desire for a moment's escape. It had only been three weeks since she'd lost her beloved father.

"Hi," she said softly. "Mind some company?"

Seth turned. The stiff lines she'd seen in his posture didn't show on his carefully blank face. When he caught sight of her, he pasted on a smile and opened his arms. "Angel, come here. I always want your company."

She complied, trying to decide what to say next. They should talk about his outburst. But if she pressed too hard, she'd already seen how he would react. If she went on as if nothing had happened, she might never hear the truth. She didn't have to know everything right now... but soon. He was hurting, and getting it out could only help him manage the pain.

Seth wrapped an arm around her shoulders and dropped a kiss to her head. "If you're coming to check on me, you don't need to worry. I just had a moment. I'm okay now. I'm sorry for the outburst."

The tension in his body said otherwise. Was he trying to fool her? Or himself?

"I understand." She sidestepped the topic with a wan smile. "I just came to tell you that Beck and I packed everything up, and he's loading the car. We thought it best if we all headed home."

Seth blinked in surprise. "I assumed we were going to stay and help Liam clean up the place."

If that was the case, why had Seth been out here, doing his utmost to put distance between himself and the massacre in the front yard?

"Beck wants to look in on Dean, see if he can help in any way. And we're both a little worried about River falling apart."

"I should have thought about that. And you're both ready now?"

She nodded. "We just said goodbye to everyone. Beck is probably waiting in the car."

He seemed taken aback but plastered on another happy expression and took her hand. "Okay. Let's go."

Inside the lodge, he bid a quick farewell to the others. Liam pinned him with a long, probing glance. Seth responded with the same plastic smile. Heavenly didn't like it. She really hoped that getting away from all the dead bodies and settling in at Beck's house—their new shared home—would help soothe him.

After a last wave at the front door, Seth followed Heavenly outside, wrapping an arm around her and all but dragging her to the SUV. He helped her into the backseat, then followed, planting himself beside her and shutting the door.

She frowned. "You're not going to sit up front?"

"Is it okay that I'd rather cuddle with you?" He flashed her his most charming smile, his gaze focused on her.

To avoid looking at the corpses littering the yard? Honestly, she couldn't blame him. They made her queasy. She especially hated knowing that every one of those now departed was somebody's child, parent, spouse, sibling, or friend. But as Gloria had pointed out, Seth had been a homicide detective. Compassion aside, dead bodies shouldn't bother him.

"Of course it's okay." She buckled her seat belt and met Beck's frown in the rearview mirror.

He looked worried.

Seth buckled up, then took her hand, bringing it to his lips for a kiss as Beck put the car in reverse.

"Stop. There's a pile of crispy critters right behind you," Seth warned as he glanced out the back windshield.

A woman wearing a drab blue FBI windbreaker appeared, stepping behind the SUV and holding up a hand to protect the charred corpses. Beck stepped on the brakes, put the car in gear, then headed down the gravel road. Seth continued peering out the back window.

Clearly, bodies didn't bother him.

"Thanks for packing up, man." He clapped Beck's shoulder, then sat back. "If I had known you wanted to leave, I would have helped."

"No problem. Heavenly and I managed pretty quickly."

Silence fell again as Beck turned onto the paved road. The atmosphere in the car wasn't awkward...but it wasn't comfortable, either.

From the front seat, a phone buzzed, breaking the quiet. Beck swore and unlocked the phone with his face, then passed the device back to Heavenly. "It's a text. Would you make sure it's not from the hospital?"

She opened his messages, then read the most recent with a sigh of relief. "It's from River. He says Dean just got out of surgery and is heading to recovery. All went well. They're going to keep him overnight. River will send details when he has them."

"Thank God." Beck heaved out an audible breath. "Tell him I'll be there as soon as I can."

Adam's death was probably weighing on him. Losing one person who had helped save him from his biological family's vengeance was difficult on Beck. Losing another, especially a friend, would be almost unbearable.

"Of course." Heavenly laid a gentle hand on his shoulder. "Sounds like he's going to be fine."

"And River should have his tag-team partner back soon," Seth quipped.

"So they can pick up random women in bars for the night." She wrinkled her nose. "I don't know whether to be grateful or insulted that River refused to take my virginity."

"Be grateful," Beck groused.

"Absolutely," Seth cut in. "Or I'd have to kill him."

Beck nodded. "I'd have to help you."

"And that might make strife between you and your bestie." Seth raised a brow at her.

Heavenly rolled her eyes. "You think?"

The moment felt almost normal. The smiles, the quips, the gentle teasing… She'd grown used to conversations like this with her men.

Was it possible she'd overreacted at the lodge? Seth was keeping secrets, no two ways about that. But maybe he'd just been too overcome to talk about it in the moment. He'd explain everything in time, right?

As if Seth could read her mind, he cleared his throat and took her hand, regret all over his face. "I owe you two an apology. I was out of line this morning. I don't really talk about Autumn and Tristan with anyone. It's still painful. When you asked me for details, I wasn't braced, and I lashed out. I'm sorry for upsetting you."

Heavenly softened. "Of course it's painful. I'm sure the grief has been difficult to overcome."

He swallowed. "I was a widower at twenty-four. It was inconceivable. And losing a child, too? There isn't even a word in the English language for someone whose child has died. You said earlier that it must have been devastating. It was beyond that. Honestly, my family was really worried about me. My mom had been raising us boys alone for years, and by then I was grown and married, so she thought she only had my younger brothers to worry about. But after Autumn and Tristan were gone…I wasn't okay for a long time. I know she worried and prayed and tried a hundred ways to make me want to live again—with good reason. I went off the deep end for a while and did things I'm not proud of." He paused. "It took me over a year to find any peace. It was several more before I could even talk about them without anger threatening to swallow me whole. For a long time, everyone I allowed in my life knew what had happened, and they all knew I didn't want to talk about it. I've known for a while I would have to explain this to you. I just didn't know what to say or how to say it. The details are still just…"

In every corner of her soul, she ached for him. "Too difficult? Oh, Seth…"

When she threw her arms around him, he dragged her against his body and held tight, as if he could take her strength through their embrace. She soothed a palm across his back and whispered words of reassurance, wishing she could erase his suffering.

Finally, he broke away, pressing a soft kiss to her forehead, then her lips before he cast a glance up to Beck in the rearview mirror. "Thanks for understanding. It means the world to me. I'm sorry I made today about me when you just went through a whole ration of shit with the people you used to call family. You okay, man?"

"Much better now that I know the past can't come back to haunt me anymore," Beck assured.

Seth shifted in his seat, his nod noncommittal. "What are the odds the rest of The Chosen come looking for revenge?"

"Against me?" Beck shrugged. "We won't know until after the raid on Messiah City tonight. Right now all those freaks and pedophiles are living their disgusting lives, twisting the word of God into their justification for violating little girls. After the feds shut them down, we'll see what happens. But as far as they know, Gideon is dead. I plan to keep it that way."

"Sure, but if they got wind you had anything to do with killing their Messiah and shutting them down…"

"There would be hell to pay, and I'm worried they wouldn't just take their anger out on me." Beck glanced her way in the rearview mirror again.

Heavenly shuddered. She couldn't imagine what girls in that horrible town suffered or why their parents condoned and encouraged such depravity. She was grateful Beck had found his way out. Hopefully, he'd never have to deal with any of The Chosen again, and anyone violent enough to seek vengeance would be behind bars.

Except Zacharias. He had decided to do the brave thing and declare himself Messiah in the wake of Jedediah's death—then let the FBI in to round up the elders and shut down their sect. Heavenly could only imagine how difficult that choice had been. She hoped the man found peace someday.

"I'm always careful," she reassured him. "And you two make sure I'm rarely out alone."

"We don't want anything to happen to you." Beck's voice sounded soft but determined over the faint hum of the engine.

Seth gripped her hand. "Ever. I can't lose you, angel."

After everything he'd been through? Heavenly could only imagine how more loss would crush him. "You won't."

They fell silent. Maybe it was her imagination, but the air between them seemed to turn heavy and tense. A change of subject might do them all good…

"Are you planning to return to the hospital on Monday?" she asked Beck.

He nodded. "But I'll probably do some quick rounds tonight. I have a few patients I should check on."

"I might go with you, see if I can catch Bridget and Jennifer," she said of her nursing director and her supervisor. "I should thank them for their flexibility. We left yesterday with so little warning, and in spite of the time I took off to deal with my dad's passing, they've been really understanding."

"They're great," Beck replied.

"You only have a few weeks left of volunteering to satisfy your school requirement, right?" Seth asked.

"Three, but I'm going to continue putting in as many hours as I can so Bridget still wants to hire me once I graduate."

"She will," Beck assured without pause. "Believe me."

"I'm proud of you." Seth kissed her temple. "Even with all the adversity and upheaval, you've managed to keep going and make great grades. Your dad would be proud of you."

His words melted Heavenly. When Daddy had been alive, he hadn't agreed with her decision to have a relationship with two men. But even before Abel Young's passing, Beck and Seth had cared for her in every way she'd needed. And, through Liam, she knew now that her father understood and approved of the path she had chosen with her men. "Thanks. I think you're right."

Seth smiled. "Just one more year of nursing school. You got this."

"If all goes well." She looked forward to finishing almost as much as she worried she'd never be ready.

"It will," he assured, wrapping an arm around her and pulling her close. "You're going to be an amazing, compassionate nurse."

"I hope. I'll do my best."

"You always do." He gave her a squeeze. "You were even brave this morning."

"Hiding in the wine cellar?"

"Relying on those of us who have been in combat to keep you safe. I know from experience that waiting and wondering for an outcome isn't any easier. But I'm also glad you and the other women didn't have to witness what happened."

She was, too. Her friends were so intrepid. During the battle, Gloria had been itching to leave the safety of the underground shelter and protect everyone alongside the men. Even Raine had seemed eager to lend her gun. Heavenly wished she had that sort of spirit. "We had no idea what was going on, and we were worried as heck about all of you. The sounds of the gunfire… It was terrifying. The not knowing if you two were okay nearly killed me."

"We're fine." He soothed her with a tender caress. "Don't think about it anymore."

Easier said than done, especially since the aftermath of the incident had affected Seth so much. He was almost back to his usual self...but not quite. He seemed a little louder, a little more animated, a little more determined to fill the conversational lulls. And what if they couldn't keep Beck's name and his past with The Chosen out of the press? They might be besieged by violent sect members or their sympathizers, some of them threatening or vengeful. That worried her almost as much as the distance she'd felt Seth shoving between her and Beck earlier.

With nothing to say, quiet pervaded the car. Beck looked deep in thought, slanting the occasional considering glance at Seth in the mirror. Was he wondering, just as she was, whether Seth was truly okay and if the tragedy in his shocking past would continue driving a wedge between them?

"Hey, man," Seth called to Beck. "Mind turning the radio up? I like that song."

Heavenly hadn't even been aware of the music playing.

Beck complied, and some suggestive, summer-themed pop song poured through the speakers. It didn't seem like Seth's sort of music, but she listened along as it filled the car and he tapped his toe. That song bled into another, a slower ballad about a couple reuniting after a long separation. He hummed along almost earnestly, as if he couldn't stand even a moment's silence.

She caught Beck's worried gaze in the rearview mirror. Without a word, she knew they both agreed that Seth might be trying to act normally, like nothing had happened. But it was a lie.

After the third song, Seth fidgeted in his seat again and glanced at the clock. "Beck, mind turning down the radio?"

He lowered the volume. "Got something to say?"

"No, but that song sucks. It's overplayed. And I need to call my mom and let her know I'm okay before the news about the raid goes public. I didn't tell her where I was when I texted her, but I told her to watch the news. Once she hears there was a gun battle, she'll freak."

He tugged his phone from his pocket and hit the button for his mom's contact.

Heavenly watched, wondering how much Seth had told his family about her. About the three of them. She didn't know much about the Cooper clan, just the basics. His mom had been widowed after his father, a police officer, had died in the line of duty when Seth was just sixteen, leaving him to be the father figure to four younger brothers—Matt, who had taken over his PI business back in New York, Danny, who was married and had made Seth an uncle last Christmas, and twins, Jack and Connor, who would graduate from college next year. His mother still lived in New York, in the house Seth had grown up in, and after all these years, she was finally engaged to a man named Carl, who made her happy. Oh, and she was very traditionally Catholic. Would Grace Cooper ever accept the three of them together?

Heavenly didn't let her worry show as Seth waited for Grace to pick up.

"Hey, Mom!" A pause. "Yeah, I'm fine. I didn't want you to worry, so when you hear the news tonight, yes, I was in Big Bear, but I don't have a scratch on me. And no, I'm not in Messiah City, so don't worry about that. I'm headed back to LA now."

The woman had plenty to say, if the earful spilling from Seth's phone was any indication, but he let her talk, answering with a single syllable or a grunt whenever necessary. Then he started asking the woman questions. Actual curiosity on his part…or intentional deflections to avoid real conversation? Heavenly hated to be suspicious, but it was as if their earlier argument had given her a new lens through which to view Seth.

Whatever his mother said made him grumble, then laugh. They exchanged what sounded like some inside jokes. Then suddenly, he turned serious. "Sure, I'm listening. And before you ask, yes, it's *way* too early to be talking about Christmas."

Vaguely, Heavenly heard his mother sass back, then her voice softened.

A few moments later, Seth's face tightened. "You and Carl already picked a date?" He paused to listen. "October fifth? Of course I'll be there. Absolutely. Keep me posted." When Grace spoke Seth froze, looking floored. Then he smiled. "Oh, Mom… Are you sure?" Another pause. "Hell, yeah, I'll walk you down the aisle. I'm honored you asked."

His mother rattled on for a few minutes, and Heavenly heard emotions in the woman's murmurings, even though she couldn't hear the words. Then she suddenly said something that sounded like a question. Seth turned Heavenly's way. "I'll talk to her. You know she's in nursing school…" Grace cut in briefly. "Yeah. I'll get back to you as soon as I can. Congrats, Mom." Another pause. "Of course. I love you, too. I'll talk to you soon."

"Everything okay back home?" Heavenly asked as he ended the call.

Seth sat in silence before turning her way. "Yeah. How do you feel about coming to my mother's wedding to meet my family? She's dying for you to join us. She can't wait to meet the girl who convinced me to move to Cali and start living again. What do you say?"

Chapter Two

So Seth wanted to take Heavenly home for his mom's wedding? Great. Since the PI hadn't once mentioned his name, Beck had a bad feeling he wasn't invited.

He glanced back in the rearview mirror, watching Seth take Heavenly's hands with an expectant smile. She merely nibbled her bottom lip in return. She wasn't jumping at the chance to meet the Cooper clan?

For a brief moment, Heavenly met Beck's stare. Yeah, she was aware Seth hadn't invited him.

"I'd love to meet your family," she finally said. "But are you sure this is the right occasion?"

"Absolutely. Everyone will be there for Mom's wedding. All my aunts, uncles, and cousins… They're dying to meet you. Mom specifically asked if you'd come."

"I don't know if—"

"They're going to like you? Angel, don't worry. They're going to love you."

"That's a given," Beck added. "But…where am I in this picture?"

Seth's smile flattened. Guilt skipped across his face. "It would be great if you could come, too, man. It's just…"

"What?"

"I don't think the wedding is the time to bring our relationship out of the closet. My mom is traditional. Hell, she's a devout Catholic… like, really devout. She believes in the whole one-man, one-woman thing. If the two of us showed up together with Heavenly, she'd lose it."

"How do you know? She might be more open-minded than you think," Beck pressed.

"She's not. Trust me." Seth sighed. "When I went home last Christmas, I told her about Liam, Raine, and Hammer. To say she was shocked would be an understatement. Then she dissected me with that mom stare and made me swear I wasn't in any kind of polyamorous relationship. At the time, I wasn't."

"So that's it?"

"I'd truly love for you to be there with us. But try to understand. Mom's waited sixteen years to find love again. If we showed up as a throuple, it would overshadow her wedding day. I can't do that to her."

So where did that leave him, being the dirty little secret?

"Maybe we could call her and explain before the wedding? So it wouldn't be a shock when we arrived." Heavenly's helpful suggestion melted Beck's heart. "October is a long way off. That gives her time to adjust."

"Good idea," Beck praised, then glanced Seth's way. "Have a heart-to-heart with her. Since your family worried about you in the past, I'm sure they'd be thrilled that you're happy now, especially your mom."

"She wants me to be happy, for sure…but this isn't the kind of news I should break to her over the phone. I would have to explain this delicately, in person."

Beck tried to understand, but it felt like excuses. Then again, he hadn't given a shit what his family thought about him in nearly two decades.

"All right. So go for a visit. You have almost six months, so you should be able to find a time to tell her," Beck countered.

"If I thought it would be that easy, I'd be on a plane tomorrow. But I know my mom. It's going to take her a long while before she approves of this." Seth swept his hand over the three of them. "If she ever does."

A worried frown knitted Heavenly's brows. Granted, she hadn't been forthcoming about her hardships earlier in their relationship. But Seth rejecting every well-meaning suggestion to tell his mother the truth felt different, at least to Beck. Heavenly had hidden her problems from them out of misplaced pride and a desire to preserve her independence. So what was Seth's issue? That wasn't clear. And the fact he was pushing Heavenly to play a part in his subterfuge clearly worried her.

It worried Beck, too. And it pissed him off. If Seth wasn't going to tell his stick-up-her-ass mother about them anytime in the next six months, when did he envision telling her…if ever?

"So I'm supposed to…what? Stay in LA with my dick in my hand while you and Heavenly fly off to New York to meet your family and play the happy couple?"

Beck gave zero fucks that he sounded somewhere between petulant and combative when Seth's refusal to even broach the subject with his mom seemed ten times more childish.

"That's not what—"

"Guys. Guys. Hold up," Heavenly intervened. "None of us wants Grace upset on her wedding day."

No. Beck simply wanted Seth to grow a pair and be honest…with everyone. "Listen, when we took Heavenly to visit her father in the hospital, she didn't ask one of us to stand in the hall to avoid upsetting Abel. And he was on his deathbed. So what's your excuse?"

"She went to say goodbye. We weren't confessing that we were both in love with his daughter," Seth scoffed.

"The hell we weren't. Maybe we didn't say it out loud, but we both had our hands on her as we promised to take care of her. What other interpretation was the man supposed to have?"

"That's true." Heavenly frowned. "And at the time, I was angry. Not only about him dying but because we spent some of our last precious minutes together discussing my life choices. He died worrying about me. He was disappointed. Thanks to Liam channeling my dad, I know now that he understands how much you both love me and he's resting peacefully because I followed my heart. But I was gutted for weeks because I thought I'd failed him."

Shit. Beck hadn't known that, while Abel lay dying in her arms, Heavenly had been drowning in guilt for being in love with both him and Seth. None of them had handled that well. Regret pressed in.

How had she not resented the hell out of them these past weeks? Only because she had a huge heart and an unending gift for forgiveness. Maybe it was time he followed her lead and showed some compassion, instead of throwing a righteous fit.

"I'm not trying to be a dick. I'm just trying to figure out how you envision telling your family about us."

"I get it." Seth sighed. "But you know better than anyone how religion can color your view of the world. How something good and loving can be seen as something obscene and wrong."

"Don't preach to me about religion," Beck bit out, gripping the steering wheel tighter. "Especially since I'm convinced this is about more. But you can't not tell your mother."

"I know. And I don't need you to goddamn tell me how to deal with my family."

"Enough!" Heavenly spat. "Clearly, we're not going to resolve this right now. So, just...drop it. Both of you. Please. There's been enough fighting for one day."

Beck swallowed the ugly retort he'd cued up for Seth and saved it for later. He wasn't about to let Cooper sweep this wedding bullshit under the rug, but he also didn't want to upset Heavenly. There really had been enough bullets, bloodshed, and bombshells. At least for today.

"You're right, little girl." Beck nodded.

"Sorry, angel. I didn't mean to upset you. Let me think about this." He patted her thigh, then shoved a pair of buds into his ears.

Glancing in the rearview mirror, Beck watched Seth tap his phone, lean his head back, close his eyes, and tune them out.

Cursing inwardly, he met Heavenly's stare in the mirror. He saw his own unsettling worry etched on her face.

"We'll get everything worked out." At least he hoped they would.

She nodded, doubt shimmering in her eyes—along with pooling tears—before she inched to the far side of the SUV and stared out the window.

Damn it. Somehow, he had to save them from falling apart. They'd come too far together to give up.

As the miles slipped away, Beck called on the knowledge he'd gained during his psych rotation. While Seth wasn't presenting any serious mental disorders, he had a slew of defense mechanisms. His favorite? Denial.

Beck was still tossing a theory around in his head and trying to decide what to do when Seth started snoring.

Heavenly shot him a concerned stare, then shed her seat belt to climb over the console. Beck watched from the corner of his eye until she settled in the seat beside him. Then she leaned in to softly kiss his cheek—melting his heart—before buckling up again.

He sent her a smile and threaded his fingers through hers, drawing her hand to his lips and brushing them across her knuckles.

"I'm sorry I barked at you both," she murmured. "The way you two were snarling at each other worried me."

"Don't be sorry. We weren't getting anywhere but angrier."

She nodded. "True, but I don't know what I'd do if I lost either of you."

It was ironic that Seth had helped teach Heavenly how to voice her fears so openly, yet he couldn't find the courage or trust to do the same.

"You're not losing me, little girl. You're stuck with me forever."

"I'm glad, but this wedding thing…" She sighed. "I'm torn. I see where you're both coming from. There's no right or wrong. I get why Seth doesn't want to disrupt his mom's special day. I also understand how it would crush you if we just jetted off to New York and left you behind."

"That's not what's upsetting me. I'm a big boy. It's the fact that Seth seems determined to hide our relationship. How's that going to work?"

"I don't know. Since he's also a big boy, he needs to come clean with his mom, just…not on her wedding day. But if he doesn't, what happens in the future? What about when the holidays roll around? Is he going to stay in LA with us or fly home to New York? If I meet his family at the wedding, they're going to expect me to come with him. But I can't do that without leaving you alone. And I don't plan to spend Thanksgiving and Christmas without both of you."

"I don't want to spend any day without you both, but especially holidays. I'm not sure Seth considered those ramifications."

"Raine warned me that finding common ground with two strong-willed men would sometimes be a challenge. I had no idea it would be this hard."

Beck smirked. "Seth and I don't hold a candle to the fights Liam and Hammer had before they decided to share Raine."

"I heard they were ugly. You two better never get into a fistfight or so help me…" Heavenly pinned him with a warning scowl.

Beck decided not to tell her how cute she looked when she was irritated. "I won't let it come to that, especially since Seth fights mean. The lead-fisted bastard would kick my ass, and a surgeon with broken hands can't do shit in the operating room."

"I just wish I understood what's going on in Seth's head." She frowned. "After blurting out the news about his wife and son, he just shut down and clammed up. Now he's back there sleeping, like he's desperate to avoid us."

"Or desperate to avoid the truth."

"Why? He was there when you told everyone you know and love about your crazy childhood and the fact you were forced to kill your own father. After he watched you pour out your soul, why should he be afraid to tell us what happened to his wife and baby boy?"

"He's not just afraid; he's fucking terrified."

"Why? He can't possibly think that whatever he says will make us stop loving him, can he?"

"Fear isn't rational. And I'm not sure, but I suspect there's more at play than fear alone."

"Like what?"

"He's full of denial, right?"

She nodded. "It seems that way."

Beck wasn't a gambling man, but… "I'd bet money Seth is stuck in the grieving process. On the surface, he knows Autumn and Tristan are gone, but somewhere in his soul—probably where his guilt lives—he can't believe they're gone. I don't know if he's made his way through any of the other stages—anger, bargaining, or depression—but it doesn't seem like he's really accepted that they're gone. I'm not sure if or when he will."

"Everyone grieves differently, but I know a thing or two about grieving since I've been working through it after losing my dad." Heavenly stared out the windshield. "I was in denial. You two had to physically drag me out of bed."

"You were escaping, kind of like he is." Beck jerked his head toward the backseat.

"But Seth functions day to day. He's moved on in some ways, moved here, started a new business and a new relationship..."

"That doesn't mean he's worked through all the stages. He might not need us to physically haul him out of bed, but he clearly needs our help to finish grieving."

"What are you saying? That we've got to... I don't know, talk him through his feelings and reassure him that we're here for him?"

Beck nodded. "And that we always will be, regardless of his past. At least we start there."

"That makes sense. I'm glad we're on the same page," Heavenly said, then yawned.

"Me, too. But like the wedding, we're not going to resolve this today." When she yawned again, Beck chuckled. "Lay your seat back and take a nap, little girl. I'll get us home safely."

"I just need to rest my eyes for a couple minutes."

She yawned again as she lowered the seat, then curled up facing him and closed her eyes. Beck had barely driven another two miles before Heavenly was sound asleep.

As the hum of the tires droned through the vehicle, Beck replayed every minute of the horrific day—from waking sated and secure with Heavenly and Seth, through the senseless battle and its resulting anger, fear, and sorrow, to the worry now plaguing him. As he continued following the ribbon of the road, Beck sent up a silent prayer that the three of them could still find happiness together.

Long hours later, Beck pulled into the garage and killed the engine. The lack of road noise worked like an alarm clock. Both Heavenly and Seth woke, bleary-eyed and blinking, before they all climbed from the SUV.

"Sorry. I didn't mean to zonk out on you two." Seth rolled his shoulders and stretched.

"I fell asleep, too." Heavenly blushed.

As they met at the back of the vehicle, Beck smirked and pushed the fob to open the back hatch. "Thankfully, I didn't."

"Hey, before we start unloading, I need a hug." Heavenly opened her arms, eyeing them pensively.

Without hesitation, he and Seth sandwiched her between them, the big PI against her chest, while Beck pressed himself to her back. Closing his eyes, he buried his face against Heavenly's neck and breathed her in, watching Seth lay a soft kiss across her lips.

His gesture was so natural, so earnest, Beck almost forgot their relationship was showing cracks.

"I'm sorry for barking at you in the car," Heavenly murmured against the PI's lips before easing back to stare up at him. Openly. Honestly. "I'm not used to you two fighting. It upset me. It made me worry about scary things…like losing you two."

"Oh, you don't need to worry, angel. I know I fucked things up this morning. I need to work through some stuff, get my head on straight again. But I love you, and everything is going to be fine."

Beck didn't know whether to believe him or call bullshit. All he could do was take a wait-and-see attitude.

He wanted to be more optimistic than he was.

"Promise?" she whispered.

Seth nodded and kissed Heavenly's cheek, then eased away from her soft body to begin retrieving their suitcases with a plastic smile. The fact he didn't verbalize his vow unsettled Beck.

After he handed Heavenly her tote full of toiletries, she flashed him a smile, as if comforted by the brief connection the three of them had just shared, then hurried into the house.

How long would the peace last?

Seth watched the door close behind her before turning to Beck. "Look, I know you're both worried, but like I told Heavenly, I just need to work some stuff out in my head. In a day or two, I'll—"

"Don't blow smoke up my ass or hers." Beck snapped. "You've kept those secrets wrapped tight for eight long years. Will a day or two really change a thing? Until you open up and purge, you'll never get your head on straight, man."

Before Seth could respond, Beck's phone rang. He pulled it from his pocket and glanced at the caller ID.

"Hey, Jericho," he greeted the FBI agent, tensing.

Seth stood beside him, watching and listening, as if he, too, was waiting for the other shoe to drop.

"How are things going at the lodge?" the agent asked.

"Fine, I think. Seth, Heavenly, and I left. We just got back to LA. Everything all right there in Messiah City?"

"For the most part, yeah. Raid starts soon. The recovery groups you asked us to contact are waiting in the wings with representatives and transportation."

"Good. How's Zach holding up?"

"That's why I called." Jericho hesitated.

Beck's gut twisted. "Not good?"

"He's doing his best, but he's struggling. He knows that he's doing the right thing, but once it's over, it can't be undone. His life will be forever changed. So will all of The Chosen's. It's a lot for him to process."

Beck scrubbed a hand through his hair and held in a curse. Even as a kid, Zach had been the quiet one, the nonconfrontational one. He'd always tried to blend into the background so he could escape Mother's scrutiny. More often than not, it had worked.

Now, he had to put himself out, front and center, for the judgment of the entire congregation as he ended their way of life.

Fuck, going with Zach to take down Messiah City hadn't been an option, but Beck wished he could be there to help his brother.

"What can I do?"

"Nothing right now, but he's going to need you when this is over."

Exactly why he'd given Zach his card. "Don't let him go with any of the recovery groups, okay? When he's done identifying those child-raping elders, send him back to LA. We've got plenty of room. He can stay with us. We'll help him acclimate to the real world."

From the corner of his eye, Beck saw Seth stiffen, jaw clenched, then grip the suitcases in his hands tighter before striding into the house, the door slamming behind him.

What the hell was that about?

"Will do," Jericho replied. "He needs family, someone he can trust. Since I'm heading back that way, I'll bring him back myself."

"Thanks. Tell Zach to stay strong and that we'll be waiting for him."

"Will do. What the—" Jericho huffed. "Son of a bitch."

Beck tensed. "What's wrong?"

"Shut that shit down now!" the agent bellowed. "Motherfucker. I hate the press."

"They're already there?"

"Yep. I've got a damn news van pulling up. Clearly, someone tipped off the press about the raid, so I've got to put out this dumpster fire. I'll text you when Zach and I get back to LA." Without waiting for a reply, Jericho ended the call.

Beck stared at his phone, worry circling his brain. Zach was still reeling from the death of his wife and daughter, and now he had to end Messiah City? Yeah, and if he was losing his shit before the raid even started, what shape would he be in when Jericho brought him here?

"Beck?" Heavenly called, looking concerned. "Seth said you were on the phone with Jericho. Is Zach okay? Is the raid over?"

He strode across the garage, then brought her warm, soft body to his chest. "Not yet. It should be starting soon."

As he led her inside, Beck relayed his conversation with the agent. That prompted Heavenly to rush downstairs and prep the guest room for Zach. And as Beck snagged a drink from the fridge, the sound of footsteps upstairs told him Seth had retreated up there.

They'd been home for two minutes, and they'd already gone their separate ways. How well did that bode for their future?

Ignoring the obvious answer, Beck pulled the keys from his pocket. "Heavenly?"

She appeared, looking up the stairs at him. "Yeah?"

"I'm heading to the hospital to check on my patients and see how Dean is doing. Do you still want to come so you can talk to Bridget and Jennifer?"

She shook her head. "I'll talk to them Monday. I need to get everything set up for Zach. But give Dean my best and tell him to get well soon."

"I will. Hey, when I get back, let's plan on a movie and some popcorn if Seth is up for it."

As the PI's heavy footfalls echoed from the floor above, Beck looked up to see the guy descending the stairs.

"Up for what?" he asked.

"A movie and popcorn." Heavenly leaned forward, craning her neck to see him on the top floor.

"Sounds good. I should be back soon."

Beck scowled. "Back from where?"

"Since River and I have both been gone for a few days, I've got to check on one of my clients. It shouldn't take long. In fact, you won't even miss me."

"Yes, I will," Heavenly insisted. "I'm looking forward to a quiet night with you two."

"Then it's a date, angel." Seth paused to smile her way, then clapped Beck on the shoulder before hurrying out the door.

"He'll be back," Heavenly assured as if sensing his trepidation.

Beck hoped that was true. "So will I."

"See you soon." She blew him a kiss, then disappeared downstairs again.

Beck left. Thirty minutes later, he lost himself in work, scanning the charts of the half-dozen patients admitted while he'd been at the lodge. Thankfully, the attending vascular surgeon had updated the status of each case. But he'd likely be performing back-to-back surgeries in the next few days.

More time away from home, separated from Heavenly and Seth. Damn it.

While he took the elevator to the med-surg unit, he tried to figure out how to impact them as little as possible. Worry plagued him until he tapped on Dean's door, plastered on a smile, then stepped inside.

Beck was surprised to find the cop sitting up in bed, watching television—something he shouldn't be doing with a concussion—and even more surprised to find him alone.

"Hey," he greeted.

Dean quickly turned off the tube with a sheepish grin. "You didn't see that on."

"You watching TV? Yeah, I did. And clearly you know better."

"Watching the wall is boring as fuck."

"I'd like to argue with you, but I can't." Beck chuckled. "How are you feeling? You look a hell of a lot better than the last time I saw you."

"I'm good now. How are you holding up? River told me what happened after I…"

"I'm fine. Honest. Speaking of River, where is he? I thought he'd be here."

"He was, but he looked like hammered shit, so I told him to go home and rest. He called me a few minutes ago and said he'd napped, but he was too wired to sleep more, so he headed into work." Dean rolled his eyes. "I told him he was a dumb ass for not hitting the club and enjoying another night off."

"He probably wouldn't have any fun without you, man."

"That's what he said." A sentimental smile tugged Dean's lips.

The cop was a lucky bastard. He'd bet Dean's wingman wasn't hiding anything so major it would rock the foundation of their friendship. And they damn sure didn't have a woman to keep calm and happy in the midst of upheaval.

Beck didn't have it that easy. All he knew was, if there was any chance Seth was going to walk away, he'd better fucking do it before they put a ring on Heavenly's finger and a baby in her womb.

At least he understood Seth's reluctance to get Heavenly pregnant. He was obviously worried that another child would be killed— murdered?—like the first. That's why he'd been so fucking obsessed with condoms. Except last night, of course. In the hours before when it seemed possible they could all die, Seth had put the past on hold. Despite the danger, Beck had been filled with hope for the future. Now? He wished he knew exactly how Seth's wife and son had died so he could help the man lay his ghosts to rest.

Suddenly, a conversation they'd shared a few weeks ago plowed through Beck's brain.

Did losing your dad have anything to do with the reason you hung up your badge?

You said your past was a long story. Mine, too.

He'd avoided discussing Autumn and Tristan from the start.

As long as it won't bite us in the ass, I can live with that.

It's all ancient history.

Seth had sounded confident. But if the past wasn't a problem, why all the hang-ups? Unless, as Beck suspected, he was still stuck in his grieving process.

"Beck?" Dean called.

Jolting from the memory, he blinked at the cop. "Sorry. Just remembered something. What were you saying?"

"It's not important. You sure you're okay?"

"Fine." It was an obvious lie.

"Hmm." Dean dissected him with a stare.

An awkward silence hung in the air. It was time to leave.

"Well, I better get going so you can rest."

"Take care of yourself, man. If you need to talk, call me. I've been forced to kill more than a couple perps over the years. It never gets easier." Sympathy and understanding filled Dean's face.

Beck didn't correct him. Better to let him think that killing Jed was the issue.

"Oh, and thank you. River told me how you worked on me at the lodge before I came to in the chopper," Dean said, extending his uncasted hand.

"No thanks needed," Beck assured with a solid shake. "I'm just glad you're still with us."

"Me, too, brother. Me, too."

As Beck left the hospital and headed home, the evening traffic was surprisingly light, unlike his thoughts. Despite being worried, he was looking forward to their date night. It would be good for them all if he and Seth cuddled their girl between them.

But when the garage door opened, the PI's SUV wasn't there. A string of curses rolled off his tongue, but he tamped down his disappointment—until he headed inside to find Heavenly sitting on the couch, hugging her knees to her chest.

"Little girl?"

She turned and looked up at him. "You're here. It was getting late, and I wondered if you were both going to get caught up at work."

He could have, and before her he probably would have, but... "No. It took me a little longer to make my rounds, but there was nothing urgent, so I came home. I was looking forward to date night with you and a bowl of popcorn."

"Me, too." But her smile was halfhearted at best. "I'm worried about Seth. He didn't seem like himself before he left. And he hasn't shown up yet."

"Has he called?"

"No."

Her lost expression gutted him. His worry ticked up a notch.

Seth should be here to clean up his mess, but since he wasn't, Beck wouldn't let her mope.

They'd start date night without him.

"Well, you know what that means, don't you?" Beck asked.

She shook her head. "What?"

"More popcorn for us." He winked, extending his hand.

With a fragile smile, she placed her slender fingers in his palm.

CHAPTER
THREE

Beck woke and stared at the clock on his nightstand. Four forty-three a.m. It was too damn early to be up on a Saturday morning, especially since he and Heavenly had waited until nearly midnight for Seth to come home.

Apparently, he never had.

When Beck reached beside him to bring Heavenly closer, he felt nothing but cool sheets. He sat up with a frown and flipped on the lamp. The bed was empty.

Cursing, he tossed his covers aside and vaulted to his feet. A quick glance at the alarm panel next to the bedroom door—a system Seth had insisted on—proved it was still armed. That meant Heavenly hadn't left the house, but where was she?

After tossing on a pair of nearby shorts, he padded out of the bedroom and down the hall, peeking into the other rooms. No sign of her.

He picked up his pace as he made his way down the stairs, guided by the nightlights she had asked them to install in case she got the late-night munchies. Funny, until a couple of weeks ago, he'd lived alone and he'd thought he liked it. Now he saw evidence of the people he loved all around. When they were gone, he felt out of sorts, like his life was out of place.

It will be a fucking wreck if you can't pull everyone together.

Beck hated that the voice in his head was right.

At the bottom of the stairs, he crept into the great room and found Heavenly on the sofa, bathed in moonlight. She wasn't seeking an early-morning snack, but had curled up with a blanket, her head resting on a throw pillow. Silver tracks ran down her cheeks. His heart twisted.

She'd come down here—and given up her comfort—to wait for Seth. Despite his many all-night cases, she had never done that before. Clearly, she was worried.

Beck sank beside Heavenly in the shadows, bringing her sleep-soft body against him and tucking the blanket around her. Instead of cuddling up to him with a sigh, she stirred, her lashes fluttering.

"Wha…" She peered through the dark with a frown. "Beck?"

He kissed her forehead. "What are you doing down here, little girl?"

"Did I wake you up? What time is it?" She glanced back at the clock on the microwave in the kitchen. "Almost five?"

"Yeah."

"Oh, my gosh." She sat up. "I woke up a little after three and, um… came down to get some water."

Did she think it would hurt his feelings if she admitted she'd been worried about Seth? "And you decided to wait up for the big guy?"

She bit her lip…then gave up her subterfuge. "Yeah."

Beck noticed she clutched her phone and glanced at the screen. "Did you text him?"

"A couple of times." She shook her head. "Nothing."

Goddamn it. What was the son of a bitch thinking?

"I'm sure he's fine, just tied up."

She nodded…but she didn't look convinced. "Probably. Go back to bed. I think I'm going to get up and…"

When she trailed off and shrugged, it was clear that she didn't know what to do. "Worry? Don't do that. Why don't you sit with me while I flip on the news? Let's see if news of the raid on Messiah City has broken."

Heavenly looked relieved that Beck had given her something else to think about. "Okay. Want me to make coffee?"

"Please."

A few minutes later, she returned with two steaming mugs and settled beside him. Beck wrapped his arm around her and curled her against his side as he reached for the remote. Before he could turn on the TV, Heavenly laid a soft hand over his.

"Do you think he's okay?"

He knew she didn't mean Zach. "It's a dangerous city, but Seth is more than capable of taking care of himself."

"He is. That's not what I was asking."

Mentally. Emotionally. She was worried.

Beck sighed. "I don't know. I'd suggest a counselor if I thought it would do any good."

"He thinks he's fine."

"Yep, just like he's convinced himself he's protecting us by withholding the truth about his wife and son. But it's himself he's protecting."

Heavenly nodded. "It's the same with his mother and this wedding stuff. Somewhere in his head, he genuinely believes he's shielding his mother from the truth about our relationship so he doesn't spoil her wedding day. But I've been thinking… By keeping the three of us a secret, he's really protecting himself from her disapproval."

"You're right." Beck hadn't thought about it quite like that, but yeah.

"What should we do?"

"Point out that he's being an ass?"

She sent him a sassy shake of her head. "I was thinking that gentle suggestions, support, and patience stand a better chance."

Probably, but it sounded painful as fuck. "Let me think about it, okay? In the meantime, let's see what's happened in Messiah City."

So I can figure out just how messed up Zach is going to be.

As Beck lifted the TV remote again, the garage door opened, then shut again. The electronic beeping of the house alarm being disarmed and reset told him all he needed to know.

Heavenly rose. "Seth?"

He appeared in the doorway, wearing last night's clothes and a scowl. "What are you two doing up?"

"You're back. I was worried—"

"About Zach," Beck cut in. Now wasn't the time to air Heavenly's concerns. Seth would only give them some BS excuse, and Beck didn't want to have to resist the urge to pound sense into him. "So we're going to see how the raid on Messiah City went. Want to join us? We'll make you some coffee."

Seth hesitated, looking between the two of them and the darkened TV. Then he sighed with exhaustion. "Yeah. It was a long night. I could use some java."

As Seth approached, he paused beside Heavenly, whose worried expression practically begged for reassurance. The big lug at least did one thing right and kissed her.

Afterward, she smiled and headed to the kitchen to brew him a mug.

Beck leveled him a pissed-off glare. Yeah, he might have smoothed things over with Heavenly, but this conversation was hardly over.

Seth swore under his breath and looked like he grappled for something to say when she returned and handed him his cup of joe. They all sat.

This time, Beck flipped on the TV. A grim-faced reporter filled the screen, breaking the news about the raid on Messiah City to the world. When footage of terrified women and crying children scurrying in the streets rolled across the big flat-screen, Beck leaned in, elbows on his knees, fingers clasped, his stare glued. The camera panned over the cult members. Some looked scared, some confused, and a few—probably the elders' sons—looked furious.

The camera focused on a reporter with a huge microphone, who summarized the situation, then panned back to reveal a cluster of Chosen being escorted into FBI vans. One woman, wearing the traditional long dress and braids, guided others away from the press. Beside her, a girl who was maybe all of thirteen had a pregnant belly that looked far too swollen for her tiny frame. It made Beck sick.

When he zeroed in on the woman's face, he froze. She looked hauntingly familiar. His gut twisted. He grabbed the remote and smashed the pause button.

That's what Blessing would have looked like if—

"What is it? Do you know her?" Heavenly asked softly.

"That's Blessing's little sister, Harmony. I'm betting the pregnant girl beside her is her daughter, Amity. And the asshole who planted a baby in her belly was not only nearly three times her age but her own father."

"Fucking pervert," Seth muttered in disgust.

"Oh, that poor girl," Heavenly whispered.

The familiar guilt for failing to protect Blessing chewed Beck up. Would she have lived to adulthood and been at least somewhat happy if he hadn't impulsively asked for her hand? He'd never fucking know, but he'd live with the question—and the regret—forever.

Shoving down the demon of his past, he pressed play. A portly gray-haired man, restrained by FBI-issued cuffs, wandered into the frame. Beck sat up straighter, watching the man rail and sob as law enforcement escorted him away. He'd know those beady eyes anywhere.

"Looks like slimy Uncle Peter isn't dead after all," he drawled.

"That guy is your uncle?" Seth pointed at the TV.

"Yep. I had no idea that cowardly piece of shit was still alive. I'm sure he was still fucking underage virgins in the name of the Lord, too. When Zach told me Peter had been ousted as Messiah after Jed turned sixteen, I assumed Esther had him killed. But he must have proven extra spineless if Mother let him keep breathing. On the bright side, there isn't a more fitting punishment for Uncle Peter than being repeatedly ass raped in prison."

His father would have looked a lot like Peter now—all thinning gray hair, crow's feet, and judgmental glower—if Beck hadn't slit the cocksucker's throat years ago.

Next, Zach's drawn face filled the screen. He looked both exhausted and wired tight. And no wonder. He was doing the right thing, but everyone in Messiah City would view his choice to end the sect as the ultimate betrayal.

Beneath Zach's photo was a printed chyron proclaiming FBI Raid on Fundamentalist Sect.

"After the early-morning raid, the leaders of the religious splinter group who call themselves The Chosen have been arrested. Authorities say this group has been on their radar for years, but they had no probable cause to search Messiah City until one brave resident, Zacharias Kimball, who found himself the leader of the sect after the previous one's death during yesterday's deadly shoot-out in Big Bear, came forward. The rest of the followers will be taken in for questioning before being released. Volunteer groups have pledged to help those who wish to acclimate to the outside world. No word yet on—"

Beck's cell phone chimed, interrupting the newscast. He paused the feed, grabbed the device off the coffee table, and read the message from FBI agent Jericho Waters.

`Just landed at Van Nuys. Be there shortly.`

Beck tapped out a reply that he'd be waiting, then sighed, rubbing the back of his stiff neck. The good news was, the cesspool of depravity he'd grown up in would soon be relegated to the dustbin of history. The bad news? Zach's difficulties were just beginning. Beck knew that from experience. Learning how to function in this world would be a long, frustrating process. Thankfully, Zach had agreed to stay with him, at least temporarily, so he'd have help adjusting to life outside the sect. Beck was damn glad he could help his brother...but the timing sucked.

Seth still wasn't acting like himself. Had he stayed home last night to talk about any of their problems? No, he'd clammed up, ditched their planned date night, and stayed out until just before sunrise. If River was already snooping on the cheating spouse, why hadn't Seth come home? Did the case really require both of them? Beck had no idea because Seth hadn't bothered to explain, much less called or answered any of Heavenly's texts. Hell, he hadn't even asked Heavenly how she was doing, despite her obvious exhaustion and worry. Instead, Seth had merely slid onto the sofa to watch the news unfold and carried on like they had no problems at all.

That was bullshit. He'd created a strain in their relationship that hadn't existed before.

On top of that, Beck's patient load had gotten more difficult virtually overnight with the addition of more cases, some incredibly complex. Piling Zach's needs onto this powder keg of stress would be a lot to handle. Thankfully, he'd found a top-notch psychologist—if Zach needed it—who specialized in cult victims to guide his brother through the upheaval and grief while he adjusted to his new life, but Zach would need family, reassurance, and time—time Beck worried he needed to shore up his relationship with Heavenly and Seth.

Worry wrung him as tight as a fucking tourniquet.

"Zach is back in LA?" Heavenly asked expectantly.

"Yeah." He turned off the TV. He'd seen enough of this media circus. Besides, he'd hear the unvarnished truth from the ringmaster himself. "He should be here soon."

Seth fidgeted in his seat like he was itchy, then checked his phone.

Beck scowled. What was up his ass? If Cooper thought he was slipping out again without them exchanging words, he was sorely mistaken.

Heavenly sent Beck a reassuring smile. "It's good Zach will be coming here. He looked…"

"Haunted," Seth finished, his voice edged with something hard.

"Yes. I'm not surprised, after dealing with all that." Heavenly gestured to the darkened screen. "I'll bet he didn't sleep all night. I doubt he's had a decent home-cooked meal in ages."

Beck nodded. "You're probably right."

"I don't pretend to understand everything he's going through, but I can at least feed him." Heavenly stood and headed toward the kitchen. "I'll have a hot breakfast ready shortly after he arrives."

As the clatter of pots and pans floated from the kitchen, Beck glared at Seth, his stare drilling into the side of the big PI's head.

Seth turned his way. "What?"

Though Heavenly had turned on some soft music, Beck still lowered his voice. "So it took all night to 'check' on the case?"

"Cases often take me out that long. What are you bitching about?"

"But you usually tell us up front how long you'll be gone, and if things change, you call. Last night, Heavenly thought you were coming back. And you ignored her texts. She was really fucking upset and worried."

That took Seth down a notch. "Sorry. Hurting her is the last thing I ever want to do."

Sure. Great. But like Seth's apology yesterday, Beck noticed what he *didn't* say. "So you'll communicate with us from now on?"

And Beck didn't just mean about his comings and goings.

"Yeah."

"Good. Want to start by telling me what's been bothering you since you dropped the bombshell at the lodge?"

Seth sucked in a breath. "Look, man. Let it go. I've already told you everything important. I made mistakes, and my family died." He stood. "I haven't slept all night, so I'm not really in the mood to rehash all this. I'm going to grab a shower."

Before he could walk off, Beck yanked him back down. "You don't want to talk about it right now? All right, but don't drag her through your emotional shit. Either wrap up this case you're working on or take tonight off and talk to us. After everything that's happened, she's feeling insecure. She needs you. We both do."

Seth hesitated, then nodded. "I'll do my best, but this case suddenly jumped up and bit me in the ass."

Beck admittedly hadn't considered that, like his own practice, Seth's had gone to hell while they'd been holed up at the lodge. "Complicated?"

"Time sensitive. Wife number six hired me to catch her cheating husband before she starts divorce proceedings."

"So she can take him to the cleaners?"

Seth nodded. "River hadn't had any luck on this case before all hell broke loose. Yesterday afternoon, the client chewed me a new asshole for disappearing while we were at the lodge. So I promised to personally step in and wrap this up. That's why this case went from a mere check-in to an all-nighter."

Beck downshifted. Since Seth had dropped paying clients' needs to help him, he couldn't be an ungrateful prick. "How'd that go?"

Seth scoffed. "Shitty. Her horny husband used the five previous wives to perfect his adultering skills. I thought I'd caught him last night when I followed him to a hotel. While we waited for the elevator in the lobby, I pretended to look at my phone. Once the doors opened, we both stepped inside. He pressed the button for the penthouse. I pressed the seventeenth floor, and I felt him watching me, but I never looked his way. As the doors started to close, the cagey son of a bitch mumbled something about leaving his card key in his glove-box and hustled out. After that, River and I both tried to find him, but no luck. I'm sure he was holed up somewhere, fucking the brains out of the woman who will be wife number seven." Seth heaved a frustrated sigh. "I don't know if this guy has Liam's sort of woo-woo or if he smelled my PI cologne. But now that he's seen my face, I've got to come up with a new plan—fast."

"PI cologne, huh? What's that smell like?"

"Bitter coffee and strong suspicion." Seth sent him an acidic grin. "Nothing as good as the mouthwatering scent coming from the kitchen."

"Right?" Beck chuckled, then patted his stomach. "I'm not sure what's worse, the fact I love to eat or that Heavenly's such a damn good cook. All I know is, if I'm not careful, she's going to turn me into a fat old man."

"Dude, you're already old."

"Fuck you." Beck grinned, relishing the easy banter and sliver of normalcy.

Maybe Seth wasn't completely closed up. Maybe he could wrap this case in the next day or two, then spend some time at home so they could get to the bottom of his past, solve the wedding conundrum, and refortify their trio.

Seth's phone and the doorbell ringing in tandem put a dent in that hope.

While the PI drifted out through the kitchen and to the back patio to take his call, Beck strode to the foyer and opened the door. Zach stood there, looking like he'd just crawled to hell and back. Beside him, Jericho wore a grim expression and gave a subtle shake of his head.

Yeah, it was that bad.

Beck wrapped his arms around his brother and hauled him across the threshold. Almost instantly, Zach fell apart, his body quaking with silent sobs. Jericho watched with mute empathy on his face.

Behind him, Heavenly raced from the kitchen to greet Zach. But when she saw him falling apart, compassion replaced her welcoming smile. Without hesitation, she moved in and wrapped a comforting arm around his brother, whispering words of encouragement and promises of better days.

"How about some breakfast? You look like you could use it," Heavenly said to Zach, her voice full of soft empathy. Then she turned to Jericho. "You're welcome to join us. I made plenty."

"I'd appreciate it. Thanks." The agent lifted a small plastic suitcase before easing past Beck and Zach, into the house. "Can I do anything to help?"

"Set the table? I've already put everything you'll need on the counter."

After Jericho set Zach's suitcase in the foyer, he sprang into action.

Beck gave his brother another reassuring squeeze. "It will get better, man. I know your grief over Faith's and Joanna's loss is overwhelming now. But what you did to stop the cycle of abuse in Messiah City took real guts. It was the right choice."

"The only choice," Zach choked out, wiping his face with his sleeve.

"The hard part is over. Take a deep breath. I promise, everything is going to be all right."

"I wish I was as sure about that as you, brother."

"You will be soon. Trust me." Beck ushered him toward the kitchen. "Let's get some food in you, then we'll sit and talk."

"I'm not sure I can eat anything."

"You need to try, Zach," Jericho coaxed, setting the last of the plates on the table. "You haven't eaten anything since we left the lodge. The nightmare's over. Focus on yourself now. You've done all you can for the others."

"Way to hustle, River. I'll be there in ten," Seth announced as he strode back into the house, ending his call. "I have to get back to work. Sorry."

"But you haven't slept." Heavenly frowned, clearly concerned.

"It'll have to wait. I'm hoping to catch this son of a bitch at a supposed meeting. On a Saturday. In Palm Springs." He kissed her softly. "I'll be back, angel."

"When?" Beck asked, probably more pointedly than he should.

"I'll be home as soon as I can." Seth shrugged, then sent Zach a sidelong glance. "Um…welcome. Sorry for all you've been through."

With that, Seth clapped Beck on the back, kissed Heavenly one more time, then strode to the door and slammed it behind him.

Beck bit back a curse. He would gladly reimburse the retainer wife number six had paid, along with a fat check to hire a better divorce attorney, if it meant Seth could stay home tonight. But Beck let it go. He needed to focus on the problem in front of him.

He gestured a mute Zach, now staring around his angular, modern home with wide eyes, to a chair at the kitchen table, beside the one Jericho grabbed. Beck slid in next to Heavenly, drawing her hand to his lips. "Thanks for making a hot breakfast." Then he glanced at the steaming casserole in the center of the table, sent her an imperceptible head bob toward Zach, followed by a wink. "Um...what is it? Mush?"

"Mush? Really?" Heavenly huffed.

Beck reared back. That sassy tone had come from his sweet little girl? If it had been real and they'd been alone, she'd already be draped across his lap for a hearty spanking. Instead, he suppressed a smile.

Beside him, Jericho snickered. Zach's mouth tugged upward for a split second.

That did Beck's heart good, so he heaped on some more. "Well, at least this mush looks better than the low-grade slop you usually fix."

Heavenly gasped indignantly and wagged a finger at him. "Oh, just wait. You haven't even tasted slop yet, mister."

At that, Zach actually smiled.

Mission accomplished.

Then Beck burst out laughing and squeezed her hand. "I'm teasing you. Everything you cook is amazing."

Jericho looked at him like he was insane. "You like living on the edge or something, Beckman?"

"You could say that..."

"Guess I'll have to pick up some low-grade slop tomorrow so you can taste the difference between that and my French toast casserole." Heavenly slanted him a cheeky stare.

Beck laughed. "You know this is one of my favorites. Let's dig in."

He handed Zach the spoon and held his breath. After a moment's hesitation, his brother loaded two big scoops onto his plate. Relief wound through him as he reached under and gently squeezed Heavenly's thigh, mouthing a silent *thank you.* She cupped his hand and returned the gesture with a loving smile.

While they ate, they talked about everything but nothing at all. They completely sidestepped heavy topics like the massacre at the lodge, the raid on Messiah City, and the losses his brother was struggling with. And when Zach spooned out another helping of casserole, the concern on Jericho's face eased.

After breakfast, the agent clapped Zach on the back and stood. "You've got my number. If you need anything or receive more threats, call me right away. Understood?"

Zach nodded.

"Who's making threats and what kind?" Beck asked.

"Some of the elders' sons vowed to end me in the name of God after their fathers were arrested." Zach tried to look calm, but his eyes were bright with fear.

"I've got agents keeping eyes on them," Jericho assured.

"Good. We'll keep ours open, too," Beck promised, unable to miss the worry skipping across Heavenly's face.

They both knew if any of The Chosen discovered Gideon was still alive, there would be another war.

"Thank you for breakfast, Heavenly. That was the best 'mush' I've ever eaten." Jericho grinned as he headed for the front door.

After a quick goodbye, Heavenly started clearing the table. "As soon as I clean up, I'm going to take a long, hot shower and do a little studying so you and Beck have some privacy. If you want a shower, too, your brother can show you to your room downstairs. There are clean towels in the bathroom and some toiletries I set out, just in case. Help yourself to anything you need. I know this isn't the home you're used to, but we want you to feel at home while you're here."

Beck settled a wistful stare on her. Just when he thought he couldn't love Heavenly more, his little girl stole another piece of his heart.

Zach blinked back tears. "Thank you both. For everything."

"You don't have to thank us, man," Beck assured. "We're family."

His brother let out a shaky breath. "The only family I have left."

"Good thing we're the sane ones." Beck grinned.

"Amen." Zach managed another ghost of a smile.

"Go relax in the family room. I'll be right there." Beck gestured across the open first floor.

As Zach settled into the chair facing the television, Beck pulled Heavenly against his chest and nuzzled her ear. "Thank you for welcoming him. I love you."

"I love you, too. You don't have to thank me. We're all he's got now."

Beck pressed his lips to hers, pouring all the emotion lodged in his throat into their kiss. "I'll be with you as soon as I can. I don't know how long this will take."

"Don't worry about me. I have school stuff to catch up on. And he really needs you right now."

"You sure? I hate to leave you alone." Because he didn't want to remind her that Seth was gone. Then again, she was probably painfully aware of it.

"Positive."

"Just make sure you need me later, huh?" He pressed a lingering kiss to her soft mouth once more.

She gave him an extra squeeze. "Deal."

He watched the sexy sway of Heavenly's ass as she hurried back to the kitchen before he snagged a bottle of bourbon and a couple of glasses, then joined Zach in the living room. Beck eased onto the couch and, despite the early hour, poured them each a double shot. Then he passed a glass to his brother.

Zach sniffed it and shook his head. "I-I can't drink this. It's Satan's brew."

"Not in this world. Here, it's just a shot of liquid courage so you can say the things you need to unburden yourself and heal." Beck tossed back the amber liquid and welcomed the burn.

His brother took a tentative sip, then coughed and sputtered like he was choking to death. With a grimace, he set the glass down and shook his head. "I'll find my courage through God."

Beck shrugged. "All right. Tell me what happened after you left the lodge."

Zach blew out a breath, as if he was reluctant to open this can of worms. "We headed to an airport and boarded a private plane to Las Vegas. I didn't enjoy flying."

"Was that your first time on a plane?"

He nodded. "And hopefully my last. After that, we met up with dozens of other FBI agents. Jericho ushered me into an SUV, introduced me to the special agent in charge, then we led a convoy of fifteen or twenty similar vehicles to Messiah City. Traveling down the roads to the place I've lived all my life, knowing I was the Messiah and that I was going to end everything wrong with our community, was surreal…but freeing."

Beck understood. "You had nothing left to lose."

"They'd already taken everything that mattered to me."

"So you loved Faith?"

"Eventually we developed feelings for each other. When we first married, she was only eleven. I was barely eighteen, but our father wanted an alliance with a sect in Montana, and Faith's father insisted that his first daughter be someone's first wife. So a deal was struck. Faith and I met for the first time at the altar at our wedding. She was dressed like a bride…but she looked like a child."

"She *was* a child."

Zach nodded. "It was one reason we didn't consummate our marriage for over a year. I would have waited longer, but the elders began probing us for the reasons Faith wasn't breeding. She got anxious and worried since she always felt out of place in Messiah City."

Beck knew exactly how unwelcoming the sect had been to outsiders. "I assume it wore on her?"

"Yes. One day, she came to me in tears because some of the women had asked questions she didn't understand. I knew if they figured out we hadn't consummated our marriage, everyone would blame her."

"Then she would be shunned."

"Exactly. But I still hesitated. I was haunted by Blessing."

That took Beck aback. "Why?"

"The night Father took her as his spiritual wife, he called Jed and me to their bedchamber. He told us that because we would soon be men, we needed to understand how we were to deflower our wives." Grim apology filled Zach's face. "Then he showed us."

Beck went icy all over. That son of a bitch… He'd always known his father was bent, but this was a new low, even for him. "Holy shit. You couldn't have been more than…what, ten?"

"Yes, and I was horrified. I knew you had feelings for her. I saw you kiss her between the clotheslines when you thought no one was looking. Before Father even took her to wife, I suspected he married her to hurt you. That night, I knew it. He was neither gentle nor considerate with her." Zach grimaced. "Blessing had always been so sweet. I wondered why God was punishing her, why Father paid no heed to her screams of pain or her tears. Then he told her that he was teaching you a lesson. After that, I closed my eyes. I just couldn't watch anymore."

The ice in Beck's veins turned to rage. "That bastard deserved exactly what I gave him when I slit his throat. I'm sorry he dragged you into his bullshit. No wonder you weren't in a hurry to consummate your marriage to Faith."

"But after she worried about her place among The Chosen, I did. She got pregnant almost immediately." He swallowed like he had to shove down something painful. "Her pregnancy was normal. Her delivery wasn't. The baby was breech. Faith almost didn't make it. The blood…"

"At that age, the body isn't fully ready to bear children. That's one reason it's illegal in the real world to have sex with anyone under eighteen."

Zach nodded. "That's about when Faith and I started sharing a bed again. After she gave birth, we didn't… I couldn't. I just kept hearing her screams. But after a few years, I developed genuine feelings for my wife. Unfortunately, God didn't bless us with more children. I was okay with that because my Joanna was such a beautiful, warmhearted girl, like her mother. I can't believe I'll never see my baby smile again."

When Zach broke down, Beck rubbed his brother's heaving back.

Heavenly turned out the kitchen lights, then tiptoed into the room and set a cold bottle of water beside Zach.

"Thank you," he croaked.

"You're welcome." She sent them a compassionate smile before disappearing upstairs.

Zach watched her go as he took a long pull from the bottle. "Heavenly is lovely, and she seems so kind."

"She's beautiful, but I fell for her because she's got such a big heart."

His brother frowned. "I know you and Seth both lie with her. Why? It's so counter to the teachings you grew up with. Do you do it to rebel against The Chosen?"

"I can see where you'd think that, but no. The truth is, we both fell in love with her and it was tearing her up to choose between us. We tried to make her, but she was so torn that she let us both go. Since neither of us wanted to live without her...we compromised."

Zach's frown deepened. "Do you lie with Seth, too?"

"Never," Beck insisted. "We're friends and partners in Heavenly's care. That's it."

Understanding dawned on his face. "So it's like The Chosen, only in reverse. You each have scheduled nights with her?"

Beck shifted uncomfortably. He really didn't want to answer, and he didn't owe Zach explanations. But if his brother was going to live with them, he would acclimate better if he understood the dynamics in the house. "No. We're with her together in all things."

"At the same time?" Zach's shocked expression made it clear he was trying to sort through the logistics of that.

"Yes. I'll explain if you need me to, but let's get back to the raid." He wanted details. After all, if they were going to deal with potential threats, he needed to know what had happened.

"It went smoother than expected. Since we'd killed most of the God Squad at the lodge, there were only a handful left who tried to stop us, but when they saw the onslaught of FBI vehicles, they retreated and disappeared. Predictably, they went to warn the others, but it was too late. Everyone surrendered."

"Without a shot being fired?"

"Thankfully, yes. The God Squad Jed left behind were mostly teenagers, and they were afraid. So Jericho and I waited in the church until the agents rounded up the rest of the Chosen. Finally, when everyone was inside, the FBI closed the doors. The flock stared up at me, and I could practically hear them wondering why I was preparing to address them and not Jed. Or even Esther. Most sat quietly, afraid of the agents and what their presence meant. Others, mostly elders, demanded to see Jed, their Messiah. I stood there, knowing I was about to destroy the only way of life I'd ever known. But I was destroying theirs, too. The realization made me so nervous I felt sick, but the sooner I said what I needed to, the sooner I could find Faith and Joanna."

He paused to gather himself. Beck fought the urge to comfort his brother, but if Zach was going to heal, purging his pain was the first step.

"So I stood before The Chosen and announced that their Messiah and Esther were dead. The shock was palpable. The elders called my claims blasphemous. So I held up a photo of Jed's and Esther's bodies. They were all shocked. Some of the women fainted. Others wailed.

"Next, the elders accused me of killing Jed. They said that, like you, I'd been possessed by Satan. I pointed out that since you had perished long ago and Jed was now gone, *I* was their new Messiah, and I demanded they kneel down and beg the Lord's forgiveness for spewing lies. They grumbled, but they dropped to their knees. Then I made sure the FBI knew who the elders were.

"On the way in, I had given them names and the number of their wives, along with their ages. The agents arrested the elders and carted them away. Pandemonium broke out. I did my best to keep everyone calm, explain what was happening, and ensure they would be given the choice to either join a similar sect or transition to the outside." He let out a shaky breath. "The hate they spewed shocked me. These were people I'd known my whole life, the *only* people I'd ever known…"

"I understand," Beck soothed in comforting tones. "It can't have been easy."

"No. About a third of the flock decided to try the outside world. The rest… They're either too blind to the evil of this way of life or too afraid to try something new."

"It's not like the elders ever encouraged independent thinking," Beck drawled.

"You're right. And that should have been my first clue something was very wrong in Messiah City. But eventually I wondered why I'd been taught to hate people and a way of life I knew so little about. I'd even seen the elders vilify people I actually liked or agreed with."

"None of what you learned in Messiah City was about God. It was about control."

"You're right. As the agents were dealing with The Chosen, Jericho led me to Jed's office. Together, we searched it. I found things… He'd obviously learned his underhanded ways from Mother, because he'd become a master of spying on his flock and blackmailing his people to manipulate them. He also had drugs, alcohol, and pornography—things he railed against in every sermon." He shook his head like he was still in shock. "I was horrified. I had no idea…"

"It was the same way with Dad and all the elders. Do as I say, not as I do."

"I supposed I was somewhat shocked to realize how true that is. I had suspicions, but…"

"Now you know."

"We also found money, jewelry, gold, stock certificates, and other valuables in a safe under Jed's floorboards. Jericho told me to take it all so I could start my life over."

Beck's esteem for the agent went up. "That's against regulation."

"He said as much, but he also told me it was my reward for stopping the evil in Messiah City. Perhaps I should have resisted the temptation for worldly goods, but he told me I would need it, so I took it, along with a few other things…and here I am."

And he would be here for a while, adjusting to a completely different way of life, with different morals, values, and norms. It wouldn't be a smooth transition. "Did you find Faith and Joanna?"

Zach's expression turned bleak. Fighting tears, he frowned as if trying to ward off pain. "Agents followed a trail of dried blood from our house to shallow graves out back. Jed had them bludgeoned to death, probably in their sleep since they were both wearing nightgowns, and had them buried in the backyard. Then he told everyone that they had left with me to do God's work and that we might not be back."

"He intended to kill you, too."

"I think he did. Mother probably told him to." Zach's pain was both soul-deep grief and soul-deep fury. "How could either of them claim to be pious and serving God's glory and do the things they did?"

Beck felt sorry for his youngest brother. He knew precisely what Zach was going through. "Because they love power above everything, even God. You doing okay?"

Zach shrugged. "How does anyone recover from this sort of hate and betrayal? How did you?"

"It's going to take time, and you have to be patient with yourself. I don't know how much you remember, but before I killed Dad and left Messiah City, I'd already stopped believing most of their shit. I refused to be anything like them, and I knew the outside world was my only chance to survive. That didn't mean it was an easy transition."

"But you got through it."

"You will, too. I'll help in every way I can. So will Heavenly and Seth."

His brother nodded like he wanted to believe that more than he did. "Did you continue with religion?"

"As I've gotten older, I've made peace with my faith, but I'll never engage in organized religion again."

"I've already come to that conclusion."

"You'll have to find a belief system that works for you."

An ironic smile tugged at Zach's mouth. "It feels odd to have the freedom to believe whatever I want."

"I know. But give it some thought. Make some decisions about your spirituality. It will help you make peace sooner."

His brother hesitated, as if he had a subject he was reluctant to bring up. "You're no longer married?"

"No, but I plan to get married again." *This time for real.*

"To Heavenly?"

Beck nodded. "It's complicated since I share her with Seth, but we'll figure it out."

"What did you do before you were married? I assume you had… relations with other females?"

"No one calls it that in the outside world. They have sex. Make love. Fuck. All those phrases have slightly different connotations, but… You want to know how finding a woman works out here?"

Zach winced. "It sounds so selfish to think about my gratification now, but I've been weeks without Faith's comfort, and now that she's gone…"

"Yeah." Beck blew out a breath. He should have seen this coming. "I'll make a phone call and set you up with a woman."

"I-I don't see myself getting married again."

"You don't have to. That's not what I'm saying. I'm just going to hire you some company for the night."

His brother reared back. "A paid woman? I don't think—"

"Listen, I know that goes against your moral code. But think about it this way: it's more honest than marriages among The Chosen. You need sex. She needs money. No one is lying about piousness or God's will or spiritual devotion. Everyone gets what they want and they go their separate ways, happy. No harm. No foul. No pretenses."

"Except it's fornication, pure and simple."

"You'll have to decide when you're ready to unshackle yourself from that moral stricture and find your own values."

"But the word of God…"

"Isn't the only word to live by. Out here, you have to make peace with yourself, too."

Slowly, Zach nodded. "Can I think about it?"

"Absolutely." Beck wondered if he'd be calling Gloria to send Zach one of her girls sooner rather than later. He also suspected his brother would find kinky coping mechanisms, like he had. "Just let me know. And if you're not ready for that, you should know that masturbating isn't really a sin."

Zach didn't look convinced. "Do you mind if I sleep now?"

Beck nodded and rose. His brother probably needed it. "I'll show you to your room. We'll talk more later."

"I can't thank you enough."

"You don't have to. Just get some rest."

And once Zach was settled, Beck intended to peek in on Heavenly, make sure she was okay, and check her pulse about Seth's behavior. Then he'd focus on how to get behind the man's barricades so they would finally get the truth.

CHAPTER FOUR

"So glad we caught that son of a bitch," River repeated beside him as they approached the glittering lights of LA. "He's going to be really damn surprised when his soon-to-be ex-wife presents those indisputable pictures in court. And damn, for an older guy, he's got game. And a really limber back."

"No doubt," Seth said absently, glad they'd put this fucking case to bed. But now that they had, a mountain of other problems was waiting for him.

"What's funny is, the last time we were in a hotel room, exposing someone's sex life, I had to take one for the team. I'm so glad I was behind the camera this time." River slapped him on the shoulder, grinning through the shadowy dark.

Seth did his best to snap out of his stupor. "For sure. Too bad we can't introduce our client's husband to Marlie."

"Exactly. Since he's a cheating jackass and she's a manipulative whore willing to spread her legs to see the man who spurned her go to prison, they deserve each other. It would be a race to see who could fuck the other over the fastest."

River wasn't wrong, so Seth nodded. "When we get to the office, I'll call the client and send her the pics. You go on home."

"You sure?"

"Yeah, we're less than an hour away, so I got it. I'm assuming you and Dean have big plans to cozy up in his hospital bed." He winked. "Going to try to sneak a woman in between you?"

"Fuck no. He's been discharged, but he's still recovering, so he's not up to banging any woman, between us or otherwise. And that's cool. I've got more than easy pussy on my mind."

"You've got a *specific* pussy on your mind, I'll bet. Pike's girlfriend?"

River's expression turned thunderous. "Why won't he just go the fuck away?"

"Maybe for the same reason I wouldn't stay in New York when I'm sure Beck wanted me to. Feelings, man. You can't escape them. When you've got them for a girl—"

"I don't. I just want to talk to her."

"Uh-huh. You keep telling yourself that."

River shrugged him off and changed the subject. "So are you going to head home and have a fucking good night after you call the client?"

Seth shook his head. "I've got some paperwork to finish and a few inquiries to follow up on. Kiddie Kares sent me a few more background checks, so I'll probably start those."

"I can do that, man."

"I got it. I'm…um, giving Beck's brother a little time to settle in."

"Zach is living with you?"

"Yeah, at least for a while." It hadn't been Seth's first choice. Then again, the house they lived in belonged to Beck. Since the surgeon paid for it, Seth could hardly tell him who should and shouldn't stay there.

"That guy has had it rough."

More than River would ever understand. The loss, the sense of failure, the suddenly feeling adrift, of having his whole life change in the blink of an eye through every fault of his own. How long would Zach second-guess his decision to cross The Chosen and try to save his daughter from hell only to lose her for good? Seth's guess? The rest of his life.

"Yeah."

And therein lay Seth's problem. Just looking at Zach brought back all the worst of his memories after Autumn's and Tristan's deaths. All his guilt, remorse, and contrition. The harsh, inescapable reality that it was too late to make different choices. The knowledge that the suburban home he'd scrimped and stretched financially to buy for his little family was nothing but an empty house haunted by memories he couldn't bear to confront. Even looking at Zach's tormented expression reminded him of looking in the mirror after his world had fallen apart and the police had been unable to come up with any hard evidence to prove who'd killed them. He remembered staring at his reflection and vowing to find the truth himself, then to kill the dirty motherfucker responsible. He'd turned in his badge in disgust and struck out on his own. He'd never forget the seedy clubs he'd visited, the dirty mobsters he'd confronted, or the low-down deal he'd made with the king of the Russian underworld in New York just to find some resolution.

He'd fucking tried to tranquilize his grief with booze and drugs, with anonymous fights and even more anonymous fucks. He'd become someone his family hadn't recognized, someone they had feared. Hell, he'd even become someone he hadn't liked.

But he'd finally found the answers he sought, meted out his revenge, laid his wife and son to rest for good, then tried to pick up the shattered pieces of his life. Until he'd met Heavenly, he'd only been taking up air and marking time. Now that he had her and he shared a great kinship with Beck, he had a reason to live again. He didn't want to fuck that up.

If you love them, don't you owe them your trust and your truth? Give them some answers…

So they could look at him like he was a violent monster? No. Beck had exposed his secret to everyone, and no wonder his loved ones hadn't blamed him. He'd been born to those fucking religious cult crazies, stuck in the thick of their fanaticism through no fault of his own. He'd had to do something horrible to escape; no denying that. But if Beck hadn't killed his father, the zealot would have killed him. As far as Seth was concerned, Beck's act of patricide had been nothing but preemptive self-defense.

His own situation had been merely cocky, self-righteous idiocy.

"You okay?" River frowned.

"Sure," he lied because he didn't want to open this can of worms with River—or anyone. "Why?"

"You haven't been yourself the last couple of days."

"A lot on my mind."

River nodded. "The action at the lodge was a lot."

True, but that hadn't bothered him. In fact, it had almost been cathartic, even if Beck didn't realize what a lucky son of a bitch he was to have both vengeance and closure. So Seth groped for something else to blame his sour mood on. Thankfully, he didn't have to reach far. And maybe River could even help with this issue.

"My mother is getting married this fall in New York. She wants me to bring Heavenly to the wedding so she can meet the family."

"But not Beck?" River raised a brow. "Oh, she doesn't know about you three."

"Nope, and I don't know how to tell her. She's super traditional. Catholic. Protective. Well-meaning, but…" He shrugged. "I just don't want to make strife at her wedding. How does your sister handle this shit?"

"Hammer doesn't have any family, and Liam's welcomed their triad with open arms."

He'd known that but hoped there had been some behind-the-scenes machinations to bring that about. Then again, he should have realized that Bryn and Duncan O'Neill would never want anything but sublime joy for their only son, no matter what that looked like.

River frowned. "Doesn't your mom want you to be happy?"

Sometimes he swore Raine's older brother could half read his mind. "She does. Totally. But I don't know that she'll ever understand why that's with both a woman and a guy I definitely don't fuck. Honestly, if I told her I was gay, she would take it better. But I also know I can't hide my relationship with Heavenly and Beck forever. I don't want to."

"I get that. I mean, not firsthand. Dean and I tend to find a hot girl for the night and lose her number the next morning, so we don't deal with the issues and problems in a real relationship. But my sister has talked about the stares and the judgment, about the difficulties of balancing the guys' needs with her own. And now that she's having twins, there will be even more to handle. But she also says she's never been happier, and it's worth it every day."

No surprise. Raine was a survivor. Heavenly was, too…but in a much different way. She'd only ever fought her dad's vicious disease, never the violence of the real world. Would she understand his failure? Would she ever look at him the same again if she knew how horribly he'd handled everything? How terribly he'd reacted afterward?

"She looks happy," he said noncommittally. "I'm happy for them. After Liam's divorce from that viper—"

"I didn't meet his ex-wife, but she sounded like a real peach."

"If you mean the rotten kind, yeah. But after Gwyneth, I didn't think Liam would ever find this kind of bliss. Raine brought him back to Hammer, and they're all where they belong now."

Just like he felt as if he'd found his forever in Heavenly and Beck. But they wanted more from him. They wanted the truth.

Seth was fucking terrified of how they'd take it.

He and River filled the rest of the ride with small talk about sports and food. When he parked at the office, Raine's brother dashed to his truck and drove off with a wave. Seth headed inside, talked to the client, worked on paperwork, returned a few phone calls…then realized he could go home.

But should he if he didn't have his head screwed on straight?

Suddenly, his phone dinged with a message from Heavenly in their three-way chat. `I'm keeping some dinner warm for you. Any chance you're coming home soon?`

Then Beck chimed in with, `It's time for dessert. Come get it while it's hot. I am…`

Swearing, Seth glanced at the time on his computer. It was already past ten p.m. By the time he locked up here, headed home, and showered—because he needed to—it would be nearly eleven. She and Beck would already be busy—if they weren't now. He'd love to be there with them, sandwiching Heavenly between him and Beck, making sweet love to her.

Forgetting about the past.

But afterward, they would ask him questions he didn't have good answers for. He would only put them off again. And he'd risk jacking up their relationship even more. Until he figured out how he could find the right way to say what they wanted to know, he was better off keeping his distance.

With an exhausted sigh, he plucked a pillow and one of his mom's old quilts from a storage closet, turned out the lights, and tossed himself onto the long sofa against the wall. He'd barely slept in three fucking days, and he was beat.

As he settled into his makeshift bed, he gripped his phone and tapped out the safe answer.

`Sorry, you two. Really wrapped up here. I'll see you in the morning.`

But when he closed his eyes, it didn't take long before the nightmare he hadn't had in years—of cold winter, hate, screams, and death —started haunting him.

P ropped up in bed beside Heavenly, Beck read Seth's reply when it appeared on his screen—and nearly lost his goddamn temper. Seth was turning down pleasure with their girl?

Fine. I'll eat all the dessert myself.

When he turned to Heavenly, she drew back from the screen in hurt. Her smile fell. With one sentence, Seth had managed to kill whatever serenity she'd found today. Beck wanted to strangle him. What the hell was that dipshit thinking?

Instead, Beck banked his fury and plucked the cell phone from her hand, then settled it on the nightstand beside his. She needed love and reassurance, and he'd give them to her, especially since Seth wasn't going to. "Well, it's his loss. Come here." He brought her close. "I told you to make sure you needed me later. It's later now…"

He layered his seductive murmur with a caress across her shoulder as he brushed her silky-soft hair aside, fanning it across her pillow, then dragged his tongue up her slender neck.

She turned his way, eyes hollow with uncertainty. "Beck…"

"Shh. I'm here for you, to give you whatever you need. And I need you, too."

He waited, letting his words sink in. She blinked as if she fought tears, then gave him a little nod and threw her arms around his neck, her eyes sliding shut. Yeah, she definitely needed him.

Beck rolled on top of her and claimed her lips. She opened and gave herself over to him. Thank fuck. He slid a hand up her body, settling at her waist. Since they'd been getting ready for bed, the only thing between her berry nipples and his mouth was her faded pink camisole. Nothing but her matching ruffled shorts kept him from the juicy spice between her legs. Everything inside him urged him to get as deep inside her as he could right now.

But she suddenly eased from their kiss and closed him out.

"Talk to me, little girl."

When she opened her eyes, they were swimming in tears. "It's not you. I love you. I—"

"I know. You don't have to reassure me. Tell me what's in your head." Though he had a pretty fucking good idea.

"He's pulling away. I know he's been through a lot, much more than I imagined. But what if he doesn't—"

Beck laid a finger over her lips, stopping her. "Don't assume the worst. It's only been a couple of days, and he said he needed some time to get his head together."

"But I think you're right. He hasn't finished grieving the family he lost, and we're pushing him to...I don't know. Get past it? Move on before he's ready? Something. But it's been eight years. Why should he still be so hung up he can barely talk about it?"

"I don't know. If he'd told us more, maybe I could figure it out and help." But Seth would have to stop running.

She nodded softly. "What do you think set him off? For months, he gave no indication he was suffering from this trauma. He seemed fine the night before the battle. Better than fine, actually. Then suddenly... he wasn't."

Beck had been trying to figure that out, too. "He was even fine *during* the battle. Something afterward triggered him."

"As we left the lodge, I thought it might be the dead bodies."

He scoffed. "It wasn't that. He had no problem adding to the body count. And after it was over, I didn't see what happened. I was busy taking care of Dean. Most everyone else was comforting Ngaire."

"Do you think it was her losing her husband that set Seth off?"

Beck sat back on his heels and thought through yesterday morning. Suddenly, the truth smacked him. "Oh, fuck. It's Zach. I was standing right beside him when Esther said they'd killed his wife and daughter. I saw Seth's face."

Heavenly pressed a hand over the silent O of her lips, more tears pooling in her eyes. "Oh, my gosh. I didn't think..."

"I didn't, either. And I just asked my brother to move in with us. No wonder Seth is avoiding home." Beck stood and paced. "What the fuck did I do?"

Heavenly climbed out of bed and followed, laying a gentle hand on his shoulder. "What you thought was right. You can't blame yourself. You didn't know, and you were just trying to help your brother. Why didn't Seth tell us?"

"He probably didn't know what to say. He probably thinks of this place as my house, so he felt like he didn't have any right to tell me who could live here." Beck reached for his pants and stepped in. "Fuck."

"Where are you going?"

"To find him. I've got to talk to him. It can't wait until morning." Beck didn't want to even whisper the possibility to Heavenly, but Seth might decide never to come home and he'd drift away for good.

And it would all be his fault.

She reached for the yoga pants she'd stripped off a few minutes ago. "I'll come with you."

He plucked his shirt from the back of a nearby chair and tossed it on. "No. Stay here in case Zach needs something. And if Seth comes back, you can text me."

Not only that, when I find him, we might exchange some blunt—maybe even brutal—words.

Heavenly's shoulders drooped as she dropped her pants. Clearly, she didn't like it, but she saw the wisdom. "All right. You'll keep me posted?"

"Absolutely." He pressed a kiss to her lips.

When he would have stepped into his shoes, Heavenly stayed him with a gentle grip. "Wait. You have to be at the hospital early in the morning. You need sleep. Since I'm volunteering, my schedule is more flexible. Let me go."

"No. I made this mess. I need to fix it more than I need sleep, and if I have to hunt him down in some seedy part of town, I'd feel better knowing you're here and safe." He pressed one last kiss to her soft mouth, swiped his phone off the nightstand, and slipped on his shoes. "I'll be back."

He tore down the stairs and picked up his keys, then set the alarm and flew out to the garage before burning rubber down the driveway. He'd barely put the car in drive before he whipped out his cell and called the one person who should know exactly where to find Seth.

River answered on the first ring. "Hey, Beck. What's up?"

"Where are you two? I need an address. I've got to talk to Seth."

"You sound upset. What's wrong?"

"I just need to talk to him ASAP. Where are you?"

"He never came home? I left him at the office about two hours ago. We got back from Palm Springs after closing the case. He said he was going to call the client with the news and do some paperwork. Since Dean's sister apparently brought him home from the hospital, then had to go back to work, I thought I'd come over here and check on him, so I jetted."

Dean had a sister? First he was hearing of that. The guy had never mentioned her, but whatever. "So you haven't seen Seth since?"

"No, man. Have you tried calling?"

Some things were better said in person. "As far as you know, he's still at the office?"

"He must be. I get the feed around the perimeter. It's like a video doorbell on steroids. Hang on."

Beck waited impatiently, hoping that River could tell him something useful. Finally, Raine's big brother sighed. "Yeah. He's still there. No one has opened the door since I left, and his SUV is still in the parking lot. He seemed pretty wiped. Maybe he fell asleep."

Yeah, on purpose. "I'll check there."

"You're going to need the code to get in."

"Code?"

"Yeah, he's got layers of security around the place."

Of course Seth did. If he'd even fortified his temporary bachelor pad, then he'd put super, impenetrable security around his office. "Lay it on me."

River did. Beck had to pull over, find a pen, and jot down the precise instructions, including a twelve-digit code.

"That's all," the guy said.

"All?" Beck huffed as he surged into sparse late-night traffic. "If there'd been more, I would have wondered if I'd need Houdini to get in."

"Seth is...particular."

"Try paranoid," Beck drawled, wondering if Autumn and Tristan were the reasons.

But his wife and son were dead. Why should he still be paranoid? Seth had claimed his past was ancient history that would never bite them in the ass.

Maybe that's not true...

"Yeah, more like that," River admitted. "You need me to come out there? Dean took his pain pills and passed out, so he doesn't need me to stay. He farts in his sleep. He swears it's his dog, but..."

The joke was funny, but Beck wasn't in the mood to smile. "Nah, I got this. Thanks for your help, man."

Before River even said goodbye, Beck hung up and gunned his engine.

He reached Seth's office a handful of minutes later, grateful he hadn't encountered any cops running speed traps on his way. Jerking his Mercedes into the first available spot, he hopped out, barely remembering to click the button on his fob to lock the vehicle, then marched to the door. He swore like a motherfucker as he punched in the ridiculously long code, agitation eating at him until the door finally snapped open.

The foyer was empty, the stairs leading up to Cooper Investigations West dark. At the top of the landing, he paused, letting his eyes adjust to the blinding light from Seth's desk lamp until he could see beyond it.

And there he was, sprawled on the couch, his head on a pillow that had seen better days, bundled up with an old blanket, his feet hanging over the side. One arm dangled and dragged the floor. And with his next breath, he snored like a chainsaw.

Seth was dead-ass asleep.

Shit.

Sighing, he approached the slumbering PI and nudged his shoulder. "Hey, wake up. We need to talk."

Seth jolted upright and blinked, bleary-eyed. "Beck? What the hell are you doing here?"

"That's what I want to ask you. When you told Heavenly you were all wrapped up, I didn't think that meant with your blanket on your too-short sofa in your office. Want to tell me why you're not at home in bed with us?"

"What time is it?" He glanced at his watch. "Almost midnight? Shit... I was working here. Still more to do, but I hadn't slept in days, so I lay down to nap for a few minutes. I didn't think I'd be safe to drive home, otherwise. I didn't mean to conk out."

Yeah, Seth probably hadn't slept in days. He definitely hadn't last night since he'd come in from the cheating-spouse case, then left immediately for Palm Springs. He hadn't slept much the night before the battle, either. Beck would concede that, but... "Why didn't you call? We would have picked you up and brought you home."

"I thought a twenty-minute power nap would be enough. Then I planned to tackle the rest of my to-do list. It's not a big deal. Why are you here, up my ass?"

Really? "Up your ass? Oh, I haven't even started to put my foot up your ass yet. You didn't see Heavenly's face when you said you weren't coming home. Again. Are you avoiding us because you know we're going to ask questions you don't want to answer?"

"No, man. Work is just fucking busy. This case..."

"You mean the one you and River solved today?"

Surprise crossed Seth's face before he banked it. "He told you that?"

"Yep. When he told me how to get into this place. So if it's not the case anymore—"

"I still have paperwork. I still run a business. That shit takes time, you know."

"Yep. I deal with paperwork and patient charts every fucking day. I still manage to come home to our girl most nights." Beck leaned in, pointing a finger in Seth's chest. "Want to know what I think?"

Seth rolled his eyes. "Even if I say no, you're going to tell me."

"Damn straight. You opened your mouth at the lodge and said something you wish you could take back. Now you're trying to backpedal by lying to us—and yourself. For some reason, the truth bothers you. I don't think you finished grieving your family and—"

"The fuck I didn't. I went through days of denial. I buried them, still trying to grapple with what the hell had happened. You think I wasn't angry? Oh, fuck, was I ever. Furious. Lava-hot, gut-churning rage like I'd never felt in my goddamn life. I tried to bargain with God and anyone I thought would listen. I would have gladly slit my own throat if I thought it would bring them back, but that shit never works, and we all know it. So I moved on. I spent the next few years depressed as fuck. I stopped going to Graffiti. I couldn't stand Christmas. I just wanted every well-meaning friend and family member to leave me the fuck alone. Of course they wouldn't, especially my mom. And finally, I accepted that the wife and child, who were my responsibility, were gone and that they had died on *my* watch." Seth poked Beck in the chest and sent him stumbling back a pace or two. "So fuck your theory that I haven't finished grieving."

"Okay." He held up his hands. "So you have survivor's guilt?"

"Wouldn't you? Didn't you have survivor's guilt about Blessing? Imagine that shit times a hundred."

"Yeah, I did. And I ended the bastard who killed her. What did you do? Because I know you didn't kill your family yourself and you didn't let their deaths go unpunished. Is that why you 'went off the deep end and did things you're not proud of?'"

"Yeah. But that's all water under the bridge now."

"Is it?"

"I did what I needed to do and I walked away over six and a half years ago, so yeah. It's over and done. Leave it the fuck alone."

Beck was dying to know what Seth had "needed to do", but if it had been that long ago, the steps he'd taken to understand their deaths or avenge them or whatever were moot now.

Seth's feelings, however, weren't. Those were causing them problems.

"I can't. If it's over and done with, why are you sleeping here? Why does it seem like you're avoiding us? Does this have anything to do with Zach?"

Cooper blanched. "I don't care if you moved your brother in. He needs help, and there's plenty of room."

"So being around him while he's processing the murders of his wife and daughter doesn't bother you at all? It doesn't exhume the fury and anguish you dealt with after losing Autumn and Tristan?"

"Is it comfortable? No. But he's not the reason I'm at the office instead of home. I. Have. Work. I know you get that."

"I do. But I'm sorry I moved Zach into the house without asking you or Heavenly how you felt about that and without thinking about how that might impact you. It was a knee-jerk reaction because I remember crawling out of Messiah City and feeling alone in a world I didn't understand. I wanted to spare my brother some of the difficulty and confusion—"

"And you should. If that was one of my brothers, I'd do the same. Besides, it's your house. Do what you want with it."

"It's *our* house. I've said that enough that you ought to know it. So if Zach being there is a problem for you, I'll find somewhere else for him. The condo, maybe. Just say the word."

"It's not a problem, man. I'm just working. If it will make you feel better, I'll come home right now and help you fuck Heavenly so you two can sleep nice and sound tonight. Would that make you happy?"

Beck restrained the urge to break his jaw—or at least try. But he needed his hands for surgery tomorrow. And he must be getting uncomfortably close to Seth's hot-button truth, because the big guy was lashing back. So he tamped down on his violent urge and shook his head. "No. I'll fuck her by myself. I wouldn't want to inconvenience you. But what would make me happy is for you to grow a set, get honest, and tell us both what the hell is bothering you. Until you can do that, maybe it's best if you don't come home."

After giving Seth the ultimatum, Beck stormed from Cooper Investigations West, slammed the door behind him, and peeled out of the parking lot. Fury lit up his system, crowding his head and firing his blood. He resisted the urge—barely—to flatten the accelerator to the floorboard and leave this bullshit in the dust.

Goddamn, he was tired of Seth shutting them out. Tired of him being unable to deal with his past and get his shit together. And tired as fuck of him hurting their girl. Didn't the stupid asshole see he was throwing away the people who loved him and wanted to help him? Didn't he give a shit that his avoidance was wreaking havoc on their future?

"Motherfucker!" Beck banged on the steering wheel.

It didn't make him feel better.

Swallowing his rage and helplessness, he turned off Wilshire and aimlessly cruised side streets. He couldn't let Heavenly see him this angry. She was already worried, but when she found out that Seth had chosen to sleep on his office sofa instead of their bed? She would be devastated. Still, she needed the truth. Worse, he couldn't give her any assurances. And Beck hated that he had to be the one to break her heart—yet another task Seth's refusal to face his feelings forced him to endure.

Beck just hoped like fuck that the PI's love for Heavenly would be enough to bring him back.

"No use procrastinating," he muttered as he drove home.

Beck had barely pulled into the garage when the door to the house swung open and Heavenly stepped into the portal. Expectation filled her face, offset by an unsettling swirl of fear and hope in her eyes.

Cursing Seth under his breath, Beck clenched his jaw and climbed from the car.

Heavenly rushed to his side. "Did you find him?"

"Yeah."

Her anxious glance at the driveway almost killed him. "W-where is he?"

"At the office. Alone." Beck wrapped his arm around her waist as he reached up to close the garage door. When the rollers squeaked and the panel met the concrete with a definitive thud, Heavenly let out a shaky breath and pressed her forehead to his chest.

"He's not coming home, is he?"

"Not tonight." He scooped her into his arms and cradled her to his chest, carrying her inside the house.

Tears pooled in her eyes and slid down her cheeks as he climbed the stairs and headed into their bedroom. When he set her on her feet, Beck fought the urge to pull out his phone and FaceTime the prick so

Seth could see how much he was hurting their girl. Right now, he didn't think it would do any good, so he nudged the pillows against the headboard, eased onto the mattress, and pulled Heavenly up beside him, nestling her close.

"Is this case really more important to him than us?"

"That's not it. He and River solved that a few hours ago." Beck dragged in a tense breath and went for broke. "Seth isn't coming home because I told him not to."

Heavenly reared back and gaped at him. "What? Why would you do that?"

Beck brushed the tears from her cheeks, wishing she was more ready to hear the truth he had to tell her. Then he crushed her as gently as possible. Once he'd explained everything, he held her close. "I'm sorry."

"I don't understand." The anguish in her voice eviscerated him. "He'd rather sleep on a couch in his office than come home to us. Why?"

"Because he knows that he can't come home until he's honest with us. And he's not ready."

"What if he's never ready? What if he never comes home?" A sob caught in her throat. "What if he leaves us for good?"

Beck hugged her tighter. "We have to think positive."

"But telling him not to come home? How can he know that we'll still love him, no matter what, if you told him to stay away?"

Goddamn it, he wasn't the bad guy. He was trying to protect her. "Seth needs to understand the consequences of his choices. And I didn't kick him out of the house; I told him that, until he could be honest with us about his past and his feelings, he shouldn't come back."

"What if he never does?" The desolation in her voice tore at him.

"Then he never loved us enough in the first place."

Her face twisted with refusal. "I don't believe that."

"I don't *want* to believe it. But until Seth decides to tell us how he really feels, I don't know what to think."

Heavenly didn't say anything for a long moment. Finally, she wiped her cheeks. Defeat crept into her voice. "You're right."

At least she saw his point, though he wished like hell he hadn't had to make it. "Come on, little girl. It's late. Let's try to get some sleep. If you need, we can talk again in the morning."

Heavenly nodded as he eased out of bed.

After he changed out of his clothes and autopiloted through his nightly routine, they climbed back between the sheets. Beck extinguished the light and held her in his arms, tucking her close, then shutting his eyes.

Normally, Heavenly's warm breath on his chest soothed him to sleep, but not tonight. The unanswered questions dive-bombing Beck's brain only reignited his anger and angst. Beside him, Heavenly wasn't faring any better. He could feel her lashes fluttering against his skin with every blink.

"I'm scared," she confessed in the dark.

"Don't be. And don't give up hope. Seth fought too hard for this—for us—to just walk away. He loves you, and love is the most powerful emotion on the planet."

"Maybe he just needs more time. I can give that to him. What about you?"

"No, not if he keeps ripping out your heart this way. Seth isn't the only protector in this relationship."

She tightened her arms around him. "I know, and I love you for it."

Beck kissed the top of her head. "It's killing me to sit back and do nothing, especially when my job is to fix people."

"I'm sure. But I know firsthand that grief is hard. Even though I had months—years, really—to prepare for Dad's death, I wasn't ready for him to go, especially not so quickly. But Seth had zero warning, no time to brace himself to lose his wife and baby. They were just ripped violently from his life."

"I don't pretend to understand everything he went through—or what he's dealing with now that those memories have resurfaced. Seriously, I'm not trying to be a heartless prick, but he's dodging us. On top of that, his refusal to tell his mom about us isn't okay."

"Well, I'm sure it's not easy to—"

"Fly your freak flag in front of a parent? I know you struggled, and I didn't appreciate how much until you explained. But you lived through it—in the worst possible circumstances. What really pisses me off is that he's not willing to compromise. How can any relationship last without give and take? Think about what happens if he doesn't come clean with his family. We'll always be stuck—every birthday, every holiday, every visit—hiding or lying or pretending to be something we're not. We'll be stuck in limbo. I fucking hate that."

"Me, too. I spent years there, every day between my father's diagnosis and the day he died. The not knowing almost killed me."

"Exactly. After I left Messiah City and ended up in Vegas, I lived minute to minute, digging through dumpsters for food and searching for safe places to sleep where I wouldn't get raped or killed."

Heavenly squeezed him again and pressed a soft kiss to his chest. "I'm so grateful Gloria found you."

"Me, too."

Several minutes passed before Heavenly's broken whisper cut the silence. "I wish I hadn't wasted so much time."

"With your dad?"

"No, with us. It shouldn't have taken me months to realize that I love you both. I wish I would have admitted that instead of sending you two away. We could have had more time together, been building a stronger foundation…"

"Seth and I pissed away weeks fighting each other for you, rather than embracing you together."

"We're both right. If we hadn't been so stubborn, maybe Seth wouldn't be holding back now." She sighed. "So many maybes, what-ifs, and regrets. Lots of those."

"You can't blame yourself. You couldn't have known. I couldn't, either. There's no reason to feel guilt." Beck cupped her cheek and tilted her head back, staring into her beloved face in shadow. "Seth is responsible for his emotions and his choices. It's on him to decide whether he's going to walk away or commit. And he needs to decide soon. If he can't, we're better off without him."

CHAPTER FIVE

After Beck left, Seth tossed on the sofa as the words they'd exchanged turned over in his head.

Maybe it's best if you don't come home.

Wow, he'd always known Beck's tolerance for BS was low, but even Seth hadn't expected him to hit so hard or so quickly.

If the shoe was on the other foot, what would you do?

Seth winced. And Heavenly? What must she be thinking? Beck hadn't been shy about the fact his failure to come home and his excuses had hurt her. Seth felt ashamed. The last thing he ever wanted to do was upset their girl. But he'd asked for a couple of days to get his head together.

Yeah, at their expense. Nice move, asshole.

Damn, that voice in his head wasn't wrong. Heavenly had lost her father less than a month ago. Of course she still spontaneously cried. She had good days and bad days. And he suspected she "talked" to the man every so often. But she was coping with his passing far better than Seth was dealing with the loss of his family, despite the fact he'd had eight years to do it. Then again, he wasn't grieving anymore, not the way Beck meant.

Still, he wasn't ready to spill all. He didn't want to—ever. How would they look at him? Seth knew the answer. They wouldn't. They would just run away screaming in terror. And they seemed determined to pry his violent past out of him.

What the fuck was he going to do? Seth grimaced into his third mug of bitter coffee, knowing full well it wouldn't give him any answers.

River walked in, saving him from his circular reverie, and spotted him, then stopped short in the door. "Jesus. You look like hell." He glanced at the pillow and blanket folded on the sofa and his brows furrowed. "Did you stay here all night?"

"None of your business." He rose and handed River a piece of paper. "Here's the new code for the building. Don't ever give it to anyone again, for any reason, or you're fired."

"You're pissed I gave it to Beck? He was worried about you. Hell, I was, too. You—"

"Didn't give you permission to give out the code. I didn't tell you not to—mostly because I didn't think I had to—but that's the only reason I'm letting it slide. Are we clear?"

River was every bit as tall as he was and probably outweighed him by twenty pounds of muscle. Unlike Beck, River knew how to fight dirty and wouldn't hesitate to throw a punch. The only thing stopping Raine's big brother now was the fact he needed this job. "Crystal. Next time Beck is worried about you, I'll tell him not to bother because you don't want anyone to give a shit. He'll take that okay, I suppose. But I doubt Heavenly will. Then again, maybe you don't care about either of them anymore. That's how you're acting."

Ouch. That fucking hurt. The worst part? River wasn't wrong.

"Can it. Here's some shit that needs following up on." Seth scooped up some paperwork from his desk and flipped it against River's chest. "I'm going home to take a shower, change clothes, and find some decent fucking breakfast. You can catch me up when I get back."

"Sure. But whatever's eating at you? It's like a parasite. It won't stop gnawing until you get it out. I'm all ears if you can't talk to Beck and Heavenly."

He'd been an absolute dick, and River was still offering to be his friend. Goddamn it. Then again, hadn't his whole family tried to reach him when he'd fallen off the deep end and let anger swallow him years ago? Yep. And he'd been too mired in grief, fury, and self-loathing to let anyone help him. The result? He'd spent nearly two years mostly alone and isolated from everyone he held dear.

Was he really going to hang on to the past? Or would he choose the new future he'd worked so fucking hard to cobble together with Beck and Heavenly?

Seth sighed. "Thanks. I appreciate the offer, but I've got an ear who will be plenty willing to listen."

And kick his ass. Seth couldn't forget that part.

He shut down his computer and grabbed his keys, then waved

River's way before heading out. Beck was probably at the hospital, and Heavenly would be leaving to put in some hours there, too. But Zach would be there, probably confused, lost, angry... And Beck had made himself clear that he wasn't welcome there until he word-vomited up the shit in his past.

There was a reason he hadn't given up the crappy bachelor pad he'd rented when he'd first made his way to LA a couple months back. Good thing he had it to go back to now.

But entering the nine hundred square feet of white boxy walls was depressing as fuck. His kitchen looked dusty. The sectional he'd picked up on clearance sat unruffled, its pillows perfectly straight, in front of a TV that hadn't been flipped on in weeks. In his bedroom, the bed was made, but he'd taken most of the clothes from his closet. What the hell was he going to put on after he showered? For that matter, how the fuck was he going to shower when he'd taken his shampoo, gel, and razors to Beck's?

Sighing, Seth decided he didn't give a fuck. He found an old bar of Dial in the soap dish and a travel-size shampoo in the medicine cabinet. Close enough. A handful of minutes later, he emerged and toweled off, trying not to care that even his towels smelled musty, as if they'd been sitting in the linen closet a bit too long to be fresh.

Seth rushed into the hodgepodge of clothes he'd left behind and finally let in the thoughts he'd been avoiding for the past hour.

He had to get his head screwed on straight. And of all the people in his life who would bend over backward—and there were thankfully a bunch, because despite everything, he was blessed—one person was at the top of his list.

Cursing under his breath, he grabbed his keys, hopped in his SUV, and headed to the palatial house Liam shared with Hammer and Raine, well aware he was about to get his ass handed to him. Paybacks were hell, and neither he nor Liam candy-coated advice.

This was going to suck.

Seth lifted his hand to ring the bell, then waited. The irony of the situation wasn't lost on him. A few months back, he'd flown across the country to dispense advice so his old pal could more successfully navigate the twisting trail of polyamory. Now he found himself stumbling up a similarly uneven path.

What were the odds that his Irish pal wouldn't rub his nose in the same well-meaning words he'd dished out months ago? He didn't have time to wonder before the door swung open.

In the portal, Liam arched a brow. "I was wondering how long it would take before you came to see me."

"You should have asked your crystal ball," Seth quipped.

"Didn't have to. I knew you were coming. I simply didn't know how long it was going to take you to swallow your pride and actually do it."

"Christ, I'm not even inside and you're already busting my balls."

"No. I'm just ribbing you a bit, mate. I'm saving the real ball bustin' for when you need it."

"Great."

Liam chuckled. "Come on in. Let's sit by the pool. No offense, but you look like you need to take a load off."

"What I need is an undo button. A big, fat one like the one on my fucking computer."

Liam grunted as he strode to the kitchen and grabbed a couple bottles of water from the fridge.

"The house is so quiet. Where is everyone?"

"Hammer's at the club, and Raine is upstairs napping."

Seth trailed him onto the deck by the pool, completely surrounded by lush foliage. They each grabbed a chair beneath the umbrella of a round patio table under the shimmering sun. Seth was too keyed up to enjoy the view.

"That undo button you wanted?" Liam began. "If you could push it, how far back would you go?"

Seth tensed. "Wow. No warm-up, huh? Just straight for the jugular?"

Liam shrugged. "You didn't come to see me toss on a tutu and dance around the elephant in the room, did you?"

"No, but that would probably trend like a motherfucker on social media."

"How far back would you go?" Liam doggedly repeated.

Seth swallowed the lump of emotion suddenly lodged in his throat. "Far enough to save them."

"Of course you would. There's not many people on the planet who'd pass up a chance to go back in time and save their loved ones."

"What would you change?"

"The list is long. I'd like to save Raine from being kidnapped and having to kill her father." Liam took a gulp of water. "But if I did that, Bill would still be alive and a threat to our girl."

"The butterfly effect."

"Exactly. If you'd saved Autumn and Tristan, you wouldn't be in LA. You certainly wouldn't be building a life with Heavenly or Beck."

Imagining living without them for the rest of his life carved a gaping, aching hole in Seth's chest.

"And you wouldn't be here with me, trying to find a way to keep your fears and worries from eating you alive."

"Are you reading me or is it that obvious?"

"Both. Talk to me, Seth. Your secrets are always safe with me."

"I know. And I appreciate that, man. I truly do." He turned and stared at the pool and worked to gather his thoughts. Finally, he dragged in a deep breath and faced Liam. "I fucked up at the lodge. I told Beck and Heavenly that I killed my wife and son."

"So I heard."

That shouldn't have surprised him. After all, if the shoe was on the other foot, Seth would be hitting Hammer up for every detail he could weasel out of the man.

"Beck or Heavenly?"

"Beck. He asked what really happened to Autumn and Tristan. He wanted to know why you said you killed them because neither he nor Heavenly believe you did."

"I might not have killed them with my own hands, but—"

"You didn't. It's time to stop guilting yourself. Are you intentionally pushing Beck and Heavenly away for a reason?"

"I'm not pushing them away," he snapped. "It's just...I can't bring myself to tell them what happened, especially what I did after Autumn and Tristan were gone."

"Why?"

"I'm worried it will put a wedge between us that none of us can ever fix."

"Oh, so keeping secrets that damn near destroyed you isn't putting a wedge between the three of you now?"

He should have seen that question coming. "Shut up."

"No chance, mate," Liam said with a smug smirk. "And if that's your best comeback, that tells me you know I'm right."

"Are we keeping score?"

Liam shook his head. "You're glum enough. The final tally would only depress you more."

"Then let's skip the rest of this chat. You'll just tell me to spill my guts and let the chips fall," Seth drawled as he scooted his chair back and stood. "And I'm telling you I can't."

"Sit down," Liam chided. "I'm not through."

"What's left to say except that I was a fool for opening my mouth in the first place? That part of my life is over. Done. There's nothing to be gained by digging up the past. It's where it belongs. It needs to stay buried."

Liam didn't say anything for long seconds, simply held him with a piercing stare. Finally, he took another drink of water. "You're aware that our girls talk, right?"

"Sure. Raine is the only girlfriend Heavenly really has."

"Then it's no surprise I'm privy to the fact that, while you and Beck haven't taken Heavenly to Shadows, you two are giving her quite an education about Dominance and submission."

A crooked smile tugged at Seth's lips. He would have loved being a fly on the wall when sweet Heavenly described all the kinky things he and Beck enjoyed doing to her. "It's been brief but thorough."

"Rumor has it that, after you and Beck discovered Heavenly was working at Bazookas, you two had hard words for her all the way home because she'd lied about her job."

"River has a big mouth. Heavenly didn't lie, but she omitted the truth."

"Like you're doing now?"

"It's not the same thing."

"Not exactly. What you're doing is more deceitful. If you expect

Heavenly to be open and honest, to communicate all her feelings, and to give you her trust, you have to give her the same in return. If you don't, your relationship with her and Beck won't be built on solid ground. And how long do you think it will last?"

People can't be in relationships with partners who aren't honest. The words Seth had once spoken to Heavenly zipped through his brain—and bit his ass like a shark.

He scrubbed a hand over his face, then stared at Liam. "This is the part where you start busting my balls for real, right?"

"Indeed. Now stop avoiding my question."

With a sigh, Seth settled into his chair again. "I can't tell them the truth."

"You can. You simply don't want to because you're afraid it will change how they feel about you."

"If you already know the reason, why are we playing twenty questions?"

"Because I was hoping you'd find the courage to tell me yourself, you daft prick," Liam said in exasperation. "Clearly you've no intention of being honest with anyone, even yourself."

"Don't pull that reverse psychology crap on me. I know the truth."

"Do you, now? Then I'll ask question number twenty-one. Did you think less of Beck after he shared the news about killing his father?"

"Of course not."

"What about Raine? She killed her father, too. Do you think less of her?"

"You know I don't." In fact, he admired the hell out of her.

"Good. Hammer and I don't, either. We're proud that our girl is a lot stronger than we'd given her credit for."

"Beck's and Raine's pasts aren't like mine. They killed in self-defense. I *chose* to dive into that cesspool of violence."

"I remember well. I was there. I was also there when you climbed back out, haunted, broken, and barely human."

Brutal memories flooded Seth's brain. His stomach knotted.

"But you fought your way back to reality, to sanity, and to the love of your family and friends because you wanted to live again," Liam continued. "Beck and Heavenly are your future. Everything that's happened has been a part of the plan."

Liam's words exposed a possibility he'd never considered —until now.

White-hot rage seared Seth's veins. Launching to his feet—and sending the heavy wrought iron chair crashing to the concrete—he squeezed his hands into fists and clenched his jaw. "You knew? You fucking knew they were going to die and you didn't tell me?"

Liam scowled and shook his head. "No. Bloody hell, mate. Do you actually think if I had known Autumn and Tristan were in danger I wouldn't have told you? I would have helped you move them some-place safe. Hell, I would have driven them myself—whatever you needed. I wasn't listening to my inner voice then. Besides, decisions hadn't been made. The future hadn't been written. I was as blind as you."

Panting, Seth dropped his chin and tried to force the rage from his system as he righted the chair and sat again. "Yeah."

"I can't explain why my gifts have grown stronger and sharper recently," Liam said, his voice low and calm. "I think it has something to do with embracing my life with Hammer and Raine. Finally being happy."

Seth had seen that in action. "Probably. I'm sorry, man. I shouldn't have accused you. And I didn't mean to lose my shit."

"Been doing that a lot lately?"

"No." Seth shook his head. "I've just been running away."

"From what? The past, the present, or the future?"

"I haven't exactly been choosy."

Liam clucked at him. "And how's that working out for you?"

"It hasn't. That's why I'm here, asshole."

"Well, it's one of the reasons." Liam smirked.

"Jesus, man. Do you know what I had for breakfast, too?"

"Black coffee," Liam replied dryly before pinning Seth with a dissecting stare. "I'm not convinced you're ready to hear the truth yet, but I'll give it to you anyway. You've convinced yourself that the sins of your past are unforgivable. They're not."

"If I tell them everything, Beck will be horrified. Heavenly will be afraid of me. And she should be."

"Bollocks. Beck and Heavenly will understand. And they won't love you any less."

"That your opinion or your spidey senses talking?"

"Neither. It's common sense. You're trying to talk yourself out of doing what's right, and you'll completely fuck up your life." Liam frowned. "If you realized that you deserve to love and be loved unconditionally and that you already have the tools to live happily ever after in the palm of your hand, you'd trust Beck and Heavenly enough to be honest with them."

Seth scoffed. "You make it sound so simple."

"Because it is, you bull-headed bastard," Liam growled. "If you address the reason the past is pouring over you like hot lava, the blistering flow will stop."

"You mean Zach."

"Precisely." He nodded. "He's the reason your dormant volcano erupted and the reason you're running away."

Liam knew him so well. Seth had taken one look at Beck's younger brother, fresh from the shock and pain of his loss, and seen himself eight terrible years ago. He hadn't been able to yank himself back to the present since.

"Yep," Seth whispered.

"You've got to confront it. And you've got to come clean with the people you love—completely. All the ugly, sordid details. It's the only path forward."

Seth heaved out a ragged breath. His old friend was probably right. He didn't know how he was going to do that...but he had to try.

He stood again and held out his hand. "Thanks."

Liam took it and dragged him in for a hearty, back-slapping hug. "I'm here for you anytime, especially if you need your balls busted."

At his Irish friend's wink, Seth found himself laughing. "Asshole."

"You're welcome."

Heavenly finally slept. She woke with the sun beaming on her face, her back pressed against Beck, whose arm was wrapped around her. Her head hurt. She opened her still stinging eyes.

Seth's empty side of the bed was a stark reminder that the happily ever after she'd tried to embrace was slipping through her fingers.

Last night, she'd cried until she'd run out of tears. After a restless night, she had more to shed. But she swallowed them back and tried to cling to hope. Seth grappling with his past couldn't last forever. He would eventually realize how much she and Beck loved him and want to come home, right?

Maybe...but she had no guarantee.

Heavenly closed her eyes again and dragged in an uneven breath to stave off more tears. She missed Seth so much.

Refusing to wallow away the day, she turned and pressed a grateful kiss to Beck's forehead. Last night, he'd tried so hard to steady and bolster her. Honestly, she didn't know how she'd ever do without him. But clearly, he was suffering, too. Seth had asked him to compromise more than once without any reciprocation. That couldn't go on. Eventually, the stubborn PI had to let them in.

Or they were doomed.

Pushing the horrible thought aside, she extricated herself and crept out of bed. Easing the door to the attached bath shut, she went through her morning ritual. But her mind wandered. Had Seth slept last night? Did he miss them, too?

As she reached for her toothbrush, she zeroed in on his sitting beside hers in the holder. The sight wrenched her. How would he perform this everyday task when he'd left his behind? Yes, there was a drugstore not far from his office. But what about shave cream? Coffee? A shower? Fresh clothes?

Her first instinct was to call him and offer to bring him his things. Maybe he'd want to talk...

No matter how tempting that idea was, Beck had been adamant about Seth needing time to figure out his feelings and priorities. If she got in the way, would she make things worse?

Heavenly rinsed her mouth and set her toothbrush aside. As

painful as it was to wait for Seth to want them more than he wanted to avoid the pain of his past, she had to.

After a quick shower and a change of clothes, she made her way to the study corner she'd set up down the hall. Even with her head and heart in turmoil, she had school to think about. Finals were coming up...

But forty minutes later, Heavenly lifted her head from her textbook. She'd probably read the same page a handful of times and retained nothing. She needed a caffeine infusion.

Rising, she tiptoed to the stairs and made her way to the kitchen. She was surprised to see Zach sitting at the table, staring down into a cup of coffee.

"Good morning."

He turned and scanned her cautiously. "Morning."

"You're up early."

"Habits of a farmer." He shrugged.

Despite the fact she was fully dressed, he seemed uncomfortable. Because they were alone?

"Did you sleep?" she asked.

"Some. Thank you."

He cast his gaze back to the coffee, as if it held all the secrets of his future. Or as if he didn't know what else to do.

Suddenly knowing he'd have to spend the rest of his life without his wife and daughter must be like a bulldozer to his heart. After missing Seth so much, Heavenly would have sworn she didn't have any more capacity to hurt for anyone, but she ached for him. "Can I make you some breakfast?"

"Don't trouble yourself. I'll be fine."

Something else occurred to her. "Do you know how to cook?"

He hesitated, looking like he wanted to set her at ease. Instead, he snapped his mouth closed and sighed. "Not really."

"I can give you a quick lesson in eggs and toast if that sounds good."

Zach's smile was faint but real. "That would be helpful."

"Let me grab some coffee and we'll get started."

He swallowed more from his mug and rose. "I appreciate it."

After Heavenly put together her own cup of nirvana and took a few swallows, she turned to Zach, now looking out the glass door to the back patio, seemingly lost in thought.

"Do you wonder if they're looking down on you?"

"I'm sorry?" He turned back to her.

"Faith and Joanna. Do you wonder if they're somewhere, watching over you?"

"It's crossed my mind. The notion that your loved ones are still with you in some way is tempting to believe. The Chosen frowned on the idea of spirits lingering in the earthly realm. A less selfish man would wish them to be resting peacefully in God's arms."

She cupped his shoulder. "But you need more time to let them go. I understand. I'm sure whatever God you believe in understands that, too. Ready to get started?"

"Sure."

It took a while to explain the mechanics of the stove and toaster, then to walk him through the cooking, but fifteen minutes later, they sat to a light breakfast. The silence was awkward, so she tried more conversation. "Any thoughts about what you'd like to do today? Tour of the area? Take in a movie? Go for a swim?"

"Gideon—I mean Beck—said something about shopping. Not my idea of a good time, but I understand it's necessary since I didn't leave Messiah City with much. Other than that... I've never seen a movie, and I don't know how to swim."

Heavenly tried not to gape. Somewhere along the way, she remembered hearing that outside influences were frowned upon in Messiah City. Of course he'd never had a chance to visit a theater. But swimming? Wow.

"Let's rectify that, then. We have a bunch of cable channels and streaming services." She reached for the remote and flipped on the big TV affixed to the wall. "What interests you? Sports? Documentaries?" She intentionally avoided the news, and he wouldn't have the faintest idea what a sitcom was. "Or I can just flip around until something appeals to you."

He had no interest in morning shows, home improvement, or

reality TV, but something bright and flashy that made lots of clinking noises got his attention. "Stop. What is that?"

It wasn't familiar to Heavenly at a glance except in the most general sense. "It's a game show."

Zach's brows furrowed as he stared in concentration. "What does that mean?"

"Um...people register to play games on TV to win prizes, like trips and cars and cash."

He scarfed down the last of his breakfast, then took his plate to the sink—his eyes never leaving the TV. Then he wandered to the sofa with the last of his coffee. "Mind if I watch this for a while?"

Not what she would have chosen, but... "No problem. I'll be upstairs studying if you need anything."

Zach gave her a vague nod as he sat, his stare glued.

Heavenly headed back upstairs, shaking her head. Game shows. Go figure.

When she settled back at her desk, she was more awake than before...but not more focused. Beck rose and came to check on her. After assuring him she was fine—well, as fine as she could be in these circumstances—she half listened as he showered, called to check in on his patients, then rounded up Zach to head out for their errands.

Soon after he left her with a lingering kiss and a promise not to be longer than necessary, her phone dinged on the desk beside her. She took a sip of her water, lifted the device, and glanced at the screen, praying Seth had decided to reach out to her. But no. This text was from one of the last people she'd ever expected to hear from.

Pike.

What the devil did he want?

`That favor I asked you for? She's available today. Can you talk to her?`

A few weeks ago, Heavenly had gone to Pike for help with her late father's hospital bed. In the end, she hadn't needed him to intervene, so she'd completely forgotten about his quid-pro-quo request to tell the girl he was interested in that, despite his tattoos, piercings, and bad attitude, he was a good guy. But he'd been willing to lend her a hand—well, kick in a door—when she'd needed it. Besides, she was curious about the kind of woman who would snag Pike's attention. And apparently, River's, too.

But Heavenly hesitated. Her head was a mess and her finals were so close... On the other hand, she had managed to catch up in the last couple of weeks after missing so much class. Her professors had been lenient when she'd explained her father's death, but she'd also worked her butt off to bring her grades back to straight As. It helped that Bridget Lewis, the hospital's nursing administrator where she volunteered, had written a glowing letter to her online university, saying that she had continued to be a passionate, dedicated volunteer, even in the midst of her own loss. So maybe she could afford an hour or two away. Besides, she wasn't accomplishing much this morning, worrying and wallowing. Fresh air would help, right? Not only that, it wasn't even ten a.m. She'd have all afternoon alone, most likely.

Sure. When and where?

After some back-and-forth, they agreed to meet at a sidewalk cafe at noon. Pike promised he'd make the introductions, then leave the ladies to talk.

Heavenly had no idea what to say. Since she'd only spoken to Pike a handful of times, none of them pleasant, she didn't know the man well. She needed info from someone who did.

There was only one person she could ask who would give her answers, so she dialed her bestie.

"Hey!" Raine picked up right away, sounding surprisingly chipper for someone pregnant with really active twins.

"Hi, did I catch you at a bad time?"

"It's the perfect time, actually. The guys are watching some war movie that's so gory it's making my stomach turn. I headed upstairs to cuddle up with a supposedly juicy book."

"Supposedly?"

Raine laughed. "My life is juicier. I'm sure yours is, too."

It used to be. Lately...not so much. Beck was trying to help Zach settle into his new life. And Seth... Who knew? Since the emotional upheaval at the lodge and the resulting disagreements, there had been a total drought in her sex life.

"You know how it is..." she muttered vaguely, trying to sound upbeat. "Listen, I just got an unexpected text. From Pike, of all people." She explained the situation. "What do I say to this woman? I don't know much about him."

Sheets rustling told Heavenly that her bestie sat up in bed, now fully invested in this conversation. "Is this the same girl my brother is totally pretending he's not hung up on?"

"Yes, but I don't know her name."

"Neither do I." And Raine didn't sound happy.

"Is River really interested? Seth told me your brother claims he just wants to talk to her."

Raine scoffed. "And I'm just a little bit pregnant. Please... Even before Dean's injury, River had all but stopped trolling bars with him for their nightly hookups. I overheard Dean grousing to him about it right after they arrived at the lodge."

That surprised Heavenly. "So you don't know *anything* about this girl?"

"Nothing, and I'm dying for details. If she made a significant impact on my manwhore brother in one night, she has to be special."

True. "Does Pike have any good qualities? Ones I haven't seen?" Heavenly winced. "I don't want to stab him in the back...but I don't want to lie to this woman, either."

"Good qualities? Um..." Raine paused.

The fact her bestie couldn't think of a single one wasn't a good sign.

"There must be something," Heavenly prompted.

"Actually, yes. He's really loyal. I mean, he was always staunchly in Hammer's corner, even when it looked like he might go to prison. Pike never once asked if the allegations that Hammer forced me into a sexual relationship as a minor were true. Considering he wasn't a member of Shadows then, much less a DM, maybe he should have. But Pike just threw his support behind Hammer as if he knew Macen was innocent."

Or as if Pike didn't care, but Heavenly kept that to herself. "Anything else?"

Raine paused again. "Depending on the girl, the fact he's super creative in the dungeon may or may not be a selling point. Then again, shouldn't she know that?"

"I don't think she does. When I talked to Pike, I got the impression she had friend-zoned him."

"And she managed to bang my brother yet escape without him knowing anything? He's a freaking PI, and he can't find her anywhere." Raine laughed. "That's epic. I kind of want to shake her hand."

When her bestie gasped like she'd just had the best idea ever, Heavenly cut in. "Whatever you're thinking, no."

"Don't say that before you've even heard my idea. What if I just happen to wander by while you're talking to her? It would be perfect."

"For who?" Heavenly said suspiciously, but she giggled.

"For all of us. Maybe neither Pike nor River deserves her, but let's find out. I can tell her more about both of them while we figure out what's up with her."

"You're stirring the pot. No offense, but Pike didn't ask you to talk to her. He asked me, probably because you're a well-documented troublemaker."

"I am not. I'm…intrepid. Pike would have asked me if he'd thought of it."

"I doubt that." Heavenly grinned.

"Well, he should have. Text me when and where you're going to be. Once Pike leaves the scene, I'll meander that way, like, by accident."

"But on purpose?" Heavenly returned tartly.

"Of course. It'll be fine."

"I must be crazy." She sighed, but Raine had a good point. She knew both River and Pike way better. If anyone was going to tell the mystery woman whatever she wanted to know, it would be Raine. "But why not?"

After she gave Raine the details she and Pike had agreed to, Heavenly found a sundress appropriate to wear to a sidewalk cafe, then, just as she would any other day, she texted both Beck and Seth to tell them she was going to meet a woman she knew for lunch. Maybe Seth wouldn't care, but until he said that, she would assume he did.

The story she sent them wasn't exactly a lie… She hated to skirt the truth. But some things—if they even wanted to hear it—were best explained in person.

Thirty minutes later, she found the quaint little restaurant with stylish outdoor tables that took advantage of the California sun, each topped with a jaunty umbrella. Heavenly spotted Pike right away in the growing crowd, shoulders crammed in a tight black T-shirt, camo pants paired with combat boots, and black hair arranged into a trendy "mess." Across the table from him sat a gorgeous redhead with thick lashes, a pert nose, and a pouty lower lip. She was young, probably old enough to drink—but barely. Her soft green sundress tied between her breasts and left a peekaboo triangle of pale flesh visible between the bow and the waistband. Gauzy ruffles ended just above her knees. She finished the look with rattan wedges, a couple of bangles at her slender wrist, and some dangling hoop earrings.

"Pike?" Heavenly called.

He stood quickly and turned to face her. She'd never seen him look nervous before, but he definitely was. "Cullen."

"What?"

"My name. It's Cullen," he murmured somewhere near her ear. "That's what she calls me."

Heavenly blinked. Of course he had a first name...she'd simply never been curious what it was. But apparently that's what the C in C. A. Pike stood for.

"Got it. Anything else?" she whispered.

He shook his head, then turned, tossing an uncharacteristic smile at the redhead. "This is Heavenly. She's the girlfriend of that doctor friend I told you about, and she's studying to be a nurse. She hasn't lived long in LA, either. You two have that in common." Pike swallowed and turned her way anxiously. "This is Jasmine. She moved here last month. She's helping to take care of some of my neighbors. We met walking dogs."

Actually, that sounded...cute—something she'd never imagined Pike would want. Wondering how River had met Jasmine, Heavenly held out her hand. "Nice to meet you."

The redhead smiled, looking almost girl-next-door, but there was something about her... Heavenly couldn't put her finger on it. Was it that her mouth looked too lush to be wholesome? Or that her eyes, an interesting shade between blue and green, looked just a tad too cynical to be sweet?

"Nice to meet you, too." Jasmine said the words, but she looked more cautious than thrilled.

"You two need anything?" Pike asked.

A script? Since that wasn't going to happen, Heavenly shook her head. Obviously, she'd be winging this luncheon.

"No. Thanks for introducing us, Cullen." Jasmine sent him a faint smile.

Pike looked lovestruck. Heavenly tried not to gape. This was a Dominant who did whatever constituted super-creative stuff at Shadows? The same guy who had ugly propositioned her a few months back?

"Of course." He turned to her, his face full of question.

"We're fine."

"Lunch is on me. Enjoy." Pike stuck his hands in his pockets, then looked Jasmine's way like he wanted to fall into her eyes. "Let me know when you're ready. I'll come pick you up."

"I can Uber."

He shook his head. "Let me pick you up. Really."

Pike could be a gentleman. Who knew?

Jasmine shrugged. "All right. Thanks."

With a nod, he held up an awkward hand and stared, obviously reluctant to leave. But he finally did, pulling his keys from his pocket and disappearing around the corner to wherever he'd parked.

Once he was out of sight, she turned her attention back to Jasmine, only to find the other woman staring. "You must think this is really awkward, coming to meet the new girl in town who's looking for friends. I told Cullen not to bother, but..."

So was that how Pike had pitched this meeting to Jasmine, as an opportunity to expand her social circle? It was smart. It made sense. Heavenly was surprised he'd even thought of it. What rationale had he given Jasmine to explain her own reason for being here? "Not at all. I've only been in LA a few months, and making friends in a city this size is hard."

Jasmine relaxed a little. "Especially without a nightlife. I don't know how much Cullen told you about me..."

"Almost nothing." A way to win Pike brownie points zipped through her brain. "I assumed he didn't want to break your confidence. He's really good about that."

"He told me next to nothing about you, too. Where are you from?"

"Wisconsin. I moved here to get my dad more advanced medical treatments last fall. But he died a few weeks ago."

Jasmine's expression softened, and Heavenly felt as if she was finally seeing the real woman. "I'm so sorry."

"Thanks. Me, too. So you've only lived in LA for a few weeks?"

"I'm the full-time caretaker for an older couple, hence the lack of nightlife."

So how had she met River?

"The weather back east got too cold for them, so they decided to move where it's warm year-round," Jasmine went on. "I'm really glad they chose LA. My brother lives here. I haven't spent much time with him in a decade. He's older than me, and we've grown apart. So...I'm hoping we'll get close again."

"I hope you do, too. You didn't want to meet any of his friends?"

"I don't want to intrude. Besides, he works in a male-dominated environment, and I'm not looking for dates. Honestly, I really intended to make my own friends over time. Then Cullen stepped in. You met him through your boyfriend?"

"Yeah. They've been friends for years." Heavenly smiled. "Tell me more about you."

"Not much to say. I didn't want to go into my family business back home. Neither did my brother. While I was in high school, I worked part-time at a senior care community. There, I met the couple I work for now, Jane and Arthur. Jane's brother and his wife lived at the facility, and after they passed, Arthur started having some health problems, but they wanted to stay at home. Long story short, they hired me. I've been with them since. They're amazing, and I love what I do. They're more like family than my own."

"You're not close to your parents?"

"God, no. Honestly?" Jasmine sighed. "My dad is a philandering asshole and my mother is a professional victim, full of wine and martyrdom. Together they're toxic. Aren't you sorry you asked?"

"No. I'm just sorry your relationship with them isn't good. My dad and I were incredibly close. But my mom ran out when I was fifteen. I've never seen or heard from her again, so I understand." Heavenly smiled wryly. "You didn't even ask, so aren't you sorry I opened my mouth?"

Jasmine gave her hand an empathetic pat. "Not at all."

The waitress came to drop off glasses of water and take their order. Afterward, the young woman with the long braid brought their iced tea before she disappeared again, apron swishing.

"Have you eaten here before?" Jasmine asked.

"No. Pike picked this place."

"You call him by his last name?"

"My boyfriend does, so…"

"Makes sense." Jasmine sipped her drink. "What do you know about Cullen?"

"He's"—Heavenly tried to think of something that wouldn't be a lie—"quiet. He's surprised me a time or two. The tattoos and the piercings, the camo and the attitude? I think they hide a decent guy." *Maybe.* "He doesn't date around, from what I can tell." But she had *no* idea what—or who—he did at Shadows.

Jasmine shrugged. "That's not really my concern. We're just friends."

Heavenly nibbled on her lip, trying to decide if she should say more. "I think he's hoping to be more than your friend."

"I know. He's made that clear." She grimaced.

"You're not interested?"

The redhead took a long time answering. "Right after I moved here, I met someone else. The circumstances were really unusual. We hooked up, and…"

Did she mean River? "You're seeing that guy now?"

"No." She winced. "I kind of…ran out on him in the middle of the night. He doesn't even know my name. But I admit, I'm a little hung up on him."

Heavenly tried not to gape. She hadn't seen that coming. How much did she dare say?

"What is it?" Jasmine drilled. "Your face… What's that expression about?"

Drat. She'd never been good at hiding her emotions. "Are you talking about River?"

Jasmine's eyes went wide as she reared back and blinked. "H-how do you know?" Then her face soured. "Cullen told you."

Heavenly shook her head. "He's never said a word to me about that. But River has said plenty."

Now her eyes bulged. "You *know* him?"

"Yeah. I've made one girlfriend since moving to LA. She just happens to be River's sister."

Her jaw dropped. "Seriously?"

"I'm afraid so." Heavenly heard the clicking of heels and looked up to find a gorgeous brunette with killer sunglasses, a hot pink sundress, and an ever-growing baby bump sashaying in their direction. "And here she is. Hi, Raine."

Jasmine stood and whirled, seemingly taken aback when River's younger sister stuck out her hand. "Hi. Have I been wanting to meet you. My brother hasn't shut up in weeks."

The redhead gaped. "You know?"

"That you had a one-night stand with him? Yeah. Did I overhear you say that you ran out on him in the middle of the night?" Raine laughed. "Serves him right. Builds character."

Jasmine looked Heavenly's way, clearly not convinced she'd heard Raine correctly. "Are you kidding?"

"Not at all." Raine took off her sunglasses, grabbed a nearby chair, and settled into it. "Women come way too easily to River. He needs to struggle a little."

"Oh, my gosh. You have his eyes," the redhead said, staring as she took her own seat.

Heavenly followed suit. "Doesn't she?"

Jasmine looked overwhelmed or worried…something Heavenly couldn't identify. "Does River know either of you are with me?"

"Of course not," Raine assured. "Heavenly is too nice. She would

THE CONFESSION | 91

never rat you out. And why would I make anything easy on my annoying big brother?"

At that, Jasmine smiled. "Why do I get the feeling you're a shit stirrer?"

Raine didn't answer, just turned to Heavenly. "See, she knows me already."

Heavenly smiled. "You're not exactly subtle."

"Oh, well." Raine shrugged, then leaned across the table to Jasmine. "Now tell me everything. Because River and Pike—not that they're friends, anyway—have been at each other's throats about you."

The redhead blinked. "Why? Cullen and I aren't involved romantically—"

"If he has his way, that will definitely change. And between you and me, he is a dirty, dirty boy. According to what I hear," she added hastily. "I don't know firsthand."

But she'd seen it, Heavenly would bet.

Jasmine looked somewhere between trepidatious and confused about that. "And I haven't seen your brother since that night."

"It's driving him insane. He says he wants to talk to you." Raine raised a dark brow. "Yeah, with his dick. Men... I should know. I'm involved with two of them, so of course I'm pregnant."

"Two men?" The redhead gaped, then stopped herself. "I'm sorry. I've just never..."

"Known anyone in a polyamorous relationship? Now you know two of us." She gestured to Heavenly, then winced. "Sorry. I shouldn't have outed you."

Heavenly shook her head. "I hadn't thought of a graceful way to say it." And she hadn't wanted to say anything in case Seth decided not to come home ever again. "It's fine."

"So you both have two boyfriends?" Jasmine looked shocked.

"Well, I have two fiancés now." Raine flashed her giant engagement ring. "I'm betting Heavenly will soon..."

A few days ago, Heavenly would have agreed. Now, she had huge, flaming doubts. If Seth couldn't even open up to her about his past, why would he ever want to make her his wife? And if he couldn't bare his soul, why would she say yes? For now, she pasted on a smile and kept her mouth shut.

"And we couldn't be happier," Raine went on. "So, what kind of info do you want about Pike or River? I've known them both for years. Ask me anything."

"How well do you know Cullen?"

"That name makes him sound so distinguished." Raine snorted. "But he's worked with one of my fiancés for probably five years."

"Doing what? I thought he was just good at inheriting money."

The question made Raine falter. She could out Pike on a lot of things, but admitting to someone else without his consent that he was in the BDSM lifestyle was a no-no. "He helps with...crowd management at my fiancé's nightclub."

Heavenly merely nodded in agreement and changed the subject. "So, is there anything you want to know? Raine really is the expert. I hope you don't mind that she joined us."

Jasmine shook her head. "I don't usually like this much interaction with strangers, but I think you two could be a lot of fun to know."

"She hasn't lived in LA long and she doesn't have any friends," Heavenly filled in for her bestie.

"Now she has us."

The waiter came by and asked Raine what she'd like to order. Since her stomach could still be iffy at times, she merely asked for a club soda with a twist of lime and dessert.

They talked some about the city. Raine gave Jasmine the lowdown on an awesome hairdresser in the vicinity. Heavenly shared what she knew about a good doctor near the hospital. And before they knew it, lunch had arrived. Lots of laughter went along with it. It was a nice interlude from worrying whether Seth would soon rip her heart out.

Thirty minutes later, they'd finished eating, exchanged phone numbers, and made plans to get pedicures in a few days. Then Jasmine's phone beeped.

She lifted it and read with a grimace. "I've been gone longer than I told Jane and Arthur I would be."

"Who?" Raine asked.

"The older couple she cares for," Heavenly explained.

Jasmine nodded and stood. "They live a few doors down from Cullen. I have to pick up a prescription for Arthur, and Jane can't remember how to work the microwave in this new place, so I need to help them with lunch. This has been so much fun. I'm looking forward to seeing you two soon."

"I can't wait," Heavenly said. And she genuinely meant it. During lunch, Jasmine had proven she was funny, witty, interesting, a good sport, and someone who rolled with the punches.

"Same, girl." Raine smiled. "Last call—at least for today. Anything more you want to know about Pike or my brother?"

Jasmine texted Pike for a ride, then looked up with a shrug. "I think Cullen is a pretty open book."

Raine raised a brow. "Is he?"

"Isn't he?"

Heavenly didn't answer. If Jasmine didn't know about Pike's proclivities, then she didn't know her "friend" as well as she thought. Oh, to be a fly on the wall for that revelation…

"Hmm," Raine hummed. "And River?"

Jasmine bit her lip as she plucked up her purse. "Is he angry with me?"

Heavenly hadn't expected that question. Clearly, Jasmine cared about him more than she wanted to.

"I don't think angry is the right word," Raine answered carefully. "Miffed, yes. Confused, for sure. And surprised as hell at the impact you made on him, which he's still trying to deny."

Heavenly would have said obsessed, too, but she kept that to herself.

"Please don't tell him you ran into me," Jasmine implored.

As Heavenly set her napkin on her plate, she wondered why the redhead seemed so upset.

"I can do that, at least for now." Raine paused. "You know my brother is a private investigator, right?"

Jasmine paled. "I didn't."

Raine nodded. "It probably won't take him much longer to figure you out. So you've got a choice. Do you want to wait until he catches up with you and let the chips fall? Or do you want to manage this and do what damage control you can? Up to you. If you choose the latter, I'm happy to help."

"You seriously think he's looking for me?"

"I know he is." Heavenly hated to distress Jasmine, but she deserved the truth.

"And pissed every day he can't find you. River isn't a patient man. And he can be unpredictable. It's the former soldier in him. So when he finally catches up with you…"

Jasmine let out a breath. "Damn it. You give a guy your virginity and he thinks he owns you."

"Is *that* how it went down?" Raine asked, looking almost gleeful.

"Yeah. It wasn't planned or anything. It just…happened."

"Take it from me," Heavenly cut in. "It can be a lot like that. You give guys your virginity, and yes. Suddenly, you find yourself tangled in a relationship you never expected."

Clearly, that wasn't the answer Jasmine wanted to hear. "Then…I guess I should let you arrange a conversation between me and your brother. I'll let you know when I'm free."

"Probably your best choice." Raine rounded the table to hug her. "I'll make sure he doesn't get out of line."

Heavenly rose and hugged her, too. "Raine is right. I'll help."

"So…I guess I'll be in touch about a time and place." Jasmine already looked nervous.

The smile that spread across Raine's face was full of mischief. "Great. I've already got ideas…"

CHAPTER SIX

"**S**teaks are done," Beck called as he shouldered his way through the patio door and into the kitchen.

"Salad and fruit are on the table." Heavenly pulled garlic bread from the oven and set it on the stove, trying to tamp down her nerves. "When Seth called to say he wanted to come home and talk, did he say anything else?"

Shutting the door behind him, Beck shook his head. "Just that he'd be here for dinner and that he wants to talk to us."

The sound of the door from the garage opening and closing had her head snapping up and her stomach tightening. After a brief jingle of keys and the click of dress shoes, Seth appeared at the end of the foyer, looking incredibly masculine in a sharp gray suit.

Heavenly's heart leapt into her throat. Was he coming home to repair their relationship and stay? To tell them he needed more time apart? Or, god forbid, had he come to say goodbye?

He loosened his tie. "Sorry if I'm late. Jesus, what a day. Want me to set the table?"

"Please." She handed him plates, napkins, and silverware, her gaze clinging to him.

Seth took everything, not kissing her hello and not quite meeting her stare. Instead, he glanced down with haunted eyes at what she'd given him. His expression made her throat tighten.

She cast a worried frown at Beck, who stood, watching.

"Glad you're here, man," he finally greeted Seth.

"Hey. Thanks," Seth responded with a bob of his head before he turned to her. "You only gave me three plates."

His unspoken question hung in the air. *Where's Zach?*

Tension hummed in the room.

"It's just the three of us eating. My brother is downstairs, asleep. He said he'd see us tomorrow. Apparently, he stayed up until four this morning watching game shows and WWE."

Seth visibly relaxed and arranged three place settings like it was any other evening, like the conversation they had tonight might not decide their entire future. "Interesting combination. Anything else need to go on the table?"

"No." She put the last piece of bread in the basket, then set it between the guys' plates before skimming her hand across Seth's shoulder because she couldn't help herself. What if tonight was her last to touch him? The thought broke her heart, but she had to keep herself together and hear him out. "So, you had a rough day?"

He sighed. "Yeah. And long. Just ready for it to be over. But I'm glad I'm here."

"Hard case?" Beck asked, setting down the meat platter and taking a seat.

Seth shrugged and helped her into her chair. "No, just shitty. I fucking hate cheating spouses. This dude was banging his wife's sister. I had to tell my client today. She's eight months pregnant."

Heavenly gasped. "That poor woman…"

"Did you castrate the son of a bitch?" Beck grunted.

"I'd love to. When I broke the bad news, she cried all over me. I felt horrible for her, and this asshole… He's destroyed her family. And the thing that pisses me off most? He has no idea what he's thrown away. If he'd had a wife and child ripped from him, he would have learned to value them damn fast."

Heavenly's heart hurt for him. Of course cases like this affected him. He might be a badass, but Seth also had a tender, surprisingly sentimental side. Having to comfort that woman had clearly taken a toll on him and reminded him of his loss, but he'd done it, even sacrificing his own mental safeguards to take care of her. She loved him all the more for it. "But you were there when she needed you."

"What damn good does it do when I don't have any answers to give her?"

"Man, that's not your job." Beck forked a steak onto his plate and passed the platter of meat. "She asked you a specific question: is my husband a cheating asshole? You gave her the truth. It's like patients who come to me and want to know if their vascular issues are fatal. I hate having to tell anyone the answer is yes...but I do it. They need to know so they can proceed and prepare. The existential stuff, like why and how will this be okay? That's for them to find. You've done your part."

Seth took a steak, then dished one for her. "I guess. It just sucks."

"It does." Beck took a spoonful of fruit and gave another to Heavenly. "But when this woman decides she wants to be happy again, she'll take another chance on love. Hopefully, she'll have learned her lesson and she'll find the right someone and the happiness she's lacking now."

With a shrug, Seth loaded salad onto his plate. "Maybe so. How was everyone else's day? Hopefully less shitty."

"Is it less shitty to take your brother, who's rarely seen the real world, out there so he can assimilate? I don't know..."

Beck grabbed a beer out of the fridge and held one up for Seth, who raised his hand. A toss later, Seth caught it and popped it open.

"What happened?" Heavenly hadn't gotten the chance to ask Beck earlier.

"When the barber whipped out the hair clippers, he freaked. I finally talked him off that ledge, then she came at him with a straight razor for a shave. You have to understand; he'd never shaved in his life. He still had that Chosen BS in his head that his beard was a sign of his masculinity and his dedication to God. I thought I was going to have to sedate his ass to get it done, but the barber was amazingly patient."

"What finally convinced Zach?" Seth's brow furrowed.

"I reminded him that, the second we walked in, the barber recognized him from the news."

"Yeah, that would do it." Seth shook his head. "Damn..."

"Then we went to the mall. He was fascinated by the escalator. I watched him ride up and down for a good twenty minutes. I figured if he loved that, he'd dig the arcade. So after we shopped, we went to Santa Monica Pier. I took him on a few rides, then turned him loose with all the video games. A hundred bucks later..." Beck shook his head.

Heavenly smiled. She could picture that.

"But it took his mind off of Faith and Joanna for a while." Beck sighed. "So I'm calling that a win."

"You should," Seth said solemnly.

"He's right." She nodded, cutting into her steak.

Seth said nothing more, just focused on his plate and shoveled in a forkful of salad.

Heavenly met Beck's stare across the table. His frown worried her. Obviously, Zach's loss was reminding Seth of his own. She could practically feel him crawling back under his hard outer shell, like a turtle, ducking for protection. If he was pulling away, what did that mean for their relationship?

Beck's expression turned grim, but he kept the conversation rolling. "Why don't you tell us about your mysterious text earlier today, little girl?"

Heavenly didn't know whether to thank him or scold him for changing the subject, but Seth didn't seem ready to blurt whatever he'd come to say, so she might as well dish. "You won't believe who I had lunch with."

Seth raised his head. "You mentioned a woman you know. Who?"

"Raine?" Beck asked.

"She was there…but I had lunch with Pike's girlfriend. Well, Pike's friend who's a girl. A woman. That's more accurate."

Beck looked surprised. "The one River banged?"

"The one he's hung up on and can't find?" Seth added.

"That one. Her name is Jasmine. She's absolutely gorgeous. Super sweet. She just moved here from somewhere back east a few weeks ago."

Seth set his fork down with a clatter. "There are something like thirteen million people in the greater LA area. How the hell did she get hooked up with Pike?"

"Exactly my question," Beck seconded. "If she's so gorgeous and sweet, why is she even friends with him? And why did she fuck River? She must have horrible taste in men."

Heavenly swatted at his arm. "She and Pike are neighbors or something. I don't know the story about River yet, but when Raine plopped down in the chair next to Jasmine—"

"Exactly how did that happen, angel?"

"I invited her to come along. After Pike, who Jasmine calls by his first name, which is Cullen—who knew?—she asked me to—"

"Cullen? Seriously?" Seth shook his head, then swiveled his gaze at Beck. "Did you know that?"

"No. Hammer probably knows, but I've never paid much attention to Pike."

Heavenly frowned. "I thought you two were friends."

"Not really, and especially not once he started hitting on you. But he's always been a loner. At the club, he plays with a lot of different girls, but he almost never takes one to bed."

"Well, he really likes this one."

Beck snorted. "Yeah? I really like islands in the South Pacific, but that doesn't mean I'm going to get one."

"Right?" Seth swallowed a bite of steak. "So what were you going to say? Pike asked you to what?"

"Have lunch with Jasmine so I could put in a good word about him to her."

"So you lied to her?" Beck spouted off.

"No. I might have skirted the truth a little, mostly because I don't know him that well."

Seth raised a brow. "And he asked you to use that pretty mouth to 'skirt the truth' because you owed him a favor and he knew everyone else would have been too honest?"

Heavenly rolled her eyes. "You two are horrible."

"We're right," he groused.

"Anyway, Raine and I both liked Jasmine. We're going to grab pedis together later this week. And Raine talked her into having a conversation with River."

Seth sat up straighter. "Oh, that will give him a...um, big thrill."

Beck scoffed. "You mean a big boner?"

"Well, yeah. He's dying to get his hands on her again."

Beck smirked. "That's not all he's dying for."

Heavenly winced. "The feeling isn't mutual. Raine had to twist her arm for this meeting, and Jasmine only agreed because Raine told her that River is a private investigator. That scared her. She doesn't really want him to find her."

"But he will," Seth said. "Just a matter of time."

"That's what Raine told her, so it looks like River will get his wish at some point."

"Wait. Let me get this straight." Beck leaned in. "These two brainiacs are fighting over a woman who doesn't want either of them?"

A smile cracked Seth's previously solemn face. "That's priceless."

"She isn't looking for a relationship," Heavenly volunteered.

Beck shrugged. "That won't stop either of them."

Heavenly bit her lip. "I didn't have the heart to tell her that."

"Poor bastards…"

She couldn't disagree. River and Pike had a hard road ahead if they each wanted her, especially if River intended to invite Dean into bed with them. That could have disaster written all over it…

Silence fell. Reality came rushing back to Heavenly. Their conversation had seemed so normal, so much like old times, she'd almost forgotten about the elephant in the room.

"Did you do anything besides work today?" she ventured, glancing Seth's way.

Did you think about us?

Instantly, he got quiet. "Let's finish dinner. Then we'll talk."

What little appetite Heavenly had suddenly vanished. Her stomach tightened. With a trembling hand, she set her fork on her plate. She felt Beck's eyes on her. Seth wouldn't meet her stare.

That terrified her.

For the next ten silent minutes, she pushed food around her plate and gulped water to wet her suddenly parched mouth. Beck finished his beer in tense silence. Half his steak went untouched.

Seth ate slowly, grabbing a second piece of bread before he finally pushed his plate away and raised his gaze to them. "Let's go to the couch."

His handful of blunt words stopped Heavenly's heart—just before it slammed into her chest. She swallowed nervously as she rose, impatient to know what he intended to say. But dread prodded her to postpone what she feared would be his inevitable goodbye.

"Let me clear the dishes." Her voice wobbled.

"Leave them," both men demanded, then shared a glance—a moment of unity?—before heading to the sofa.

With a nod, she returned her plate to the table, then followed them.

Her thoughts raced. Would Seth leave them for good? Was breaking away the decision he'd come to overnight? Heavenly was terrified he had, but he reached out for her, guiding her across the room with a warm hand at the small of her back. His touch felt so normal. So right. Then he situated her between him and Beck, as he always did. He had even talked to them over dinner like it was any other day, as if they had no problems at all.

Testing the waters to see if she and Beck would still welcome him? Or was he softening the blow?

Her legs trembled, threatening to give out underneath her as she slowly sat, perching on the edge of the cushion and folding her hands tightly in her lap. To her right, Beck didn't look much more comfortable. He leaned forward, like he was ready to fight at the slightest hint of trouble. But he still comforted her, resting his hand on her thigh in silent reassurance.

Seth fidgeted and cleared his throat. "After I told you about Autumn's and Tristan's deaths, I left you both with a lot of questions and I didn't give you any answers." He addressed Beck directly. "I know you're worried I'm not willing to give you my whole truth, and that's a sign that I'm not committed to us. That's not true."

Heavenly's heart fluttered with hope at those words when he faced her. "I suspect you think I don't love you enough to be honest. That's not true, either."

Before she could stop herself, her thoughts slipped free. "Then why have you shut us out?"

Seth swallowed and leaned over, steepling his fingers between his spread thighs. Then he looked down with a sigh. "Because I hate telling you how badly I failed—as a husband, a father, a cop, and a human being."

"Someone else killed your wife and son, right? You couldn't know—"

"There was any danger? I did. The perpetrator gave me plenty of warning. I just ignored it." As if he couldn't sit a moment longer, Seth vaulted out of his seat.

Beck met her bewildered stare, then watched him pace. "Ignoring it doesn't sound like you."

Exactly. Seth was a protector. From almost the moment they'd met, there hadn't been a day he hadn't done his utmost to look after her. In fact, he'd been overprotective at times, always tracking her phone. He'd even resisted her trip to Wisconsin alone to spread her father's ashes because he'd been concerned about her safety.

At the time, it had seemed like overkill. Now she had an inkling why.

"The summer I made detective, I started working a cold case. It was a murder that had been unsolved for a little over eight years. The precinct kept my caseload light while I learned the ropes, so I had some time on my hands. But this case sucked me in, and I ended up spending every moment I could spare on it. It wasn't long before I stumbled onto something I shouldn't."

"The truth?" Beck asked.

"Pieces of it, yeah. At least that's what it seemed like. I never could get my head around the whole thing. But I was onto something, and I knew it. So did whoever wanted to keep it quiet. In the middle of August, a witness 'suddenly' had a heart attack. Over Labor Day, another supposedly decided, three years after his wife's death, to commit suicide. I'm sure the killer was tying up loose ends. He probably thought the loss of witnesses would discourage me, and if I'd been thinking about it from the perspective of trying this case in a court of law, I would have been. Instead, it emboldened me. I was getting so close I could taste it."

"But people were dying," Heavenly protested, feeling a wave of fear for him clear to her core. "The murderer could have hurt you."

Slowly, he nodded and faced her. "And when the threats started, that's who I assumed he meant to hurt. I stopped investigating in September because Tristan had just been born, and Autumn was overwhelmed. Being a new mom was more…decision-making than she was used to. She got mastitis and had to go to the hospital for a few days until the infection eased up. My mom helped me juggle the baby while my wife healed, but work stopped until our family got back to normal."

"You hadn't received any threats yet?" Heavenly asked.

"Directly? No. But the witnesses being wiped out were a message for me. I knew that."

"Yet you picked up the case again." Beck raised a brow.

"I told myself to quit, that it was getting dangerous. But I couldn't stop thinking about it. In late October, I started in again, right where I'd left off."

Heavenly gasped. "Seth…"

"I began receiving threats immediately. Direct ones, in writing. But since the killer had always targeted the 'problem' and never their family, it didn't occur to me…" He shook his head. "I'm sure that sounds stupid, but I was young and cocky. I thought I was somewhere between untouchable and invincible. I had a gun and a badge and a whole police force behind me. Even if I wasn't the most liked detective—a lot of guys with more seniority thought I'd only been promoted because of pure, old-fashioned nepotism, thanks to my dad's best friend, Gene, pulling the right strings—I was convinced the precinct would want to catch this killer. Any decent cop would, right?"

Beck frowned. "They didn't?"

Seth shrugged. "They probably did, but my cases started piling up, and the brass made it clear that my first responsibility was to the new investigations, not the one least likely to be solved. After all, the department looked bad if I didn't get someone in jail and on the DA's docket fast. But that still didn't stop me. I started using days off, taking vacation time… I was obsessed. The answer was right there. I could feel it. So yeah, I laughed at the first note that warned me to back off. I ignored the second one that told me I'd be sorry if I didn't focus my attention on something else. In fact, the killer might as well have thrown down a gauntlet. No way was I giving up."

"Did you tell anyone about the threats?"

"Sure, my old beat partner, Tony. And, of course, Gene. They both insisted I take the threats seriously."

"But you didn't?" Beck crossed his arms, almost angry.

Despite the fact Heavenly knew this was all in the past, fear for Seth assailed her. He'd thumbed his nose at danger and been incredibly reckless. Even if he hadn't known the killer would come after his family, he'd known full well a madman was coming for him. And he hadn't cared.

"I couldn't," Seth shot back. "I felt like I owed the victim…"

"Why? You were responsible for other victims, too." Heavenly shook her head, shocked to find herself fighting tears. "And your safety mattered."

"It should have. I was a new father, and Autumn relied on me in every way—financially, mentally, and emotionally. But I was too driven to just give up, so I trashed the third note that came in mid-December. By then, someone, probably the killer, was following me. I acted like I wasn't aware and tried to lead him into a dark fucking alley where I could rough him up for answers. But it was like this perp was a half-step ahead of me. Just before I'd corner him, he'd disappear."

Heavenly sat up straighter, her eyes going wide. Had Seth been insane? "Did he follow you home? Is that what happened?"

Seth shook his head. "No. But that was another reason I never imagined he'd come after my wife and son. Anyway, I'd taken the week before Christmas off that year. The holiday fell on Sunday, and since I had the least seniority, I was scheduled to be back on duty by then. So Saturday, Christmas Eve, was my last day off. I'd been up half the night, thinking. I had a hunch, so I got up early, kissed my wife and son, and told them I'd be back that evening to take them to my mom's for family dinner. She and the baby were planning to go to her parents' place for Christmas."

"You didn't spend your last day off with your family?" Heavenly didn't understand.

Clearly, Beck didn't, either. "You spent it chasing ghosts instead?"

Seth closed his eyes. "Yeah. And believe me, no one regrets it more than me. If I had a do-over… Would it have changed the outcome? I don't know. Maybe I was already in too deep. Probably. Even Liam's mom called me from Ireland a few days prior to warn me I was into something too dangerous. Back then, I thought her psychic shtick was shit. So that morning I was stupidly ignorant of the tragedy about to unfold.

"Evidence that had previously been overlooked sent me to a warehouse in Jersey, near the docks. Most of those operations are crooked as hell, and I didn't have any authority to be crawling inside the location, but...yeah, that didn't stop me."

Beck looked stupefied. "Isn't that mob territory?"

Even his question made Heavenly's gut twist. She hadn't been aware of that, but Seth's expression said he had.

Despite the fact she already knew the end of this story, the sense of angst and impending doom made her squirm and her heart ache.

"Definitely. But the Mafia wasn't my problem. In my experience, if I left them alone, they'd return the favor."

"You were damn cocky." Beck sent him a disbelieving stare. "Jesus..."

"I was. Weren't you at twenty-four?"

Beck shrugged. "Pretty much."

"I'm not that old yet, and I would be terrified," Heavenly objected.

Both men sent her smiles that were at once amused and protective.

"A sweet angel like you has reason to be," Seth pointed out. "I was a pissed-off motherfucker with a gun and I wasn't afraid to use it. Anyway, I didn't find anything at the warehouse, but I knew in my gut the place was somehow important. When I got back to my car, there was a note on my windshield. Another threat. But this one was different. This one made my blood run cold."

Seth choked on his last words and turned away. Heavenly rose from the sofa to comfort him, but Beck grabbed her arm and pulled her down with a shake of his head.

"He needs to do this himself," he whispered.

She shook her head. "He's all alone."

Beck nodded. "He has to tell us if he doesn't want to be."

That low-voiced murmur knocked the breath from her. As much as she hated it, Beck was right. Seth might love them and he might be telling them the story of Autumn's and Tristan's deaths, but that didn't mean he wanted to come home and have a future with them.

That realization was crushing.

"What did the note say?" Beck asked.

Seth clenched his fists. His body went taut, his shoulders so tense Heavenly held her breath. Had she ever seen him so close to breaking down?

"Seth?" She needed to know if he was all right.

He stood unmoving, refusing to face them.

She pressed her lips together, resisting the powerful urge to comfort him and tell him it was okay if he didn't finish his explanation.

But it wasn't. They all knew that.

Instead, she waited beside Beck, grabbing his hand tightly, praying Seth found the strength to go on.

Finally, he took a step, exhaled, then pivoted to them, his face a shockingly blank mask. "It was a picture of Autumn and Tristan in our kitchen, taken the day before through the window. It said 'You should have listened. Merry fucking Christmas.'"

Heavenly gasped and gripped Beck's hand so tightly her own went numb. He squeezed her back, looking shocked and sickened. Neither of them spoke a word. She felt faint and had to remind herself to take a breath.

"I got in my car and hauled ass out of there. I called Autumn on my way home, relieved as hell when she answered. I told her to grab the baby and get out of the house that minute, to drive to her parents' place. I promised I would pack them some essentials and meet them there."

His wife must have been panicked. Heavenly could only imagine how terrifying the urgency in Seth's voice must have been. And the horror of knowing that someone wanted to harm her and their child…

"Oh, my gosh," Heavenly squeaked, near tears.

"Autumn did exactly as I asked. I talked to her while she slipped on her coat, picked up Tristan's diaper bag, and ran to the car. She strapped him in, backed the car out of the garage, and put it in drive. She was telling me that the streets were icy when I heard a deafening bang. The call went dead. I tried to reach her again at least ten times.

She didn't pick up. Then my scanner erupted with chatter. Car explosion. My address. No survivors." He took a ragged breath, then finally looked their way. "My family was gone."

Heavenly couldn't move. The horror he'd been through sickened her, and she'd merely heard about the incident. Seth had *lived* it. At Christmas.

How had he ever survived?

And last holiday season, when he must have been reliving that nightmare again, she had told Seth in the checkout line at the grocery store that she liked Beck as more than a friend and sent him packing back to New York. She'd left him alone to deal with his annual grief and guilt, along with what he'd perceived as her rejection.

She tore free from Beck's grip. It didn't matter right now that Seth hadn't agreed to come home. He needed comfort, and she was a human being. One who loved him, yes. But even if he'd been a stranger, she would have been compelled to throw her arms around him as she did right now and offer the only words she could think of. "I'm so sorry."

Thankfully, Beck was right beside her, palming Seth between the shoulder blades and sending him the most sympathetic of gazes. "Jesus, I had no idea. I'm sorry, too."

Seth stood stiff, unyielding and unmoving for the span of a few heartbeats. Finally, he buried his face in her neck and clung to her as if he couldn't make it another moment without her. His fingers bit into her waist, his exhalations desperate pants against her skin. Everything inside her ached for him, and she offered herself up—strength, fortitude, and heart. Whatever happened next between them, in that moment, she was his, however he needed her.

Behind them, Beck eased closer, clutching them both, reaffirming the circle of compassion and understanding. He gripped Seth's shoulder with one hand, squeezing to convey his silent sympathy. He clutched her hip with the other, giving her another lifeline of support to pass on to Seth.

Everything about the moment—both its beauty and heartbreak—filled her eyes with tears.

"Shh." Seth pulled away before she was ready to let him go. "Don't cry for me."

Did he really think she wouldn't sob for all he'd lost?

He cupped her face and looked deep into her eyes as he thumbed her tears away. "I'm okay. It was a long time ago. And I have no one to blame but myself."

"That's not true. You didn't blow up your family."

"I might as well have."

"Man, you're not the only one at fault," Beck insisted. "Granted, you didn't listen to the warnings, but the killer did all the heavy lifting."

"Maybe." Seth shrugged and stepped away. "But I'm not at the end of the story."

When he gestured them to the sofa again, he clasped his hands behind his back and paced away, separating himself from them again. Heavenly cast a worried glance at Beck. What more could he have to say after he'd already ripped out their hearts? She felt more than a little guilty that they'd pushed him to open up about something so horrific and painful. But to understand him, they'd needed to know.

Beck took her hand and helped her settle on the sofa again as he addressed Seth. "From conversations we've had, I know you didn't just grieve and go on with your life."

Seth smiled acidly. "I didn't. Autumn and Tristan were barely in the ground before I dove back into the case. This time I was unrelenting. Even though a psych eval cleared me to return to work, I took a leave of absence. I was going to catch this motherfucker. If he thought taking my family out would stop me, I aimed to prove him wrong. Now I had nothing to lose."

"Except your own life."

Seth shrugged. "At that point, I didn't care. But resuming the case wasn't that easy. Tony warned me to back down because the brass was worried about me. They thought I was a loose cannon, and he'd heard whispers they were considering placing me on administrative leave. I cleaned up my act for a bit—on the surface. But really I just took my investigation deeper underground. Gene figured me out, and those same strings he pulled to get me an interview after I passed the detective exam? He pulled them to have me locked out of the cold case. Then he sat me down and told me I was on a suicide path. And since my father wasn't there to stop me, he would. He reminded me that my mother couldn't handle losing me, too. My captain absolutely ripped me a new one. Everywhere I turned, the people around me became roadblocks. They meant well, but I wasn't giving up. This killer had taken everything from me. And goddamn it, I was going to have revenge."

Horror filled Heavenly. Had he gone insane? Maybe so. Grief could do that to a person. She knew that firsthand.

"What did you do?" Beck asked.

"Eventually? I quit. I hung up my badge, walked away from everyone in my life—my mother and brothers, my friends, even Graffiti—and I dedicated my life to getting even." Seth hung his head, then turned once more to stare sightlessly out at the pool. "What happened next was…ugly.

"I started prowling New York's seedy underbelly until I made the right connections. From there, I greased the right palms and did the right favors until I was allowed to ask the right people the right questions. Finally, I did a few favors for someone I was never supposed to know, much less exchange intel with. He gave me the name I wanted. I went to the asshole's seedy apartment deep in South Bronx." He glanced over his shoulder at them. "In case you don't know, if you can't take care of yourself, you should never go to that neighborhood. I found the son of a bitch home alone, and I cuffed him to a chair in his dirty-ass kitchen. I pressed my gun to his forehead and forced him to tell me exactly how he'd rigged the explosive in my wife's car. He babbled. He apologized. He claimed he had no malice against me; he merely wanted to stop me from exposing him as the killer in the cold case. After that, he started crying and begging. But he wouldn't tell me anything else and his usefulness was at an end. So I blew out his brains, walked away from his apartment, showered, and waited for the sun to rise. Then I called my mother for the first time in months. She honestly hadn't known whether I was dead or alive. I went to see her, and we had breakfast. I apologized but refused to answer questions. She still doesn't know what happened to this day."

Heavenly covered her mouth in shock. What should she say? Do? Did he want comfort? After he'd just confessed to killing another man in cold blood, could she even give it to him?

On some level, she'd always known he was capable of doing whatever he needed to protect those he loved. After all, he'd knocked Pike out with one punch after he'd come on to her a few months ago. But he'd been defending her. Heavenly hadn't realized he would murder—become the very thing he'd once hunted and jailed—for revenge. She hadn't believed him capable of that.

Seth scrubbed a hand down his face and spoke into the silence. "The following week, I got my PI license and hung out my shingle. Everything stayed static for years." He finally turned to her, his face closed tight, his eyes carefully blank. "Until I met you. You brought me back to life."

Their stares connected. Fused. Her hand trembled as she pulled it from her face. She knew this man intimately—knew his laugh, his kiss, his likes, his habits, the way he flirted, the way he slept, the way he thought.

But after his confession, she had to wonder… How well did she really know *him?*

Swallowing, Heavenly struggled to find not just the right words but *any* words. On the one hand, she ached for all he'd lost when this killer had ended his wife and son. Anguish for the time, love, and normalcy that were forever gone panged her. But he'd given up his humanity for vengeance. No, he'd given it away—with glee. With both hands. Without thinking twice. He'd shot a human being with zero remorse. Worse, Heavenly suspected that if he could go back in time, he would still make the same choice.

On some level, that shattered her view of Seth. To her, he'd always been the noble protector. Now she saw his relentless, savage side.

"I've shocked you." His raised brow challenged her to refute him.

Heavenly didn't want to, but she found herself judging him, just as he'd known she would. The longer she stared, the more his expression felt like a crowbar, trying to force an acceptance and understanding she wasn't sure when—or if—she could ever give him.

With a shaking hand, she balanced against the table and rose to her feet. Her head swam. Her heart pounded. She was painfully aware that, with every moment, with every movement, Seth watched her.

"Heavenly?" Beck rose beside her, looking wary and worried.

"I-I need a minute." She couldn't look at either of them. "Excuse me."

"Angel!" Seth called after her.

She ignored him, darting into the powder bath at the front of the house before she locked the door with trembling hands. She sucked in giant breaths, closed her eyes, and leaned against the door for support.

One thought burned through her brain over and over: Seth had hunted down a person and killed him without remorse. How was she supposed to feel about that?

On the other hand, he'd killed a man who had marked a woman and infant for death because Seth had sought the truth. A man who had killed before. A man likely to kill again. A man who clearly thought little of human life.

Where did that leave her?

Slowly, she flipped on the bathroom light. The too-bright bulbs beamed in her face. She recoiled, then stared at her image in the mirror. She looked pale and stunned, her eyes shell-shocked and dilated.

On automatic pilot, she turned on the water, then splashed some on her face. The cold jolted her. Some of her shock receded. She had to start thinking. Both Seth and Beck were out there, wondering what was running through her head.

Honestly, Heavenly didn't know.

What would she have done in Seth's place, knowing the identity of this horrible, dangerous man? The system had seemingly been willing to sweep his crimes under the rug in favor of solving new and shinier murders. The very people who should have wanted him behind bars had apparently resisted Seth's attempts to put him there. Should she cast him in the role of villain for having the fortitude to see justice done, despite the fact it hadn't been legal?

Heavenly still couldn't answer that.

What if this killer's victim had been *her* loved one? Her father, for instance? Would she still condemn Seth for making the perpetrator pay in whatever way he could?

She was less certain of that.

A sudden knock on the door had her jerking toward the sound.

"You okay, little girl?" Beck asked softly.

Heavenly wasn't sure. "I need a minute."

"I know," he said in a low voice. "I'm shocked, too. But Seth is pacing like he's about to come out of his skin. He's falling apart without you."

Now she understood exactly why Seth hadn't wanted to tell her. He'd feared her reaction. He'd feared their backlash. He had feared breaking them apart.

Maybe he'd been right.

But if they managed to move forward—and if she ever wanted him to be honest again—she couldn't shut him out like he was a monster.

Seth was still the same man who had brought her the most thoughtful gift ever when he'd merely been the acquaintance of a broke, overstressed nursing student. The same hero who had cobbled together a lovely picnic at a scenic park for their first date. The same lover who had given her her first kiss, full of the kind of passion and promise she'd been aching for. On top of that, he had worked with Beck, then his rival, to slay her Kathryn dragon because he'd been worried about her. He had pulled her from bed to face life again after her father's passing and ensured that she both looked presentable for his service and that his final goodbye had been dignified. Then he had moved mountains to help her spread Daddy's ashes when she had been overcome by indecision and grief.

Seth Cooper was a man who cared, who had compassion, who would do anything for those he loved.

Should she condemn him for avenging the woman he had pledged his life to and the child they'd created together?

Heavenly sighed. It was the violence itself she didn't understand. He had relished that killing and made no bones about it. But she had never lived in his world. She had, however, lived with *him*. On some level, she grasped Seth wanting to put the past behind him and move on...but being unable to leave that chapter of his life without ensuring justice had been served.

Then she remembered the way he and Beck had beat the landlord, who'd demanded she pay rent on her back, to a pulp. And she realized… Seth hadn't gone after the fight until it had come for his loved ones. Then, he hadn't flinched or backed down. If she was the victim of a predator tomorrow, did she think for one moment that Seth would sit back and let others ensure the proper sentence was meted out?

No.

He would take matters into his own hands. And if she loved the man, didn't she have to accept that about him?

Yes.

Dragging in a deep breath, she reached for the knob, resolved to face Seth, and figure out what should happen between them next.

S eth tried not to fidget as he paced the kitchen from counter to table and back again. He was aware of Beck eyeing him, leaning against the island a few feet away. Staring. Dissecting. Judging? Yeah, probably. Heavenly certainly had.

Not that he was shocked. Not that he blamed her. This was exactly why he'd avoided telling her the ugly truth. And the surgeon might spend a lot more time in hospitals than back alleys these days, but he'd lived part of his adolescence in Vegas on the streets. He was too smart not to read between the lines. If he hadn't already figured it out, once the big sadist put a few minutes of thought into the situation, he'd realize there were holes in the story—and he'd start asking questions.

Seth cursed under his breath. There were parts of his past that no one fucking needed to know.

Finally, he couldn't stand the silence anymore. "What did she say?"

"Not much. She's thinking. Everything you laid out there…it was a lot for her to take in."

Of course it was. In Heavenly's world, people were nice. Everyone meant well. In Bayfield, Wisconsin, where she'd grown up, that had probably been true. Other than a few months of living in an LA ghetto, where she'd miraculously managed to remain unscathed by violence or crime, her wholesome upbringing was all she knew. For him, New York City had been vastly different, especially as a former cop willing to do anything for vengeance. The criminal element had come out of the woodwork to help—for the right price. And by then, Seth hadn't cared much about the law.

"I shouldn't have come here."

Beck's eyes narrowed. "So it would have been better if you'd just given up on us?"

Seth scowled. "She's horrified by me now."

"She's processing," Beck corrected.

No, she was making a crucial decision. "She's trying to decide if she can live with a killer."

The surgeon didn't sugarcoat. "Yes."

A rough breath left Seth's chest as he resumed pacing. Then something else occurred to him, and he pinned Beck with another stare. "Despite the fact you save lives every day, what I did doesn't bother you?"

Beck didn't hesitate. "No. But let's be honest. You didn't kill your family's murderer that easily. There's no way you popped in, had a ten-minute interrogation, blew his brains out, then whistled your way out the door."

Just as Seth suspected, the doctor saw right through him. "I didn't."

"How long did you torture him for answers?"

Seth hesitated, then shook his head. The truth couldn't lead anywhere good. "Why does it matter?"

Beck shrugged. "If you offed him in less than twenty-four hours, I'll be disappointed."

He should have guessed that the doctor, despite his Hippocratic Oath, was bloodthirsty. "Two hours shy of four days."

And when he'd started peeling off the killer's skin layer by layer, Silas Nichols had finally admitted everything he'd done.

"How did you feel afterward?"

He whirled at the sound of Heavenly's question across the house. She stood just outside the powder bath, staring at him with big, uncertain eyes. Fuck, she'd heard his admission.

It took everything inside Seth not to rush across the space between them and wrap her in his arms. Instead, he swallowed and forced himself to be honest. "Exhausted. Empty. Soulless."

She bit her lip. "But you would do it again?"

"Yes." He didn't hesitate, and he didn't prevaricate. Neither would do him any good. As much as he hated to give her the truth, he'd come this far. She deserved as much as he dared to give her.

"I see."

"Tell me what you're thinking," he demanded in the softest voice he could manage with his guts twisting and his world falling apart.

"Logically, I know you're a dangerous man. I think I've always known on some level. But the details…"

Were too much for her tender heart. He didn't know how to be anyone else. "I'm sorry."

She shook her head. "On the other hand, you lived through something tragic. Of course it affected you. I suspect you even saw getting revenge as your duty."

"I did." For more reasons than she would ever know.

"Another way you take care of those you care about."

What was she getting at? "Yes."

"Do you love me, Seth? Really?" Heavenly looked so vulnerable, standing a dozen feet away, fingers clasped in front of her as if she was afraid of the answer.

Though conversation about his past had frozen his insides, the uncertainty in her words melted his heart. "You have no idea. I think I've been in love with you from the moment we met."

She exhaled, releasing a pent-up breath, then she glanced at Beck. "Do you have anything to say?"

"Objections? Concerns?" The surgeon shook his head. "No. In his place, I probably would have done something very similar."

"We're men," Seth felt compelled to add.

As soon as the words were out, he realized that might not explain anything to her at all. But seconds later, she proved he'd underestimated her.

"You're protectors," she murmured.

"Yes," he rushed to agree, ridiculously grateful she grasped that fact.

"I know."

But she was still hesitating, and Seth grappled to understand why.

"If you think I would only go to such lengths for Autumn because she was my wife, you don't understand."

"What do you mean?" Heavenly cocked her head, her pale curls sliding across her shoulders and down her bare arms.

The sun slanted through the windows, lighting her up like the angel he always called her. He clenched his fists and quelled his urge to cross the floor, take her in his arms, and nestle her body under his until he reminded her in the most thorough, pleasurable ways possible that he belonged to her, now and always.

"I love you more." At her gasp, he went on. "That sounds like a terrible thing to say. But Autumn and I had problems. We met in high school. I was the only man she'd ever known. In some ways, she went straight from her father's care to mine."

And he'd sucked it all in. They'd fit together because she hadn't liked decisions and thrived on structure. He'd relished having complete control over her…at first. But even before Tristan's birth, the weight of her day-to-day care had begun to drain him. He'd tried his best to ease back, but she'd merely cried and heaped guilt on him, then accused him of not loving her anymore. After every such fight, he'd inevitably resumed being the master to her slave, while assuring her that her fears weren't true. But he'd been lying, and deep down, they'd both known it. The breaking point had been coming. Tristan had been a temporary Band-Aid, a vehicle—he'd hoped—for Autumn to grow into a fully adult role. Instead, she'd crumpled under the weight of duty. So had he.

Together, they had been a disaster.

Heavenly lifted a trembling hand to her mouth. "What are you trying to say?"

"There is nothing I wouldn't do to keep you safe." He couldn't stand the distance between them another moment. He rushed her, wrapping hard fingers around her soft shoulders and hauling her body against his, ignoring the way she tensed. "I would go to the ends of the earth for you. And if anyone ever dared to touch you, what I did to the motherfucker who ended Autumn and Tristan would look like a scratch."

"You would kill them." Heavenly sounded shocked, but it wasn't a question. She knew.

He didn't pretend otherwise, merely nodded. Now that his secret was out, he might as well be clear about her protection. Better for her to know exactly who she claimed to be in love with. "In ways so terrible, even the most hardened criminal would be afraid to whisper about it."

Her eyes widened. "You're scaring me."

"I'm sorry. That isn't my intent. You know I can be gentle. I can love you softly, sweetly—in whatever way you need. Everything that happened is in the past. It was years ago—"

"But that part of you still lives and seethes under your surface."

Seth couldn't refute her. Instead, he glanced over her shoulder at Beck for help.

"He's not pretending otherwise." The surgeon pushed away from the island and made his way toward them. "He's only saying that there's more to him than violence. And you know that. Come here."

When Beck fitted his hands around her waist and tried to pull her away from his grip, Seth resisted, pinning the doctor with a warning glare. Beck met his stare, his eyes full of calm. They asked for trust. Seth hesitated, then released her into the surgeon's care. Heavenly exhaled and relaxed against Beck when he fitted her back to his chest.

Then he banded his arm around her middle and dipped his head, caressing the shell of her ear with his lips. "Do you trust me?"

"Yes." Her reply sounded steady, sure.

Seth hoped like fuck the surgeon didn't ask Heavenly if she trusted him. After everything he'd admitted today, he knew the answer and he couldn't hear the terrible truth. "Beck—"

"It's fine," he insisted, wearing an expression that told him to shut the fuck up.

It went against his grain, but Seth did it. In Heavenly's eyes, the doctor had the moral high ground.

"Would I ever steer you wrong?" Beck asked her.

"No," Heavenly admitted.

"Have I ever hurt you?" A smile quirked the corner of his mouth. "Unless you asked me to."

"No."

"Have I shown you that I only ever want what's best for you?"

She let out a shaky breath. "Yes."

"I have," Beck agreed. "I always will. You said you trust me, little girl."

"I do."

"Good. I trust Seth. I trust him with my life. And I trust him with the most important thing in my world." He skimmed his lips down her neck, cascading them across her shoulder as he caressed the strap of her cheerful sundress down her arm. Then he repeated the process with the other strap, leaving her bodice clinging to her breasts. "I trust him with you."

Heavenly gasped. "Beck—"

"Shh." He lifted the hair away from her neck and settled the mass of waves across one shoulder, leaving her nape bare and vulnerable to his questing lips. "Let us prove your trust isn't misplaced."

The words had barely cleared Beck's mouth before he tugged on her dress and her breasts bounced free, naked and supple and topped with hard berry tips that tempted Seth to throw caution to the wind. But he held back, his stare burning its way across her pale skin and beautiful, familiar curves.

Thankfully, she didn't protest. In fact, the uptick in her breathing suggested that she was aroused.

Lava flowed through Seth's veins while he waited for Beck's next move. It wasn't long before the doctor skated his fingertips across the top of her shoulder, then glided over her collarbones, before diving slowly down, down, down just beside her nipple, skimming very near her cleavage, before rounding underneath—then lifting her whole breast in his palm.

Heavenly inhaled into his touch, her flesh filling his hand. He thumbed the sensitive tip. Her exhalation turned shaky as her eyes slid shut. Bliss washed over her uncertainty.

"How does that feel?" Beck asked.

"Good," she admitted breathlessly.

"Tip your head back on my shoulder. Just like that," he praised when she complied. "Keep your eyes closed. Just pay attention to sensation, nothing else. Can you do that for me, because you trust me? I won't let anything happen to you."

She hesitated, probably because she knew Beck wouldn't be the only one touching her. Finally, she bit her lip and nodded. "Yes."

"Good girl." He palmed her other breast, then plucked at the tips with his fingers, hardening her nipples even more. "What is your safe word?"

"Freedom," she breathed.

"That's right," he crooned, his voice buttery.

Watching them was a fucking turn-on, but Seth was dying even more to touch Heavenly, to reaffirm himself as not merely her violent protector but as her lover.

Apparently, Beck had the same idea since he motioned Seth closer with a bob of his head.

He could hardly wait. Heavenly was half spread out in front of him like a buffet, but he wanted her fully open to him. After she'd nearly turned him away, he was eager to insinuate himself inside her again as deep as he possibly could, in every way she would let him.

But Seth forced himself to be patient. If he pounced on her, she might balk or safe word out.

Instead of fitting his mouth over her upturned lips, filling his hands with her tits, and consuming her, he stepped closer, letting her feel his body heat, nothing more.

Her inhalation wobbled. Her lashes fluttered open.

"Didn't Beck tell you to keep your eyes closed?" Seth corrected her.

"Yes." She shut them again immediately.

But she was deliciously aware of him, as evidenced by the fact her nipples in Beck's palm turned rosier and harder, her breaths turned even choppier.

"Good," Seth praised.

Then he took her hips in his hands—and pulled on her dress. She bit back a gasp as the thin garment floated down her thighs and skimmed her knees before falling to the floor.

She stood before him, trembling, in nothing but tiny, transparent white panties with a feminine filagree design, lace trim, and a little pink bow.

Seth swallowed. "You're beautiful."

"What are you going to do to me?"

She sounded anxious, and he tried to decide how best to answer her honestly while still putting her at ease.

Beck intervened. "Stop. You trust me, and I trust him. You have a safe word. Unless you want to use that, he'll do whatever he wants to you. Do you understand, little girl?"

Her breathing turned increasingly uneven. Her nipples hardened more. Her chest flushed with a fresh splash of rosy color. Seth would bet that, if he touched her pussy right now, she'd be soaking wet.

Holy shit. This was bent enough to excite his kinky heart; no surprise about that. But it was turning her on, too?

"Yes, Sir."

Her whisper whipped through Seth.

Oh, it was *so* on.

"Excellent," Beck murmured in her ear, then gave her a little nudge in Seth's direction. "Now go upstairs with him."

For a tense moment, Heavenly stood in the no-man's-land between him and Beck. Slowly, she opened her eyes. They were a dark, dilating blue as she tried to cover herself with her hands, almost as if it was a modesty reflex, but Seth caught her wrists in his grip and exerted just enough pressure to prevent her from concealing her flesh.

"I didn't tell you to hide yourself," Beck scolded, bending to pick up her discarded dress and drape it across his arm. "I told you to go upstairs with him. Are you safe wording out?"

"No, Sir."

"Then why are you still standing there?" Beck turned away and headed downstairs, likely to check on Zach.

He was alone with Heavenly.

She swallowed hard and offered him her trembling hand.

Fuck that.

Seth bent and scooped her into his arms. It was all he could do not to swallow her little gasp of surprise with his kiss. Instead, he climbed the stairs two at a time until he reached their bedroom. Then he settled her on her feet just beside the mattress and blocked her route to the door, ensuring she only had two places to go—onto the bed or into his arms. Either worked for him.

"Heavenly, you know me," he reminded solemnly.

She met his stare with cutting doubt. "I thought I did."

"You still do. I'm every bit the man you met last December. I'm still the man you fell in love with. I'm the man you moved in with. I'm one of the only two men you've ever allowed inside your body."

She closed her eyes. "In my head, I know all that."

"Let me remind your heart." He clutched her shoulders, dragged her against him, fell into her scorching blue stare, and took her mouth.

For an instant, she stiffened and fought, but he kept on, working his lips over hers until slowly, bit by bit, she softened under him, clinging to him.

Seth needed her—to be with her, tasting her, on top of her, plundering her. He stayed patient, plying her with slow, drugging kiss after slow, drugging kiss. Finally, she stepped into his embrace, her arms creeping around his neck, allowing him to press every inch of his body against hers.

Footsteps up the stairs alerted Seth that Beck was coming for them. When Heavenly would have backed away, he held tight, keeping the lock he had on her lips and prying them apart with his own until he tasted the recesses of her candied mouth.

"This is a promising development," Beck praised, approaching while he shucked his T-shirt. "Be a good girl and take off Seth's coat."

When she pulled her lips away and lifted her lashes to peer at Seth with hot eyes, electricity pinged through him.

But Beck wasn't having it. "Did I say to stop kissing him?"

Heavenly turned the doctor's way, her lips parted in surprise. "N-no, but I—"

"Didn't think?" he cut in. "Give him your mouth and take off his coat."

And just like that, her breathing turned erratic again. Seth watched the pulse surge and thrum at her neck.

He yanked her against his body and delved past her lips, tongue sweeping through every corner until she melted against him. Her fingers clutched at the lapels of his suit as if that alone could keep her wobbling legs upright.

Beck squeezed in behind her and gripped her hips like he meant business. "Last time I'm going to tell you. Coat off."

Seconds later, she let go of Seth's lapels and swept the jacket from his shoulders. He rolled and wriggled until it fell to the floor. He hated wrinkling such an expensive suit, and it fucked with his OCD nature to leave Hugo Boss there, but Heavenly was far more important. God had invented dry cleaners for a reason.

Suddenly, he felt the good doctor's hands sweeping up and down her body. He cracked an eye open and caught sight of the man's lips at her ear again. "Good. Shirt next. Be quick."

She shuddered between them.

It was obvious that her instinct was to verbally answer the command—something Seth would normally applaud—but he kept her mouth far too busy for talking, crushing her lips under his again and again. She gave in to him, opening to him, allowing him wherever and whatever he wanted. It was heady.

She fumbled her way down the buttons of his dress shirt, then slid the garment from his body as he worked the buttons at his cuffs free. The starched cotton fell to the floor near the forgotten coat.

Now they were both bare from the waist up, and he took hold of her, bringing her in until her warm breasts pressed against his bare skin. At the contact, they both groaned.

Seth grabbed her delicate jaw in his big hands, slanted his head above hers, and swooped down to consume her now pliable lips. She was almost his again…

Behind her, Beck dropped the rest of his clothes, then turned his attention to her, kissing his way down her body as he peeled her underwear past her hips and tugged them to the floor. "Step out."

Automatically, she did. Beck pulled the tiny little garment free and held it up with a smile.

Immediately, the sweet spice of Heavenly's pussy hit Seth's nose—and triggered every feral instinct inside him. He shook with the effort to find his self-control and dial back his hunger.

"Good," Beck praised, then eased her back against his chest as if he somehow knew that Seth had reached his limit. Then he took her breasts in his hands and pinched the tips as he murmured in her ear again. "You're doing well. I think you enjoyed Seth kissing that pretty mouth of yours."

"It's swollen," he told the doctor.

And it was. Her lips were plump and rosy and tempting as fuck.

"Good to know. Let's see what else you can make swollen with your mouth, shall we?" Beck sent him a wolfish grin as he sat back on the bed, taking Heavenly down with him. He settled her pert ass between his spread legs and tugged on her hair until she lay back against him.

The move thrust her tits and their succulent pink berry nipples in the air, right in his direction.

God bless the motherfucker for being so perverted and devious.

The doctor pressed teasing kisses up and down her neck. "Seth?"

Fuck, yes.

Planting a knee between Heavenly's spread thighs, he lowered himself onto the bed, braced his hands on either side of them, and kissed his way across her velvety tits, skimming his lips around the sides and tonguing his way near the stabbing points, now begging for his touch.

Nothing was sweeter than Heavenly's eyes sliding shut and her back arching in invitation.

Some subversive part of him wanted to make her wait the way she'd made him, but he was too desperate for games. Instead, he leapt on her offering, latching onto her nipples with a greedy hunger that had her gasping. And the doctor helped right along, nipping at her lobe and breathing hot in her ear.

Heavenly whimpered.

"Does that feel good?" Beck growled. "Do you like his mouth on you? Do you like the way he sucks you deep and gives you pleasure?"

"Yes," she breathed.

"What was that? I can't hear you."

"Yes!" Her cry was a soft sob of pleading.

"Are those your nipples or mine?" Beck asked her.

"Y-yours."

"That's right. Arch more. Give them to Seth. Make sure he gets all he could want in his mouth. Do you understand?"

"Yes, Sir," she gasped out.

It turned Seth on even more.

He switched from one breast to the other, nipping, laving, and tugging. True to her word, she pulled her shoulders back and lifted in offering to his waiting mouth, searing him with her willingness. Some corner of his brain tried to tell him that she was merely pleasing Beck, but he knew better. She wanted him, too. And when she wrapped her arms around him, tunneling her fingers in his hair to keep him at her reddening, distending nipples, Seth was convinced of that.

Between them, she started shifting restlessly, uttering little whimpering wails of need. He couldn't stop himself from swallowing the sounds and pinching her hard points relentlessly. For a moment, she tensed, and Seth worried he'd gone too far, but she went wild in his arms, writhing and moaning for more.

"I'm watching him devour you," Beck murmured intimately. "It's arousing as fuck to see you give yourself to him. But I'm greedy. I want more. I want you to surrender. Spread your legs for him, little girl."

With a tiny whine, she complied, and Seth eased back, staring down at the most beautiful, glistening pale pussy he'd ever clapped eyes on. Right now, that wasn't all he wanted to put on her cunt. His mouth watered.

"The good detective has a very singular talent I think he needs to remind you of."

Heat blasted Seth's bloodstream like a furnace. Fuck, it was as if the doctor could read his mind.

Then he stopped thinking about Beck as he knelt on the ground beside the bed, cupped Heavenly's hips in his hands, and yanked her to the edge. Her yelp turned into a long, tortured moan as Seth fastened his mouth over her wet folds. He didn't bother wasting time teasing her or sampling her. He sucked her in, pulling on her hard clit and tonguing it savagely.

In seconds, she was fisting the comforter, clawing at Beck, and keening for mercy. Seth didn't have any, especially after her taste hit his taste buds. Having her ride his tongue felt a lot like coming home.

In that instant, he didn't know what the fuck he'd been thinking when he'd genuinely considered not coming home to them, to her, to this. He couldn't live without these two. Heavenly was the perfect woman for him, and Beck was proving why he was the best possible partner in her pleasure.

"Beck," she pleaded with him. "Beck..."

"Don't beg me. That's not my mouth on your pussy. It's his. Ask him for what you want."

She hesitated, wriggling on his tongue like she wanted to him to guess that she ached for the orgasm she wasn't quite willing to beg for.

Yeah, that wasn't how he worked.

"Better start talking, angel," he taunted, thumbing her little pebbled clit in intentionally slow, frustrating strokes.

"More."

He sped up his teasing circles...but not enough to do anything but make her twist and cry out louder. "Of what? Tell me what you need."

She bit her lip, her pants audible as he increased the speed of his stroke and jacked her up even higher. "You know."

"I do, but if you want it, you have to beg for it."

Heavenly let out a trio of frustrated exhalations, as if she thought she could breathe past the pleasure overwhelming her. Seth made sure she couldn't.

"Please."

"Please what?" he demanded.

She didn't answer right away, and he fastened his mouth on her again, this time toying with her, lashing her with his tongue and backing away until she subconsciously spread her legs wider and dug her fingers in his hair as she pressed him against her pussy.

But she still hadn't given him the words he wanted to hear, and he wasn't about to give her any quarter.

Seth lifted away and spread her pussy open, breathing hard and hot on her distended button. "Please what?"

Heavenly bit her lip again, wriggling and fighting. "Let me come."

"No, I won't let you. I'll *make* you. But you have to beg me nicely." She needed to acknowledge that *he* was giving her pleasure before he'd grant her release. "Tears will help."

And in case she needed extra incentive, he bent and plowed his tongue up her slit again, moaning as he licked up her juices. He targeted her most sensitive spots, lingering over her clit until she panted and huffed…and gave in. "Please make me come. Please…"

"That's some pretty begging, little girl," Beck murmured as he took her breasts in hand, strumming and pinching her nipples. "You're making my cock ache."

"*Please!*"

"Yes, I know. But Seth is the one with his mouth on that pussy. Remind me… Who does it belong to?"

"You," she wailed.

"And tonight, I gave it to him. He alone decides when—or if—you deserve orgasm."

In response, she cried and writhed, looking at Seth with helpless, beseeching eyes. He felt her silent pleading in every corner of his body. But it wasn't enough. He might not deserve it, but he needed her to acknowledge him as her Dominant. He needed her absolute surrender. Only that would help him put them back together.

He speared her with two blunt fingers, plunging deep, relishing the way she gasped and clamped her swollen tissues around his intruding digits and begged with her circling hips.

Slowly, he stimulated that spot inside her, just behind her clit, with one hand. With the other, he grabbed the hair at her nape and forced her to look at him. "If you want this orgasm, you'll get it from me—and me alone. Beg me for it."

Heavenly fell into his stare, her breaths harsh, her cheeks red. Perspiration dotted her hairline. Her neck was damp with it. Between her breasts dripped with it. Everything about her screamed how badly her body needed what he could give her, but her mind had to comply, too. He couldn't force this on her.

"Angel." He pressed his lips to hers. "Stop fighting us. I love you—more than anything. And I'm sorry."

Tears filled her eyes then. She closed them as drops ran to her temples and her face softened with something between love, exalta- tion, and—finally—surrender. Then she lifted her mouth to his and whispered against his lips, "I love you, too. I'm sorry. Make me come, Seth. Please…"

Relief poured through him. Finally, they might be happy and whole again, hopefully for good. "With pleasure."

He didn't waste a moment bending to the wet heat between her legs and drinking her in with his tongue while he tormented her depths with his digits. Immediately, she gasped. Beck smothered the sound with his kiss, taking her lips over and over as he fondled her breasts, teasing the tips with his thumbs.

Everything about being with them again, about having her between them, felt right. This was where he belonged. His relief in being here and accepted again was momentous. If Heavenly and Beck had walked away from him, Seth didn't know how he would have moved on, especially if they'd left because of his own stupidity.

But the perfection of the moment made ramping her up until she writhed, until her skin sheened all over, even sweeter. Her cheeks turned rosier. Her cries got louder. Her desperation felt visceral. Her need spoke to the man in him, stoked the Dom in him. Her torment wrapped around his cock. But the way she gave to him now, so openly and completely, tugged on his heart until there was no saving him from the inevitable tumble of falling more in love.

"Now, little girl. We're dying to be inside you," Beck growled.

"Yes. Yes. *Yeeessss!*" she screamed, her body contorting with ecstasy as she let go, releasing onto Seth's tongue. He could all but feel her lowering the barricades around her heart and putting it back into his keeping.

She shuddered and shattered between them for a small eternity, and Seth kept at her until she slowly, slowly fell from the stratosphere and back into their arms.

When she opened her eyes, their stares connected. Her face twisted. Tears pooled and fell. She lurched for him.

Love slammed through Seth's chest as he enclosed her in his embrace. The need to fuse with her slammed down his spine. If he didn't get inside her in the next thirty seconds, it would crush his soul.

Beck surged up behind them and wrapped his arms around her

middle as Seth meshed her body to his for a lingering moment, feeling their hearts beat together and their breaths meld as one.

Then the surgeon broke their moment by tugging on her hair and muttering in her ear. "I need inside you, little girl."

She turned to glance at him over her shoulder. "Hurry."

Beck plucked a kiss from her mouth, then lay back. "Lube?"

"On it." Seth hopped up and rummaged through the nightstand until he found the mostly empty tube. They would need to restock soon. He tossed it the surgeon's way.

By the time Seth finished shedding his pants, Beck had finished lubing up and had positioned Heavenly on her hands and knees. He wasn't wearing a condom.

Seth let the observation pass. As long as the doctor didn't go bare in her pussy, they wouldn't have any problems.

Then he got caught up in the erotic sight of Beck aligning his fat purple crest with her tiny back opening.

Watching them made Seth's blood pump harder and his anticipation surge. He settled onto the bed, right in her face. "Open up, angel. Take him."

She nodded, the long, damp tendrils of her hair sliding seductively over her naked body. Their stares met again, and the blue of her eyes slammed deep into him.

"While you do, look at me," he told her. "Don't look away."

"I'll try." Her voice caught, ending on a gasp as Beck nudged her, teasing.

"You'll *do*," Seth corrected.

In his periphery, he was aware of Beck parting her cheeks, of Heavenly bearing down. She gasped as the doctor invaded and slid deep. Her eyes widened. Twin splashes of color rose on her face before she closed her eyes and let out a throaty moan.

Heavenly might be one of the kindest, sweetest females he'd ever met, but at heart she was one of the dirtiest. She loved anal sex. *Thank fuck.*

"Beck!" she cried out as he tunneled in to the hilt.

"Oh, fuck. You're so tight around my cock, little girl." The surgeon threw his head back with a groan, jaw clenched.

As he established a hard, fast rhythm, Heavenly wriggled to take more of him, clutching at the quilt beneath her as her breasts jiggled with every rough thrust. Her nipples hardened to enticing points.

The sight galvanized Seth into action. He grabbed a condom from the nearby nightstand. "Get her on her back and spread her legs."

"Yeah." Beck sounded strained. "Hurry, man. This is going to go fast."

For sure. It had only been two days since Seth had been inside her. It felt like two fucking centuries.

Seconds later, he rolled the condom on, then looked up to find Beck sprawled on his back, his feet braced on the mattress, with Heavenly on top, faceup, her back entrance speared by the surgeon's cock. He clutched her hips, rocking up underneath her as she rolled her head from side to side in sensual distress. He'd slung her thighs over either one of his, leaving her spread wide and her pussy totally open.

Seth swallowed hard. "Oh, that's pretty. I need to defile her."

Then he climbed onto the bed, toying with her slick button as he worked himself into position. It was a good goddamn thing that he was tall and his arms were long. He was able to slide between their spread legs, anchor himself on his knees, and grip her thighs. Then he fitted his sheathed staff at her glistening opening and, with a single surge of his hips, shoved himself deep in a stroke that had them all groaning, long and loud. Electricity zapped his system. Hot pleasure swelled. Already, he was stunned and shaking.

"Fuck. Me," Seth ground out.

"Nothing else feels this good..." Beck's voice sounded like well-worn gravel.

"Nothing," Seth agreed to the backdrop of Heavenly's high-pitched pleading.

"Help me. Hurry. Please. I'm begging..."

And she was. The whining desperation in her voice kicked Seth into high gear. Teeth bared, he drove into her, sank seemingly forever inside her, filling her with every inch he had in one ruthless stroke. Reluctantly, he eased back. Beck, bless the bastard, was right there, shoving her down on his cock as he lifted up into her. A chorus of her moans and broken pleas filled the air.

Need climbed, built. He and Beck worked to establish a tempo that solidly and steadily pushed her toward bliss and drove her out of her goddamn mind. He was losing his, too, shuddering with every thrust, haunted by the last time he'd been balls deep inside her—bareback and not giving a damn about the fact she could get pregnant. He'd come in her depths heedlessly. Happily. Even though it fucking terrified him, some part of him still hoped his seed took.

The other part of him—the part still using his brain up top—knew every reason that was a horrible idea.

Still, he closed his eyes and pretended he was about to unload deep inside her. Together with images of Heavenly round and pregnant, that fucking turned him on like nothing else.

What the hell was wrong with him?

"Now," Beck ground out, settling his fingers over her clit.

"Now," Seth growled back, angling his hips to abrade that spot inside Heavenly that never failed to launch her into climax.

She tensed. She held her breath and clutched at him, burying her nails in his shoulders as desire bloomed across her face. Her whimpers turned to a scream of ecstasy. Then she clamped down on them, pulsing long and strong, destroying Seth's self-control.

Seconds later, orgasm slammed his system, rolled down his spine, and threatened to dismantle him altogether.

Jesus, every time with Heavenly and Beck just got better.

Under them, the surgeon's strangled moans said he'd also bowed to the pleasure. Seth closed his eyes and basked in their waning sounds of satisfaction. A languid, gratified buzz hummed through his veins.

With them was where he belonged. Rightness swelled inside Seth as he fought to catch his breath.

As much as he hated to, he untangled himself from Heavenly, rolling off of her so she could catch her breath. The ceiling fan above swayed lazily as Beck lifted her off his cock and settled her between them. As Seth reached to take her into his arms and bring her close, she curled into a ball at his side and sobbed.

What the fuck?

"Angel?" He gathered her close, sliding the curls from her face as he kissed her damp forehead and willed her to look at him. "What is it? What's wrong?"

She sniffled and opened those wide eyes that threatened to rip his heart from his chest. "What happens next? Are you leaving again? Or are you home for good?"

Beck rolled onto his side and propped his head onto his upturned palm. "I think we deserve an answer."

Despite the fact Seth had known this was coming, just as he'd known he had to tell them the details of Autumn's and Tristan's deaths, he flinched. Time to be painfully honest again. If he couldn't be, they were right; they had no prayer of lasting.

"I want to."

"What's stopping you?" Beck demanded.

A couple of things. First, he addressed Heavenly. "Can you live with what I did? I can't undo it, angel. It will always be a stain on my past."

"I won't say it didn't shock me, but you would never hurt me."

He nodded emphatically. "Ever. I would never lift a hand to you. I would die protecting you."

"I know." She kissed him softly.

Pressed against her back, Beck let out a tense breath and pasted on a smile. "So it's settled?"

Seth winced. "I have another problem. It's something I don't have the right to ask you for. But if I don't, I'm not sure I can stay."

The surgeon sent him a challenging glare. "Try me."

"I-I lied." He squeezed his eyes shut, feeling guilty as hell. But the sounds of Heavenly crying urged him on. "I can't live here if Zach does. His tragedy hits too close to home. The memories... I thought I'd handled them. I thought I could deal. But I—"

"We know." Beck reached over Heavenly to clap his shoulder. "We already figured it out."

Relief curled through Seth. They had? Why hadn't they said so?

She curled against his chest and looked up at him with imploring eyes. "We were just waiting for you to tell us."

"Why? Angel, I can't tell Beck who he can and can't have living in his house. And Zach's loss is so much fresher. Asking him to accommodate me is shitty and...I feel fucking weak. But not communicating with you two only made it worse. I retreated and got in my head...and I'm sorry."

As Heavenly kissed his jaw in absolution, Beck shook his head. "I understand. But we all live here. We all need to be comfortable here. This should be our sanctuary, not someplace you try to escape by sleeping on the too-short sofa in your office."

"You're right." Seth felt more than vaguely guilty. "I fucked up. But he's your brother. He's suffering, and he has nowhere else to go. He can't stay on the streets, and every minute he's out there, he could be recognized, harassed—"

"I have an idea that I'm hoping will suit us all. But first things first. Put Zach aside for a minute. Do you want to come home and be with us?"

Put Zach aside? How? "It's not that simple—"

"It is. Yes or no?"

Seth gaped. If Zach wasn't in the picture... "I never wanted to leave in the first place. I've never been happier than when I was here." He glanced down at Heavenly. "I love you."

She beamed up at him, her cheeks still rosy with satisfaction. "I love you."

Finally, Beck smiled. "Then I know what to do. Just promise me you won't abandon us again."

That seemed like the simplest promise in the world to keep. "I won't."

And if he stayed with them, he'd reconcile what their future looked like—commitment and babies and forever. He just needed time to get it all straight in his head.

"Then I got you," Beck promised. "Leave the situation with Zach to me."

CHAPTER SEVEN

Despite the fact he and Seth had reaffirmed their bond with Heavenly and managed spine-bending satisfaction all around, sleep proved to be an elusive bitch. Though having her between them again felt right and finally gave Beck some optimism, his brain refused to let him rest. He'd spent hours dissecting everything Seth had confessed about Autumn and Tristan, the way they'd died, and his subsequent revenge. Beck had come to one inescapable conclusion.

There were holes in Seth's story.

Oh, the PI had been thorough—even self-castigating—up through their murders. After that, the explanation had turned murky. Why had Seth gotten obsessed with that particular cold case? What about it had made him unable to let go? Unable to care about other cases? Newer cases? And once he'd gone down the dark road with that case, whose palms had he had to grease? Who in the seedy underworld had he asked questions of? And what sort of favors had he done for them in exchange for the name of his wife's and son's killer? Nothing legal, that was for fucking sure.

Beck didn't blame Seth for wasting the asshole who had killed his family, but why had the murderer done it? Simply to cover up his cold-case killing? Or was there something deeper at work that would motivate a stranger to off a homicide detective's wife and infant boy? If there wasn't, why wouldn't the killer simply end the detective hunting him down?

Other things didn't add up, too. Once upon a time, Seth had knocked Pike out cold with one punch. The police academy hadn't taught him that shit. Who had? Beck didn't like the possible answers.

And the biggest question of all? Why would Seth have bared so much pain about the loss of his family, then given them double-speak to explain everything else?

Pieces of this story weren't fitting together, and he'd get to the bottom of it. But right now, Beck had to deal with the situation in front of him. He had to talk to Zach.

He'd rehearsed ways to explain to his brother that, after inviting him to stay at the house, Beck was now asking him to leave. No, he wasn't casting Zach onto the streets. His brother would have a place to stay. But if he wasn't here, how was Beck supposed to help guide him through this new existence? On the other hand, if Seth couldn't handle being around Zach, what choice did he have?

None. He fucking hated this. Guilt weighed heavily on Beck's heart and shoulders.

Plucking his cell phone from the nightstand, he checked the time. Just after four a.m.—an hour earlier than he wanted to be out of bed. But trying to drift off now was pointless. He had rounds to make. Might as well get to them. If he finished early, maybe he could approach Zach about moving out this afternoon and get him settled at the new place before Seth returned from work.

Carefully easing away from Heavenly's warm body, he tossed back the covers and crept to the bathroom. After a quick shower and shave, he dressed, then headed to the kitchen for a much-needed caffeine infusion. But when he reached the bottom of the stairs, he found Zach sitting at the kitchen table, sipping a cup of his own.

"Hey," Beck greeted in a low murmur.

"Morning."

"If you're hungry, I can make you some breakfast. Or Heavenly saved you a steak and some salad from dinner last night. They're in the fridge."

"Thank you. I'm not hungry now, but I'll probably have that for lunch."

"Sounds good. I'll leave you directions for reheating it," Beck said, filling his mug with coffee. "Heavenly would help, but she's studying for finals." Besides, she wouldn't be around to cook for Zach in the future. His brother needed to learn kitchen skills so he could eventually take care of himself.

"I'll figure it out," Zach snapped, then he sighed. "Sorry, I don't mean to sound ungrateful."

He didn't, but something was clearly bothering him.

Like losing a wife and daughter?

"It's all good," Beck assured as he eased onto the chair across from his brother. "You okay?"

"Fine."

Bullshit. But Beck was trying to figure out how to broach the topic that had kept him up half the night when Zach broke into his thoughts.

"What are you doing up so early?"

"Couldn't sleep, so I decided I'd get up and start my rounds. Did you sleep okay?"

"I did, until..." He glanced upstairs, then Beck's way with a pointed stare.

Zach had heard him and Seth making love to Heavenly? Beck grimaced. "Ahh. Sorry, man. We...forgot we weren't alone."

"Don't apologize. It's your house, and I'm not complaining. I'm grateful you offered me a place to stay."

Unwittingly, Zach had given Beck the perfect opening. He wished he didn't have to take it.

"About that... You don't know Seth well, but eight years ago, while he was living in New York, he lost a wife and child, too. They were murdered."

"Like mine." Zach scrubbed a hand down his face.

"Yes. Watching you deal with your loss and grief has caused his to resurface. He's not handling it well."

"Is that why he's rarely around? Because of me?"

Beck heaved a sigh. "Yes and no. It's not *you*. Being around you is simply a reminder of all he lost. He knows exactly what you're thinking and feeling. It's like looking in a mirror and reliving the most horrific time of his life all over again."

"If you think it will help, I'll talk to him."

Amazing. Zach was suffering, but he was still willing to help someone whose pain was years old, while Seth couldn't seem to find a fucking ounce of compassion to help his brother, who was currently enduring the worst of his grief. The fact that Zach might interpret his insistence to move elsewhere as him choosing Seth over his own brother added another layer to Beck's guilt, along with a boatload of anger.

"Thanks for the offer, but that's not what he needs. You ever heard the adage 'out of sight, out of mind'?"

"Of course." Zach's nod slowed as he digested Beck's question. "You want me to leave."

"I don't *want* you to, but—"

"It's okay, brother." Zach sent Beck a crooked smile. "It's ironic you brought this up. I woke this morning, pondering the kindest way possible to ask if I could find a place of my own."

That took Beck aback. "You did?"

"Again, I don't mean to sound ungrateful, but..." Zach scanned the room and frowned. "I don't feel like this is where I'm supposed to be. It's hard to sort everything out here. You and Heavenly are so attentive and worried about leaving me alone that it's hard to just be with my thoughts."

Shit. As a kid, Zach had always been the quietest of the Kimball brothers. He'd preferred his own company, especially when something troubled him. "I'm sorry for not realizing..."

"How could you? And I would never want to upset you or Heavenly. I don't pretend to understand your relationship, but I know my first assumption, that any woman involved sexually with two men at once must be a harlot, is wrong. Heavenly is a genuinely sweet and kind person. I would never want to upset her or seem ungracious, but she often tries to engage or distract me, asking if I want to watch a movie, swim, talk, or..." He shrugged. "Right now, I'd rather be alone."

"She means well," Beck assured. "A few weeks ago, she lost her dad. They were very close. Even though he was sick and his death wasn't unexpected, he passed suddenly. She took it hard. I think she's trying to make sure you don't fall into the same mental chasm of grief she did."

Zach's face softened. "I'm so sorry. I didn't know."

"You couldn't. My point is, Heavenly wasn't trying to be pushy. She was just trying to help you find a path forward and show you that life goes on."

His brother raked a hand through his hair. "And I came at the worst possible time. I didn't realize you had a houseful of mourning people."

Ironically, Beck hadn't either until Zach pointed it out. "You came when you found yourself at a crossroads, and I'm still here for you."

"I appreciate that. But I need time—*quiet* time—to reflect on everything that's happened."

"I understand. I know you feel completely lost."

Zach nodded. "All my life, I knew what was expected of me, what my role in Messiah City was, and how I fit into God's plan. I don't anymore. I'm still not sure what I believe about God right now."

Beck ached for Zach's obvious confusion and struggle. "One day at a time. That's how you'll figure everything out. If you keep yourself open and stay receptive to what's around you, you'll find this life has advantages and blessings. You'll eventually find happiness, too."

"You should know." He smiled faintly. "But to get there, I need space and solitude so I can figure out where to go next, to take the right path so I can find where I belong."

The guilt in Beck's chest eased. Thank fuck that his needs and Zach's dovetailed. But that didn't lessen his resentment at Seth for putting him in what could have been a terrible position.

"I'll give you as much solitude as you need and a place to be alone."

"You will?"

"Yeah. Seth has an apartment sitting empty. It's not far from here."

"If he lives with you and Heavenly, why?"

"He rented it when he first moved from New York, before the three of us got together."

"Why does he keep it if he's not using it?"

There were so many real-world things Zach had no way of understanding. Beck explained the concept of a lease in the most basic terms, along with the consequences of breaking one, before he described Seth's one-bedroom unit with state-of-the-art security.

"It sounds like a good fit," Zach mused.

"It's a great complex with a swimming pool, fitness center, and a clubhouse. There's a grocery store and tons of restaurants right around the corner, so you won't go hungry."

Zach nodded. "Are you sure Seth won't mind me staying there?"

"Not at all. We talked about it last night, and he offered to let you stay at the apartment. Would you like to see it?"

"Sure. I don't have a schedule to keep, so let me know when you're available."

"We can go now. It won't take more than a few minutes."

"It's that close?"

"Yeah," Beck assured. "It's just a few minutes by car, so if you'd like company or want to visit, all you have to do is call. I'll slip over and pick you up." Beck frowned. "But you'll eventually need your own set of wheels."

"Wheels?"

"A new truck."

Zach didn't look happy. "Do I have to get a truck?"

The question took Beck aback. Living with The Chosen, his brother had no doubt driven nothing but high-utility vehicles for years, so he'd assumed... "No. You can get whatever kind of car you want."

"I want one like yours."

That shocked him. "A sports car?"

"Yeah. A red one, sleek and flashy."

Beck was about to let Zach down gently and tell him he couldn't afford a Mercedes convertible when he remembered their raid on Jed's safe. "How much money did you take from Messiah City?"

"Everything in Jed's office—stacks of cash, bars of gold, stocks, and jewelry."

"What did you do with it?" Beck mentally kicked himself for not asking sooner.

"It's downstairs, in my suitcase."

Seriously? "Did Jericho give you any idea how much all that is worth?"

"On the flight here, he took stock of everything. He said that, after selling the land Messiah City sits on, which I'll eventually inherit, I'll have around twenty million dollars."

Beck nearly choked on his coffee. "Are you shitting me?"

"No. And after watching many episodes of *The Price is Right*, I realize that's a lot of money. I-I wasn't sure before. But I gave a couple million to Jericho to pass on to those who have left The Chosen's way of life. They'll need a solid start, too."

Quick math told Beck he'd given each of the survivors close to a hundred thousand dollars—way more than most people leaving a cult had to begin again.

"Maybe I should give them more." Zach frowned. "I'm not greedy."

"You're not. You did fine," Beck assured.

Still, it was obvious he had a lot to teach Zach about money.

"And you can buy any car you want," he told his brother. "You could buy a house, too. A damn yacht even."

"I-I don't think I need all that."

"You don't. But you do need a bank account. Then I'll set up a meeting with my investment broker. After that, we'll find you whatever red sports car you want." As he thought through that paperwork, something else occurred to Beck. "Except...do you have a driver's license? Or a birth certificate?"

Beck hadn't stayed long enough in Messiah City to know if the townsfolk had submitted to the state's laws. "I do. I carry my license. In Jed's office, we found everyone's birth certificates. Those leaving the sect got theirs, me included."

"Good. We can get you hooked up with banking and investments right away. The question is, do you want to remain Zacharias Kimball? You can, but I have to warn you, everyone you meet will know where you came from." And if they didn't off the top of their head, a simple internet search would tell them. "If you want to avoid potential altercations and ensure your privacy, it might be better to change your name."

"Like you did?"

"Exactly. But it's your call."

Zach fell silent and stared down into his coffee cup for a long moment. "If I changed my name, could I be a Beckman, too? We're brothers. After so many years apart, I'd like to keep it that way."

His words filled Beck's heart with a love for family he'd never felt. But he had to be honest. "Sure. That's Gloria's last name, but if that doesn't bother you..."

"It doesn't. Before I met her, I simply thought of her as a whore. I also assumed she would be a bad person. After Jed and Mother attacked us and she comforted that grieving widow—"

"Ngaire."

Zach nodded. "She had just suffered a terrible loss."

"Like you had, yes."

"Gloria was doing her utmost to hold the widow together. And I began to think... Why was I judging this woman? Who am I to believe I have the moral authority to do that? The only person I should stand in judgment on is myself. Everyone else? That's God's responsibility... whoever He is."

Beck was proud that his brother was breaking out of The Chosen's mindset so quickly and so well. "You're damn right. Despite being raised by Esther and constantly exposed to Jed, you turned out good."

"Thank you." Zach flashed something that almost looked like a whole smile. "You did, too."

Though Beck's to-do list had suddenly grown longer, the grin lighting up Zach's face was more than worth the work.

May

A couple of weeks later, Heavenly piled her hair on her head in a messy bun and stepped back, casting a critical eye in the bedroom mirror at the pink high-cut bikini with its clinging bandeau top. A little frown wrinkled her brow. She was probably showing off more skin than Zach would be comfortable with, but this was the only swimsuit she owned...and the first time she'd ever worn it. Beck and Seth preferred her naked when they enjoyed the pool in the backyard. But today, Heavenly would be giving Zach the swim lessons she'd promised him at Seth's apartment complex. Her only saving grace was that she and Zach would be in the water most of the day. He shouldn't have time to look twice at her.

"You're not wearing that in public, angel." Leaning against the doorframe, arms crossed over his wide chest, Seth wore a disapproving scowl.

While she loved the times when he and Beck let out their inner cavemen, she frowned back at Seth now. Of course she'd been relieved he had opened up and explained the circumstances around Autumn's and Tristan's deaths. Yes, she suspected there was more to the story than Seth had revealed, but that was okay...at least for now. The three of them were on fairly solid footing again.

Except he hadn't quite been himself since he'd come home. Mostly he was fine, and the three of them had slipped back into a daily rhythm that felt normal and wonderful. He still worked cases overnight more often than not—the nature of cheating spouses, she supposed. But the fuse on his temper seemed shorter than usual, and that edge often appeared when she least expected it.

"Of course not. I'm wearing this over it." She slid on the gauzy, see-through cover-up.

"That doesn't hide anything."

"It's fine," she assured with a smile.

"It's not. Wrap a blanket around you."

Heavenly tried to hang on to her composure. "Seth, be reasonable. It's hot out there."

His scowl deepened. "Then use a towel. Better yet, use two."

"I've already packed them." She lifted the canvas bag she'd also filled with water, sunscreen, and her cell phone. "Let's go. I don't want to keep Zach waiting."

Especially since she was hoping to see Jasmine for a quick pedi and hug before the woman left with Jane and Arthur for nearly a month back east. Now that their house had sold and their granddaughter was graduating college, they'd be gone for a while. Though she and Raine had only had a few outings with the sweet redhead, Heavenly already considered her a friend. She was going to miss Jasmine.

Grumbling something undecipherable under his breath, Seth slung his arm around her waist and escorted her down the stairs, through the garage, and into his SUV.

As he backed out of the darkness and into the bright afternoon,

Heavenly slid her sunglasses on, then rested her hand on his thigh. "Thank you for doing this."

"You don't have to thank me, angel."

"I know being around Zach isn't easy for you. That's why I told him I'd text him when I got there. This way, you can drop me off and head to the office, and he can just meet me at the pool. You don't have to see him at all."

"I don't dislike him. Neither you nor Beck has to hide him from me."

"I know." She squeezed his thigh. "I just want to protect you."

He scowled. "Don't. It's my job to protect *you*."

"You do. Every day." She leaned over the console and kissed his cheek.

He sighed in agitation, but he let it go. "It shouldn't take me more than a couple of hours to run these background checks. If you want to leave before I'm done, just call. I'll come right over and pick you up."

"No worries. I'll be fine," Heavenly assured. "It will take at least that long to teach Zach to swim. He seemed intrigued with the idea, but I think he's afraid. Then again, I'm sure there's a lot of things in our world that scare him."

Seth nodded. "To be sure. But swimming is a good place to start since most people can. Where did you learn to swim, angel?"

His change of subject was too pronounced for her not to notice, but Heavenly played along. "On the farm. We had a big pond nearby. Though I was too young to remember, my dad told me he'd taught me before I could even walk because he worried I might wander off, fall in, and drown."

"Smart man."

"Where did you learn to swim?"

"The Y. To save her sanity, Mom enrolled us boys in their summer camp each year."

"Smart woman." Heavenly grinned.

"Do you ever wonder what Zach thinks of the real world?"

She was stunned he'd brought Beck's brother up again. Progress? "All the time, especially the things he's never seen before, like the microwave. It seems so silly and common to us, but he's fascinated by it. I've seen him let his coffee get cold just so he can warm it back up."

Seth chuckled. "It boggles my mind how many things he's never experienced, like his trip to the barber."

"And he looks completely different with a good haircut and shave. So much like a younger Beck."

"Exactly. The barber did a great job. Since Zach's picture has been plastered across every media outlet, maybe he'll get some anonymity now."

"Fingers crossed. Let's also hope that the men who want to hurt him don't recognize him."

Seth squeezed her hand. "Yeah. But the good news is, the media attention has finally died down, and Zach has proven he can take care of himself."

"I know, but..." Heavenly hated to bring up a sore spot, but she couldn't dismiss the truth simply because it was inconvenient. "It's just...he's at the apartment by himself all the time, and—"

"He says he prefers the solitude, and my security system would put Fort Knox to shame." Seth's tone sounded more like a warning than a conversation.

She steered away from pointing out that Zach was alone because of him. It wouldn't do any good. "Beck said that when he took Zach shopping for clothes, the poor guy didn't know there were styles of underwear besides briefs. And that when they stopped for lunch, Zach had never been to a restaurant with a waitperson before. He thought restaurants cost a lot of money, and that he wouldn't fit in wearing jeans and a work shirt, so he lived on fast food while he was in Vegas and LA looking for Beck. I ache when I think about how overwhelming all this change must be for him."

"Yeah," Seth said solemnly. "It's going to take time, but he'll eventually adjust. Beck will give him plenty of guidance. And you'll give him swim lessons."

Heavenly nodded as Seth turned into the apartment complex and pulled to a stop at the curb near the pool.

"Call me if you need me, angel," he murmured against her lips, then cupped her nape and pulled her in for a long, slow kiss, as if he intended to brand himself on her.

"If you keep that up, I'll be calling before you even leave the parking lot," she joked to keep things light, then hopped out of the SUV.

Heavenly could feel Seth's eyes on her as she strode across the sidewalk, past a pair of tall, potted palms, and through the black metal gate surrounding the pool. After plopping her bag onto a thickly padded chaise, she pulled out her phone, then smiled and waved to Seth. It took a few moments, and she could feel his protective stare, but he drove away.

"All right, let's get these lessons started," she murmured, sending Zach a text.

Three minutes later, as she sat unloading the things from her bag, he strolled from beneath a stucco archway. Heavenly couldn't help but grin. With a clinging white tank perched on top of his bulging shoulders, muted blue swim trunks, black flip-flops, and aviators, he almost looked as if he'd been born and raised in LA.

Once he'd eaten up the distance between them, Heavenly stood and wrapped her arms around him awkwardly. Zach still tensed each time she hugged him, but that didn't deter her. The man needed some form of affection besides the brotherly slaps on the shoulder Beck gave him. She didn't want Zach climbing so far inside himself that he couldn't find his way back out.

"Ready to learn how to swim?" she asked encouragingly.

Sliding the sunglasses to the end of his nose, Zach eyed the water warily. "I don't know. I understand people swim for fun, but I've heard of those who have drowned in mere inches of water."

"I promise, you won't drown today. I won't let you. Okay?"

"Okay," he replied doubtfully.

"First, we need to put on sunscreen."

"That's not necessary," he pushed back. "I've worked outside in the desert my whole life without it."

He probably had if the bronzed bulges of his arms were any indication. "Maybe so, but water increases the reflection of the sun. You don't want to get a horrible sunburn. Trust me. Besides, I need it. Otherwise, I'll be burnt to a crisp in five minutes."

As Heavenly applied the sunscreen to her arms, chest, and stomach, Zach did the same, staring at the water suspiciously.

"Think of the pool as a giant bathtub," she offered, hoping to alleviate his angst while working the lotion onto her legs. "The only difference is that the water is cooler. It's refreshing."

Zach's grunt said he wasn't entirely convinced.

Heavenly was beginning to wonder if she'd even be able to convince him to stick his big toe in before Seth picked her up again.

"Would you mind putting some on my back?" she asked, holding out the bottle of sunscreen to him.

"I-I'm sorry." Zach shook his head adamantly. "I can't touch you. It would be disrespectful and wrong. You belong to my brother."

She hadn't realized he'd see it that way, but she should have. "He won't consider you helping me with sunscreen an inappropriate touch, but he'll definitely be mad if I go home with a sunburn. And I'll have to pay for that sin."

Zach blanched. "He beats you?"

Only when I beg him to.

But she bit back the confession. There was no sense confusing the poor man even more.

"Absolutely not! I meant he wouldn't be pleased that I didn't protect my skin." Heavenly glanced around the pool area and spotted a middle-aged lady sitting beneath a big umbrella, reading a book. "I'll go ask that woman if she'll do it."

"Do you know her?"

"No, but if you can't—"

"I will do it to placate my brother."

"Thank you." Heavenly presented her back to Zach.

She heard him swallow. And when he settled his rough, calloused hands on her back, his touch was tentative. To ensure she didn't spook him, she held perfectly still while he applied the lotion. When he was done, she thanked him politely.

"Go ahead and take off your T-shirt. I'll apply some sunscreen to your back, then we'll get in the water."

"I'd rather leave it on in the company of strangers." He skimmed a glance over the woman reading and a thirty-something man catching rays on the other side of the pool.

"Whatever you're comfortable with." Which was probably sitting inside Seth's apartment, watching TV. "Zach, we don't have to do this if you've changed your mind."

"You said this is an important skill, and I promised I would let you teach me. Promises cannot be broken."

Too bad my mom never learned that lesson.

"All right. Let's do this."

After placing their flip-flops and sunglasses beneath the chaise, Zach followed her to the shallow end of the pool. Heavenly stepped in first, sighing as the cool water enveloped her feet and lapped at her ankles. She stepped down a few more times, until the water brushed her thighs. She turned to find Zach still standing at the edge and motioned him to join her.

Gripping the silver railing like a lifeline, he cautiously stepped into the water. As he descended the stairs, a childlike surprise crossed his face. Then he smiled.

When she stepped down to the shallow end, he followed, his arms flailing in the air while he took exaggerated steps. "I feel like I'm walking through mud, but it's…thinner."

"It's called buoyancy. The water is trying to keep you afloat."

"It feels strange."

She let Zach get used to the sensation before teaching him how to float, then dog-paddle. His tank clung to every muscle and ripple of his body, especially his ridged abs, and even though the middle-aged woman on her chaise staring made him uncomfortable, he was doing well. He was even starting to get brave…until she tried to teach him how to hold his breath. After the fifth time he submerged himself, he jerked his head above the surface, choking and gasping and wearing an angry scowl.

"I'm done," Zach growled. "If God had wanted me to swim, he would have made me a fish."

"You did great for your first lesson," she placated. "I promise, when you try again, it won't be as difficult. And the good news is, you've learned enough to ensure that, if you ever fall into a lake, you won't drown."

"Try again?" He blanched.

"Not today. Not tomorrow, if you don't want. When you're ready," she assured. "Do you want to get out and dry off?"

"Yes."

They returned to the chaise, and she handed him a towel. Zach shook his head. "I have towels upstairs. Would you like to come with me and have something to drink while you wait for Seth?"

"No. I still have water in my bottle. Besides, he'll be picking me up soon. I'll hang out in the shade and read my book while I wait."

"Are you sure? We can watch *The Price Is Right*. Have you ever seen that show?"

"I have."

"Isn't it interesting? They give away the most wonderful gadgets." His face lit up with more childlike excitement.

"What kind?"

"Toaster ovens, motorized scooters, and golf carts. They even have a toothbrush that uses water instead of toothpaste. So many awesome things… In fact, I want to buy a golf cart one day."

Heavenly wasn't sure what he'd do with it, but… "Then do it."

"I really can? No one will tell me no?"

A valid question, considering how much the elders had controlled his life. "As long as it's not illegal and you can afford it, you can buy or do anything you want."

As if she'd just given him permission to live, a brilliant smile stretched his lips.

"I understand why Beck chose you. You're sweeter and kinder than most in this world." Zach hugged her impulsively, then immediately released her and stepped back. "I'm sorry if that was untoward. Thank you for everything, especially not letting me drown."

"You're fine. And you're welcome. Want to come for dinner next week?"

"I'd like that. Tell my brother and Seth that I said hello."

"Will do."

As Zach turned and headed back to Seth's apartment, Heavenly spread both towels across her chaise, then positioned it under the nearby overhang, sat, and found her dog-eared paperback in the bottom of her bag.

She began reapplying sunscreen so she'd be covered once she was ready to cool off in the pool again. As she spread some lotion on her shoulders, she glanced up to find two tall guys about her age strolling under the arch and into the fenced area. Heavenly didn't pay them any attention until they approached and stopped beside her, blocking her view of the pool with matching wide shoulders, piercing green eyes, and dark blond hair.

They're identical twins. And they're staring at me.

A flutter of unease rippled through her. "Are you lost?"

"Nah, baby," the twin on the right murmured. "Just enjoying the view."

Oh, she'd heard this shtick before. When she'd worked at Bazookas, drunken frat boys who loved to flirt, proposition, and grope had been the bane of her existence.

Flashing the same plastic smile that used to generate good tips, she nonchalantly clasped her cell phone and arched her brows. "The pool is really nice. Don't you think?"

The twins exchanged cocky grins, then dragged their hungry stares up her body.

"Sure. Can I ask you a question?" The twin on the right leered.

You just did. Instead of pointing out the obvious, Heavenly sighed and hoped she didn't regret this. "Sure."

It was obvious the guys weren't from LA. In fact, their accent was almost like Seth's, but thicker and stronger, so it was possible the pair had gotten lost and needed directions.

"That's a sexy swimsuit, but you wanna know what you'd look better in?"

Here came the pickup lines. She should have known better. "I have a feeling you're going to tell me."

"Our arms," they growled in tandem.

She burst out laughing. "Really?"

"Yeah. Do you know what we have in common with the Little

Mermaid?" the other twin finally spoke up with the same thick East Coast accent.

"I'm afraid to ask."

"We both want to be a part of your world."

Heavenly moaned and shook her head. "Do these lines actually—"

"Wait. Don't shut us down yet. We're just getting warmed up," the first twin pleaded.

"Yeah. Hang on." The second one held up his hand. "Yo, man. I thought we were at a swimming pool, but we must be in a museum because you, baby, are truly a work of art."

The first twin sat beside her with a seductive smile. "Do you have a name or can we just call you ours?"

Heavenly rolled her eyes and laughed again. "You can call me flattered. But sorry, guys. I'm taken."

"He's an idiot for leaving you alone."

Suddenly, the second twin, the one who seemed slightly more reserved, plucked up the tube of sunscreen and squeezed a big dollop in his palm before flanking her. "Let me get your back for you, beautiful. We don't want all that milky, smooth skin to burn. Do we?"

"Actually, I was going to—" She gasped when the cool lotion met the warm flesh directly below her neck and sent him a side-eyed glare.

He just flashed her a crooked smile, kept right on gliding his palm over her, as he leaned close to her ear. "You know, you're proof that aliens exist, because you've abducted our hearts."

She laughed again. Despite being overeager, they were somehow charming. "Like I said, I'm taken."

"Maybe, but you haven't lived until you've been taken by two men at once. Men who know how to blow your pretty little mind," the first one groaned, sliding his hand over her back to help his brother spread the lotion. "Trust me, baby, once you've had twins, you won't go back."

"Jack. Connor. What the fuck are you doing here with your hands on my woman?" Seth bellowed behind her.

They're his brothers?

The twins jolted and jumped to their feet, then immediately

backpedaled as the PI prowled toward them wearing a murderous scowl.

Heavenly slapped a hand over her gaping mouth and stared at the trio of siblings in shock. Now that Seth was standing beside them—looking like he wanted to rip out their hearts with his bare hands—she saw the striking resemblance.

"Seth. Hey, bro." The first twin sounded nervous.

"Shut up, Jack," Seth barked.

"Surprise! We're here," the second one added.

"I see that, Connor," Seth drawled derisively. "But you didn't answer my question. Why are you hitting on my woman? And which one of you idiots came up that ridiculous line, 'Once you've had twins, you won't go back'? Christ, you better not have meant that the way it sounded."

"I-it was just a joke," Jack stammered. "We weren't serious."

"Yeah. No, not serious at all," Connor added.

Jack nodded. "We don't actually do that."

"Never." Connor gave the same head bob.

"We were just…saying hello to your girlfriend, bro. Creatively."

Seth rolled his eyes. "No, you asswipes were hitting on Heavenly because you didn't remember the picture of her I showed you at Christmas. And if you want to keep all the protruding parts of your body attached, you better stop now."

"Okay. Yeah. Calm down." Jack held up his hands. "You're right. We didn't recognize her from your photo. We saw a pretty California girl and—"

"And what? Decided to tap her here, next to the pool, in front of God and everyone?"

"No," Connor insisted before lifting an apologetic wince Heavenly's way. "Sorry for being so—"

"Rude?" Seth barked.

"I was going to say forward," his brother corrected before turning back to Heavenly, his expression softening. "We didn't mean to—"

"No need to apologize." She eased beside Seth with a gentle smile, then extended her hand. "It's nice to meet you, Connor."

The younger twin darted a questioning glance Seth's way, silently asking permission to touch her. At least one of his brothers was getting smart... Seth nodded curtly, then watched Connor shake his girl's hand.

"You, too, Jack." She greeted him with the same gesture.

The hell-raising rebel didn't seek Seth's permission, simply shook her hand and took his sweet time releasing it.

Gnashing his teeth, Seth drew his barely dressed girl closer. "Now that introductions are over, what the fuck are you two doing here in LA?"

Not that he wasn't happy to see them. He was. But he'd been sitting at his office, working himself into a self-loathing froth at the realization that he'd dumped his angel off with Zach because he still struggled to be around Beck's brother. It made him feel weak and ridiculous. And when he'd stumbled on to the twins trying to pick Heavenly up, it hadn't improved his mood.

Jack shrugged. "Well...we told you we wanted to surprise you for spring break, but that didn't work out, and now it's summer, so like I said...surprise!"

Was he serious? "You're here for the whole summer?"

"Yeah. Don't send us back. These plane tickets weren't cheap."

That was a monkey wrench he hadn't foreseen. How would that work with Beck and Heavenly? There was no way he could have the twins underfoot for months without them realizing that he shared his girl with the surgeon. *Fuck.* "And you're planning to do what while you're here? Sit on my couch, eat all my food, and bring different women to my apartment every night?"

Connor grappled for an answer. "Isn't that what summer breaks are for?"

Heavenly shook with silent laughter.

Jack pinned his twin with a what-the-fuck glare, then slanted Seth the puppy-dog eyes he'd perfected as a toddler to get an extra cookie at snack time. "C'mon, bro. You're not happy to see us?"

"I am," Seth admitted. And he was, but… "You might have called first. Does Mom know you two are here in LA?"

"Yeah. We already checked in with her, like we promised," Connor assured.

"When did you arrive?"

"Our flight landed about three hours ago." Jack answered. "It took a while to get our luggage and the rental car—"

"Since we'd never seen the Pacific, we stopped at the beach on our way here," Connor offered.

"We checked out the babes, too." Jack grinned wolfishly.

"Then we came here. We knocked on the door, but no one answered, so we wandered to the pool—"

"Wait," Seth interrupted, turning his glance to Heavenly. "Where's Zach? Did he already learn to swim?"

She sighed. "No. We tried. He got frustrated and left to watch *The Price Is Right*. He must have passed your brothers in the alcove."

"Who's Zach?" Connor frowned.

Shit. How was he going to explain this? "A friend's brother. He just moved to town, so he's staying in my apartment for a while."

"How many bedrooms you got?"

"One."

"So where are we going to sleep if he's crashing on your couch? Or are you living with Heavenly now?"

"Don't you think I would have told Mom if I was?" He skirted the truth.

"True, but I'll bet you didn't mention sleepovers." Connor leered.

That just annoyed Seth and he tried to hold on to his temper, but… no dice. "Shut up."

Jack turned to drill Connor with a glare. "I told you we should have called and let Seth know we were coming. But no. You wanted to *surprise* him. Where the fuck are we gonna stay for the summer, Einstein? On the floor?"

Connor scowled. "How was I supposed to know he'd turned all Mother Teresa and let someone else have his sofa?"

"Stop squabbling. I've been staying with Dr. Beckman temporarily. He's a friend. Zach has been sleeping in my bedroom here at the apartment. I've got a sectional sofa that turns into a king bed. You bozos can have it." Seth squeezed the back of his neck, trying to ward off the headache beginning to throb in his skull. "Now go get your luggage and meet us back at my apartment before I change my mind and make you two cockbags find your own place to crash."

"Awesome!" Connor cheered, fist pumping the air. "Thanks!"

"Yeah!" Jack barked out, grin wide. "Thanks a bunch, bro. We won't eat all your food. Promise."

"Liar," he drawled, fighting a smile.

The twins laughed, then Connor clapped Jack on the back. "Come on, man. Let's get our shit."

As they raced toward the parking lot, Seth peered down at Heavenly with a sigh and shook his head. "I'm sorry about them. They're…"

"Funny and weirdly sweet."

"They're demons who did everything possible to make my life hell growing up."

"Boys will be boys." She grinned.

"Yeah. Even if they're supposed to be grown men." He chuckled, then sobered. "Gather your things, angel. I need to prep Zach before the twins return."

"Prep him?"

"He knows about the three of us. I can't risk him saying anything about it to Jack or Connor. Or my mother will know in two point two seconds."

Heavenly looked away and nodded, but he couldn't miss the disappointment in her expression as she started shoving her things back into the canvas bag.

Biting back a curse, he moved in behind her, wrapped his arms around her waist, and nuzzled his lips against her ear. "I don't want my mom to find out about us from my bigmouthed brothers, angel. I want to tell her myself, the right way."

Heavenly tucked her cell phone into the bag, then turned to faced him. "Zach won't lie for you, me, or Beck. You know that, right?"

He hadn't considered that, but she made a good point. "I get it and

I'll figure something out, but this isn't the right time for me to talk to Mom about us."

"Are you sure? She's happy right now. Maybe it's the perfect time."

At Heavenly's expectant gaze, guilt splintered his composure. He had to break the news to his mom. He knew that. He simply wasn't sure how to manage that, not without her losing her shit.

"Not yet. But soon, angel. I swear," he assured before brushing his lips across hers, then giving her ass a playful swat. "Get moving so I can talk to Zach."

"Do you want me to talk to him for you?" she asked as they reached the archway.

She was trying to keep him from falling into the black abyss of the past again, and he loved her for it, but he had to start manning up. "No. They're my brothers. I'll be fine. Trust me."

Mentally walling off his memories, Seth dragged in a breath as he made his way to Zach, repeating one important litany: *He's Beck's brother. He's Beck's brother.*

The mantra was still spooling through his brain when he and Heavenly entered the apartment where Zach sat on the sectional, yelling at a game show contestant on the big screen. "Pick the cake mix. It's less expensive than the cold medicine."

As the door snicked shut behind them, Zach whirled around with fear-filled eyes as he launched off the couch.

"Easy," Heavenly murmured softly. "It's just us."

"Sorry," Seth added. "We didn't mean to scare you."

Zach let out a pent-up breath. "It's fine. I just wasn't expecting you two. I always worry it's—"

"The Chosen can't find you here, and I should have knocked." Seth offered an apologetic smile.

"No. It's your place and I'm really grateful that you're letting me stay here. Sorry I'm jumpy."

"It was just sitting here empty. But…" Seth cringed. "Um, it's going to be kind of full now. I know you're trying to get your life together, and I hate to invade your peace, but my twin brothers, Jack and Connor, just arrived from New York. They didn't tell me they were coming because they wanted to surprise me. They don't have anywhere else to stay, so I hope you don't mind some roommates."

"I don't mind." Though he kind of looked like he did. "But are you sure you don't mind me staying? If you need me to, I can pack up my stuff. Just give me a few minutes and—"

"You don't need to leave. In fact, I don't want you to. It might be a little tight, but there's room for all three of you here since the sectional makes into a king bed. The twins can suffer the sofa, and you can keep the bedroom so you still have privacy."

"Are they all right sharing space with me?"

"If they're not, too bad. Otherwise, they can find someplace else to stay on their dime." Seth smirked, hoping to reassure Zach. "Where they sleep is a minor problem. The bigger one is that my family thinks Heavenly and I are a couple. Just a couple. They don't know about Beck yet. They're not ready for that."

"Oh." Zach's brows slashed as he digested Seth's words.

"I'm not asking you to lie for me, and they have no reason to ask about Beck since they haven't even met him yet. I simply need you to not say anything about the three of us being a throuple."

"That's what it's called?"

"It's slang, but yeah." He gripped Heavenly's hand. "Will you do it? Will you keep the information about Beck and me being in a relationship with Heavenly to yourself?"

He hesitated, then nodded. "Sure. No problem."

"Thanks, man. I really appreciate—"

A loud knock interrupted him.

"I got it." Heavenly hurried to the door and pulled it open.

"We gotta make one more trip," Connor announced as he and Jack each dumped two large suitcases in the tiled entryway.

"Hold up a sec. Let me introduce you two clowns, then I'll help you haul in the rest." Seth waved his brothers into the room.

Zach, a few years older, eyed the twins, as if sizing them up.

"Jack, Connor, this is Zach." Seth forced a smile, hoping this shit didn't blow up in his face. "Zach, these are my boneheaded brothers Jack and Connor."

As the trio shook hands, Zach scowled. "How am I supposed to tell who is who?"

"I'm Jack." He pointed to himself. "I'm the nice one. Connor is the asshole."

"Fuck you," Connor groused. "We both know I'm the one with the bigger dick."

At Heavenly's soft giggle, Seth scowled. "Hey. Knock it off. There's a lady present."

"Sorry," Connor mumbled. "In all seriousness, Zach, don't worry about telling us apart. People have called us by the wrong name our whole lives. We're used to it."

"Okay." Zach's expression softened with visible relief.

"Let's go get the rest of your luggage, boys," Seth prompted. He really was trying to get used to being around Zach…but Beck's brother made him anxious.

As he herded the twins out the door, he glanced over his shoulder to find Heavenly sinking beside Zach on the sectional, focused on the game show.

When he stepped outside, Seth dragged in a deep breath and slowly released it.

"Hey, um…is there something wrong with Zach?" Jack asked as the three strolled toward the parking lot.

That didn't take long. "What makes you think something's wrong?"

"He's quiet. Like, he's upset or…I don't know. Something."

"Have either of you seen the coverage on the news about the FBI busting up a cult in a place called Messiah City?"

"I think I saw something about it on TikTok." But Jack didn't look convinced.

Connor elbowed him. "Yeah, it was on the TV while we were packing."

"Zach is Zacharias Kimball, the guy who helped orchestrate the FBI raid after the cult killed his wife and daughter."

Jack gaped. "Are you shitting me?"

"No." Seth paused and sent them both a warning glare. "I don't want either of you bringing it up. Understand? He's mourning, not only the loss of his family but the only way of life he's ever known. He doesn't understand how the real world works, so don't be assholes. I need you to act like considerate, responsible adults. Be respectful of what he's going through. That means my apartment will *not* be party central. No acting like frat boys. No keggers. No booze. No hookups. No pussy in the apartment."

"C'mon, man." Jack huffed. "Are you out of your mind?"

"Seriously?" Connor chimed in. "No booze? No beer? No banging?"

"None," Seth bit out. "The rules of my apartment are the same as Mom's rules back home. If you want to party and get laid, do it somewhere else. Understand?"

Jack heaved an infinitely disappointed sigh. "We get it. We promise not to mess with Zach. The poor man is probably messed up enough."

"He is," Seth put in.

And every time I see him, all I see is my past. So clearly, I am, too.

Chapter Eight

It was late when Beck finally left the hospital and stepped out of his Mercedes in the parking lot in front of Seth's apartment. In the past few weeks, he'd been in frequent contact with Zach, checking on his transition from The Chosen to the real world. His brother seemed okay...but Beck still felt guilty as fuck for inviting him to stay at the house, then asking him to leave the very next day. It had been imperative for Seth's mental health and the survival of their trio, but he'd hated it for Zach.

Thankfully, his brother had seemingly been okay for the past couple of weeks on his own, cautiously exploring his new world. Whenever he'd asked questions, Beck had given him straightforward, sometimes blunt answers. That had been working pretty well. But two days ago, Seth's twin brothers had invaded the space he'd hoped would be a haven.

Zach had barely had time to find his footing in this totally foreign world, and now he was sleeping mere feet from strangers. Beck needed to check in with his brother, face to face.

Dashing off a quick text to Heavenly and Seth to let them know, Beck promised to advise them when he was on his way home. Seth responded with a thumbs-up emoji and a picture of his current location, the lobby of some swanky downtown hotel. Heavenly sent a heart and a quick message to say hi to Zach for her.

Sighing, Beck pocketed his phone and headed through the balmy night to Seth's apartment. He knocked, not surprised when Zach answered right away. His brother's appearance, however, shocked the hell out of him.

Two days of scruff covered Zach's jaw. He'd shed his usual starchy button-down shirt for a dark graphic tee seemingly plastered to his body, hardened by years of work. His faded, serviceable jeans had been replaced by basketball shorts. And instead of boots, he wore trendy sneakers.

Had Zach gone shopping again?

"Hey. I thought I'd stop by and check on you. How are you doing?" Beck gave him another once-over. "You look...good. Different, but I like it."

Zach stepped back and silently invited him in. "I'm well. As you can see, Jack and Connor insisted I find clothes that didn't make me look, in their words, Amish as fu... Well, Amish. I didn't know what that meant until I looked it up online. I like the internet. And I really like these clothes. Far more comfortable."

"Good." Beck followed his brother through the narrow foyer, past the kitchen, and into the living room, filled with the king-size sofa bed with pale, rumpled sheets. "Have the twins been sleeping here?"

"They have." Zach hesitated as he sat on the edge.

So they'd left him the apartment's lone bedroom? Good.

"Then what's wrong?"

His brother didn't answer right away. "Are they typical men of this society? I know they're a few years younger than me, but..."

What the hell was Zach really asking? "I haven't met them. Where are they?"

"Out grabbing food. They said they would bring some back for me, but that was a few hours ago."

Beck frowned. Were they going out and leaving Zach behind because he didn't want to tag along? Or because they were assholes, intentionally excluding him? "How are you getting along with them?"

"Jack and Connor? Good, I think. They're trying to understand what I've been through, but they don't have a frame of reference, except their father's unexpected death. They were just children, though. They don't remember much."

If Seth had been sixteen, the twins had been five or six. They likely didn't recall the loss itself, so yeah, they probably struggled to relate. "Listen, if being here isn't working for you, I have another place. A condo on the beach. It's really secure, so you wouldn't have to worry if the press finds you. And you'd have the place all to yourself—"

"Don't trouble yourself, brother. I'm doing fine here with Jack and Connor." Despite the fact they were alone, he lowered his voice as if he didn't want anyone to overhear him. "The struggles I'm experiencing are purely mine. I don't understand where I fit in."

"With the twins?"

"With this new world as a whole...but with the twins, too. I realize they go to college. I don't think that's for me. You know I'm used to working the land, maintaining a farm, and caring for my family. I felt aimless until I found that community gardening project I was telling you about." He wrinkled his nose. "But I've been surprised by all the chemicals they're willing to put on the food they grow. I've tried to teach them the old ways..." He sighed.

Beck figured that had been unsuccessful, based on his expression. "Out here, people want what's fast and easy. So...did Jack and Connor poke fun at you for helping with the gardening project?"

If they had, Beck didn't care if they were Seth's brothers, he would smash their heads together.

"Not at all. They didn't want to participate, and that was all right. They said they were city boys, which I took to mean they know nothing about farming."

"I doubt they do. I'm serious, if you want to move to the condo, we'll make that happen. It's a bit farther from my house, but—"

"Thank you, but I'm fine here. I'm just trying to understand if this society expects me to be more like them than like me."

That question set Beck back. Of course Zach knew who he was—in the context of The Chosen. For the first time in his life, he had the power to think what he wanted, do what he wanted, and be who he wanted. That much freedom all at once could be confusing, maybe even scary.

"You don't ever have to be anyone but you, Zach."

"Without the structure of the church and the town, I'm not sure who that is. I don't believe what I once did. I still think God exists, but He's not the deity Father, Jed, and the elders paid lip service to because they wanted to marry more and younger women."

"I understand. I found this counselor, someone experienced with situations like yours. I'll call her if you want to talk to her and—"

"No. I'm not so much confused about this world, just my place in it. If I'm no longer a farmer or a husband, what am I supposed to do? I have enough money to last the rest of my life, according to Agent Waters. But I have no purpose. I worried about that...until I realized the twins don't, either. At least not that I've seen."

No wonder Zach was confused. "Unlike Messiah City, few students here go to school year-round."

"They explained that they were on summer break." But he still seemed perplexed about what that meant.

"Seth says the twins are planning to get jobs while they're here this summer."

"They told me." Zach frowned. "But so far, their top priorities have been drink, women, and baseball."

"Then, yeah." Beck smiled. "That makes them pretty normal for their age."

"Don't they want more out of life?"

Of course Zach had never seen behavior like this. Hedonism and idleness had never been tolerated in Messiah City, but the fact he wasn't outright rejecting Jack and Connor or their behavior said that his mind was opening. "The thing about out here is that most people mind their own business. As long as you're not breaking laws—you know, killing or stealing and the like—there's no right or wrong way to do life. You just do what gets you where you want to go, whatever makes you happy. Have the twins brought women here?"

Zach nodded. "Both the night they arrived and last night."

Jesus, they'd been here two days and they'd gotten laid twice? Good for them, but...confusing as hell for Zach. "Are you uncomfortable?"

"I was at first. Now I'm...curious."

Three weeks ago, Zach had admitted that he'd been without his late wife's "comfort" for weeks. If he'd been horny then, how desperate must he be now? "And that's okay. There's no value judgment here if you find a woman to spend the night with. Make sure she's over eighteen."

Zach grimaced. "I'd like to spend time with someone closer to my age."

The fact his brother didn't want to get naked with a female the law had recently considered a child was fantastic in Beck's book. "Then do that. You'll find plenty of women in their twenties who are single and fun and…"

"Not expecting a man to marry her in order to have sex with her?"

That was a change in Zach's vernacular, which must be the twins' doing. "Exactly."

His brother nodded. "I drank a beer last night."

Wow, Jack and Connor really were having an influence on him. "And?"

"I didn't hate it. If I drank another tonight…"

"No one would think anything of it." And from everything Beck was hearing, the twins just might be perfect for showing Zach how to do life in the outside world. "Whatever makes you happy."

Zach sighed, seeming to consider his options. "It's that simple?"

"Pretty much."

The opening of the apartment door, followed by a female giggle, brought Beck's head snapping around. It wasn't long before the twins appeared at the end of the foyer, a twelve-pack in one hand and a pair of clinging ladies by their sides who looked more like Instagram models than college students. Then again, Jack and Connor were dead ringers for their older brother, and Seth had always been popular with the ladies.

The twins stopped short when they spotted him.

"Shit. You must be Zach's brother," said one, setting the beer down to offer his hand. "Hi, I'm Jack."

Beck shook the guy's hand. "Nice to meet you. I'm—"

"Seth's friend. Dr. Beckman, right?"

Since the twins had no idea he and their brother shared Heavenly, that was probably the safest answer. "Yeah, but just call me Beck."

"Cool. That's Connor." He pointed to his twin, who waved. "This is Lacey and Katie."

"Kaitlyn," corrected a blonde wearing a skirt so short she should fear a stiff breeze.

"Sorry. Yeah. Um…Zach, we brought you back some grub, man. Up to trying Mexican food?"

Connor forked over a to-go container from a nearby restaurant. "It's all yours."

Zach stood and accepted it. "Thank you."

"No problem. There are cold waters and sodas in the fridge."

"Can I have a beer?"

The twins exchanged a surprised glance.

"Sure." Jack ripped into the twelve-pack and tossed one. "Bought 'em cold."

Zach caught it, but his stare was glued to the blonde. He swallowed hard.

"This is Kaitlyn," the chattier twin said to Zach. "She's Lacey's friend. You remember Lacey from Saturday night?"

A petite brunette in an equally small micro-dress waved with one hand, now clinging to Jack's arm with the other.

Zach nodded, still fixated on Kaitlyn.

Beck watched with interest. Apparently, one of the twins, probably Jack, had gotten busy with Lacey a couple nights back and had now brought a friend so they could both get lucky. Which made Zach the third wheel. That was going to suck, especially since he seemed attracted to her.

Jack took the beer and the food from Zach's hands and put them into Kaitlyn's. "Would you mind setting this up at the kitchen table for Zach?"

So he'd be out of their way while everyone else fucked in the living room? Zach would still be able to hear them. If he stood and peeked over the bar between the two rooms, he'd be able to see them, too. If his brother was still processing how he felt about premarital sex, getting an eyeful of it could put him over the edge.

"Or I could take you out for dinner, just the two of us," Beck suggested. It was something he should have done sooner. "How about a nice steak?"

Zach watched Kaitlyn brush past Connor, who murmured something in her ear. She turned back to look at Zach—and she eye-fucked him hard.

Whoa.

"I think I'll stay here and give this a try," Zach muttered, never taking his eyes off the flirty blonde. "If that's okay."

He wasn't talking about the Mexican food. Zach was asking Beck if it was okay to fuck this girl. If she actually followed through on that expression, why not?

Beck smiled and clapped his brother on the back. "Sure. Great. We'll do dinner another time."

"Awesome. Nice to meet you, man." Jack stuck out his hand, not at all subtle about rushing him out the door.

Beck repressed a smile and shook it again. "Same."

With that, Jack disappeared into the bathroom. When Beck looked to Connor again, he was lip-locked with Lacey, his hand slipping under her mostly backless dress to grab her pert ass. He hadn't seen that coming. Were the twins tag-teaming her? Sharing her?

Doubtful. Liam and Hammer aside, most guys didn't do sex the way he and Seth did with Heavenly. It was stupid to project his own life onto them. More than likely, Jack would emerge any moment and seduce Kaitlyn. Where would that leave Zach?

As if he sensed they were being watched, Connor broke away and had the good grace to look sheepish. "Thanks for stopping in. We're taking good care of Zach. I promise."

Beck wasn't totally convinced, but he nodded while Connor and Lacey bumped their way to the sofa bed, barely keeping their hands off of each other.

As Beck headed into the kitchen, he almost ran into Kaitlyn. He steadied her with one hand and an apology.

She gave him a chagrined little smile. "Sorry."

"It was my fault." Beck glanced across the room at Zach, who had settled at the kitchen table with his beer and his food, then he dropped his voice. "Are you here to spend the night with Jack?"

She shook her head. "He and Connor asked me to meet Zach. I like him."

That was good to hear, but who the hell was Jack planning to fuck tonight? Not his problem. "He likes you, too."

Kaitlyn blushed. "They said he was different."

That was one way of putting it. "Yeah. Listen, do you know how to put a condom on a guy?"

She blinked as if the question surprised her, but finally gave him a little nod.

Thank fuck. "My brother is…rusty. If you two get naked, will you help him with that?"

Her face softened. "The twins said he just lost his wife. That's so sad. I want to comfort him."

With her pussy? Perfect. "He could use that. Thanks."

She nodded and headed back toward the door, where she kicked off her high-heeled sandals. Beck turned his attention to Zach, who peered at the Mexican food with a skeptical face. "Try it. You'll like it." He lowered his voice. "That goes for everything tonight, but call me if you change your mind. If not, I'll talk to you in the morning, buddy."

His brother nodded. "Sounds good."

Then Kaitlyn entered the room again, barefoot. Zach fixed his stare on her. In that moment, Beck ceased to exist for his brother, so he let himself out of the apartment, grateful to the twins for helping Zach take the next big leap into the outside world.

Thankful that another grueling week of work was behind him, Beck pulled his Mercedes into the garage, gathered his purchases from the passenger's seat, then headed for the door. It was Friday evening and he was no longer on call. Already cause for celebration, but he had another reason to be excited.

He might have found the solution to a nagging problem. Or he might be making a giant mistake.

Beck wasn't sure which.

Dragging in a steadying breath, he stepped inside the house. A delicious, savory scent lured him to the kitchen. Lingering nearby, he found Seth in front of the island, cutting chunks of watermelon. Behind him at the stove, Heavenly stirred something mouthwatering, wearing a pale yellow sundress and absolutely nothing on her feet.

"The stroganoff is simmering. I hope it tastes as good as it smells." She sounded uncertain.

"I'm sure it will be delicious," Seth tossed over his shoulder.

"Fingers crossed. Trying new recipes off the internet is risky." She gathered placemats and napkins, then piled them on the kitchen table. "So we'll see."

"If it doesn't work out, no sweat. We can just have something delivered." Seth prowled after her, a chunk of watermelon in hand. "Open up, angel."

Obediently, she complied, her plump lips parting. Seth painted her bottom one with the melon before setting it on her pink tongue.

Closing her eyes, she moaned. "Hmm, that's sweet."

Seth licked up the juice dripping from her chin. "It is."

Then he covered her lips with his own.

Watching intently, Beck crossed the room to them on silent footfalls and settled the grocery sack of items he'd bought on the corner of the kitchen island. "How sweet?"

They snapped apart, and Heavenly gasped as they zipped their stares in his direction.

She flashed a happy grin and hugged him. "Welcome home."

"How sweet?" he repeated.

"Very," she answered.

"Yeah? Let me taste." Beck dipped his head and kissed her, savoring her sugary-stained mouth.

Seth washed and dried his hands, his lazy grin a greeting, before he sidled up to them, eyeing the grocery sack on the nearby island. "What's all this?"

Reluctantly, Beck pulled away from Heavenly. "Just a few things to help celebrate some news I have."

"What?" Cooper prompted. "Let's hear it."

Here goes nothing… "I signed up to attend a medical conference."

"Where? Someplace awesome, like Hawaii?" Heavenly looked beyond excited by that possibility.

Beck winced. With everything happening these days, he and Seth had been shirking the vow they'd made to her dying father to show Heavenly the world. The PI's grimace said he realized it, too.

"No. But if you'd like to go sometime, we'll plan a vacation."

"Really?" Her big eyes lit with thrill. "I would *love* that."

"Then we'll make it happen," Seth promised.

"Definitely," Beck seconded. "But the conference I registered to

THE CONFESSION | 167

attend—and subsequently got wrangled into speaking at—is in New York."

"My old stomping grounds." Seth chuckled. "When?"

Now for the tricky part… "October second through fourth."

Cooper arched his brows. "The same week Mom and Carl are getting married. Is that a coincidence?"

Beck didn't pretend innocence. "No."

The PI might reject his plan, but after he'd invited Heavenly to the wedding to meet the family, Beck had pictured her making inroads with the in-laws-to-be since there was no way Grace Cooper and Seth's brothers wouldn't love her. Then he'd visualized himself rattling around the house alone while the pair played in New York. And he'd hated that. So he'd begun to plot. If he was close by, maybe Seth would find some pretense to invite him, too?

Normally, Beck wouldn't push himself on anyone, but this was their future. He didn't want to be left out.

"I see." Seth's pause was lengthy and inscrutable. "Did it take you long to find a conference in the city that same week?"

"To find one that had anything to do with vascular surgery took more than a few minutes," Beck admitted, wishing he could get a read on Seth's reaction. "Look, I figured we could fly out together. I booked a room at the conference hotel, which shouldn't be more than a taxi ride from your mom's place."

Seth frowned. "So you're planning to crash the wedding?"

"No," Beck assured. "I wouldn't do that. I'm not a raging asshole."

Seth heaved out a sigh. "I know. It's just, I thought—"

"That I intended to show up and force our relationship down your family's throat? I understand the reasons you'd rather wait to tell your mother about us, and I get it."

Heavenly stroked a hand down Seth's arm and sent him a placid smile. "Everyone—your aunts, uncles, siblings, and cousins—will be at the wedding, right?"

Cooper nodded, looking guarded. "Yeah."

"I'm guessing that means a lot of people will be staying at your mom's house?"

"Yeah." He frowned suspiciously.

"Since your mom is traditional and we're not married, I doubt she'll be okay with us sharing a bedroom. I'd rather not spend my nights without you, and it seems silly for each of us to take a bedroom while someone else, probably one of your brothers, will be relegated to a sofa."

Beck bit back a smile. He knew where Heavenly was leading the conversation...which was exactly where he'd hoped to take it.

Seth snorted. "After I walked in on her and Carl fucking on our kitchen table, she can't object too loudly."

"You caught them having sex?" Heavenly gasped.

"Yep. On the same table I ate every meal and did my homework on as a kid. Seeing some strange man bang my mother was"—he shook his head as if he hoped to shake the vision free—"traumatizing."

"I'm sure." She cringed. "But even so, with all those people coming to celebrate her big day, wouldn't it give her—and us—some breathing room if we stayed at the hotel with Beck?"

While Seth digested her suggestion, Heavenly cast Beck a conspiratorial smile. Idly wondering if she was spending too much time with meddling Raine, he nodded her way.

"There'll be plenty of room," Beck added to sway Seth. "I booked a suite."

Moments passed. Finally, the PI stopped frowning and slowly started nodding, as if he saw the wisdom of Heavenly's argument.

"During the day, I'll attend the conference, while you and Heavenly enjoy all the family things. At night, we'll hook up in our hotel room and do all the *pleasurable* things." Beck underscored his suggestion with a lascivious grin.

"I love that plan. I like doing pleasurable things with you two." Heavenly fluttered her lashes at them.

"So do we," Seth assured with a wolfish curl of his lips. "But I know my brothers, especially the twins. If they think they might miss out on a party in the city, they'll want to come with us."

"Let them." Beck shrugged. "I'll tell them I'm staying in a room down the hall or something."

Seth looked surprised. "You wouldn't mind?"

"Bending the truth? I don't love it, but I can live with it temporarily."

And if they happen to go to the bathroom and see both of our electric razors on the counter, just tell them the second one is for your balls." Beck grinned.

"And the day of the wedding?" Seth fished.

Beck shrugged. "That's up to you, man. I can come with you as your good friend who happened to be in town or not at all—whatever you're comfortable with. Whatever you think your mom will understand."

"It just might work. You may not believe me, but I want you to meet my family. It's important that they get to know you, so that, down the road, when I tell them about our relationship, they'll understand—"

"That I'm not just some perv banging your girlfriend with you?"

"Exactly." Seth nodded.

"If Beck happened to be in town and his conference ended that Friday, no one would question you inviting our good friend to your mom's wedding," Heavenly pointed out. "Plus, meeting some of your LA friends would give your family more insight about your new life."

"That's a good point..." Seth conceded, then pinned Beck with a stare. "Would that be okay with you?"

"Yeah. The cover story will work—for now."

At least he'd get to attend with them and meet the PI's family.

"That's not exactly what I was asking." Seth rubbed at the back of his neck. "Will you be okay not touching Heavenly at the wedding? For this to work, you can't give her any affection. You can't even look at her the way you normally do."

As if he was dying to fuck her?

"To be honest, I'm not sure *I* could do it if the roles were reversed," Seth admitted.

Beck did a gut check. Could he actually treat their girl as a mere friend?

You can do anything you have to, as long as it's not forever. Gloria's voice, along with the sage advice she'd given him years ago, echoed in Beck's brain. Besides, the three of them had no future if they couldn't get Seth's family on board. The reception would probably be torture. He'd simply have to focus on their long-term good.

"I can nix the PDA for a few hours," Beck conceded. "I don't know if I can change the way I look at her, but I'll do my best."

Seth nodded. "That's the best I can't ask for, especially since I know I look at her the same way."

Heavenly frowned. "Like what?"

With a low growl, Seth brushed Heavenly's hair aside before raking his teeth down her neck. "Like I'm the Big Bad Wolf and you're Little Red."

She shivered beneath Seth's sensual assault, her eyes drifting closed.

"Exactly," Beck murmured. "So it's settled?"

"Yeah," Seth whispered against her skin. "You're coming with us to New York. Let's celebrate."

Thank fuck they'd come to an agreement—and overcome what could have been a giant hurdle. After Grace Cooper's wedding, they could come clean with Seth's family. Hopefully, they would accept the three of them someday. Sure, they still had obstacles to overcome, and Beck still had questions about Seth's story he needed to ask…in good time. When they were more settled. When it seemed like Seth was in a better place to answer them. Soon. It had to be since he'd already waited weeks. But not now.

"Good idea," Beck murmured. "That's why I thought ahead and brought the party with me. Look in the bag."

Rustling plastic told him Seth was doing just that. "Strawberries, whipped cream, and champagne. Hot damn, we have everything for a decadent strawberry shortcake." He glided his hand over her dress and palmed her breast. "As long as you'll be our cake, angel."

"I'd love to," she assured them.

Beck claimed her mouth in a slow, sultry kiss. Her lips parted in welcome. Heat jetted through him. His cock thickened.

As he swept inside her mouth and lapped up more watermelon flavor, Seth nipped at her shoulder, skimming his hands down her curves before settling on her hips and pressing himself against her with a groan. A little whimper escaped Heavenly's throat as she caressed her way up Beck's shoulders and looped her arms around his neck, her fingers furrowing through his hair.

"How much longer until dinner?" he muttered, breath hot against her lips.

"The stroganoff has to simmer for forty-five minutes," she whispered.

"Plenty of time." Beck covered her mouth again and reached blindly into the nearby grocery sack for the strawberries, managing to lift the lid and pluck one out.

"Don't worry, angel. We won't make you simmer that long," Seth promised, cinching his hand in Heavenly's hair and tugging her head back.

Beck lifted from her lips and watched as Cooper melded his mouth over hers. He wasn't sure what turned him on more, watching the other man eat at her so voraciously or hearing her kitten-soft moans.

The second Seth lifted from her, Beck tapped the berry to Heavenly's lips, shuddering with thrill as she sank her teeth into the plump fruit and chewed. He fused his stare to hers as he tossed the stem onto the bag. Her breath caught. The pulse at her neck jumped. The instant she swallowed, he slanted his mouth over hers again and barged deep. As their tongues tangled in the shared juice, his cock lurched and raked his zipper.

Beck eased from her lips and cupped her other breast, slowly brushing his thumb across her pebbled peak. Inwardly, he cursed the clothes between them. He couldn't wait to undress her and latch his mouth over her sweet, stiff peaks.

"Promise?" she gasped out.

"We have no intention of stopping, little girl."

"At all," Seth assured, bending to gather the hem of her dress and lifting it over her head, exposing her one luscious inch at a time— adorable knees, slender thighs, a flare of hips concealed by tiny pink panties, her flat belly with a pronounced inward curve at her waist, and finally her breasts, barely hidden by a matching lace bra.

Beck's mouth went dry.

Seth groaned. "She needs to be naked."

"Oh, she does," he agreed, peeling her panties down her legs and dragging his tongue over her milky flesh.

Cooper unhooked her bra. It flitted down her arms before he took her tits in his palms with a moan of appreciation. Heavenly melted against him, eyes closed.

Beck stood slowly, watching Seth pinch her nipples while nibbling at her neck. The sight scalded his blood. He couldn't merely watch them anymore. He was dying to touch her, too.

Seizing Heavenly's nape in his palm, Beck took her lips in a hot, urgent stroke. Their kiss, filled with damp sighs and feverish need, felt like an addicting slide into Shangri-La. But he needed more.

Insistently, he swept his tongue into her mouth, demanding she yield. She did, allowing him deeper inside her spun-sugar sweetness and keening at the back of her throat. Beck drowned in her.

Then he heard the crinkle of condom wrappers.

He pulled back from Heavenly, watching the PI dig into his pocket and toss several packets on the table. Beck tamped down his disappointment.

After Seth's tragedy, it was no surprise he wasn't in a rush to father another child. But Beck was on the downhill slide to thirty-seven. He wanted kids ASAP, and he wanted them with Heavenly. Unfortunately, Seth's family would ask questions he wasn't ready to answer if their girl attended Grace Cooper's wedding five months pregnant. So, at least for now, Beck had to wait.

But just like Zach moving out, he was bending to accommodate Seth again. Yeah, relationships were about give and take. But it felt like he'd done a whole lot of giving lately.

"Angel…" Seth's husky growl snapped Beck out of his thoughts.

He refocused on Heavenly, seizing her mouth again and cupping her breast in his hand. There would be time to think about their problems later.

A cry slipped from her throat and she arched, filling his palm with her supple flesh. He dragged his thumb across her distended nipple in a slow tease, then swallowed her gasp. Seth didn't waste time, moving in behind her and sliding his fingers through her sweet pussy, shielded by sparse golden curls.

"She's so wet," Seth murmured.

Beck lifted from her mouth, only to be snared by the arousal glowing on her face. "Then dessert will be extra tasty."

Seth gave a low, filthy chuckle. "You got that right."

Beck brushed a curl from her flushed face. "Is my little girl wet because she wants us to fuck her?"

She whimpered, her blue eyes darkening as she moved her head restlessly.

He raised a brow in rebuke. "Is that a yes?"

"Yes," Heavenly breathed.

"I'm sure you meant to say please, too," he prompted, thumbing her nipple slowly again.

"Yes. Please…"

"You beg so sweetly," Seth murmured in her ear, his fingers slowly strumming her clit.

"She does. And we know what she wants," Beck murmured, sliding his lips up her neck. "The question is, should we give it to her?"

"I need you both. Please!" She melted between them.

Seth ignored her. "I'm not sure. I was thinking we'd eat our dessert… After all, it's not nice to play with our food."

"True." Beck pulled back, leaving her pouting nipples untended. "It looks so delicious, and I could eat at her all night."

Almost instantly, she cried out, silently begging with her eyes. "But you put condoms on the table."

"In case *we* feel like fucking you. Right now, we just want to nibble, sample, taste, and lick."

"Amen," Seth agreed as Beck cupped her shoulders and turned her to face him.

The big PI stared at Heavenly with searing desire, but the love on his face was unmistakable. Relief wended through Beck. When Seth had pulled away last month, Beck had counted on that love to lure him back. And while they still hadn't worked through all their issues yet, that expression reassured him they were on the right path.

Then he stopped thinking as Seth crushed Heavenly's mouth beneath his in a hungry kiss. Beck flung the nearest chair away from the kitchen table, then snagged a couple of clean beach towels from the adjacent patio and draped the thick terry cloth over the smooth wooden surface. Finally, he set the berries, cream, and champagne beside them.

Pressing himself against Heavenly's backside, he leaned close to her ear. "It's time for dessert, little girl. Get on the table."

As Seth lifted from her lips, he flashed her a lascivious smile. "Hurry. We're going to have our cake and eat it, too."

Cinching his hands around her narrow waist, Cooper hoisted Heavenly onto the table. She clutched his arms and held tight as he positioned her right where he wanted her.

"Lie back on the towel." Beck smirked as he helped her recline. "That's it. Now spread your legs."

She complied with a soft cry and a pleading stare, heels gripping the edge. The earthy scent of her slick spice filled his nose and made his mouth water.

Gripping the bottle of champagne, Beck popped it open before repositioning the strawberries and whipped cream on either side of her for easy access. Then he raked his hungry gaze down her pale, naked body.

"Hmm. Where should we begin?" Seth taunted, dragging a finger down between her breasts to the wet blond curls between her legs.

She arched up to him, spreading herself wider. "Anywhere."

"I'm looking forward to coating your cunt with whipped cream and mixing the taste with your arousal."

"Oh, my gosh," she whimpered, her eyes sliding shut.

"Eventually. I'll save the best for last."

"Seth…" Heavenly moaned in protest, hips writhing.

She looked delectable. But as much as Beck wanted to dive face-first between her thighs, he loved tormenting her into a begging, desperate mess. "Good call, man."

"No," she entreated.

"Yes," Beck insisted, his gaze locked on her taut nipples, straining toward the ceiling.

An evil idea bloomed in his brain.

He plucked up a pair of strawberries, pinched off the stems, then pried the cap off the chilled can of whipped cream and handed it to Seth. When the cold metal met his palm, the PI's eyes widened.

"Oh, this is going to be fun."

"It is." Beck softly chuckled.

Holding the can over her breast, Seth laid his finger against the nozzle and arched a brow at Heavenly. "This might be a little chilly, angel."

As the white fluffy cream sputtered from the tip, Heavenly gasped, then screeched, her back arching. "Chilly? That's freez—"

Seth stole whatever she meant to say when he covered her breast with his mouth and sucked deep. Heavenly let out a needy mewl that made Beck's blood jet thick and scalding hot through his veins.

"That's so fucking hot," Beck groaned. "But you forgot something, man."

When he held up a strawberry, Seth released her nipple with an audible pop and smiled. "You're right. But I'm going to need more cream with this." The PI plucked the berry from his grip. "You should join me. Nipples and cream are mighty tasty."

"I think I will." Beck smirked.

She shivered. "But…but that stuff is *cold*."

"But you liked the way I warmed it up." Seth arched a brow, daring her to refute him.

She didn't, merely bit her lip and whimpered.

"Spread those pretty thighs wider, little girl," Beck drawled as he glided his hand down her torso.

Obediently, she did. He skated his palm straight to her pussy. Seth seemed to have the same idea since their hands collided between her legs. Her wet heat had both men groaning. Together, they toyed with her.

Heavenly gasped. "You're *evil*."

"Oh, you haven't seen evil yet," Beck warned with a predatory grin.

Seth shook the can again, a fiendish smile tugging at his lips as he quirked a brow at Beck. "Ready?"

"Hell, yeah."

Heavenly held her breath as Seth pressed the nozzle, depositing a cold dollop of cream over both nipples. When she arched up and gaped in shocked pleasure, he drove his fingers into her slick pussy. In the same moment, Beck settled his thumb over her clit and slowly stroked. Instantly, her quiet gave way to squeals, shuddering moans, and broken pleas as she rocked to the rhythm of their busy hands. He and Seth watched her together, sharing a triumphant grin.

Heavenly's rising pleasure pinged through his system. Even his hand shook as he swiped a strawberry and nestled it in the heap of whipped cream covering her nipple. Seth did the same. With his other hand still between her legs, Beck continued driving her higher, working her until she gasped. After another shared glance, he and Seth nodded. Then, together, they leaned over her restless body and sucked her berry-and-cream-topped peaks deep into their mouths.

The tart fruit, sugary cream, and warm flesh blended to explode over Beck's taste buds. He mashed the plump berry and Heavenly's hardened nipple to the roof of his mouth and pulled harder.

Her cries of bliss made his cock throb.

Beck licked away the last of the cream as he reached blindly for the champagne. Tilting the bottle, he drenched Heavenly's distended nipple in a slow stream of chilled bubbly. Agonized pleasure twisted her face. As he lapped the liquid from her flesh, she sank her nails into his scalp, her begging a litany in his ears. Then he passed the bottle to Seth, who did the same to her other breast, wringing more broken wails from her.

Beck worked his way down her body, squirting whipped cream everywhere that looked inviting—under her tits, across her stomach, just above her pussy—then licking her clean.

Above him, Seth slurped and tongued a puddle of champagne from Heavenly's navel. With a smoky, half-lidded gaze, she tossed her head back, her hips writhing restlessly. Her feminine scent saturated the air.

Beck's restraint snapped.

Rounding the table, he grabbed the chair he'd discarded and positioned it between her legs. His possessive stare zeroed in on her slick cunt.

Impatiently, Beck yanked on the towel, sliding her hips to the very edge of the table. Then he took her thighs in hand, positioning them over his shoulders. A feral growl rumbled from his chest as he leaned in and inhaled her earthy, feminine spice. "The way you suffer for us is so pretty."

"I could watch you all day." Seth laved her hip.

"Please. Help me. I'm on fire," she begged.

Beck slid a thumb up her puffy, pink folds and grazed her distended clit, working a hungry whimper from her. Then he reached for the whipped cream.

Seth's gaze latched onto her cunt. "There's the best part of dessert, man."

"Absolutely." And since that was true, why frost Heavenly with anything that would change her taste?

Instead, Beck set the whipped cream aside and parted her folds with his thumbs. The cool air combined with his hot breath hit her overstimulated flesh. She was a thing of beauty as her back twisted, her nipples stabbed the air, and she moaned. More nectar spilled from her narrow slit.

He wanted that.

Heart drumming ferociously, Beck dragged his tongue up her flowing furrow. His taste buds exploded. More cries tore from her throat and filled his ears. Her hips lifted in entreaty.

Pressing his palm above her mound, Beck held her in place as he tormented her thoroughly, scraping his tongue over and over her sensitive clit.

"You like his mouth on you, don't you, angel?" Seth cajoled as he rolled, pinched, and tugged on her nipples without mercy.

"*Yessss*," Heavenly hissed.

Good. Beck loved having his mouth on her. And he wasn't going to stop, not even to tell her that, until he wrung every bit of pleasure he could from her.

Ravenously, he ate at her. It wasn't long before her peachy-pale skin turned rosy, her whimpers morphed into mewls, and her small opening fluttered.

"Oh, she's close," Seth murmured between swipes of his tongue across her erect nipples.

"She is." Satisfaction blistered through Beck.

"You're going to be a good angel and come for us, right on his tongue, aren't you?" Seth goaded.

"Yes. Yes!" She tossed her head back in abandon.

"Good. I'll help you along," he murmured. "And help him drag every last ounce of bliss from you."

Beck watched through heavy lids as Seth nestled the rim of the champagne against Heavenly's golden curls. A second later, he tipped the bottle, spilling the liquid over her clit and straight into Beck's mouth.

As the bubbles met her flesh, Heavenly yelped and wriggled against Beck's firm hand.

Her muscles seized. Her clit turned to quivering stone. She sucked in a gasp and screamed his name as she shattered with a sensual thrash and roll of her body.

Fuck, he couldn't wait to be inside her.

Beck kept at her, licking and sucking at her pussy, to the soundtrack of her orgasmic cries while he grabbed a condom, ripped it open, and fisted the latex down his angry cock. She was still roaring out as he lifted from her, gripped her hips, and drove balls deep into her. Her cunt clamped down on him instantly. He clenched his jaw, his eyes rolling to the back of his head, as he forced his way through her taut muscles and fought for control.

As he thrust in and out of her gripping heat, he watched Seth suck, nip, and pinch her nipples. It was erotic as fuck, and Beck beat back the urge to follow Heavenly into climax. But he refused to end the pleasure this soon.

"Send…her…back up…man," Beck panted.

Grinning around her nipple, Seth skated a hand down her quaking body and circled her twitching clit. Heavenly clamped around Beck's driving cock like a vise. An agonized sound between a whine and a moan escaped her rosy, swollen lips.

"That's it, angel," Seth cooed.

Lost in her liquid heat, Beck raced headlong toward oblivion.

Seth must have sensed it, too, as he quickly gloved up. "Let me know if you need to—"

"Yeah, I'm tapping out," Beck growled, gathering all the willpower he possessed to pull from Heavenly and step aside.

Seth was right there, driving deep inside their girl like a freight train in a single thrust. "Christ, angel. You're so fucking tight."

"Seth. Seth…" she chanted mindlessly.

"Take me," he groaned as he shuttled in and out of her relentlessly. "Like that. Oh, fuck…"

Beck moved in close, still panting as he savored the sight of her half-lidded eyes, heaving chest, and glistening pink skin. She belonged to them. He wanted her breathless, mindless, and defenseless against them. Beck couldn't explain why he needed for him and Seth to arouse her until she could no longer deny the sharp pleasure and tumbled into bliss for them. It just was. Part sexual thrill, part primal instinct, and one-hundred-percent possession.

Perverse excitement lurched through him as he glided his fingers down to stroke her swollen clit. At his touch, Heavenly inhaled sharply through her nose. Her whole body went taut. Then she jolted and gripped the towel under her with a sensual moan of anguish.

Beck bent to lave and suck her sensitive nipples—and shoved her to the edge of ecstasy. "Give it to him, little girl. Yes. Yes… Right now."

Her cry turned sharper.

Her body bowed.

Her muscles strained.

And her mouth stretched in a perfect, so-tempting O.

"Just like that," he encouraged. "Oh, that's pretty."

Sinking his fingers deeper into the flesh of her hips, Seth clenched his jaw. Sweat dripped down his cut chest as he plunged through her clenching muscles. "She's fucking killing me."

Beck knew the feeling well, but… "Hang on. She's got more to give."

Then he stroked the tiny head of her clit, the pearl as hard as a diamond. Half a heartbeat later, Heavenly's screams ratcheted up as her body did the same, shuddering in thunderous orgasm as she gushed out in ecstasy. He did his part to guide her through the climax, leaning over her panting, quaking body and circling her reddened nipples with the tip of his tongue while murmuring praises and promising that he and Seth had more in store for her.

"Fuck!" Seth slid free from Heavenly and flung himself away. "Finish her."

Seth didn't want to? Because he didn't want this to end yet? Or was there another reason?

Beck shoved the questions away. He was reading too much into Seth's retreat. Of course he wanted to prolong the pleasure. Who wouldn't?

When Beck positioned himself between Heavenly's splayed thighs, he knew that getting inside of her would be the end of his restraint. And he didn't fucking care. He was ready to lose himself with her. So he cinched his hands around her waist and bulldozed into her fist-tight depths.

His thick invasion had Heavenly gripping the towels and thrashing under him in abandon as he stroked deep, hard, and fast.

"One more orgasm, little girl. You'll give us that, won't you?"

"Yes." She nodded helplessly.

"We'll help you." Seth darted around the table to Heavenly's head, his hot eyes focused on them. He tugged on the towel beneath her until her neck hung over the edge of the table, then he tore off his condom, fisted the hair at her crown, turned her to face him, and brushed his fat crest against her mouth. "Open and take me deep."

She didn't hesitate, parting her plump lips as her stare leapt to his.

He sank inside, nestling onto her tongue with a hiss, never once looking away. "Yes. Like that. Hmm... Now suck me dry."

As Beck watched Cooper fuck her mouth faster, he increased his tempo into her pussy. Heavenly's eyes slid shut as she dissolved into a wriggling puddle of need. Her swollen nipples, feral sounds, and rosy glow told him she'd never quite come down from her last climax. Her fluttering, clamping pussy told him she was primed for another.

She broke from Seth long enough to pant and whine, "I... can't...hold—"

"Back?" Seth groaned. "Oh, fuck. Fuck."

"Me, either," Beck grunted, their pleasure sending him roaring to the brink. "Heavenly..."

Since Seth filled her mouth with his cock again, all she could do was moan, but when she tightened on him, he knew. Heavenly was gone—and she was theirs.

Sweat dripping, lungs working, Beck banged into her without restraint, thumbing her hard clit one last time.

He wished like hell he wasn't strangling his cock with this condom so he could unleash his seed inside her and start their family. The idea of getting her pregnant and tying their futures together sent his desire soaring past his self-control.

Demand slammed down Beck's spine as he growled and pinched Heavenly's clit. "Come now, little girl."

"Come hard," Seth commanded, voice rising as he launched like a rocket. "Now. Fuck!"

Those words incited a chain reaction, hurtling Beck over the edge, too. Sucking in a deep breath, he released a deafening roar that merged with Seth's bellow. Lights exploded behind his eyes as waves of bliss crashed through him. But he took a gasping, keening Heavenly with him, blood pumping hard as he filled her with stroke after savage stroke. Her pussy tightened impossibly before she spasmed, shuddered, and sobbed out one last release.

Together, he and Seth basked in her screams of ecstasy.

When the thunder finally passed, Beck lifted Heavenly from the table and cradled her limp, sated body against his chest, staring into her glassy eyes as he brushed strands of sweat-soaked hair from her face. Contentment settled in his soul.

Before Seth had come clean—well, mostly—about the deaths of his wife and son, Beck had been worried he'd have to take care of Heavenly on his own. Not that it would have been a hardship, but it would have been a challenge to fill the void Seth left in her life. He'd need to leave Heavenly daily lists designed to help her structure her life, and he'd do whatever necessary to love her enough for both of them. Hell, Beck would die trying to give Heavenly everything she needed, but it appeared as if he wouldn't have to. It seemed as if Seth was back…mostly.

But again, why had Cooper pulled free from Heavenly's pussy when he'd had her right there?

Red-faced and dripping sweat, Seth moved in to wrap an arm around their girl and press a kiss to her damp forehead. "That was amazing."

She smiled softly. "It was."

"Amen," Beck murmured. And it was true.

Joined in body, heart, and soul, they silently held each other while aftershocks zipped and twitched through their systems.

Long minutes later when their breathing evened out, Heavenly lifted her head and licked her lips, then turned a bleary-eyed gaze at the stove.

"I think dinner's wasted," she said in a raspy voice.

"It's all right, angel." Seth smirked. "We'll order in."

Beck slowly eased out of her. "That was so fucking worth it."

When he set her feet on the floor, Heavenly moaned and whimpered. The PI stepped away, reaching for his pants. And as Beck discarded his condom in the nearby trash, he wondered again if Seth had chosen Heavenly's mouth because he'd wanted to lose himself there...or because he refused to run the risk of impregnating her. Sure, he'd had her pussy since spilling his secrets, but Beck had also noticed that, more and more, Seth was opting for oral and anal. Coincidence?

Beck didn't know. That question, along with the nagging gaps in Seth's past, haunted him as they called for pizza. They were happy right now, yes...but he had a terrible suspicion there was more to uncover, and once he did, it would rock them all.

The following evening, Seth stood at the base of the stairs beside Beck, gazing up at the second floor with impatience. He checked his watch for the fifth time. "Angel, are you almost ready? We're going to be late."

"Almost done. One more minute."

"That's another twenty minutes in woman-speak." Beck smirked.

Seth chuckled. "At least."

"I heard that," Heavenly drawled as she descended the stairs.

When her pretty pink toenails, peeking from a pair of white

wedges, came into view, Seth's heart rate kicked up a notch. Gliding his gaze up her bare, slender calves, he licked his lips as he caught sight of a pink floral ruffle kissing her silky thighs.

Then she rounded the landing, allowing both men an unobstructed view of the airy, wraparound dress that clung to her body, held together by nothing more than a tiny bow. Beck groaned. The hint of her cleavage just visible above the sexy V-neck bodice made Seth do the same. It didn't matter that they'd made her their erotic dessert last night or that he'd slid into her tight little backside this morning while the good doctor had been making rounds. He still wanted her.

"Fuck the cookout." Beck breathed hard. "I'd rather stay home to devour you, little girl."

"I second that motion." Seth stepped up and took her hand.

Her soft giggle morphed into a breathless moan as he and Beck surrounded her, pressing her between them. While feasting on her neck, lips, and every inch of exposed flesh, their questing hands cupped and caressed every dip, swell, and curve.

"I thought you were worried about being late," Heavenly teased as she melted between them.

"Late for what?" Seth nipped his way down her neck before pressing his lips to her fluttering pulse point.

"The cookout Raine, Hammer, and Liam are hosting for… Ahh"— she groaned as Beck pinched her nipples—"to welcome Zach and the twins to LA."

"You feel feverish to me." Beck dragged his tongue across the swells of her breasts. "Maybe you should quarantine this weekend in bed with us."

"Is that your professional diagnosis, doctor?" Heavenly writhed, dragging her lush ass against Seth's hungry erection.

"I can't give a correct diagnosis without a thorough exam. In order to do that, we both need to be balls deep inside you." Beck thrust his hips, driving his cock against her pussy and pressing her sweet cheeks around Seth's shaft.

"Please…" she whined.

"With pleasure." Seth kissed the sensitive spot behind her ear, loving the way she moaned.

They could make this quick. Maybe. Hell, did it really matter if they were an hour late? Or two? Everyone would keep his brothers occupied.

As Beck leaned in to claim Heavenly's lips, the emergency chime on his cell phone pealed. He cursed.

Seth stilled. "Do you have to get that?"

"Yeah. I'm on call." He released Heavenly with a curse and yanked the device from his pocket. "Beckman."

"I hope he doesn't have to go in," she murmured to Seth. "Especially after you went to all the trouble to ask everyone to pretend Beck is just our friend in front of the twins."

Seth winced. Yeah, he was sure that had been a bitter pill for the doctor to swallow. And Seth had hated to sideline Beck that way among his own friends. Thankfully, he'd been a decent sport, probably because they'd devised roughly the same strategy for his attendance at Mom's wedding this fall and they'd discussed telling his family the truth afterward. Still, guilt pricked Seth. If the shoe was on the other foot, he'd hate it.

"What's the ETA on the chopper?" Beck asked, glancing at his watch. "Get him prepped when he arrives. I'm on my way."

"Dang it." Heavenly's shoulders slumped as Beck ended the call.

"Sorry, you two. There was an ugly wreck on 210. Out of an eight-car pileup, there's only one survivor. If I don't get moving, he won't make it, either." Beck kissed Heavenly quickly before running for the garage. "I'll meet you two at the party if I can."

"I'll keep my fingers crossed," Heavenly called. "Be careful. I love you."

"Love you, too. Tell everybody I said hi."

"Will do," Seth assured as the door closed behind Beck.

Gathering Heavenly in his arms, he claimed her lips with a soft kiss. "We'll pick up where we left off when we all get home."

She smiled like that would mean the world to her. "Promise?"

Fuck, had she been feeling insecure about his love for her? Things between them had been improving since his confession about the past, but he had to do better. "Absolutely." He tugged his keys from his pocket. "Are you ready to go? I'm sure Raine is dying to see you."

"I can't wait to see her. Let me grab my purse."

Once Heavenly plucked the little bag off a nearby counter, he guided her to the garage and helped her into his SUV before climbing in behind the wheel.

"I hope Beck makes it in time to save the patient," she said as he backed out.

"He'll do his best, angel. Just like I'm sure he'll do everything he can to make it to the cookout."

"I know. And I know he's doing something amazing by saving lives. It's just…nothing is the same when one of you is gone. And that's been a lot lately."

Seth didn't hear censure in her tone, but her audible sadness flooded him with guilt. A few weeks back, Beck hadn't candy-coated the fact that Seth's absence—or rather him running away to escape his past night after night—had crushed Heavenly. But knowing that unhappiness was merely a fraction of the grief he'd selfishly piled onto Beck's shoulders and expected him to handle nearly gutted Seth. He had no clue how to make it up to his friend. To both of them, really. All he could do was keep trying.

Short minutes later, Seth pulled up to Hammer, Liam, and Raine's house, then helped Heavenly from the SUV. Wrapping his arm around her waist, he guided her to the front porch and rang the bell.

Raine answered with an excited squeal, she hugged Heavenly as best she could with her ever-growing baby belly, smiled at Seth, then scanned the porch with a frown. "Where's Beck?"

Heavenly sighed. "There was an emergency at the hospital."

"Damn you, Murphy, and your stupid law," Raine huffed.

"Language, love," Liam warned in a silky tone as he approached behind her.

She had the good grace to look chastened. Or at least she gave that appearance.

"Sorry." She squeezed Heavenly's hand. "We'll just have to have fun for him."

"That we will. Hey, man," Seth nodded and greeted Liam.

"Hello, Seth." His Irish pal shook his hand with a smile.

With a guiding arm around Heavenly's waist, Seth led her over the threshold, following Liam and Raine through the palatial place. As they passed the kitchen, people dressed in black slacks and crisp white shirts darted, busily working.

"Do you need any help?" Heavenly offered.

"No," Raine assured. "Thanks, but Hammer and Liam hired caterers so I don't have to lift a finger."

"We want you off your feet," Liam reminded.

"I know. But you two also want to be in control," Raine quipped with a sassy smile.

"That we do. And you love every minute of it," Liam pointed out with a tap on her pert nose.

Raine merely grinned as Liam took her hand and led her to the back door. Seth followed, hovering beside Heavenly as they all stepped onto the spacious patio.

The party was in full swing.

As if sensing his girl was near, Hammer lifted his head, locking the same sort of possessive stare on Raine that Liam had. Then he headed straight for them, pressing a tender kiss to her cheek.

They looked really fucking happy. Seth wanted that closeness, that same deep bond, for him, Beck, and Heavenly, forever. Hopefully, they would get there after he'd stupidly done damage to the people he loved. He still had shit to figure out. It was going to take time and effort, and he had to be patient. Too bad he sucked at that.

Raine murmured something in Hammer's ear that had his eyes darkening and her cheeks blushing before she resumed the role of hostess, pointing to a pair of coolers situated beneath a shady palm. "Beer is in the red one. Soda and water are in the blue. Most everyone is gathered around the pool. Head down and make yourselves at home. I need to check in with the caterer about dinner."

Seth nodded. "Thanks."

"Let me know if I can help," Heavenly offered.

When Raine waved her away, Seth cupped his girl's elbow and helped her down the stairs. At the bottom, he skimmed a glance over the guests—all familiar—drinking, talking, and laughing. At the far side of the pool, Dean, River, and FBI agent Jericho Waters sat at a table, engrossed in conversation. Jack and Connor filed up beside Liam, wearing familiar feigned scowls.

Seth laughed, then leaned down to murmur in Heavenly's ear. "My mischievous brothers are busting Liam's balls about something, the way they did when he still lived in New York."

"Poor Liam." She sounded both amused and sorry for him at the same time.

Then Zach sidled up beside the twins, laughing and holding a *beer*. Beck hadn't been kidding about his brother's progress. Good for Zach. No wonder Beck was pleased. The twins, despite their ability to massively fuck up, were really helping Zach acclimate to life outside the cult. Granted, drinking beer wasn't as epic as banging a stable of hookers, like Beck had done when he'd first found freedom. But he was starting to put the past behind him and move on.

Seth knew he needed to do the same—once and for all—somehow.

"Look at Zach," Heavenly whispered.

"I know."

"He seems…happy. Oh, my gosh. That's fantastic."

Heavenly was still grinning when they headed closer to mingle with the group. On the way, Seth spotted longtime Shadows members Vivian and Donald heading for the coolers. They waved to Pike, who stood alone, beer in one hand, the other in his pocket.

As if sensing his scrutiny, the pierced, tattooed DM flashed him a cocky smirk, then sent Heavenly a head bob. Was he fucking leering at her again? Seth's blood boiled. His temper, irritatingly close to the surface these past few weeks, started slipping off its chain.

"Some assholes never learn," he growled, releasing Heavenly's elbow. "I'll be right back, angel."

"Seth…" Heavenly protested.

He went on as if he hadn't heard her.

As Donald and Vivian passed him, he murmured an absent greeting, complete with pasted-on smile. But the second they were out of earshot, Seth ate up the distance between him and Pike, his jaw clenched. "If you look at Heavenly again, I'll rip your eyes out of your skull. Got it, motherfucker?"

Pike arched a pierced black brow. "Easy man, I was only saying hi."

"Bullshit. Every time you see her, you mentally undress her."

"Dude, I wasn't. Back down."

That only notched up Seth's temper again. "Fuck that."

"Look, I've got a girl...a nice one. A pretty one. I'm not trying to steal yours. I never was. I just enjoy pissing you off."

"If that's true, where is your 'nice, pretty' girl?"

Pike lifted his chin defensively. "Not that it's any of your fucking business, but she's out of town. Otherwise, she'd be here with me."

That jibed with what Heavenly had told him, but if Pike wanted to needle him, Seth was ready to give it back. "Would she? Or would she be with River?"

For the millionth time since learning that Raine's brother and Pike were vying for the same woman, Seth tried to imagine who would be attracted to a snarky, antisocial asshole *and* a cocky manwhore. It was like trying to align repelling magnets. Impossible.

Pike lunged in his face. "She's mine. Your junior PI needs to back off."

"Not my problem. Don't look at Heavenly again. Or I'll kill you."

"Are you really worried about me looking at her...or about you being able to hold on to her?" The DM's drawl dripped contempt.

That tone crawled up Seth's back. "Fuck you."

Fists clenched, he walked away, dragging in a deep breath and trying to force the rage from his system. If he didn't, he'd plow his fist into Pike's face and put a damper on Raine's party...not for the first time.

Suddenly, Heavenly was beside him, stroking her soft fingers down his arm. "What did you two argue about?"

"Nothing, angel," he lied. "Let's get something to drink."

"Okay," she replied, darting a wary glance at Pike.

After grabbing a couple bottles of water, Seth took her hand again and looked for a place to sit. Hammer was busy directing the caterers as they placed huge platters of brisket, ribs, and baked beans into chafing dishes over flaming cans of Sterno. Another group nestled huge bowls of coleslaw, pasta salad, and fruit into a wide ice trough atop the long, red-linen-covered tables.

Seth forced a smile, trying to get into the party spirit, as he sidled up beside Liam, still standing with Zach and the twins, and clapped him on the back. "Are my bozo brothers giving you trouble?"

"They're breathing, aren't they?" Liam shot Jack and Connor a crooked grin, then winked at Heavenly. "Glad you two could make it."

"Is my brother coming?" Zach asked. "He hasn't answered my text."

Heavenly tensed. She wasn't comfortable with their ruse. Clearly, Beck's brother wasn't, either. Even though Seth had done it to protect his mom, he hated it, too.

Swallowing his guilt, he answered carefully. "He's hoping to. I talked to him a little bit ago. There was an emergency at the hospital, and since he was on call, he had to go in."

Shit. Would the twins wonder why he knew where to find Beck before his own brother?

"Oh." Zach sounded disappointed.

"Don't worry." Jack bumped his shoulder. "We got you, man."

"Yeah," Connor seconded.

Seth let out a sigh of relief that his brothers seemingly hadn't questioned anything.

Heavenly flashed Zach a smile that didn't quite reach her eyes and changed the subject, bless her. "So, you like beer now?"

He nodded sheepishly. "It's actually pretty good."

"He likes vodka-Sevens, too. Don't you?" Jack laughed, elbowing Zach in the ribs.

"Not to mention Jack and water," Connor added with a grin. "Tequila shots. Scotch…"

Heavenly laughed. "Wow, you're definitely expanding your horizons. Good for you, I guess."

"Turns out, Satan's brew isn't bad after all," Zach admitted. "I just don't like hangovers."

Seth scowled at the twins. "You boneheads didn't teach him moderation?"

"It's okay. I needed to learn for myself, and I did—the hard way." Zach grimaced. "Three of anything is my limit."

"Good plan," Seth gave him a noncommittal reply and an imitation smile. He wanted to do better, but it was still hard to look at Zach and not see his own loss.

"Grab a plate, everyone. It's time to eat," Liam called.

"Thank goodness." Heavenly pressed a hand to her stomach. "The salad I had at lunch wore off, and I'm starving."

"Then let's get you fed." Seth put a hand to the small of her back.

Before they could make it to the buffet line, Jericho approached with a friendly nod. "Hi, Heavenly."

She turned and smile. "Hi, Jericho. Nice to see you again."

"You, too. The food here all looks good, but I admit…I've thought once or twice about your French toast casserole. I don't suppose you made any today?" He winked.

"I didn't. Sorry."

"Well, damn." Jericho laughed and stuck out a hand in his direction. "Seth, right?"

"Yeah." He shook the agent's hand. "Good to see you. I know you were involved in that Big Bear mess, but you're Dean Gorman's friend?" And Seth had walked right past the guy without so much as a hello the day Zach arrived at Beck's place.

"Yep. Dean and I go way back."

"Yeah? You from around here?" Seth made small talk, wondering why the agent had approached them.

"Born and bred. For the last few years, I've been working mostly in San Bernardino County, but starting next week I'll be working the west side of LA—my old stomping grounds. I'm glad to be moving back." He smiled. "But you don't sound like you're from around here."

Seth shrugged. "You can take the guy out of New York, but…"

"You can't take New York out of the guy. Got it." The agent nodded and scanned the party, then he dropped his voice. "Dr. Beckman around?"

"Surgery." Seth frowned. "There a problem?"

Jericho shook his head. "No. I was just going to give him some information."

That sounded ominous. Seth knew damn well that Beck was worried about the elders' sons hunting Zach down for revenge. Heavenly looked concerned, too. The last thing he wanted was for her to be distressed.

"Angel, why don't you get yourself a plate? I'll be there as soon as I talk to Jericho."

Heavenly obviously didn't like it, but she nodded. "All right. Do you want me to get you a plate, too?"

"I'll get it. You pick a spot to sit and I'll join you."

"If you don't mind, would you save me a seat, too?" Jericho asked.

"Sure," Heavenly confirmed, then dashed to the food table.

Seth looked around for privacy, then nodded toward the pool house. The agent followed.

Once they were out of sight and earshot from the others, he turned to Jericho with concern. "You know Beck and I are"—shit, how did he explain their relationship?—"friends with a common interest."

The agent raised a dark brow. "In Heavenly? Dean told me. You guys are lucky. She seems like a keeper."

"She is, but…" He winced. "My twin brothers are here tonight. They're the two jackasses with Zach. They don't know about the three of us."

"No worries. Raine already told me to keep quiet." Jericho shrugged. "Your brothers might be jackasses to you, but they've definitely helped Zach. Whoever thought of putting those three together was a fucking genius."

Guilt for not stepping up and helping Beck's brother acclimate warred with the pride of his own brothers providing the real-life experiences Zach needed. "It just kind of happened, but I think it's turned out for the best. Anyway, if you need me to pass some information to Beck, I'll be happy to."

"Sure. I was going to call, but I thought I'd see him tonight…"

"Is anything wrong?" Seth frowned.

"No. Actually, it's good news. The elders' sons who flapped their jaws and vowed revenge? Turns out they were all full of hot air. Most of them, when faced with the prospect of figuring out how to make their own money to live in the real world, couldn't hack it. Instead, they decided to join a sect in Idaho. The two who didn't? These class A idiots picked up a couple of hookers in Vegas. After the sex, they beat them up and took their money. Their pimp didn't take kindly to having the merchandise damaged. They're both in the county hospital and probably heading to jail as soon as they're medically cleared to stand trial. But reports are that they're both eating through straws and one is in traction, so it'll be a while, if ever, before they bother with Zach."

"That's great news. It should set Beck at ease."

"Exactly. It's better than I expected," Jericho admitted. "Now how about we get some food? My stomach is eating itself."

"Same."

As they stepped out of the pool house, Hammer met them with a smile. "Sorry I haven't had time to welcome you guys. Glad you both could make it."

"Thanks for the invite." Jericho extended his hand.

"I appreciate you, Liam, and Raine for hosting the party." Seth clapped Hammer on the back fondly. "The twins were dying to see Liam and to meet you and Raine."

"Based on the stories Liam has told me, Jack and Connor are wild as hell...in a good way."

"Well, it's not all good," Seth refuted with a fond grin. "I still think it's a miracle my mom never killed them."

After chuckles all around, Jericho skimmed the yard to see if anyone was nearby, then he faced Hammer, his voice low. "Before we return to the others, I wanted to ask you a question, Macen. I'm not sure if this is the right time or—"

"Sure. What's on your mind?"

"Following the whole Marlie debacle when she implicated you for supposedly exploiting Raine and all that shit..."

Hammer's face hardened. "You know about that? It was all lies. I've been exonerated—"

"I know. After you got arrested, Dean asked me to look at your case. I took a deep dive into your file, especially the info about your club. I knew you were innocent and that your fucking sham of a trial wasn't going anywhere."

Macen relaxed. "Thank God that turned out to be the case."

"Anyway, everyone interviewed had nothing but good things to say about you and Shadows, and..." Jericho glanced around again. "I've spent a few years playing in private with a fellow agent. She worked in another division and got transferred to Milwaukee a few months ago. I don't want to give up the lifestyle, but I need to find someone and someplace to play that affords anonymity. I can't risk my job."

Suddenly, Hammer was all smiles. "I got you covered. All play at Shadows is as anonymous as you want it to be. Come by anytime. We'll get the paperwork done, talk about what you're looking for, and I'll introduce you to some subs who might fit your interests."

"Your members all sign confidentiality agreements, right?"

"Absolutely. Binding and tight."

"Great." Jericho grinned. "I'm looking forward to it."

"Welcome to the club." Hammer clapped Jericho on the back.

"Now let's eat." Seth gestured toward the buffet tables.

As they strode toward the line, Heavenly—carrying a plate laden with brisket, ribs, beans, and salads—looped her arm through Seth's and tugged him toward a table. "Come with me. I stacked an extra plate under this one so we can share."

"I'll save you a seat, Jericho." He grinned at Heavenly. "See, there's another one of the million reasons I fell so hard for you."

"Really?" She laughed as they sat at a table under a big umbrella. "What are the others? I need examples."

He brushed a strand of hair from her cheek. "You're not only breathtakingly gorgeous but you also think of ways to make me smile." Seth dropped his voice. "To make *us* smile. I love you, angel."

She squeezed his hand. "I love you, too."

As Heavenly leaned into his kiss, her stomach growled.

He backed away reluctantly. "Eat."

By the time she slid the extra plate free and loaded it up with food, Jericho joined them, seemingly happy to answer questions about the latest on Messiah City, including the fact that each of the child-molesting elders had been denied bail. All were still sitting behind bars, awaiting trial.

"That's a perfect place for them. I know Beck will be happy to hear that." Heavenly shook her head in disgust. "What about the people who chose to leave and brave the outside world? They can't be having an easy time."

They probably weren't, and her compassion never ceased to amaze Seth.

Jericho shook his head. "A lot are struggling, as expected. But some are embracing their new freedom. Not as enthusiastically as Zach, but it's a start. The volunteers from those rescue groups are amazing. They know exactly what they're doing."

Heavenly nodded. "Thank goodness."

"Yeah. The whole situation is so tragic. The stories some of these girls told were both sickening and heartbreaking. But this is one case where I actually got to make a difference. It feels really good, you know? Like I have a little faith in humanity again—and for me, that takes a lot."

The sun was sliding toward the horizon when Raine announced dessert would soon be ready. Seth and Jericho let out a low groan and palmed their full stomachs.

"Dessert? I didn't leave room for that." Seth grimaced.

"Me, either." Jericho glanced over his shoulder. "Hey, I need to chat with Zach, catch him up. Care to join me?"

Not really. Beck's brother still brought back feelings he didn't handle well. He knew he had to keep trying, but then Pike strolled up to River and Dean's table. The pair sitting tensed.

"Oh, no," Heavenly murmured. "This won't be good."

"Didn't find Jasmine yet, did you?" Pike taunted.

River suddenly leapt to his feet, his face twisted in fury. "You motherfucking son of a bitch."

Dean was out of his chair a split second later, gripping River's shoulder and holding him back.

Hammer sprinted into the fray, slinging an arm around Pike's shoulder and leading him away with a forced smile that said, *Nothing to see here*. But near the coolers, Macen gave the caustic DM an earful. Pike merely stood and listened, wearing an impassive expression.

"You get with Zach," Seth told Jericho. "I should talk to River."

It was the truth...but it was also a damn good excuse to avoid Beck's younger brother. Seth wasn't proud of his reaction, but he needed to work through this. Pretending that Zach's loss didn't affect him wasn't possible.

"Sure. If anything changes with the case or I have more news, tell Beck I'll let him know."

"Will do. Appreciate it, man." Then Seth turned to Heavenly. "I'll be right back."

As the agent headed toward Zach and the twins, he stood and made his way to River and Dean's table.

"Hey, boss." River gestured to an open chair. "What's up?"

Seth settled beside River. "Not much. What are you two dirtbags up to?"

"Celebrating. A month ago, we were in Big Bear and I thought Dean was dead. But we just bought a house together. Paperwork and funding were final today."

As they clinked beer bottles, Dean nodded in excitement. "We move in June eighth. Soon, we'll have roots down and we'll be ready for the future."

When they found the right woman? That certainly sounded like the plan to Seth.

"And we were having a good fucking time talking about our new place—it's in Santa Monica, just a few blocks from the beach—until fucking Pike showed up."

Seth shot River a pointed stare. "You have to stop letting him get the best of you."

"Ugh. He's such a cockbag."

Dean nodded. "He is, but you let him push your buttons."

"I don't let him; he just does. He knows I have no idea how the fuck to find Jasmine. Hell, it took me weeks to even learn her goddamn name. And that motherfucker rubs my nose in the fact he sees her every chance he gets."

"Because you plucked her cherry, brother, and that eats him up," Dean pointed out.

"Yeah," River grumbled. "But I want more. And I want answers."

"Now that you have a first name, can't you look for her? You're a PI," Seth pointed out.

"You think I haven't been looking? I can't tell you how many times

I've hacked into the DMV data—" River snapped his mouth shut, guilt lining his face. He cringed Dean's way. "You did not hear that."

"Hear what?"

River exhaled. "Do you have any idea how many redheads named Jasmine there are in LA? That's all I can search for since I don't know her age or her last known address. If I could search by bra size and O face, I'd find her real fast."

"You sure she's old enough to have a driver's license?" Seth teased.

"Bite me," River groused. "She was young, but she was definitely over eighteen."

"You sure?" Dean prodded. "After all, she was a virgin..."

"I know, but underage girls don't have curves like that. They don't have that silky, tight, fucking incredible—"

"Shut up," Dean demanded. "I still can't believe you didn't call me to help you deflower her, asshole."

"You were on duty. Besides, it all happened so fast. The adrenaline was pumping. My heart was pounding. I lost my damn mind when I started kissing her. Oh, fuck, her mouth. It was so red and plush and perfect. That mouth should be illegal in every state, every country. Shit, in every universe." River glanced down at his jeans. "Fuck. I'm hard just thinking about her."

"It's been too long since you got laid," Dean chided.

"I know. But if you'd been there, if you'd had your dick inside that sweet pussy, she would have ruined you, too. She was so hot, so wet, so goddamn tight, I wanted to cry. And her tits? Christ, I've never felt anything like them. She's a tiny thing, but they were warm and heavy. They fit my hands like they'd been made for me. And her nipples?" He groaned. "I couldn't get enough. I spent hours sucking, biting, and tugging on them. They just keep growing longer and harder and—"

"Stop," Dean growled. "Now you're just rubbing it in."

"No, I'm being honest. She might have been a virgin, but she was so uninhibited. There wasn't anything she wouldn't try and didn't love. And after all the kinky shit I did to her? She begged for more. She lost her damn mind when I started teasing her ass. And, sweet Jesus... her ass. I mean, her pussy was velvety soft and perfect, but when I worked my way past her tiny rim, my eyes rolled into the back of my head. It was another level of paradise, and I—"

"Better introduce me when you find her again or I'll rain down a whole world of shit on you," Dean warned.

"I swear, man, when I find her, you'll be balls deep inside her with me."

"Damn right." Dean nodded as they clinked beers.

"I'm telling you, the more I think about her, the more I think"— River's face turned solemn, and his voice followed suit—"she's the one we've been looking for, brother."

It was obvious River believed he'd found his *one*, but he knew Jasmine didn't want to see him, right? So why did he imagine she would welcome Dean, too? Even if she was game to take on both of them, what assurance did River have that Dean would actually fall as fast and hard for her?

"Damn," the cop cursed. "We've got to find her."

"Well, you won't succeed today," Seth informed them.

"Why not?" River glowered.

"Apparently, she's out of town."

Raine's brother nearly came out of his seat. "How do you know that?"

Well, Heavenly had told him first, but he was leaving his girl out of this. "Pike."

"That motherfucker. Did he say where she went?"

"Sorry. I didn't ask."

"Go talk to him again, man. Find out everything you can."

"He isn't going to tell me shit."

"I'll bet my sister knows. She's got Jasmine's phone number and won't give it to me, so why wouldn't she keep this shit from me, too?" River grumbled. "She's convinced this is a good 'growth experience' for me. It's bullshit."

Seth tried not to laugh. He'd always known Raine was clever, if a little underhanded—usually for a good cause. But she wasn't wrong in thinking that everything came too easily for her brother. River going after something he craved badly enough to work for would be good for him. But Seth didn't say that aloud, merely smiled.

A long minute later, Jack, Connor, and Zach sprinted in their direction, skidding to a halt at the table.

"What are you hellions up to?" Seth asked, trying to find the balls to meet Zach's gaze.

Beck's brother seemed more focused on the gathering around him.

"Not much," Connor replied. "Sorry we didn't get to visit much with you and Heavenly."

"No worries. The party is for you three to get to know the people we care about and trust."

"And they're all damn amazing." Jack grinned.

"Totally. Everyone is…nice," Zach piped in.

They were. Seth figured he'd done a pretty good job reuniting with old friends and finding new ones on the West Coast.

"Hey, we're about to head out and hit some clubs. You two want to come?" Connor asked.

He was asking River and Dean. Seth wasn't the least bit miffed that they hadn't invited him. But he wasn't going to let the chance to fuck with his brother pass him by.

"Aww, thanks for the invite, but I think Heavenly and I are going to head over to her place and watch some movies."

"Oh. Cool. Um…" Connor turned toward River and Dean. "How about you two? You feel like going to find some—"

His brother abruptly shut up. The gaping panic on his face said he was struggling to recover.

"Pussy?" Seth supplied helpfully, his smile acidic.

"I-I was going to say dates, but…"

Seth stood, brow raised. "You meant pussy."

"Hell, yes!" Dean bolted from his chair.

River looked far less enthusiastic. "I don't know. I'm not sure your shoulder has healed up enough for us to—"

"I don't need my shoulder to fuck. My dick works just fine," Dean assured.

"But I'm still not sure we should—"

"Come on," Dean cajoled. "You've been out of the saddle for weeks now. It's time you stop letting Jasmine mess with your head. She doesn't own you. So let's get back on the horse. We could both use a long, hot ride."

Had River actually gone celibate since taking Jasmine's virginity? That was a first. Did the poor bastard have any idea yet that he was fucked?

"Come on, man," Dean pressed. "You can't give up your sex life for some chick who's avoiding you."

River sighed. "Fine. Let's go."

"Yeah!" Jack cheered. "Time to party!"

"Have fun." Seth chuckled. "Don't do anything I wouldn't enjoy."

"We're kinky, but we're not *that* kinky," River muttered just loudly enough for Seth.

"I'm calling bullshit," he returned as River fell in with the rest of the manwhore parade.

Shaking his head, Seth sauntered back to Heavenly, still sitting at their table, and stared at the inviting bowl of peach cobbler and ice cream she'd dished for him. "You're trying to make me fat, angel."

She shook her head. "I'm making sure you have enough energy."

"For what?"

"Anything you want," she said in a breathy whisper that threatened to undo him.

"Anything?" Seth filled his spoon with whipped cream. "Then I say we take this with us so Beck and I can do a little repeat of last night, spread this all over your body, then spend hours licking it off…"

Her breath caught. "I wouldn't protest."

Seth leaned in and skimmed his lips up her neck, to her ear. "You're a naughty little angel, aren't you?"

"Maybe."

"Maybe what?" Beck asked, suddenly sliding onto the chair beside her and wrapping his arm around her.

"You made it!" She bounced into his embrace, so obviously happy. Then she jerked back, scanning the partygoers.

"You're safe," Seth promised. "The twins are long gone."

"Thank goodness." She planted a welcoming kiss on Beck's mouth.

"So…are you going to let us make dessert of you again tonight?" Seth muttered hotly in her ear.

"Say yes," Beck breathed over Heavenly's pouty lips. "I'll show you just how sorry I am that I was late…"

Heavenly's face softened. "You don't have to make anything up to me. Duty called. I understand, and you're here now."

"But I'd rather be at home with you, naked, in our bed, and spread out between us."

Her breathing quickened. "You don't want to stay and mingle?"

Beck shook his head. "There's no one here I can't see later. We want you now."

"Absolutely. Why don't you let me get your purse, angel?" Seth offered.

Clandestinely, Beck slid his hand under the table and beneath her skirt. "You do that while I get this pussy wet and ready."

His hand must have slipped into her panties, because Heavenly dragged in a shuddering breath and a rosy hue spread across her cheeks as she asked, "How soon can we be home?"

Seth got hard just watching them. "Ten minutes."

"And in fifteen, we'll both be deep inside you," Beck promised.

"Hurry," she breathed. "Please."

CHAPTER
NINE

June

A few weeks later, Seth headed home after an uneventful day in the office, surrounded by a five o'clock full of sunshine. The official first day of summer was on the horizon, so the afternoon was still temperate. Everywhere he looked, joggers and cyclists were getting in their cardio, kids played soccer, and sun worshippers soaked up rays. People drove with the tops down on their convertibles and walked their dogs. Potential earthquakes aside, he had to admit that Los Angeles was an urban paradise. He definitely didn't miss New York's humidity. In fact, he didn't miss much about the place he used to call home, except his family. But his future was here.

He just had to fully embrace it.

Since Beck had texted to say he'd be home a couple of hours late, and Heavenly was spending some girl time with Raine and Jasmine, Seth had an opportunity to start wrapping his arms around his tomorrows. And to check on his brothers. The twins had been too quiet lately, which meant they were up to something... Seth was afraid to ask what.

But most of all, he was here to mend a fence. He just had to find his balls.

As he approached his former apartment complex, he let out a deep breath. *You sure you want to do this?*

The short answer was no, but he had to stop running and start dealing with the unpleasant things he'd been avoiding—chief among them, Zach. It wasn't that he disliked the guy. Hell, Seth didn't even know him. He felt sorry for Zach and everything he'd lost, absolutely. But being around him triggered all the dark memories of grief, sorrow, and rage Seth had tried so fucking hard to forget. That was on him.

But his avoidance had come at Beck's expense. It was time to man up and admit that ducking Zach had been a temporary solution. A Band-Aid destined to slough off. After all, Zach was Beck's brother; that wasn't going to change. Zach had stepped up and found the courage to destroy his twisted way of life—the only one he'd ever known. And what had Seth done? Run from his ghosts and his failures. No more. He owed it to Zach—and to Beck—to face his fear head on and meet them halfway. Looking back, Seth was ashamed that Beck had been forced to turn out his brother simply to shield him from his own failures. It wasn't fair, and he needed to rectify it.

Come hell or high water, Seth would get to know Zach and make peace with his own tragic past. After eight years, wasn't it time to let go?

After slinging his SUV into a parking spot at his complex, he locked up his vehicle and climbed the stairs. Once he made his way down the hall, he slid his key into the lock of his apartment. As he stepped inside his unit and closed the door, the hairs on the back of Seth's neck stood on end. It was disturbingly quiet. Considering the twins didn't know how to exist without making noise—and lots of it—the silence was deafening. But he wasn't alone; he could *feel* people here.

Something was wrong.

Seth reached inside his jacket and pulled his Glock from its holster. Then he heard a long, drawn-out moan and stopped in his tracks, heart revving. Was one of his brothers sick? Hurt? Fuck, what if Jericho's intel had been wrong and the sons of Messiah City's elders had tracked Zach down and beaten the shit out of all three of them?

Since he had surprise on his side, Seth needed to proceed carefully. It was the only way he could take down whoever might be threatening his and Beck's brothers.

Cocking his head, Seth listened for clues. A short second later, another guttural groan sounded from the living room.

Adrenaline firing his veins, he tiptoed out of the foyer and rounded the corner. When he caught sight of his brothers on the sofa bed, he stopped short. His eyes nearly bugged out of his head.

Jack and Connor were fucking the same glassy-eyed brunette.

Holy fuck!

He blinked. But the vision was still there. His twin brothers were definitely hammering their cocks into the woman, whose lips were parted and her head was tossed back in a picture of ecstasy as the sofa bed shook violently with each thrust. She moaned again.

Shock ricocheted through Seth. He stood slack-jawed, his thoughts racing as he tucked his gun away. What the hell should he do? Leave them to their devices…or confront them?

Legally, they were adults, capable of making their own decisions—in theory. It would probably make him a giant hypocrite to shut them down…but they weren't mature enough to grasp how difficult it was to mesh three lives into one. If he could guide them down a simpler path, wouldn't he be doing them a favor?

Oh, god. I should have been a better role model.

And what if they were both in more than lust with this girl? What if it was love? Fuck, that would complicate everything. As that night-marish scenario skittered through his brain, the urge to do *something* to save them from such a difficult future pressed in on him. Maybe in a few years, when they had more life experience—when they under-stood themselves and love, commitment, sacrifice, compromise, and all that entailed a lot more—they could handle it. But right now, Jack and Connor weren't ready for the long-term ramifications of loving one woman.

While Seth had miraculously found love again with Heavenly and Beck, their relationship wasn't always easy. Every day, they had to make the conscious choice to find the common ground necessary to keep moving forward. The three of them had overcome so much to be together, and Seth knew they still had hurdles to clear. He hated to think they might eventually encounter one that tripped them up for good. They were committed to working through those issues…but what if the day came when love and commitment weren't enough? It would end in obliterating heartache. Being the only father figure in the twins' lives, Seth felt obligated to steer his brothers away from these kind of difficulties. But he had to do it without revealing his own secrets.

Fuck me. This is going to be like jogging through a damn minefield.

"Didn't I tell you that once you've had twins, you won't go back?"

Connor panted, shuttling in and out of the woman's ass. "You believe me now, don't you, Emily?"

Seth rolled his eyes. The dumb ass was still using that idiotic phrase he'd spewed to Heavenly at the pool the day he and Jack had arrived. When Seth had pressed him about it, both brothers had assured him they'd been kidding.

Clearly, they'd lied.

That was nothing new. Growing up, the twins had told some whoppers to cover for one another so neither got grounded. Obviously, they were still lying as adults. They weren't fucking teenagers anymore. They needed to stop acting like it.

Emily responded with an incoherent whimper that morphed into a long-suffering wail.

At the same moment, Jack sucked in a sharp hiss. "Slow the fuck down, Connor. Every time you take the ass, you go too fast. Ease up so I can get off, too."

Every time? Oh, Jesus. Seth mentally recoiled. *They've done this before. When? Where? Why?*

"I can't help it," Connor groaned. "She's got the finest ass I've ever fucked."

"I get it, bro. Her pussy is the same, but you've got to slow down," Jack reiterated.

"Too late. Fuck!" Connor gave one last jerky thrust before letting out a strangled yelp and stilling in her backside, tendons pulsing in his neck.

Jack gripped her hips tighter, surged up even harder, and growled, "Give it to us, baby."

Emily did, tossing her head back and screaming as Jack lunged up one last time with a filthy, guttural curse, jaw tensed, teeth clenched. The sex sounds went on for long moments. Seth grimaced. Heartbeats passed. The room fell into silence.

Seth blew out a breath and prepared to open a can of whoop-ass. "What the hell are you two doing?"

Besides fucking this girl into orgasmic bliss?

Connor jerked his head up, his eyes locked on Seth's before shock and horror ripped across his face. He yanked free of Emily's backside and scrambled to cover himself with his pants. "Fuck. Fuck. Shit! We got company."

Jack's head popped up from the cushion. He blinked at Seth, then his eyes grew bigger than baseballs. Unceremoniously, he shoved Emily off him, then frantically covered her—and himself—with a sheet.

"Who's that?" she demanded, her big eyes on Seth.

And he was under no illusion. He must look as displeased as he felt.

"Um, our older brother." Jack looked nervous as he tried to maneuver Emily behind him.

Dismay crawled across her face. "You said that, other than the guy in the bedroom, we'd be all alone."

From his old bedroom, down the hall, a woman screamed in sexual bliss. Apparently, Zach was getting action, too.

Christ. This place has turned into Grand Fucking Central Station. So much for having a conversation with Beck's brother this evening…

"They lied." Seth raised a brow Emily's way. "If you have someplace else to be, now would be a good time to go."

"Aww, man," Jack complained. "Don't make her leave. Bro…"

He zipped his pissed-off stare at his brother. "You're lucky I don't make *you* leave—back to New York. Explain what you two are doing with her. Now."

"I'm out of here," Emily said, jerking the sheet off the bed and exposing Jack as she gathered it around her and plucked her clothes off the floor.

Jack and Connor grumbled as they scowled, rose, and disposed of their condoms.

"Wait." Jack grabbed Emily by the arm. "When can we see you again?"

"Never. It was fun, but, thanks to the buzzkill,"—she thumbed his way—"fun time is clearly over."

"It doesn't have to be," Connor insisted.

She arched a brow at Seth, then pinned the twins with a scowl as she finished dressing. "Yeah, it does. Lose my number."

As Emily stormed past Seth and slammed out the front door, an awkward silence descended. Connor tugged on his boxers and turned an angry glare his way. Jack looked equally pissed off.

Seth sent him a scowl designed to take control of the argument and put them in their place. "She's gone now. Explain."

Connor sent Jack an uneasy expression, then looked back at Seth. "It was just some harmless fun, you know? Experimentation. We...we were just curious and wanted to see what doing a girl together would feel like."

"Yeah," Jack nodded nervously. "We found this video of two guys and a girl and it looked hot—"

"Super hot," Connor chimed in. "Like fire."

"So we decided to try it."

"Uh-huh. This was your first time fucking the same girl?" Seth purposely baited the hook.

"Yeah. Totally," Connor lied.

"One hundred percent." Jack nodded.

"Really?" Seth probed them while they nodded like matching bobbleheads. "Then what did you mean when you told Connor to slow down because he fucked too fast every time you let him take the ass?"

Jack blanched. "Shit. You heard that?"

"Oh, I heard everything, including Connor's 'once you've had twins, you won't go back' bullshit."

His brothers exchanged mirrored expressions of *oh, fuck*.

"Okay, look," Connor tried to reason with him. "We've taken a few together, but—"

"How many?" Seth asked.

"Why does it matter?" Jack swallowed tightly.

"Because it does. How many? Five, ten, fifty? A hundred?"

"I-I don't know. W-we kind of...lost count." Jack winced.

Lost count? Jesus... "How long have you two been sharing girls?"

They exchanged another glance, both gaping and wriggling like worms on a hook.

"Don't look at each other so you can get your stories straight. I want the fucking truth."

Jack sighed. "Since ninth grade."

That sent Seth reeling. Why hadn't he ever noticed the signs? Clearly, he'd been too wrapped up in his own life, his own problems. His own bullshit. Or maybe he simply hadn't known what to look for then. Now he did. "How old were you?"

They glanced at one another for confirmation, then answered together. "Fourteen."

Good god. They'd been two years from having their driver's licenses and they'd been fucking girls together? "Have either of you ever had sex with a woman alone?"

"I have." Jack nodded. "For sure."

"Same," Connor assured.

"Yeah? How often? And don't bullshit me, guys. You're both horrible liars."

Jack flinched. "Once. With my girlfriend at the time."

Seth turned to Connor. "And you?"

He shrugged. "Yeah, once. I-I wanted to know what it was like, so…"

"So he pretended to be me, but my girlfriend figured it out."

"That was a horrible trick to play on her." Seth sent a thunderous scowl Jack's way. "And you just let your brother hop in the sack with your girlfriend? Idiot. I hope she broke up with your sorry ass once she figured out you two had deceived her."

"Actually…" Jack tried to pass off his grimace as a smile. "She didn't mind. She asked us to do her together and—"

"The rest is history," Connor explained.

"And…we like it." Jack dared to step closer, almost entreating him. "A lot."

Of course they did, but now where the hell did he take this conversation?

"We'll get back to that in a minute. This Emily I…met today, do you love her?"

"Love? Hell, no." Connor blinked. "We just met her this afternoon at work. She had lunch with her mom, and her table was in my station. I flirted. She flirted back. Jack caught her before she left the place and got her number. We called when our shift ended and…"

Thank God. If they'd been in love with her, Seth didn't know what advice he would have given them except to hang on to their hearts because they were probably destined to crash and burn. At least now he might be able to provide some words of wisdom, providing they listened.

"You two are clearly having a blast banging babes together, but have either of you stopped to think about your future?"

Their matching blank stares told him they hadn't strained a single brain cell on tomorrow, let alone beyond. He wasn't surprised.

"One day you're both going to want to settle down, get married, and raise a family. How do you think that's going to work?"

Connor reared back, his face looking like he'd sucked a lemon. "I'm not interested in that, at least not anytime soon."

"Yeah, bro. It's a no from me, too." Jack nodded.

Seth strained for patience. "You don't get it. The more time you spend carving notches in your bedposts together, the less you'll really know yourselves. And the fewer skills you'll have in making long-term commitments. Relationships don't just happen. You have to work at them every day. All the time. Keeping love and passion alive takes work and dedication. You have to want it and mean it. But once you get there, it's amazing."

"And all that sounds great…but sharing is amazing, too," Jack countered.

I know. Lord, do I know.

"Right now, we're just having fun. When we decide we want all the forever stuff, we'll go our separate ways and each find a girl," Connor said.

"Okay, but you're not going to do that with girls like Emily."

"What's that supposed to mean? She's not a whore."

"I never said she was," Seth assured. "I'm saying she was doing you both for a thrill, not an emotional connection."

"So?" Jack shrugged defiantly. "That's all we wanted."

"For now. But when you're ready to settle down, you won't find forever with a girl you've been passing between you."

Well, you might. But finding one as rare as Heavenly and Raine will be like searching for a needle in a haystack.

"Hey, don't knock it until you've tried it," Connor backed up his twin.

"Exactly," Jack piped up. "If you had any idea how awesome it feels to share a woman, you wouldn't be saying any of this shit."

"Is that what you think?" Seth tried not to laugh. "I've shared women."

The twins gaped, then turned to one another in shock.

"When? Where?" Connor frowned like the obvious question was just now hitting him. "And with who?"

"None of your business, but I've done lots of things that would shock you, even kinky things. I used to be a member of a BDSM club when I lived in New York. I used to think of it as my kinky home away from home."

"Club Graffiti? Yeah. We know." Connor nodded enthusiastically. "We're members, too."

That stopped Seth cold. *Shit, is it genetic?*

"Then you two should be well aware that the lifestyle isn't about sharing your cocks with a woman but sharing your trust, honesty, and heart with one. That's how you build your lives, separately, with a like-minded woman who shares your desires and—"

"We have plenty of time for that crap," Jack countered. "We're not ancient like you."

"Ancient?" Seth scoffed. "I was already married when I was your age."

"No offense, bro, but we're not you," Jack reminded.

No shit. By then, he'd been responsible enough to be in a committed relationship. "You're not, and I'm not trying to compare our lives. I'm simply trying to put things into perspective. When you find your soul mate, it doesn't matter how old you are. Your heart comes alive. Life takes on a whole new meaning. And the world is brighter and more beautiful than it's ever been. I want that for you—each of you. But if you don't start looking *separately*, you'll never find it."

"We appreciate your wisdom, Obi-Wan," Jack drawled. "But like we said, we're not ready to settle down, get married, and make babies yet."

"We'd rather practice." Connor grinned.

"Oh, I saw. More than I wanted to," Seth drawled. "But there's more at stake than finding your happily ever after."

"Like what?"

"Like…have you thought about what sharing a woman would do to Mom?"

Jack's jaw fell open. "You're gonna tell *Mom*? Dude, y-you can't. She'll—"

"Freak the fuck out," Seth finished for him. "I know. When I told her about Hammer, Liam, and Raine, she nearly had an apoplectic seizure."

"Oh, god." Connor blanched. "If you tell her, it might kill her."

"I doubt she'll die, but she'll probably browbeat you both within an inch of your lives. You know what she believes, what the Church has taught her since before her first communion."

"Yeah, yeah." Connor sighed. "Sex is between a man and a woman."

"It's more than that. She's going to think it's incest, and the Bible has a whole lot to say about that."

"Eww." Jack recoiled. "We don't fuck each other."

"No. That's disgusting," Connor snarled. "It's sick and wrong on every level."

"Well, in the eyes of the Church, sharing one woman is just as sick and wrong."

Which is exactly why I haven't mentioned a word to Mom about my relationship with Beck and Heavenly.

Seth knew he'd have to drop his bombshell confession on her soon. And once Jack and Connor found out, they'd be pissed beyond belief. But Seth wasn't being hypocritical out of spite or selfishness. He simply wanted his brothers to grow up before they got serious about traveling down such a hard road. They weren't yet capable of putting their own wants aside and doing what it took to maintain a stable, secure, and loving relationship. Separately, they might learn. Together? They fed one another's worst tendencies. And even if they weren't looking for happily ever after now, they would someday. Seth was doing them a favor.

Are you sure you're not rationalizing?

"All the more reason *not* to tell her," Jack bit out emphatically.

"I won't," he assured them.

They blew out a collective breath of relief before Jack spoke up. "Thanks, bro. We—"

"Really appreciate it," Connor seconded. "And we—"

"Under one condition," Seth cut into their word vomit. "You both make a concerted effort to date separately, starting now."

The twins exchanged a look that told him they didn't like the idea, but they sighed and nodded glumly.

"All right." Connor didn't sound pleased. "We will."

"Will you? Really?" Seth probed.

"We'll try," Jack answered. "Promise."

"Great. Then it's settled." Seth smiled. "You two will walk the straight and narrow from here on out, and I won't tell Mom about your deviant shit."

And when the truth about his own relationship with Beck and Heavenly came out… Well, he'd deal with that later.

"So…think Zach will be out here anytime soon? I'd like to talk to him."

Jack shook his head. Connor joined in, then added, "Once he gets a woman in his room, he doesn't come out for hours. Often, they hole up all night."

"Yeah, but damn, girls leave the next morning looking wrecked and walking sideways."

That was more than Seth needed to know. And basically, his former digs had become hookup headquarters. Nice.

He sighed. "Tell him I stopped by to talk to him, will you? It's important."

Hopefully, he and Zach could have a man-to-man later.

"Sure, bro." Jack rushed to be amenable.

Seth would think it was funny if he wasn't so worried about the twins. "Thanks. No calling Emily back."

"Nope," Connor assured.

"And no trolling for another chick together."

"Absolutely not." Jack saluted him.

Seth didn't believe them for a second, but he'd done what he could for now. "We'll talk later."

After making a mental note to schedule more surprise visits, he left, cursing under his breath.

After a shitty night of sleep, Seth came to a couple of conclusions. First, the twins were headstrong, always had been. Even birth had come on their terms—a month early, in the middle of the night, and in dramatic fashion. As if they couldn't stand being apart even then, they'd come into the world separated by a mere two minutes. They'd been allergic to being awake with the sun and loved to make an entrance. In short, they were going to do what they wanted to. Seth doubted chastising them about their sexual proclivities would do any good. His mom had been vaguely aware that he and Autumn used to play at Club Graffiti, but that hadn't stopped them. They'd only hidden their kink better.

Seth's hypocrisy didn't sit well with him. Eventually, he'd have to come clean with the twins...but not until he told Mom about his relationship with Heavenly and Beck. He couldn't trust Jack and Connor not to blab. And if the truth got back to Grace Cooper before he could preface his relationship so that she might understand it, she wouldn't accept the three of them.

But his bigger conclusion had been about Zach. Instead of ducking the grieving man who'd obviously needed help and a hand, he should have given comfort and advice from someone who had lived through the same losses and had come out on the other side. Seth felt guilty that it had taken him nearly two months to come to that conclusion. Right now, he didn't feel like a great human being.

All that changed, starting today.

Seth plucked up his car keys from the hall table on his way to the garage. "Since Zach volunteered to help River and Dean move, I'm going to pick him up and bring him to the new place. We'll stop and get donuts or something. Would you let Beck know?"

Concern settled into Heavenly's big blue eyes. "Are you sure? He'll be happy to pick up Zach. You don't have to—"

"I want to." He kissed her cheek. "And I'll be fine. See you in an hour or so?"

She nodded, then smiled. "I'm not sure how much help Beck's red convertible will be today, but he can help move furniture and I can unpack and organize. What about the twins?"

"They're working until five." And it was just as well. River and Dean were setting up house to more readily share women, maybe even one in particular if Raine's brother got his way and the elusive Jasmine appeared. Seth really didn't want to give Jack and Connor any new ideas.

"That's okay. I think we'll have enough people. From what I've seen online, it's not a big house. It shouldn't take all day."

Two bachelors moving in together? River's organizational skills were decent, though not as good as his own. And Dean? He seemed like a fly-by-the-seat-of-his-pants guy. So this ought to be fun. "We'll see. Bye, angel."

"Bye." She kissed him one last time with a smile.

Then Seth was out the door, driving down the road, blessedly empty early on a Saturday morning. After a quick stop at the donut shop around the corner from his old apartment, he schlepped back to his SUV and headed to pick up Zach.

Beck's brother answered quickly, his arm around a blonde, looking confused. "Where's my brother?"

"Change of plans. We'll be meeting him and Heavenly there shortly."

Zach sent him a cautious nod, then looked at the woman in his arms. "There's my ride. I'm glad you stayed."

The woman flashed him a shy smile. "Me, too. See you around."

She extricated herself from his embrace, sent Seth a sideways stare, then left with a wave. A few seconds later, they heard the slam of a car door and the start of an engine.

"New girlfriend?" Seth ventured.

Zach shook his head. "Just temporary companionship and comfort."

Seth understood that. "You ready to head out?"

"Sure." He grabbed his wallet and keys.

"I know River and Dean appreciate the help." Seth led Beck's brother to his SUV.

Zach shrugged. "I'm happy to. My community garden can wait a day."

Fantastic. Now what should they talk about? In theory, Seth knew. He just didn't know how to broach the conversation. Zach barely knew him, and what little he'd learned was that Seth struggled to be around him. No wonder Zach seemed somewhere between standoffish and tight-lipped.

As they slid into the SUV, Seth turned it over and glanced across the cab. "You're doing great, by the way. You've suffered a horrific loss and I can only guess, given the way you lost your wife and daughter, that you feel guilty or responsible or—"

"I do." Zach frowned. "I was doing the right thing for the right reasons, but I should never have assumed Faith and Joanna would be safe. I just figured I was the one betraying The Chosen and that…"

"They'd never take your choices out on your family?"

"Something like that."

And didn't that hit really fucking close to home?

Seth started to sweat. The black hole of rage he'd felt after Autumn's and Tristan's losses was right there, still threatening to suck him under. Yes, he'd ultimately killed the man responsible for their deaths. But when he let himself think about that time in his life, which was rare, and he was honest about the whole incident, which was even more rare, he wondered if he'd truly killed the right person when he'd offed Silas Nichols in his dingy apartment. Yes, he guessed it made sense that Nichols wouldn't have wanted his guilt in the cold case to surface…but during those dark, infrequent hours, Seth let himself wonder if he'd been off base. If the whole thing hadn't been a little too pat.

But that wasn't the point of today. Zach was.

"I got the satisfaction of ending the people who killed my family. In a way, you did, too."

Zach frowned. "I don't know if I would call that satisfaction."

Beck's brother was right. "It doesn't make the pain of your loss go away."

"No. Nothing ever will. But you know that."

"Eight years later, I do." He cleared his throat as he coasted through a green light. "Listen…I know I've been—" Seth almost said *an asshole*, but last time he checked, Zach still frowned on swearing much. He'd drink and get laid, but ixnay on the four-letter words. "Well, I haven't been very welcoming, helpful, or kind. And I'm sorry."

Zach let out a breath. "Gideon, I mean Beck—I hope that will get easier—told me about your past, about the deaths of your wife and son. He said that being around me wasn't easy."

"It isn't. But it was selfish of me to retreat into my years-old pain and ignore yours that's so fresh. I know exactly what you're going through. I know the anger you're trying to suppress so you can tell the people who love you that you're fine and at least mean it a little. I know the lying awake at night and realizing that when you wake up in the morning, you'll only be a day further away from the people you thought would be with you for the rest of your life. And I understand your head telling you that you need to figure out how to go on when all you want to do is listen to your heart that it's not fair and go back in time to make different choices."

A shocked expression froze Zach's face. "You really do understand. Wow. I didn't think anyone did. I know my brother tries."

"And you have in common the loss of Messiah City and a way of life that shaped you. But let's be real. He walked out in a fit of anger and teenage rebellion over a girl he felt guilty about but never loved. You made the grim choice to turn your back on everything, despite being an adult. And you didn't merely leave, you destroyed every-thing to ensure those horrible elders could never hurt anyone again."

Zach scoffed. "You make me sound like a saint. I've known for years that they were sick and wrong, but I didn't have the courage or strength to buck their system. I counted myself lucky to be the Messi-ah's brother. I believed that would keep me and my family safe, so if I just kept my head down and pretended not to notice what was going on…"

"They would leave you alone? Yeah, it never ends up that way. Evil always comes after what's good."

"Something I learned the hard way." Zach nodded. "How long does this horrible hollowness last?"

The one question Seth had really hoped Beck's brother wouldn't ask. Still, he couldn't be less than honest. "It never goes away. I wish I could tell you something that would make you feel better. Give you some light at the end of the dark tunnel. But no. First, you learn to breathe again. Then you learn to go through the motions until, one day, you realize that you're living without them. And that's okay. It's not the life you had before. Nothing will bring that back. But sometimes…" Seth gripped the steering wheel and gave him the unvarnished truth. "Sometimes you find something even better. And it hurts like hell to admit that, but I can sit here today and tell you that I'm incredibly happy sharing Heavenly with your brother. She is the perfect woman for me, and your brother… Well, I've got four of my own, but Beck has become a different sort of brother. I can't explain it. I just know that my life is better for loving them. So believe that something good will come your way, too."

Zach shook his head. "I'm not looking to find love again."

Seth gave him a wry smile. "Yeah, I said the same thing, too. And you've already got your hookup game down. Good for you. I mean that. Sincerely. It will get you through the next few months at least, maybe the next few years. But I'm telling you, there will come a point when you meet someone who will change your mind. You can fight it all you want…but that need for her will win." When he saw Zach's doubt, Seth shrugged. "But you're a while from that."

The other guy nodded. "A long while. You found Heavenly and my brother, and I'm happy for you all. But if I'm honest, I wasn't eager to get married the first time. I doubt I'll do it again."

Seth didn't argue, but he knew better. Someday, Zach would want his life to mean something, and he would want someone to share it with. "Understood. I just wanted to let you know that, if you ever need someone to talk to or have any questions about grieving and healing or whatever…I'm here."

Zach looked surprised. "And that won't bother or upset you anymore?"

He couldn't lie and say he'd never be upset by trekking into dark memories again, but... "I've worked through a lot, even in the last few months. When you first lost your family, I saw your face. I knew what you felt. It brought all that back for me. But now I realize how far I've come, and that I can help get you to a better place—if you need."

"Thanks." Beck's brother nodded. "I appreciate that. And I know this conversation couldn't have been easy for you."

"Fu—" Seth cleared his throat. "I mean, no. I was sweating bullets. But...it wasn't too bad." He gave Zach a mock punch on the shoulder. "Just like your brother, I guess you're not half bad."

"I'll pretend there's a compliment in there somewhere." A sly smile curled Zach's lips.

"Maybe a little." Seth reached onto the dash between them. "Donut? If you don't take your pick now, Beck will eat them."

"Will he?"

"Oh, for a doctor, Beck has a surprisingly hard-core sweet tooth. I'm telling you, eat your favorite now. Once we get there, I can't guarantee you'll get anything but crumbs."

"I'm fond of these apple fritters." Zach filched it and took a big bite.

"Just like your brother. I'm swiping this Boston cream. Let's not tell anyone. Just...mix those around. No one will know."

With a conspiratorial glint in his eyes, Zach did. "Our secret."

Just like all the feelings they grappled with following their respective losses. No one else would understand anyway.

Seth was licking the last of the donut from his fingers and noticing Zach do the same when they pulled up in front of River and Dean's new place. Beck and Heavenly had already arrived, as had most everyone who had agreed to help. "You ready?"

"I've raised a barn in a day. I think I can move a little furniture."

With a glance between Beck's brother and the new house, he shrugged. "You'd think. But never underestimate this gang's ability to take something mundane and turn it into a—excuse my language—shitshow."

Zach shrugged. "I figured. Let's go."

Beck breathed a sigh of relief as he caught sight of Seth and Zach marching up the walkway to River and Dean's new pad, box of donuts in hand and smiles on their faces. He curled his arm around Heavenly. "Look."

She did, then sent him a soft stare. "He's okay."

"Seems like they both are." And thank god. Beck didn't know why Seth had been determined to see his brother this morning, but whatever words they'd exchanged had apparently given them both some peace. "Hey!"

Seth met his stare first and responded with a thumbs-up. "I brought donuts, so if you need a little fuel before we get started..."

"Apple fritter?" Beck asked hopefully.

Cooper repressed a smile. "Sorry. They were completely out. But you can prowl through the rest and find something you like."

"What a shame." Zach looked as if he was trying not to laugh.

Clearly, those two were up to something, but if the secret helped them coexist—and even bond—Beck didn't need to know. He was just grateful.

Seth handed him the box and waved to Hammer and Liam, who stood just inside the open door.

Raine came barreling out behind them. "Donuts?"

Without warning, she plucked the box from Beck's hands.

"Hey!" he called after her. "What the—"

"Pregnant woman with hormones here. Don't mess with me." She gripped the white container of fried pastries and shot him a glare that warned him that if he touched the box, he risked losing a hand.

Liam approached. "Best to let it go, mate. You want to keep all your appendages, I assume."

"Seriously. Take our word for it," Hammer added. "The closer she gets to her due date..."

"The more you placate the princess?" he quipped.

The Irishman pulled at the back of his neck. "Something like that. We'll make it up to you."

Medically, Beck understood pregnancy cravings, but he'd been looking forward to a little sugar boost, damn it. "I'll live."

Raine turned to Heavenly. "Want one, honey?"

The brunette flashed him a saccharine grin that said she was pleased with herself, especially since she knew he couldn't do a damn thing about her attitude. The little shit.

Beck stepped closer and dropped a whisper in her ear. "I still own that rubber paddle."

Raine swallowed a mouth full of donut and stuck out her tongue. "Good for you. I have a whole box of donuts." Then she grabbed Heavenly's arm and led her inside. "Chocolate or sprinkles?"

Beck glanced up at Liam and Hammer, who both looked chagrined.

He raised a brow at them. "You boys are keeping track of this shit, right?"

"You bet I am," Hammer drawled. "And I'm looking forward to the moment the doctor clears her ass for punishment."

Liam nodded. "She won't sit right for a month. Maybe two."

Beck smiled and clapped the Irishman on the shoulder. "Excellent."

"But you won't care much about donuts in a bit," Liam promised. "There's something else going on. Watch the front door today."

He frowned the Irishman's way. "What do you mean?"

"Trouble is brewing... I can feel it."

"If anyone thinks they're going to pull some shit, I'm packing," Jericho said, appearing behind him.

"Not that kind of trouble, mate. But this should shake things up."

With that ominous prediction, Liam ambled toward the house.

"Everyone is here now, right?" River called out the front door to all the new arrivals, donut in hand.

"Almost. Psycho is at doggie daycare and—"

"You named your dog Psycho?" Zach blinked.

"Yeah, it fit when he was a puppy. He ate wallpaper, for fuck's sake. Anyway, Pike is on his way with the truck. And my sister, Miri, will be swinging by as soon as she can get free." Dean glowered at River. "Listen, she's young and a little sheltered. Be nice."

"Absolutely. I would never want to offend your little sister. I'm just looking forward to meeting her. I'm glad you two are working on your relationship."

"Thanks." Then Dean called out to everyone, "Come check out the new digs!"

Still grumbling that Raine had swiped the donuts, Beck stepped inside, watching Dean and River stand in the middle of their living room, turning in slow circles on the hardwood floors and grinning like loons.

From the outside, the house looked like a typical three-bedroom, two-bath beige stucco bungalow. But inside, the rooms were large, the layout open and inviting, even without a stick of furniture. It had the makings of a decent bachelor pad…or a solid starter home.

It would be interesting to see which prevailed.

"Dude," River bellowed. "We bought a house. A freaking house!"

"I know. It's fucking epic." Dean beamed. "No more shitty apartments. We can bring hookups to our *house*."

"*And* we have a private playroom." River slapped Dean a high five.

"We're going to get so much pussy now." Dean laughed.

"There's only one pussy I want between us, man," River said. "I'm telling you, once you have her…"

"I'll be hooked. I know. You keep saying that."

"Trust me. One taste of Jasmine's sweetness, and you'll crave hers."

Beck could relate to that. He was like a junkie when it came to Heavenly.

"TMI, guys," Raine drawled derisively, clinging to Hammer and Liam as both men massaged the small of her back while she guarded what was left of the donuts.

In all fairness, the princess looked miserable. Her pregnant belly stuck out like a damn beachball—and she still had two months until her due date. The strain the twins were putting on her petite body showed in her eyes, her attitude, and every waddling step she took. Still, the fact that Raine wasn't on total bed rest yet was one more testament to her strength and perseverance.

Outside, the blare of a horn had Dean's and River's grins widening.

"Pike's here with the truck," Dean howled like a child on Christmas morning.

"If that cockbag fucked up any of our shit, I'll break his neck."

"Lighten up, man. He's doing us a solid, borrowing the truck from some pal of his, which saves us the cash, and—"

"No. He's doing *you* a favor," River corrected. "He wouldn't bother to piss on me if I was on fire."

"Still, don't be an ungrateful prick. And for fuck's sake, don't bring up banging Jasmine—at least not before we get the truck unloaded."

River groused but shoved his animosity aside, then sent Dean a head bob, gesturing him out the door. The cop raced onto the porch. Beck heard Raine's brother curse under his breath.

"Hang tight, precious. I'll grab the first chair off the truck so you can get off your feet." Hammer pressed a kiss to Raine's forehead, then eased her into Liam's arms.

Seth frowned. "I can get you one, too, angel."

Heavenly waved him away. "I'm not seven months pregnant with twins, and I didn't come to sit."

"I didn't come to sit, either." Raine patted her round belly. "But these two have other ideas. I can still help, though. As soon as someone brings in the kitchen table, I can unpack the dishes and stuff."

"Perfect. You're great in the kitchen, so you can tell me how to organize everything. I'll put it away."

"Because lord knows neither of these two bozos will think about anything that practical." Raine rolled her eyes.

"Ever," Heavenly agreed.

"How about I find that table?" Beck offered, softly pressing his lips to Heavenly's.

As he eased back, Seth swooped in and stole a kiss of his own, then lifted with a wink. "And I'll start bringing in kitchen boxes."

Beck clapped the PI on the back as they strolled outside together. "So you and Zach had a good conversation?"

"We did. We understand each other now. And I told him he can come to me anytime the grief or the anger is too much. But honestly? He's doing decent."

"That's a relief...but it sounds like what you're saying is that he's not doing great."

"Nope, and he won't be for a while." Seth swallowed. "I apologized to him for being an asshole when he first left Messiah City. I think we're square now. But I need to apologize to you."

Relief filled Beck, even as Seth's words choked him up. "Given everything you've been through, there's no need. Feelings are feelings; they're not right or wrong. They just are. You were dealing with shit I can't even begin to fathom. When Zach first learned of his loss, I didn't realize it would trigger yours. I could have been more understanding and less snarly."

Seth shook his head. "You were worried about Heavenly and her feelings."

"I was."

"As you should have been."

Beck nodded. "But I was worried about you, too."

Seth pierced him with a surprised stare. "Me? I'm solid. I just... needed a minute."

Solid? Mostly, Beck supposed. There were still holes in the big guy's story, but just like the last time he'd thought about asking, now wasn't the right moment. "Good to hear. So...should we see what these two clowns packed for their slick new bachelor pad?"

"I'm afraid." Seth snorted. "If they brought blow-up dolls, I'm not touching that shit."

"Oh, fuck, no." Beck shuddered.

With a laugh, he and Seth approached the truck. River and Dean stood at the curb as Pike climbed from the cab.

"What took you so long?" River barked.

Pike lifted his chin. "Seriously? I didn't *have* to show up today and I certainly didn't *have* to borrow this truck to haul your crap across town."

"You didn't, but we truly appreciate your help," Dean placated, scowling at River.

"*You* do. This asshole doesn't." Pike thumbed at River. "Anyway, I would have been here sooner, but some fidiot blew through a red light and caused an accident, so I had to take a detour."

"It's all good, man. I'm just glad you weren't involved." Dean slapped Pike on the shoulder as Hammer yanked the door up at the back of the truck.

Peering at the color-coded stickers on River's boxes, Beck had to shake his head. He busted Seth's balls all the time for anal-retentively arranging his socks and underwear. It looked like River was cut from the same cloth. "Another freaking perfectionist. No wonder he and Seth work so well together."

Hammer smirked. "Are you surprised, Dr. Beckman? Surely you know that perfectionism is just another form of control."

"I do, but I'd rather express mine with ropes and cuffs." Beck grinned as he passed a chair down to Hammer for Raine.

"You and me both." Macen chuckled, heading inside to settle his girl.

Short minutes later, Heavenly and Raine were tackling the kitchen while the others hauled furniture and assorted boxes off the truck and into the house. Each time Beck entered the place, his gaze stilled on Heavenly. And each time, as if sensing his presence, she flashed him a sweet smile or a flirty wink that warmed his heart.

After depositing Dean's dresser in his bedroom, Beck and Seth retraced their steps, abruptly ducking into the kitchen to give River and Dean, who wrangled a heavy St. Andrews cross through the front door, plenty of room to maneuver. From the corner of his eye, Beck saw Heavenly pause and study the piece of dungeon equipment.

"What's that wooden thing they're carrying in?"

Her question reminded him that, while he and Seth had introduced her to a lot of BDSM play, she'd still never visited anything that remotely looked like a dungeon. Two months ago, she'd insisted they teach her about what went on at Hammer's club, Shadows. They had...but they hadn't.

He exchanged a glance with Seth, who winced. Yeah, Cooper was aware they'd held back. Beck had his reasons for hesitating. He should probably check with Seth about his, then discuss how they could fulfill their promise.

"She doesn't know?" Jericho murmured just loud enough for Beck to hear. "Wow."

Raine smothered a grin, then turned, sending him and Seth an arched brow. "Boys?"

Seth scowled at her, then took Heavenly by the elbow. "It's something we need to introduce you to, angel."

"In good time." Beck fisted the messy bun on top of her head and leaned in close to her ear. "I promise."

The tiny lines between Heavenly's brows deepened as she watched Dean, River, and the cross disappear inside the playroom. "Why not today?"

"We'll talk about it when we get home, but now isn't the time."

"I know we're busy helping the guys move, but—"

"That's not it. This house isn't that big, there's a whole lot of people here, and... River?" Beck called down the hall. "Is the playroom soundproofed yet?"

"Haven't had time."

"That's why." Seth punctuated his reply with a tight smile. "Unless you want everyone to hear you scream."

Heavenly's eyes widened and her cheeks flushed pink. "We'll wait until we get home."

"Good choice," Raine muttered.

Dean stopped short as he entered his bedroom. "Whoever hauled my dresser in, thank you."

"You're welcome," Beck and Seth replied in unison.

"I'm going to unpack my clothes from these boxes so I can move around in here. Holler if there's anything else heavy that needs lugging."

"Most of the truck is already unpacked," River announced from the playroom. "Liam and Hammer are bringing in the sofa, and there's not much left after that."

"We'll get your big-screen mounted," Beck told the guys as he and Seth gathered near the pale gray wall in the living room to assemble the mount.

At the sounds of masculine grunts, River strode from the playroom. Beck followed the noise and found Liam and Hammer wrestling a long leather couch through the front door, right behind the recliner Jericho lugged in.

"Shit. Let me help you guys." River rushed toward them.

"We got it, mate," Liam assured. "But Pike might need a hand with your mattress."

"On it."

As River raced out the door, Liam and Hammer lowered the couch, centering it beneath a big picture window against the wall. Coupled with the tables, art, and other touches, the place was starting to look like a real home.

Hammer stood upright and stretched, then frowned when Liam glanced at his watch. "You keep checking the time. You got a hot date or something?"

"He'd better not, or I'll bitch-slap a heifer into next week," Raine threatened, pinning the Irishman with a fierce glare.

"There'll be no need to bitch-slap anyone, love," Liam stressed. "Just waiting for the storm…"

Since the skies were perfectly clear, he didn't mean the weather.

"You're serious. When?" Hammer shot him a dissecting stare.

"Not too much longer." Liam glanced at the door.

"What do you see?" Raine asked pensively.

Beck wondered the same thing. Liam had called it trouble earlier. Honestly, Beck didn't need more shit in his life. No one here did.

"Something you won't believe until you see it with your own eyes. But you should be braced."

"For what?" Raine demanded.

"Hold up," River gritted out as he and Pike struggled to get the mattress through the portal, interrupting whatever Liam might have said. "I'm losing my grip."

"Lift it. Or do you need to work out more?" Pike groused.

Maybe the storm Liam was predicting had something to do with these two pricks vying for the same girl's attention? Maybe they were about to settle things the old-fashioned way—with a bloody fistfight.

While River repositioned his hands, Pike's muscles strained beneath the bulk of the mattress.

"Here, let me help." Zach dumped the box in his arms on the porch.

"I got it," Pike growled over his shoulder.

"*I* got it," River snarled.

"Whatever." Zach plucked the box up again before breezing past the pair and heading down the hallway.

He and River dumped the mattress just inside the door, the junior PI panting.

"While you catch your breath, cupcake, I'm going to hit the head," Pike announced.

"I'll alert the media," River shot back with a smirk.

Pike flipped him the middle finger as he ambled down the hallway.

"I hate that fucking douche nozzle," River muttered.

"Tell us how you really feel," Seth drawled.

While the two PIs exchanged barbs, Beck caught sight of a willowy redhead carrying a stack of pizza boxes who paused just inside the front door.

"Here we go…" Liam whispered.

Raine looked up, then let loose a squeal of surprise. "Jasmine?"

Beck pivoted. *Jasmine? The Jasmine?*

"What are you doing here?" Heavenly flashed the redhead a welcoming smile as she helped Raine from her chair. "It's good to see you."

Beside him, Seth and Hammer stared at the woman in slack-jawed surprise.

Mere feet from her, River whirled around like an F-5 tornado, locking his stunned stare on her. "Jasmine?" Before the girl could say a word, he ate up what little distance there was between them. "You're really fucking here."

She looked equally stunned. "Why are you here?"

"What do you mean? I live here." As white-hot rage overcame his initial surprise, River ripped the pizza boxes from her arms and tossed them onto the couch. Then he cinched her slender wrists in his big hand, dragged her arms over her head, and pinned her to the wall. "You want to tell me where the fuck you've been?"

"I-I…" she stammered.

"You what?"

Electricity charged the air. The flicker of panic in Jasmine's eyes had Beck's protective instincts pegging red. He crossed the room, Seth at his side, who stood shoulder to shoulder with Hammer and Liam.

Zach moved in next, Jericho right beside him, silently vowing, like the others, to intervene if River took things too far.

Heavenly and Raine raced from the kitchen to reach Jasmine. In tandem, he and Seth snagged an arm around their girl, tucking her between them, while Liam and Hammer did the same with Raine.

"Let me go. I don't owe you an answer." The redhead glared at River, looking angrier by the moment.

"I saved your fucking life. And how did you repay me? By walking out in the middle of the night. You just disappeared."

Jasmine shook her head. "The night was over. I got out of your hair. I didn't—"

"Mean to fuck my brains out, sneak out of my bed without even telling me your name, then vanish into thin air?"

As a rush of red climbed her chest and stained her cheeks, Jasmine pressed her lips into a thin, angry line. "Thank you so much for telling everyone here that we slept together."

"Oh, we didn't *sleep*, sweetheart," River scoffed. "We fucked. For hours. In every way imaginable. After you milked me dry and I passed out, you took off. No name. No number. No note. No nothing."

"Shut up, big brother," Raine snapped, still clasped between Hammer and Liam. "It would serve you right if she kneed your balls straight to your sinuses. Maybe you could try being nice?"

Beck was still grimacing when a feral growl rolled from the hallway behind him. "River? Get your fucking hands off my sister." He turned his furious gaze to the redhead. His face softened with concern. "You okay, Miri?"

River turned his scowl on Dean. "Miri? No, this is Jasmine. The Jasmine I keep telling you about."

"No, that's my sister, Miri. Wait…" His scowl turned deadly as he charged into the room and passed Beck. "*This* is the woman you spent the night with? You *fucked* my sister?"

Dean's bellow was deafening. In the wake of his demand, a terrible silence prevailed.

Liam broke it with a soft whisper. "Didn't see that coming now, did you?"

Beck hadn't, but shit was about to get real. No one said a word. They were probably trying to process their shock, just like he was.

Pike ambled into the room, the sounds of the toilet running faint in the background, and frowned. "What the... Jasmine is *your* sister?" Pike leaned against the wall near the kitchen and howled with laughter. "Oh, my god, this is epic."

It was epic, all right—an epic disaster. Ugly was written all over it.

"Why does everyone keep calling her Jasmine, for fuck's sake?" Dean tossed up his hands.

"That's how she introduced herself," Pike shot back, then he turned to her. "That's not your name?"

"That's the name I prefer." Jasmine sent her brother a withering glare. "I've told you that."

Dean winced. "You've always been Miri to me."

"I'm not a kid anymore," she snapped, then struggled against River's hold again. "I told you to let me go."

He held firm. "You're really Dean's sister?"

"Yes," Dean growled. "Now get your hands off her, cocksucker, before I kill you."

River didn't flinch—or obey. He simply seared Jasmine with a dissecting stare. "Are you?"

"Yes," she hissed, jerking free from his grasp and wriggling from beneath his body.

Heavenly lunged toward her, clearly wanting to comfort her friend. He and Seth held her back.

"Stay here, angel." She didn't belong in the middle of the drama, not when the air sizzled with fury and retribution.

"How? Why?" River mumbled, his stunned stare still bouncing between the siblings. A split second later, his confusion morphed into anger. "And what is your real goddamn name?"

"It's Miracle," Dean spat. "Jasmine is her *middle* name—something I've never called her in my life!"

"All my friends call me Jasmine," she cut in.

They both ignored her.

"How the hell was I supposed to know that?" River asked.

"Now that you do, back the fuck off! You don't touch her, talk to her, or look at her again. In fact, you don't even think about her."

"Like hell!" River challenged. "You know how long I spent trying to find her."

"Oh, I do. I also know exactly what you planned to do to her once you did." Dean poked a finger into River's chest. "And that is *never* going to happen."

Jasmine scowled. "Do to me?"

Beck hoped like fuck River had the presence of mind not to answer that question. He didn't think the redhead would take it well.

"Yeah. He intended to fuck you again—while he *shared* you with me," Dean growled.

Jasmine gaped. "Shared me...sexually?"

River sent her a sheepish stare. "That was before I knew he was your brother and—"

"But if he wasn't my brother, you were going to pass me back and forth with your buddy like a plate of hors d'oeuvres? Were you even going to ask me first?"

"Don't worry, Miri. He'll never touch you again. Ever." Dean narrowed his eyes on River. "I *know* how perverted you are. I know first-hand all the twisted shit you love doing to women. Did you fuck my sister as dirty and nasty as you do all the others?"

"Dean!" Jasmine screeched, grabbing her brother by the arm.

He shook her off. "Don't, Miri. I'm hanging by a thread here, and I need to say some things to this steaming sack of shit."

"I don't give a fuck what you say," River warned, narrowing his eyes.

"You should because I'm going to fucking kill you. You did way more than touch my sister. Shit, you popped her cherry. You stole my little sister's *virginity*. Motherfucker..."

"I didn't know she was your sister," River barked.

"And all those hours you rambled on about how hot, wet, and tight her pussy was, about all the kinky shit you did to her and how much she liked it... All that time you were talking about my *little sister!*"

"I didn't *know*," River bit out between clenched teeth.

"You *told* him?" Jasmine whirled on River, clearly livid.

"I didn't know he was your brother."

Her eyes bulged. "That makes it okay?"

"Well, I just… No, but—"

"Oh, River spent days and nights waxing poetic about your tits," Dean cut in with a sarcastic smile. "He especially couldn't stop talking about your nipples and all the hours he feasted on them."

Jasmine tensed her delicate jaw, fists clenched, as she faced River. "You're a pig."

"Yep. And you should know how impressed he was that a virgin could be so uninhibited and love all the kinky shit he did to you. I heard about it. In detail." He glowered at River, veins throbbing in his neck. "I know your MO, you sick piece of shit. You made her beg so you could get off. You made my *little sister* fucking beg you."

Suddenly, River's smile turned ugly. "You know I did. And she begged so, so sweetly."

Beck sighed and shook his head.

"You really are a pig." Raine punched her brother in the arm. "And a bastard."

"Try asshole," Jasmine grated out.

"That, too." Raine crossed her arms over her chest. "You might apologize."

River sucked in a furious breath, obviously trying to grab control of his temper. "I'm sorry."

Tears filled Jasmine's eyes. The poor girl was keeping herself together by sheer will. "No, you're not. You'd have to have feelings to actually be sorry. What you are is full of shit."

"Oh, she just handed you your balls." Pike laughed. "Classic."

Dean whipped around, slashing him with a hateful glare. "Did you fuck her, too?"

"Dean!" Jasmine objected.

The tattooed DM raised his hands, adamantly shaking his head. "No, man. I've never touched her. I swear."

"Not for lack of trying," River growled.

Beck closed his eyes and shook his head. This four-alarm blaze hardly needed more fuel.

"Keep it that way if you want to live," Dean snarled.

"I can't believe you told my brother everything we did in detail," Jasmine railed at River.

"Listen to me," he gasped. "Jasmine…"

"I heard about every whimper, moan, and"—Dean grimaced—"orgasm he dragged out of you, Miri. And he told me more than once that he wanted to cry like a baby when he squeezed his filthy dick in your—"

"Don't say it," River bellowed.

"Ass," Dean finished. "Your *virgin* ass!"

"Stop!" Jasmine screamed. "Not another word. I hate you both right now."

A humorless grin kicked up a corner of River's mouth. "You might not want to hate me until we've established whether or not you're pregnant, sweetheart."

Dean blanched and pinned his sister with a look of disbelief. Then, nostrils flaring, he turned his focus back on River, his face mottled, his chest heaving. "You took my little sister *bareback?*"

River shrugged. "It happened so fast and—"

With a roar of pure, unadulterated rage, Dean charged River.

Pike snagged an arm around Jasmine's waist and pulled her to safety as Dean landed a right hook on River's jaw. His head snapped back. Both Heavenly and Raine screamed, but that didn't stop Dean, who whaled an upper cut into River's jaw that had his teeth snapping shut with grating force and blood dripping down his chin.

"Fuck," Seth muttered.

"Good thing I brought my medical bag," Beck drawled. "Both these idiots will likely need mending."

"Stop it!" Jasmine called, struggling to break from Pike's grasp.

He held tight. "You need to let them work it out. This is what men do. They're just marking their territory."

"I'm not a fire hydrant," she spat, twisting free.

"Dude, is this how you want to settle things?" River spit blood onto the hardwoods. "Really?"

"I'd rather just shoot you," Dean sneered. "But you'll suffer longer under my fists."

River snorted. "You wish."

He was still smirking when, like a rocket, his fist launched, colliding with Dean's nose.

Then it was on. Fists began to blur as blood sprayed through the air. Blows landed. Bones crunched. Curses echoed off the walls.

Seth shook his head. "What a fucking mess."

Yes, and a horrific end to any chance that River and Dean would someday share their futures with a woman. They'd spent months planning, preparing, and saving for their special someone. In less than an hour, it was all down the toilet.

"We should break this up before they kill each other," Beck muttered.

"Sadly, yes." Jericho sighed. "My money would be on River, but if they killed each other the paperwork would be a bitch."

"True." Seth nodded, setting Heavenly behind them. "Stay back."

Liam and Hammer followed, doing the same with their princess. Then, in unison, the five of them, along with Zach, stepped into the fray. Hammer and Beck pried Dean to one side of the room. Seth and Liam pulled River to the other. Zach and Jericho stood between them as sentries. River and Dean continued glaring daggers of hate, chests heaving with rage.

Arms banded around Dean, Beck ignored the blood dripping onto his shirt sleeve and glanced over his shoulder to check on Heavenly. The horror etched on her face—on Raine's and Jasmine's too—told him they'd never witnessed this kind of caveman violence.

Sensing his concern, Heavenly sent him an unsettled half smile.

"Easy. Calm down," Hammer urged both men.

Pike, the demented fuck, leaned against a nearby wall and laughed hysterically.

"Shut up, asshole," Beck snapped.

It wouldn't be easy, but they had to defuse this situation and somehow find neutral ground.

"I wasn't done pounding his face." Dean tried to lurch from Beck's grip.

"He's not worth breaking your knuckles," Beck growled in low tones.

"You're right. Forget my knuckles. I'm going to kill that cocksucker in his sleep. I will stab a knife through his fucking heart and smile."

"No, you won't," Beck muttered. "If you did, you'd lose your job, and you wouldn't last a day in jail with all the criminals you put there. Even if you did, you're too pretty to go to prison and not end up somebody's bitch."

"Yeah, so fuck you," River hurled across the room.

"It'd be worth it," Dean bit out.

"Who will protect Jasmine if you and River are both dead?" Beck asked. "Pike?"

"You're not helping," Dean snarled.

"Calm the fuck down and I'll let you go."

Dean dragged in a handful of deep breaths, then gave him a choppy nod. "I'm good."

"Are you? Give me your word you'll behave."

"Don't push me." Dean rolled his shoulders, shrugging Beck off.

"I'm serious, fucker."

Dean ignored him.

On the far side of the room, Seth released River, who also eyed the cop as if plotting his death. But instead of antagonizing Dean again, he turned to Jasmine. "Could you be pregnant?"

She hesitated, then gave a soft shake of her head. "No."

Raine sighed in relief. "That's a good thing."

Beck agreed, but River didn't look quite so thrilled. Had he *wanted* her to be pregnant?

Jasmine looked so vulnerable, and Heavenly reached out to clasp her hands. "How can we help?"

Beck's heart filled. Damn, he loved this woman.

"Right now, there's nothing you can do." Jasmine shook her head. "I have to get out of here."

"Of course. I'll come with you," she offered, sending Beck a pleading stare.

Yeah, Heavenly didn't want her to be alone. There was his girl's tender heart again.

"You're so sweet, but... This is ridiculous. I moved away from home to escape drama. I certainly didn't come here for more."

"Don't let these jerks chase you off." Raine sent both River and Dean angry glares. "Come sit in the kitchen with us. We'll talk this out, girl-style."

"Later, okay? I-I just can't be around them right now—either of them."

Heavenly and Raine exchanged a glance, then his girl squeezed Jasmine's hand. "We understand."

"More than you realize," Raine drawled.

Heavenly nodded. "And we're here for you whenever you're ready."

"Exactly. Then we'll talk, vent, scream, or cry. Trust us, Jasmine, we've both lost our minds over men more than once." Raine smirked.

"As soon as I process all of this, I'll likely take you up on that. You two are my lifelines to sanity now."

"Good. Just…text one of us to let us know you got home okay?" Heavenly hugged her gently. "Please."

"Sure."

Dean ambled up with an apologetic grimace, wiping blood from his nose with the hem of his tee.

But before the cop could say a word, Pike stepped in front of Jasmine. "I know you're upset. Let me drive you home."

"Back off." Dean shoved Pike aside. "I need to talk to her before she goes."

"No, you back off—all of you," Jasmine huffed. "I'm not talking to anyone with a penis for the rest of the day."

"Come on, Miri, don't be like that. We need to work this out and—"

"Unbelievable." She turned on him. "Did you even hear a word I said?"

He sighed. "I know you want to be alone. Fine. I—"

"Yes, but I also don't want to be called Miri anymore. I'm not a miracle; I'm just a woman who wants a normal life."

"Fine…Jasmine." Dean raised his hands and sighed. "Will you call me once you've had some time so we can talk?"

"It may take a couple days," she warned.

"That's fine. Just promise you'll call?"

Jasmine nodded curtly, waved goodbye to the girls, then headed for the door.

Beck couldn't help but admire the woman. She had spine and grit. Even after her brother had recounted her whole night with River in detail for a roomful of strangers, she still left with her head held high.

As Jasmine neared the portal, River darted around her and blocked her path. "Don't go. Please. We need to talk."

"I have *nothing* to say to you."

"Then let me talk." He reached out to take her arm, then seemed to think better of it. "I'm sorry."

"For what? Thinking the only redeeming qualities I possess are my lady bits? Or for telling my brother, who in turn told everyone here, all the details of our night together? Or for thinking that once you fucked me, you owned me and could just share me with any of your pals?"

"Okay, I get that now maybe isn't the time to sort this out. Just… give me your number." River yanked his cell phone from his pocket. "Please. I'll call you in a couple of days, once we've both had time to think. We can meet up for—"

"You don't need my number. Since you and my brother share women and houses and god knows what else, if I need to send you a message, I'll tell him so he can pass it on. Until then, get out of my way." Jasmine flashed a brittle smile and sidestepped River before strolling out the door.

He gaped after her, jaw hanging open wide. Beck just shook his head. Clearly, Raine's brother had zero experience being snubbed by a woman, especially a strong-willed, independent one. Outside the bedroom, he had tons to learn about the fairer sex.

"Wait!" River yelled, hurrying onto the porch after her.

Dean grabbed him from behind. "Leave my sister alone."

"Here we go again," Hammer groaned.

"Yep." Beck dropped a kiss to Heavenly's forehead before trekking after them. Aware of Pike following, he glanced over his shoulder and arched a brow. "You going to shut your trap and help separate McGregor and Liddell this time?"

"Who?" Pike stared at Beck blankly.

Clearly, the man was not an MMA fan.

"I'm not helping those idiots. I'm going to watch and gloat."

"Gloat?"

"Yeah. River proved he's not only an insensitive manwhore but a dumb fuck. And he just handed Jasmine to me on a silver platter." Pike shot him a smug smile as they stepped outside.

Talk about a dumb fuck…

"You've got to get past the friend zone with her first," Beck pointed out.

"I'm working on it," Pike muttered.

With a squeal of tires, Jasmine jetted down the street. On the patch of grass in the front yard, Dean and River rolled around, exchanging punches and insults.

"You fucking leave my sister alone!" Dean rammed his fist into River's kidney.

"I'll do anything I want with her, shit stain." River slammed a fist in the cop's gut. "I know exactly how to make her scream."

Zach rushed toward Beck. "Shouldn't you stop them again?"

"We will. In a minute. Clearly, they need to bleed out some of their anger." Beck spotted a middle-aged brunette striding their way from the house next door. "Shit."

This was definitely a bad time for Dean and River to meet their new neighbor.

Zach turned and caught sight of the newcomer. "That's not good."

"Hang tight. I'll be right back." Beck hurried across the driveway, trying his best to shield the brawl with his body while forcing a fake-as-fuck smile. "Hi."

"Welcome to the neighborhood. I see you're moving in. I'm—"

"Just because you fucked every one of my little sister's holes doesn't give you any right to touch her, cocksucker," Dean bellowed.

The woman's eyes nearly popped out of her head as she slapped a hand over her mouth in shock.

"I'm not your new neighbor. They are." He gestured toward the former friends still beating the hell out of each other, then back to the woman with an apologetic smile. "Sorry."

"You keep talking about Jasmine like she's a kid. When I fucked her all night, I more than proved she's a goddamn adult," River roared. "Which is more than I can say for you."

"Excuse me. I'll just...quiet them down." Beck darted into the melee to help the others separate the pissed-off pair.

"That's it. Load your shit back on the truck and find someplace else to live." Dean shoved at River, who was being pulled away by Beck and Seth.

"And forfeit my half of the down payment for this place?" River scoffed. "Dream on, douchebag. You pack up your shit and get the fuck out."

"Suck my dick. I'm not leaving."

"Suck it yourself, asshole. I'm not going anywhere, either," Raine's brother snarled.

Dean and River's friendship—the connection they'd spent years building—was severed for good. There was no coming back from something like this. Worse, how could they possibly coexist in the house they owned together?

"Maybe you should hire a hooker to come suck you both off," Pike chimed in.

Beck pondered getting the ball gag from the toy bag in his trunk and shoving it in the asshole's mouth, but the neighbor had probably been shocked enough for one day.

Liam tsked and shook his head before turning toward Pike. "You and River should get on the same page and make friends."

The two men gaped at each other before turning matching scowls Liam's way.

"Fuck that shit," Pike barked.

River wiped the blood from his nose. "That is *never* going to happen."

A little smile played at Liam's lips. "Famous last words..."

C H A P T E R
T E N

Late July

"Buckle up, everyone," Beck quipped as he climbed into the backseat of Seth's SUV and secured his seat belt. "A weekend with Gloria in Vegas is always unpredictable, but since she's decided to get married at the last minute? Expect an epic level of crazy."

Beck certainly did. He was thrilled his ex-wife and her plumber fiancé were tying the knot...but also a little envious. He was more than ready to begin his future with Seth and Heavenly. Certainly when he'd divorced Gloria to marry his girl, Beck had never anticipated his ex would get hitched first.

Since they'd helped River and Dean move into their place seven weeks ago, he, Seth, and Heavenly had settled into something like domestic bliss. Almost. Sure, they'd all been busy, working and helping Raine, Liam, and Hammer prepare for their coming twins, due in roughly a week. They'd also spent a stupid amount of time refereeing Dean and River's battles. But they still had two unresolved issues that bugged the hell out of Beck.

First, Seth still hadn't completely come clean about his past. When he'd asked the PI to explain the holes in his story, he'd ducked, dodged, and changed the subject. Beck hadn't pried; he could give the guy a little more time. Obviously, Seth's tragedy had scarred and shaped him. Undoing that would take time. Unfortunately, Beck was getting impatient because he was almost certain that problem fed into the other. Seth still refused to ditch the condoms. Granted, he hadn't pushed to get Heavenly on the pill...but he wasn't ready for a family. Beck was—now.

Something had to give.

In front of him, Heavenly buckled up in the passenger's seat. "I can't believe she called you yesterday to say she's getting married on Saturday. Who plans a wedding in three days?"

Beck shrugged. "Gloria."

Seth started the SUV. "She doesn't seem impulsive. Obviously, you know her a lot better…"

"She's not," Beck confirmed. "But once she makes up her mind to do something, she wants it done right now."

Seth laughed as he backed out of the driveway and headed for the highway to Vegas. "Meaning she wants Buddy done right now."

Heavenly tried to frown but was clearly repressing a laugh. "That's a horrible way to put it."

"But accurate." He gestured between himself and Beck. "Trust me, we heard it."

Beck grimaced. "Don't remind me. I'm scarred for life." At Heavenly's confusion, he caressed her elbow. "Don't ask. You're better off not knowing."

"No. Now you have to tell me," she insisted.

Beck sighed. "That night you stopped in Vegas and Gloria coaxed you into drinking wine, Seth and I showed up to collect you, right? While you were sleeping off your drunk, he and I had to share the bedroom next to her and Buddy."

"They spent the entire night getting busy…*loudly*," Seth added.

Blue eyes wide with mirth, Heavenly giggled. "Really?"

"You have *no* idea. I mean, everyone deserves a good sex life, but this time our room will be as far from theirs as possible," Beck vowed.

"Amen. That way, we can get even louder," Seth drawled.

"I hope so." Heavenly blushed. "I missed you both last night."

It had been a rare occurrence that neither he nor Seth had been home.

"Sorry, little girl. That emergency surgery was a bitch. It took a lot longer than I expected. But I'm not on call this weekend, so the next mangled artery is Dr. Simmons's problem."

"Will the patient be okay?" she asked.

Heavenly always had a soft heart.

"Yeah. And I'm pretty sure that kid will think twice about skateboarding in an abandoned factory while he's high again."

"Let's hope," Seth remarked. "But I still think you had it easier. When I dropped River off at his place after last night's stakeout, I ended up playing peacemaker again. I swear, those two are like petty old women."

"Another argument?" Heavenly rolled her eyes. "Raine says River constantly complains about Dean. What started this one?"

"Dean ate River's leftover pizza—on purpose. So at four a.m. when I dropped him off, that snack he'd been looking forward to was gone. Fireworks ensued."

"Jesus, the idiot couldn't make a fucking sandwich?" Beck asked.

"I'm not sure they do anything as practical as shop for groceries. They're both too focused on one-upping each other." Seth groaned. "You ought to see the place now. Let's just say that Dean took over the decorating, and that isn't a good thing."

Heavenly gaped. "What did he do?"

"Hang *Dogs Playing Poker* everywhere?" Beck drawled.

"Worse." Seth shook his head. "He's slapped up pictures of Jasmine —as a little girl with pigtails and braces and missing front teeth. In a Girl Scout uniform and at dance recitals, way before training bras, and doing things like playing with Barbie. They're on every wall, every surface. There's even one of her as a toddler in the john. Dean told me that was in case River felt compelled to jack off to thoughts of his sister in the shower."

Beck howled. "It's horrible and underhanded. I like it."

"Right?" Seth agreed. "But River got the last word in. He snapped a picture of Jasmine, um…post-coital, looking all soft and sated in his bed. He blew it up to poster size and hung it in his room, where it's totally visible from the hallway. So every time Dean has to use the can…he has to walk past that image."

"He didn't!" Heavenly looked scandalized.

"Oh, he did," Seth confirmed. "And he's proud of it."

Beck just shook his head. "So things are going really well at the swinging bachelor pad, huh?"

Seth shook his head. "Be glad you don't work with either of them. Every fucking day I hear about some new, petty disagreement. I'm ready to duct-tape River's mouth shut. I swear, there's no enemy like a former friend. They know exactly how to push each other's buttons."

"Hammer and Liam proved that before they got smart and took Raine together," Beck pointed out.

"You two weren't exactly slouches in the prank department," Heavenly scolded. "I still have nightmares about Madame Zelda and Clovis."

"Hey, maybe that would have been a good show." Beck flashed her a cheesy grin.

"Bite your tongue, mister," she scolded.

"Well, we might have pranked, but just like Liam and Hammer, we worked it out by taking the girl together. Since Jasmine is Dean's sister and River is too hung up on her to walk away, that's not going to happen."

"And they're both too stubborn to move out. Men." Heavenly rolled her eyes. "River has to stop following her like a stalker."

"I'm trying to keep him busy with cases." Seth shrugged. "But the stupid bastard is single-minded."

Beck leaned in. "Like a dog with a juicy bone. Don't you think it's interesting that he keeps insisting he doesn't have feelings for her, but he won't back the hell off?"

"He's lying to himself. One hundred percent." Seth nodded.

"Yep," Beck agreed. "Is Pike getting anywhere with her?"

They both turned to Heavenly, who shrugged. "I know she spent a lot of time with him after the disastrous move-in, but I don't know if he's out of the friend zone yet. I didn't get a chance to ask her before she left on that big cruise with the elderly couple she works for."

The conversation and the miles whizzed by as the sun sank closer to the horizon in their back windshield. Finally, the iconic, WELCOME TO LAS VEGAS sign shimmered in the headlights.

Twenty minutes later, Beck savored the familiar comfort of Gloria's tight hug. He couldn't name a time or date when her embrace had gone from inciting teenage lust to a feeling of homecoming. But watching her hug Heavenly and Seth with the same affection warmed his heart.

After Buddy greeted them with bro-hugs and gave Heavenly a

friendly squeeze, they each grabbed a cocktail and strolled out onto the patio. Seated by the pool on the thickly padded outdoor sectional, they laughed and talked while the warm desert air kissed Beck's skin.

"It's not too hot out here for you guys, is it?" Buddy asked.

"At night, with the overhead fans, it actually feels good," Seth assured while Beck nodded in agreement. "What made you decide to get married now?"

"You mean when it's hotter than Satan's balls?" Gloria grinned.

"Yeah."

"Vegas is never unbusy, and we got tired of waiting." She shrugged.

"Besides, we don't plan on being out in the heat for long," Buddy agreed. "Just into the chapel so Elvis can marry us, then out again before coming back here to celebrate."

"That sounds perfect. I can't wait." Heavenly flashed her warmest smile, complete with dimples.

"We can't, either." Gloria looked at Buddy with love in her eyes.

"Is there anything I can do to help?" Heavenly asked.

"No, honey, but thanks." Gloria pinned Beck with a weighty glance. "Kenneth?"

That had him sitting up a little straighter. "Yeah?"

"I have a favor to ask."

He couldn't imagine what, but… "Anything. What is it, sweetheart?"

Her eyes filled with tears. Then her voice quivered. "Would you walk me down the aisle?"

Him? The honor blindsided Beck. Memories of their years together flipped through his brain like pages of a scrapbook. She'd offered to take him in—three square meals and a roof over his head in exchange for protection from sometimes vicious johns—but she'd helped him heal from years of neglect and mental abuse. Gloria was one of the good ones, and Beck knew if she hadn't saved him, he'd either be dead or still searching for his place in this world, like Zach.

When he didn't answer right away, she laughed nervously. "Come on, Kenneth, most of my clients would love to give their wives away, even their exes."

He laughed. "I won't give you away if it means losing you, sweetheart. But I'd be thrilled to walk you down the aisle and give you to Buddy so you two can live happily ever after."

"Thank you." Her voice cracked. "I thought you'd say yes, if only to make sure the old ball and chain became someone else's problem."

Beck squeezed her hand. "You were never a ball and chain, and you never have to thank me. It's my honor."

Buddy wrapped his bride-to-be in his arms. "Aww, baby. Come here…"

Seth clapped Beck on the back while Heavenly sat between them with a loving smile. It was almost a perfect moment. All he lacked to be sublimely happy was for Seth to commit to a future and a family with him and Heavenly. The guy couldn't hold out much longer, right?

After dabbing at her misty eyes, Gloria sat up, gulped her wine, and smiled. "Now that we've gotten the important stuff out of the way, let's talk about the bachelor and bachelorette parties tomorrow night."

Bachelorette party?

All the warm fuzzies floating through Beck's system dissipated. Even though Seth flanked Heavenly, Beck felt Cooper tense palpably. A quick glance at the apprehension lining his face told Beck they were on the same page. It was a *hell no* from them both.

"Aren't you two a little…" He wracked his brain for a tactful way to decline. If he couldn't find one, Gloria would only dig her heels in deeper.

"Don't you dare say old, Kenneth." She scowled.

"Mature, then." He smirked.

"To have fun? Just because we're not in our twenties and not having a traditional wedding, why shouldn't we celebrate?" She smiled and reached for Heavenly's hand. "And you, my dear, will be my special guest of honor."

As Heavenly's face lit up with excitement, apprehension twisted his gut. Beck didn't even have to look at Seth. He could feel panic rolling off the PI.

"Where is the bachelorette party?" Beck somehow managed to sound calm.

"That's what I'd like to know." Seth's question came out more like a growl.

Beck frowned. He was concerned about his ex-wife corrupting his sweet little girl, but Seth sounded downright worried. No doubt, he was still struggling with his past, with the fear that if he let Heavenly out of his sight, she would be taken from him.

"Relax, you cavemen." Gloria waved her hand. "Kenneth, you know I'm not exactly welcome in most respectable nightlife establishments in this town, so we're celebrating at the apartment."

He couldn't argue with her assessment. Still, the private setting didn't make him feel better. "What exactly are you planning to *do*?"

"Nothing too crazy. We'll probably snort some blow, stream some guy-on-guy porn, then have a gang bang with the Chippendales crew. You know, the usual."

"What?" Seth barked as he stood, looking as if he was about to blow a gasket.

Buddy cackled.

"She's kidding." Beck glared at her. "At least she'd better be."

"Have you completely lost all sense of humor?" Gloria asked. "Of course we're not doing any of that shit. We're simply going to have a fun—but tame—party with my girls."

"You're not inviting any johns, I hope," Beck growled.

"Be real." Gloria bit out. "I already informed all the regulars that none of the girls are working this weekend. We're going to pop open some champagne, swap a few hooker horror stories, and celebrate my last night as a free woman."

"So there's no gang bang?" Seth narrowed his eyes at her.

Gloria sent him one of her patented chiding stares. "Last time I checked, gang bangs are yours and Beck's department, sugar. Not mine."

The PI still didn't look convinced as he turned to Heavenly. "You don't have to go, angel."

She stared back as if he'd grown an extra head. "I want to."

Shit. Like him, Seth had probably hoped Heavenly's natural shyness and modesty would assert itself. Instead, Beck could all but hear the wheels of Gloria's mind spinning. He needed to shut this down—fast—before their worries about this ridiculous party ended up ruining the happy couple's wedding day.

Like Seth is worried about ruining his mother's?

"Why don't we talk about this in the morning," he suggested. "It's getting late, and it's been a long day."

Heavenly frowned back. "I want to go. What's the problem?"

Shit.

"Have you ever been to a bachelorette party?" Beck tried to sound rational.

"No. But now that I have a chance to, I'm excited."

"Thirty minutes with your ex-wife, and look what happens to our girl," Seth groused.

"What can I say?" Gloria shrugged, grinning. "I'm a good influence."

"She is," Heavenly defended. "It's you two I'm not happy with."

"Why? We simply don't want you to be subjected to"—Beck eyed Gloria suspiciously—"what *might* happen."

"No. Because you don't trust that I can handle myself when you two aren't around." Heavenly sighed. "Now I know what Raine deals with all the time."

"That's not true, little girl. We trust you," Beck assured. "We just know how rowdy those parties can be."

"In what way?"

"Snorting blow, streaming guy-on-guy porn, then having a gang bang with the Chippendales crew." Gloria laughed, then shot Beck and Seth a quelling glare. "But that's not happening."

"See?" Heavenly shot back. "And what about Buddy's party?" She whipped her head in the older man's direction and arched her brows. "What are you boys planning to do with your last night as a single man?"

Buddy blinked as Gloria slapped a hand over her mouth and snickered.

"N-nothing," her husband-to-be stammered. "We're just going to play poker here at the house with some of the guys from the union hall."

"Poker, huh?" Heavenly drawled. "Will there be any 'ladies' present?"

Gloria howled with laughter, grinning at their girl with pure pride.

Seeing Heavenly all riled up turned Beck on like a fucking light-bulb. It also made his palm itch to take her over his knee and spank the sassy tone out of her.

"No." Buddy scowled. "All the ladies will be partying with you and Gloria."

Heavenly sat back, arms crossed over her chest, casting him and Seth an expectant glance. "See, it's possible to have a fun but tame party."

Beck cupped her chin and tilted her head back. "You've pled your case beautifully, little girl."

Seth leaned over and sank his fingers in her hair and fisted it. "Have fun tomorrow night, but not too much fun."

"And save some for us, because when you get back, we plan to wreck you with more fun than you can handle," Beck murmured against her lips.

"Speaking of fun, I think we should go upstairs and have some of our own, baby girl," Buddy growled.

"That's the best idea you've had since last night, big daddy," Gloria purred.

Beck was exploring Heavenly's sweet mouth when his ex announced, "Make yourselves at home. If you need anything, Kenneth knows where to find it. Good night."

"All we need is right here, between us." Seth's voice sounded raspy as he moved closer.

As the click of Gloria's heels faded away, Beck slowly lifted from Heavenly's lips and savored her dreamy expression. Easing into his arms, he settled her in Seth's lap. Cooper clutched her close and smiled, pressing a kiss to her mouth.

"Take our girl upstairs and warm her up. I'll lock up and be right behind you."

"It'd be my pleasure," Seth assured. "Hers, too."

With a grin, he stood, cradling her against his chest. Eyeing him with hunger, Heavenly clutched his shoulders and slid her lips up his neck as he carried her into the house and up the stairs.

Beck didn't waste any time securing all the doors, then rushing to the control panel in the kitchen to lower the drapes and set the alarm.

Then, with her sugar-sweet kiss still lingering on his tongue, Beck took the stairs two at a time and raced down the hall toward the guest room. He'd only taken a few steps when her sensual moans filled his ears.

Desire spiked.

As he opened the bedroom door, Beck skidded to a halt. A trail of clothes, shed in seconds, littered the floor and led straight to Heavenly, who lay naked on her back in the center of the bed, legs spread. Seth, equally naked, sprawled on his stomach, his face buried between her thighs. Pinning her wrists to the mattress, he ate at their girl as if she were his last meal, forcing Heavenly to take one demanding lash of his tongue after the next.

"You feel me, angel?" Seth demanded. "That good?"

"Yessss."

Her breathy whine as she fisted the sheets and tossed her head against the pillow made Beck's body ping. Her feminine scent in the air jacked Beck's need up even more.

"Then keep your legs spread for me," Seth growled. "Lie there and take it."

"Seth…"

Never peeling his stare from the erotic sight of Seth laving Heavenly's thigh, Beck reached behind him blindly and closed the bedroom door, his cock surging against his zipper. He'd seen Cooper eat their girl to orgasm dozens of times, but never this raptly.

What did that mean? What was going on in the PI's head?

Whatever it was, Beck approved of Seth's single-minded ruthlessness. The PI showed no sign of giving a thought to his traumatic past.

Maybe the worst was behind him. Maybe, with the right nudge, he would finally be willing to lock down their girl and put a ring on her finger…

Beck had a good idea how to use Seth's hunger to make that happen.

Hurriedly, he stripped and tossed his clothes to the floor with the others, then lunged for the bed. Eating up the distance in three strides, he eased behind their girl and sank a fist in her hair. Seth barely raised his head in acknowledgment before turning all his focus back to her.

"Watching him work his tongue over your pretty pink pussy is arousing as fuck," Beck growled in her ear. "I hope you didn't plan on sleeping tonight. Seth and I are going to keep you wide awake tongue-fucking your slick little slit until you beg for mercy."

"And when you've grown hoarse screaming our names, we'll see if we have any," Seth taunted.

Heavenly whimpered.

"If you're a good little girl, we'll squeeze our fat cocks inside you, stretch your tiny ass and your snug pussy, until the burn eats you alive," Beck added. "Then we'll force you to come over and over."

His words sent her thrashing restlessly, hips rocking. "Oh…"

He gripped her thighs, stilling her. His fingers would probably leave faint bruises, but she didn't seem to care.

"Shh. I told you to take it," he rebuked thickly, then trailed his tongue up her furrow. "Every lick, every stroke. That pussy doesn't belong to you. It's *ours.*"

He yanked her closer and devoured her even more voraciously, as if consuming all of Heavenly right now was a biological imperative.

Seth was so lost in the moment.

Lost enough to forget about everything except claiming their girl? Uninhibited and desperate enough to take her bareback again?

Beck fucking hoped so. Not that he was trying to manipulate Seth. Well, not exactly. But why not nudge Cooper down the path they'd collectively chosen—until the murder of Zach's wife and daughter had resurrected Seth's ghosts? That—and fear—had been the only thing stopping the PI from embracing the future. And if he'd buried the ghosts again, he should be past his fear, right?

Beck didn't mind giving Seth a little shove in the right direction.

"Yes," their girl panted, tossing her head back and forth. "Yours."

The raw pleasure playing across her face stunned Beck. She was beautiful every day, but like this, deep in the throes of arousal, she was breathtaking.

He dragged his stare down her writhing body, blushing pink as her desire soared. Her hard berry nipples strained toward the ceiling, all but begging to be licked and sucked. Wrecked, even. Beck was happy to oblige.

Before he could, Heavenly jolted and arched, fisting the sheets as Seth sucked her clit into his mouth and nipped it with his teeth. She dug her heels into the mattress and hissed.

Jesus, watching her writhe and need was fucking hot.

"Is she hard and swollen?" he asked.

Seth didn't answer, only sucked harder.

"Sweet?" Beck prodded.

"Mmm," Seth groaned.

"Throbbing against your tongue?"

Grudgingly, Cooper lifted from her pussy, his hungry gaze eating its way up Heavenly's body. "Yes. We're going to spend all night dragging orgasms out of you, angel."

"Oh, god," Heavenly wailed.

"He can't help you now. You're in our hands," Seth reminded roughly before he fastened his mouth over her again like a man possessed.

"Don't stop," Beck urged, easing to the side of the mattress. "Tease her until she fucking begs."

Then he latched onto one of Heavenly's engorged nipples. She jolted, lifting her unfocused gaze to him. Their eyes met. His heart thrummed as he drew on her stony peak, laving, lashing, and nipping. Her cries filled his ears.

"I need…" Heavenly panted. "Please."

He rewarded her pleading by pressing her pebbled nipple to the roof of his mouth and sucking even harder. Heavenly's stare turned glassy yet frantic. She mewled, clutching his arms as if he were an anchor.

Beck allowed it…but extracted a price, taking her other nipple in his mouth while he pinched the first mercilessly.

Between her legs, Seth continued to gorge on Heavenly, now filling her pussy with his fingers and rubbing her most sensitive spots.

That quickly sent Heavenly spiraling higher. Her nipples got harder in his mouth.

"She's melting all over your tongue, isn't she?" Beck taunted.

Seth growled in response as he lapped and sucked at her glistening slit without pause, seemingly without taking a breath. Beck took that as a yes.

"You going to come for us, little girl?" he coaxed. "That orgasm is ours."

Seth snarled, rocking his hips against the soft comforter and digging his fingers deeper into Heavenly's thighs. The PI's cock must be screaming for relief, just like his own.

"Ramp her up. Yes..." Beck praised when Seth redoubled his efforts. "Almost there. Now wring it from her. Make sure she can't hold anything back."

With a strangled growl, Seth captured her clit between his teeth again, then tugged. Heavenly shrieked and sank her fingernails into Beck's arms in desperation.

"Now, little girl. Come!" Beck demanded, pinching and plucking her nipples.

With her hips arching off the bed, Heavenly ground her pussy against Seth's mouth, then froze. She looked at Beck helplessly as a guttural, bone-rattling cry clawed from her throat.

She shattered completely.

It took all of Beck's willpower not to snatch her off Seth's tongue and bury his cock inside her. But he had a greater purpose than getting off. He needed to stay the course.

So he watched, jaw clenched tight, as Heavenly quaked and quivered for interminable moments. Then slowly, she dragged in a ragged breath and sagged to the bed, seemingly sated.

Seth wasn't. "Again."

"I-I need...a...minute," she panted.

"Now." That voice brooked no refusal.

"Don't ease up. Make her give us more. That's it..." Beck encouraged when Seth slammed his fingers inside her again and resumed feasting on her clit.

Heavenly wailed, wriggling as if she wanted to escape the lashing of his tongue as much as she wanted it to continue. They didn't give her a choice. Seth kept at her pussy, mindlessly driven by desire.

She tossed a look of dazed panic Beck's way, silently begging him to make it all better. He merely smiled and dragged her nipples into his mouth again, toying and squeezing without mercy.

But driving Heavenly up and stringing Seth out was taking its toll on Beck's restraint. It took everything he had not to grip his cock and stroke it until relief came. Instead, he forced himself to keep his eye on the prize.

"Look at her face, man, all rosy and full of need," Beck murmured, still pinching her swelling tips. "Hear the sexy sounds she's making? Keep drowning her in pleasure. She's nearly out of her fucking mind."

Seth lifted his heavy lids and inspected Heavenly, moaning in agreement against her flesh.

A desperate yelp of sensation rolled from her throat.

"Oh, she liked that. Do it again," Beck murmured.

When Seth obliged, Heavenly screamed even louder.

"She loves the way you tongue-fuck her. You going to lick another orgasm from her? You going to suck at her until she screams for us again?"

"Beck," Heavenly panted. "H-he doesn't...need...help."

He chuckled. "You do, don't you, little girl?"

"Yessss." She sounded pitiful and lost and half-crazed.

"You want to come all over his tongue again, don't you?"

She bit her lip and tossed her head and tried to hold back climax... but she couldn't. "Yessss!"

"Give it to us, then. Come!" Seth drove his fingers inside her and savagely sucked her clit.

Heavenly arched against his mouth and dragged in a breath, her muscles seizing up. Then she bore down on Seth's driving digits, her deafening scream cutting through the heavy air. He pinned her under him with an animalistic stare while she wailed and quivered and jerked.

She'd barely eked out the last warble of her cry when he lifted from her cunt, his eyes burning. "More, angel. I want more. Now."

"Seth..." she whimpered.

"Your little wail says you can't, but that pouting pussy says you can. And you will."

He gave her no more time to recover before he latched onto her puffy flesh again.

As Heavenly shrieked and shuddered, Beck brushed a strand of sweat-soaked hair from her face. "Don't hold out on us."

He wanted her teetering on a spine-bending precipice. And this time, he'd keep her from falling over—until her begging pushed Seth past his resistance and he mounted her snug, swollen sex, forgetting all about his tragic past.

"I'm not," she swore breathlessly. "It's just…"

"You're suffering, I know. But you do it beautifully," Beck whispered as he brushed a light kiss over her lips. "You won't disappoint us, right? I'll even help."

Cupping the back of Heavenly's knee, he lifted one leg higher. As if that gave Seth ideas, he shoved the other toward her chest. He pounced again, tonguing her manically.

Heavenly closed her eyes, a broken moan escaping her throat.

"There… She's entirely spread out for you, pussy and ass," Beck murmured. "She makes you need her, doesn't she?"

"Yes," Seth snarled between laps at her clit.

"Makes you want to get inside her?"

"Yes."

"Makes you desperate to show her that you own her?"

"Fuck, yes." Growling, Seth withdrew his fingers from her cunt. They glistened under the golden light glowing from the nightstand as he dragged the digit down to her gathered rim and stared at Heavenly with demanding eyes. "Take me. Give me more."

He didn't wait, just started working beyond her taut ring and fixed his mouth over her pussy again.

She gasped, her heavy exhalation shuddering in the air when, somehow, he ate at her with even more gusto.

As Beck watched, need and impatience jerked at his mental leash. He held on by reminding himself their future was at stake. He couldn't afford to fuck up tonight. Somehow, someway he had to convince Seth that marrying their girl and making babies with her was the right path —the only path—to happy ever after.

And he had to believe Seth was ready for that. Hell, he'd willingly taken Heavenly bareback at the lodge. Beck was convinced Seth would have continued doing it if Zach and his tragedy hadn't stirred him up. But now that the PI had made peace with his brother, it was time for their lives to get back on track, right? Beck fucking hoped so.

Soon, the rise of her keening cries echoed off the walls and rang in his ears. She was on the edge again.

It was time for Seth to make a choice.

Ignoring the condoms on the nightstand, Beck reached for the tube of lube beside them.

"Take this." He placed it in Seth's hand. "Stretch her open. Get her ready so we can squeeze inside her tight little holes and fill her with our seed."

Seth tore from Heavenly's pussy and pinned him with a stare both weighty and unreadable.

"No. No! Don't stop." Heavenly's whole body trembled. "I-I'm close. I need—"

"Us inside you. Yes." Beck looked Seth's way. "Hurry, man. She's struggling. She's suffering. She's primed. It's time to fuck her."

"Please." She jerked her head, shaking fingers pinching her own nipples before skimming down her body. She reached her swollen cunt and fumbled for her clit. "Please."

Seth glanced between his own weeping cock and the lube in his hand, then at the condoms.

Make the right choice. Come on. Let's move forward, man. Together.

"Yeah," Seth gasped out, squeezing lube over his fingers. "Let's get her ready."

As he slathered the clear liquid over Heavenly's crinkled rim, Beck watched, waiting for the PI's next move. He kissed their girl while working a pair of fingers in soft circles over her clit.

"What are you doing?" Heavenly breathed out, her unfocused eyes huge in her face. "You're making the ache worse."

Yes, he was.

"We'll make it better, little girl...eventually," Beck assured before arching a brow Seth's way. "What do you want here?"

Seth probably thought he was asking front or back, pussy or ass. On the surface, he was. But the bigger choice loomed. Past or present? Fear or bravery? Solitude or family?

Seth cursed under his breath, glancing between the condoms and the lube. Then he tossed the lube on the bed. He didn't reach for the foil squares.

Beck's heart lurched with hope.

Cooper claimed Heavenly's lips in a brutal kiss. With a moan of surrender, she wrapped her arms around his neck and gave back every ounce of fiery passion he poured into her.

Beck looked on, still manipulating her clit at a pace designed to incite, not satisfy. With Seth's naked front pressed to her side, he was so close to mounting her. Another nudge. Another few inches...

"Come on, man. It's time," Beck urged. "She needs us, and my cock is about to explode."

Grudgingly lifting from Heavenly's mouth, Seth dragged a hungry stare down her body, stalling on her pussy. He knelt back on his heels and spread her legs, lowering his hips toward the bed while gripping his cock. Wordlessly, Seth aligned his bare, weeping crest to Heavenly's slick folds.

Beck's thrill soared. Triumph thundered through his veins.

He's going to do it. He's going to take her bareback again. Thank fuck.

Beck was mentally fist-pumping when Seth froze, his expression wrenched with turmoil. Then he blinked, hissed, and jerked back as if he'd been slapped by the devil.

Without meeting anyone's gaze, Cooper plucked the lube off the bed. "On your knees, angel. I'm going to fill your sweet ass."

She complied, and as Seth slathered the clear gel over his dick, Beck bit back disappointment and eyed the condoms.

What would happen if he left them where they lay?

At the lodge, Heavenly had confessed that she wanted children. Of course, that had been three months ago, before Seth had shared the details of his horrific past. Before they'd realized they were fighting an impossible foe—his ghosts. Before they'd discovered how impenetrable his fears could be.

What would Seth say or do if he chose not to glove up? He was tempted to damn the consequences and find out...but he couldn't do that without talking to Heavenly. Not only did he have no idea if her desire to have children had changed after all they'd been through with Seth, but he didn't know if she was ready to deal with the very real possibility of the PI walking away if she conceived.

She hadn't mentioned kids in months now, and that left Beck wondering...was he the only one who ached for the pitter-patter of little feet and innocent laughter filling their house? If so, could he stay in a relationship without the chance of ever having the family he craved?

That question was a bitter pill. But now wasn't the time to dissect Heavenly's feelings or be a selfish prick. Their girl needed release, and god knew he could use one, too.

Swallowing down his frustration, he reached for the condoms and tore one open.

As he rolled the latex down his throbbing shaft, Seth stretched her sinful rosebud with his fingers again. Heavenly gasped, then closed her eyes with a sigh. Beck cupped her shoulders and eased her onto her knees, then slid into position on the mattress beneath her. Drinking in the bliss skipping across her flushed face, he guided her hands to his pecs, then gripped his shaft and aligned his eager crest to her slick, swollen folds. As the cold condom met her sweltering slit, her eyes flew open with a gasp.

"Easy. We've got you," he vowed, watching anticipation and hunger smolder in her eyes. "Now be a good little girl. Slide your pretty pussy down my cock and ride me slow."

As she slipped her scalding, narrow passage down his shaft, Beck hissed and cupped her breasts. And when he thumbed the hard points, he cursed as she clasped him even tighter.

Heavenly continued to impale herself slowly, mewling as his thick cock stretched and filled her. Undulating, head thrown back, she raised and lowered herself over Beck exactly as he'd demanded, whimpering when Seth got into position behind her.

"Bear down, angel. Let me claim your ass," Seth growled.

Without hesitation, Heavenly complied. Beck skated his hands to her waist, then lifted her off his cock, leaving his bulbous crest nestled just inside. He hissed, jaw clenched, as her slick juices seeped down his shaft.

As Seth fed inch after fat inch into her tiny backside, Beck absorbed Heavenly's helpless whimpers, gazing into her smoky, half-lidded eyes. By the time Cooper worked himself deep, sweat dripped off his face and trickled down his chest.

After what seemed like interminable hours, he slowly eased back. Beck grunted in acknowledgment before thrusting upward and dragging Heavenly's hips down, filling her sweet cunt again.

Soon, he and Seth found their rhythm, working in and out of her over and over, panting and cursing, the inescapable sensations quickly taking them all to the edge.

"Oh, god. Oh, god. Oh, my god…" Heavenly chanted, her voice turning sharp and high-pitched.

It spurred them on. They seesawed in and out of her quivering body with long, measured strokes. Beck couldn't resist working her tempting, turgid nipples, basking in Heavenly's cries of bliss that vibrated through his body.

Still, he craved more. That wasn't a surprise. Heavenly was like a drug, one Beck was addicted to, now and forever. Wedging a hand between their damp bodies, he stroked Heavenly's clit. She clamped down. Seth cursed. Beck just smiled.

Their animalistic grunts melded with her escalating whimpers. His demand for release warred with his urge to prolong the inevitable surrender to pleasure. The friction searing his cock as he and Seth drove in and out of Heavenly like twin pistons took the decision from him.

Tingles surged through his limbs. Lightning zipped up his spine. Need boiled in his balls. As Heavenly's cries grew louder, Beck tried like hell to gather his restraint and resolve…but it was no use.

"I can't…hold… Oh, god!" Heavenly wailed.

"Same. Let go," Beck barked, thrusting wildly into her fluttering cunt.

"Jesus, I'm coming!" Seth choked out, driving into her with teeth bared.

As they shattered together, their roars and screams rolled through the room.

Once the peak passed, defeat washed over Beck. He wasn't a man who liked or accepted failure, but tonight Seth's fears had won. Still, the evening hadn't been a complete debacle. Seth had nearly penetrated their girl without protection. He was wavering. Beck just had to keep nudging, figure out some way to assure Seth that the benefits of starting a family with their girl outweighed the risks. Reminding him how magical it had felt the one time they'd taken Heavenly together without a single barrier wouldn't hurt.

Either way, Beck refused to give up hope that sooner or later Seth would bury the past for good and fully commit to their future.

T hirty hours later, Beck gathered up the chips and cards from Buddy's bachelor poker party, then checked his watch for the hundredth time. It was late. He shot Seth a grim stare. While they'd spent the evening giving raunchy toasts and telling crude jokes, accompanied by booze and laughter, as the hours slid by Beck had begun to worry. What debauchery were Gloria and her girls introducing Heavenly to? And where the hell were they?

"Relax, boys." Buddy clapped him and Seth each on the shoulder. "Your girl is fine."

"Is she?" Seth's question sounded like a whip. "It's nearly two a.m. What the fuck can they be doing?"

"Who knows? Remember, that's the middle of the day for Gloria."

"But not for Heavenly," Beck shot back.

"Gloria is watching over her like a hawk. She'll know when Heavenly's had enough and bring her straight home."

The words had barely cleared his lips when the front door swung open. Beck and Seth nearly gave themselves whiplash as they whirled to the sound.

Gloria and Heavenly—both clearly shit-faced and clinging to one another while sipping booze from plastic penis-shaped bottles—staggered into the foyer.

"Son of a bitch." Seth scrubbed a hand down his face.

Buddy cursed under his breath. "I'll start some coffee."

As the groom-to-be raced for the kitchen and dumped grounds into the brewer, Gloria swayed into the room, wobbling on her stilettos and blowing at the veil of flashing neon-pink penises slipping off her head. It would be funny—if Beck wasn't so pissed.

"Oh, boyssss, we're hoooome," his ex-wife sang.

Beck and Seth raced toward the drunken pair. Beck slung an arm around Gloria's waist while Seth secured their girl, making sure she didn't face-plant on the tile.

With a loopy, bleary-eyed grin, Heavenly glanced between him and Seth. Then suddenly, she frowned. "Sumthin's wrong wiff the floor. Isss moving."

"Oh, fuck," Beck groaned. "Her hangover tomorrow…"

"One for the ages, she and Gloria both," Seth grumbled, then nodded at Heavenly. "It's all right, angel. I've got you."

"I love you," she said with a dreamy sigh.

"I love you, too," Seth assured as he and Beck began herding her and Gloria toward the living room.

"And I love you," Heavenly told Beck. "Even if Gloria got you first."

"It doesn't matter if I was first," his ex insisted vehemently. "You're his last, honey."

Heavenly nodded as she slurped up the last of the drink from her plastic penis bottle. Scowling, she reached over and grabbed Gloria's, then sipped some of her cocktail. "Mmm. Thass so good. What is it?"

"Iss vodka and crabberry juice," Gloria slurred back.

"Buddy, make that coffee extra strong," Beck called over his shoulder as he and Seth settled the tipsy duo onto the couch.

"Already did. It's brewing now."

"Buddy? Buddy?" Gloria yelled. "Where's my big daddy?"

"I'm right here, baby girl." He waved to her from the kitchen.

"How was your poker game?"

"It was great."

"Did you save some pokin' for me?" Gloria snorted and giggled.

"Always." Buddy grinned.

After flanking their girl on the couch, Seth turned to her and smiled. "Did you have a good time, angel?"

Beck smiled tightly. "It definitely looks like you did."

"I had a blast!" She tossed her arms in the air, nearly sending her plastic penis flying.

"Buddy!" Gloria yelled to her man in kitchen.

"Yes, love."

"I'm marrying your sexy ass tomorrow."

"Actually, make that later today, baby girl." He winked. "Hopefully, you'll be sober by then."

Gloria gasped dramatically. "I'm not drunk. I'm...happy."

"Me, too." Heavenly sipped more air from her penis bottle, then scowled. "Iss all gone."

"It's okay, little girl. Buddy is making you some coffee," Beck assured. "Tell us everything you drank tonight."

"Umm, lesss see. First, we had champagne, then we had sex in the sand."

"No, no, no. Sex on the beach," Gloria corrected, then dissolved into more snorting laughter.

"Oh, yeah...on the beach. Then the girls... Oh, my gosh, you guys, Gloria's girls are so sweet. I never met hookers before. But they were awesome! They gave me all kinds of tips on things to try in the bedroom." Heavenly's dimpled smile was full of mischief.

A sidelong glance told Beck that Seth's curiosity was as piqued as his own.

Beck slid a hand over her thigh. "What kind of things?"

"If you're good boys, I'll show you later." She winked.

"Good boys, huh?" Seth raised a brow. "We'll look forward to that."

"After our naughty girl gets a spanking," Beck murmured for Seth's ears only.

Seth smiled and took Heavenly's hand. "So you drank champagne and sex on the beach. Is that all?"

"Oh, no." Heavenly shook her head. "Some of the girls passed out little glasses with all kinds of yummy stuff in them. I started sipping one, but Venus stopped me and showed me how to drink them the right way."

Beck knew exactly what that meant. He whipped around and sent his ex a fiery glare. "You let her do shots?"

"Oh, lighten up, Kenneth. We were *all* doing them," Gloria chided with a dismissive wave of her hand.

"And they were *so* good," Heavenly gushed. "I had a woo woo and a kamikaze. Then I had a blow job, followed by an orgasm. That was the best."

"Excuse me? A blow job *and* an orgasm?" Seth thundered.

Beck found himself in the same camp.

"Don't look at me like that… My blow job and my orgasm weren't the real thing, silly." Heavenly grinned. "I put them in my mouth—" She stopped speaking, then started a belly-clutching laugh. "Wait. That didn't come out right. I mean, I didn't give a blow job or orgasm with my mouth. They were liquid. I drank them with my mouth. Thatss it."

"I see." Seth nodded, still looking downright pissed.

Beck wasn't at all happy, either. In fact, he wondered how the hell their girl hadn't passed out. She'd feel like hammered shit tomorrow.

"What else did you do besides drink a lot?" he quizzed, giving Gloria the evil eye.

"Well, there were firemen. It was exciting when they showed up," she said with a wistful sigh.

"Firemen? Did you have some emergency at your bachelorette party?" Beck demanded.

"Oh, the building wasn't on fire or anything. They weren't real firemen," Heavenly blurted before his ex could answer. "I mean, at first I thought they were, but they were just pretend ones. I figured that out when someone turned up the music and all the firemen started dancing. They must take dance lessons together, 'cause, holy cow, they sure knew how to move."

Beck groaned, jaw clenched, and he shoved down his anger. Nearby, a low growl rumbled from the back of Seth's throat.

Heavenly went on, oblivious. "Anyway, they were all shaking their hips"—she drunkenly demonstrated in her seat—"then they took off their coats all at once. Just ripped them off. And not a single one of them was wearing a shirt. I wondered if they worked out together or something, too, 'cause they all had muscles bulging everywhere. But having them around was fun." She sent him and Seth a crooked grin. "You two need coats like that. You're both built like them and—" She frowned. "Wait, can you dance?"

"I'm going to kill your ex-wife," Seth muttered under his breath.

Yeah, Beck was contemplating that, too.

"Why are you two frowning? It's fine." Heavenly patted Seth's hand and sent Beck a smile. "When the next song started, Gloria sat me in a chair, then all the fireman started dancing in a circle around me. I giggled and blushed a lot. I'm not used to being the center of attention. Then"—she slapped dramatic hands over her cheeks, mouth agape—"they all grabbed the front of their fireman pants and poof"—she tossed up her hands—"they flew right off. No zipper or anything. They just…disappeared. I'mma buy you two pants like that."

"You didn't say anything about having strippers at the fucking party, Gloria," Beck bellowed.

"Shhh." His ex pressed a finger to her lips. "I didn't know they were coming. My girls hired them…or traded sex with them. I'm not sure. But don't worry, I made it clear that Heavenly was off-limits. They were perfect gentlemen around her. Well, mostly."

Beck struggled not to come out of his chair and rebuke her. He would have if he thought it would do any good.

"So, you got an eyeful." Beck struggled to keep his voice level and calm.

"Not then, but later on I did. Oh, yeah. More than an eyeful." Heavenly looked shocked.

"I need the name, address, and social security number of every man who got naked for our girl," Seth bit out.

"You don't," Gloria refused.

Heavenly scowled in confusion. "Why do you need that? They were nice."

"Oh, I'm sure," Beck drawled.

"And they weren't naked," she went on as if no one else was speaking. "They were wearing these little weenie bikinis—at least at first."

"Weenie bikinis? Oh, my god." Gloria howled. "I'm gonna call them that from now on."

"That's what they looked like," Heavenly pointed out. "All the girls went wild. They started stuffing money in the guys' pouch things in places I didn't know money could stick."

"That's why you always wash your hands after handling money, honey," Gloria advised sagely as Buddy handed her a mug of steaming coffee.

"Good point." Heavenly accepted hers from Buddy with a soft smile. Pausing, she blew on the brew and took a sip, then eyed him and Seth curiously.

"Is something wrong?" Beck asked. "Are you going to be sick?"

"No. I was just wondering… Can either of you do that helicopter thing with your"—Heavenly nodded toward their laps—"you know… your penises? Peeni? What's the plural of penis?"

Beck closed his eyes, sighed, and counted to ten.

"Helicopter thing?" Seth repeated, sounding like he was seconds from losing his shit.

"Yeah. After the girls finished shoving money in the pouches, the firemen tore them off and started rolling their hips. Their…things started going round and round like helicopter blades." She waved her finger in circles. "Can you guys do that with yours?"

Buddy lost his fight to hold in his laughter and Gloria chortled. Beck and Seth simply sat, utterly speechless and gaping at their girl.

"Or maybe they had to go to some school to learn that." Heavenly paused, seeming to think it over. "Cherry said I should come to her school."

"She did?" Gloria suddenly sobered.

"Yeah. I told her I was already in school to be a nurse. But she said that once I gradda…graddadate…graduated, I should enroll in her school because she could teach me something *really* useful."

"Don't do that," Gloria warned.

"What kind of school?" Beck and Seth demanded at once.

"I-I don't know," Heavenly replied. "She never said."

"Gloria?" Beck prodded, quickly losing patience.

Glancing toward the ceiling, his ex tried—and failed—to appear innocent. "Let it go."

"That is *not* happening. Tell us," Beck insisted.

His ex-wife blew out a futile breath. "It's a…a squirting school."

"A *what?*" Seth barked, looking furious.

"Squirting school?" Heavenly's jaw dropped as pink stained her cheeks. "Does that mean what I think it means?"

"Yeah. You're not enrolling, little girl," Beck growled.

"Okay. But I bet the homework is fun," Heavenly sighed wistfully.

At that, Beck roared with laughter. And Seth finally found his sense of humor and joined in.

"Drink your coffee, angel," Seth instructed. "After that, we'll pour you into bed."

Dutifully, she did, then set her cup aside.

"I'll get her some ibuprofen and water," Beck volunteered as Seth lifted Heavenly off the couch. "You're going to feel like homegrown hell in the morning."

"You think?" She sounded disheartened, then shook her head. "Even if I do, it was worth it. Thank you for a fun night, Gloria. I love you."

"I love you, too, sugar. It *was* fun. I'll see you in the morning," she said with a grin and a wave, then cupped Buddy's chin and smiled up at him. "Take me to bed, you big stud."

As predicted, Heavenly and Gloria were in rough shape the next day. After drawing the kitchen curtains to block the bright Nevada sun, Beck doled out the ibuprofen.

The girls sat at the kitchen counter with Buddy and Seth, who were coaxing them to drink water and orange juice to flush the alcohol from their systems. Beck prepared a high-sugar breakfast of French toast, fresh fruit, and bacon to boost their blood sugar since the booze had depleted it.

"I feel like I've been run over by a bus. I'm never drinking again," Heavenly moaned, cupping her forehead with both hands.

Gloria, looking somehow both pale and green, wasn't faring much better.

Buddy patted his bride's back. "But what about the reception ceremony? I bought a case of special champagne to—"

"Shut up or I'll puke all over you." Gloria slid a bracing hand over her stomach.

He didn't look fazed. "You came close last night."

"Ugh. Don't remind me."

Beck tried not to laugh since it would piss Gloria off. Seth was less subtle, chuckling aloud.

"After you get some food in your system, you'll feel like a whole new woman," Beck assured.

"Can't you just open your black bag and give me a pill that will knock my ass out so I can sleep off this shit?"

"Yeah," Heavenly seconded. "Maybe some Thorazine or something."

Beck scowled. "Anti-psychotic medication?"

"Yes. Clearly, I must be psychotic for drinking so much last night."

Seth laughed outright, then leaned in close. "I got a better idea. Beck and I can take you upstairs, turn on some music—extra loud—and do the helicopter thing you seemed so excited about last night."

"Shh," she scolded. "Don't you dare. I have a headache."

Beck, Buddy, and Seth didn't even try to hold back, simply howled with laughter. Both girls covered their ears and glared.

"If you assholes are going to laugh at us, do it quietly," Gloria snapped.

Beck laughed even harder—until he saw anger transform Buddy's face. And when the seemingly mild plumber wrapped his beefy hand around Gloria's throat, Beck dropped the spatula. Waves of tension poured off Seth. Visions of abusive johns who'd once used Gloria as a punching bag swarmed Beck's brain.

He braced to launch over the counter and pound Buddy bloody when Gloria did something Beck swore he'd never see; she lowered her head and nuzzled her face against his forearm.

"Did you just call me an asshole, baby girl?" His voice was hauntingly calm.

"I did." She lifted her eyelids, looking almost contrite.

"So you're marrying an asshole today, huh?"

"No. I'm marrying *my* asshole today," she purred as she kissed her way up his arm, to his lips. "And I wouldn't change a thing about you."

Beck's jaw nearly hit the floor. Gloria had always claimed she wasn't into the Dom/sub scene, but their blatant power exchange proved otherwise. She might not have enjoyed it before, but somewhere along the way—probably when Buddy showed up—she'd changed her tune. The fact that Gloria, who had almost no faith in anyone, willingly handed her trust to Buddy was a shock.

Still reeling, Beck plucked up the spatula and finished breakfast.

A few minutes and feminine moans of appreciation later, he proved that whatever ill effects the alcohol was still having on the girls' systems couldn't hold out against the powdered sugar and syrup now filling their stomachs. After breakfast, Heavenly and Gloria perked up fast.

He was still plying them with orange juice and seconds while Seth and Buddy began cleaning the kitchen. Then the doorbell rang.

"Right on time." Gloria hopped off her stool, then turned to Heavenly. "Come with me, honey, and meet everyone."

She did, and a noisy minute later, they returned with an entourage of men and women toting portable tables and suitcases out to the pool.

"What the hell?" Beck frowned. Who were all these people?

"They're Gloria's beauty brigade, here to get the girls ready for the wedding. You know, massages, facials, manis, pedis, makeup, and hair," Buddy explained. "When we get finished here, we'll get our manis done."

"Awesome." Seth grinned. "I haven't had one in months."

Beck quirked a brow at the PI. "You have your nails done?"

"Don't judge," Seth flung back. "If you're too much of a caveman to get a mani, that's your issue."

Beck scoffed. "I'd rather embrace my inner Neanderthal than have my nails polished."

"You're missing out." Buddy snickered, then hurried out to the pool.

Seth nodded and followed. "I'm a Neanderthal, too. But unlike you, I'm an evolved one."

Beck rolled his eyes as he trailed after the gang. "What color are you going to have them paint yours? Something to match your eyes?"

"Oh, ha ha." Seth sent him a sardonic smile. "I'm thinking red, to match your blood dripping off my fingertips if you don't stop busting my balls."

"No need for violence."

"For your information, I'm not getting them painted; I'm getting them buffed," Seth bit out. "If you'd stop beating your chest long enough to give it a try, you might like it."

"Maybe." Beck grinned, clapping him on the back while watching Heavenly and Gloria emerge from the pool house wearing white, fluffy robes. "But I don't want to start color-coding my socks and underwear like a pussy."

"Fuck off." Seth laughed, pulling the door open and stepping outside.

The afternoon flew by like clouds on the wind.

It was past four thirty when Buddy, dressed in a classic black designer tux, paced the living room, pausing periodically to peer toward the stairs. Beck and Seth, wearing matching black suits, sat grinning at the nervous groom.

Beck imagined himself in Buddy's shoes. In fact, he couldn't wait to be pacing and crawling out of his skin beside Seth, anxiously waiting to exchange lifelong vows with Heavenly. She would make an exquisitely beautiful bride. That was one fantasy that couldn't come true fast enough for him.

He cast a sidelong glance over to Seth and sighed. Sure, they'd settled back into something like normal in the past few months, but he was beginning to feel as if they were stuck in place. Beck was beyond ready to start their future. Seth was firmly mired in the past. And Heavenly stood between them, soothing both beasts with her sweetness and honeyed touch. It would work for a while…until it didn't. Until Beck couldn't stand waiting anymore and Seth refused to budge. Then what?

"Oh, Heavenly. You look beautiful." A smile lit Buddy's face as he peered up the stairs.

In tandem, Beck and Seth stood and strode across the room, then stopped dead in their tracks. Beck nearly swallowed his tongue as Heavenly paused, flashed a shy smile, then turned to model her flirty but elegant pink dress. The top, clinging to her breasts, was a scoop-neck tease of swirling pink roses. Delicate straps crisscrossed the back as feminine flowing chiffon gathered at the waist and fell just above her knees.

Heavenly's hair was swept high on top of her head, but instead of the messy bun she often sported at home, it was artfully arranged in a delicate pile of curls with tiny coiled tendrils slipping down to tease her neck. She took his breath away—and left him no doubt she was the one.

When would Seth admit it?

"You look…amazing, little girl," he whispered.

"Like a gorgeous angel," Seth seconded.

"Thank you. You three look incredibly handsome yourselves." She smiled again as she descended the stairs, regarding Buddy. "Gloria said to sit tight. She'll be down as soon as Giorgio finishes her makeup."

The groom nodded. But instead of sitting, he started pacing again.

Beck and Seth met their girl at the bottom of the stairs and extended their hands. After placing a palm in each, she smiled as they meshed her between them. Though Beck ached to wreck her glossy pink lips, he forced himself to wait until after the wedding. As if struggling to keep from kissing her senseless, too, Seth glided his lips up her exposed neck. Beck joined in, reveling when she shuddered between them.

Was Seth too afraid to feel how right this was?

"May I have your attention please?" Giorgio, a flamboyant makeup artist with neon orange hair, called. Grudgingly, Beck peeled his lips away from Heavenly's soft skin. Seth did the same as everyone turned their attention to the slender man. "It's my honor and privilege to present your beautiful bride, Gloria."

His ex-wife appeared at the top of the stairs, looking like a vision.

Her gaze instantly locked on Buddy, who'd stopped pacing and stared up at her, slack-jawed.

"Oh, baby." Tears pooled in his eyes. "You're beautiful."

Gloria's chin quivered ever so slightly as she floated down the stairs in a billowing gray chiffon gown with a tasteful V-neck, elegant lace sleeves, a banded waist, and a bi-level hem that framed her shapely legs.

"Isn't she lovely?" Heavenly beamed.

"Yeah." Beck nodded, pushing the words past the lump of emotion lodged in his throat.

Buddy charged up the stairs and wrapped an arm around his bride-to-be's waist as the doorbell rang.

"That's our ride," Buddy announced, helping Gloria off the last step.

"You ready to get married?" she asked breathlessly, peering up at her groom.

"Baby, I've been ready for years. I was just waiting on you."

That was sweet, and Beck was happy for them...but he didn't want to wait years. His closest friends—and confirmed singletons—Hammer and Gloria, were both happy and settling down. After today, his ex-wife would be a married woman—for real. Hammer was expecting twins with Liam and Raine and they were planning a wedding in September. Beck was beginning to feel left behind, like the future was happening without him.

After they all loaded into the shiny black stretch limo, Beck reached down and clasped Heavenly's hand. She sent him a warm smile, then lifted their entwined fingers, studying his intently.

"Your nails look nice."

"Thanks," he grumbled. "I guess having them buffed wasn't as bad as I thought."

On her other side, Seth cleared his throat, wearing a cocky grin. "I told you so."

Beck eased against the seat, slung an arm around Heavenly's shoulders, and flipped the gloating prick his middle finger.

A few minutes later, they pulled up to the iconic white chapel with its pitched blue roof. Beck chuckled at the pink Cadillac parked beside the building.

Gloria and Buddy were giggling madly as everyone exited the limo and hurried inside to escape the Vegas summer heat. While Beck and Gloria remained at the back of the chapel, Buddy strolled down the gold brocade carpet and assumed his position near the podium. Seth and Heavenly followed, taking a first-row seat on one of the white wooden pews.

As they waited for Elvis to make his grand entrance, Gloria looped her arm through Beck's elbow.

"Hey." Beck smiled, patting her hand, which now clutched his forearm.

"Hey, yourself."

"Don't be nervous."

She sent him a wobbling stare. "I'm trying not to be. But this time, I'm getting married for real."

"You are. And I'm so happy for you, sweetheart."

"Thank you. I'm happy, too." Her smile turned tender. "You're next, you know."

Beck did his best to maintain his smile. "From your lips to God's ears…"

"She'll come around," Gloria encouraged.

Beck didn't correct her. Now wasn't the time. Instead, he changed the subject. "Speaking of happy…thank you again for helping Zach with his new identity. Now he's officially and legally Zach Beckman, and I talked to him yesterday. He's over the moon."

"You're welcome. He needed a fresh start as much as you did all those years ago, Kenneth."

Beck smiled. "You look like a queen. And Buddy will always treat you like one."

Gloria drew in a ragged breath and swallowed tightly, eyes glistening with unshed tears. "For the first time in my life, I feel like one, instead of a worthless hooker."

"You've never been a worthless hooker, sweetheart."

"Not even to you?"

"Especially not to me." He squeezed her hand. "You've always been my savior and my friend. You've said for years that I would have survived without you, but I don't think so. If you hadn't plucked me off the streets and showed me how many ways my life had purpose and meaning, I'd either be dead or behind bars. Your understanding, patience, and guidance made me the man I am today. And the man I'll be tomorrow. Thank you isn't enough to convey the love and gratitude in my heart for you, Gloria."

When a fat tear rolled down her cheek, Beck reached up and caught it. "Don't cry. You'll mess up your makeup, and Giorgio will beat us both with a tube of mascara."

Gloria choked out a watery laugh as she cupped his cheek. "I'm trying not to, but you don't understand."

"What, the power of mascara?"

"Stop. I'm being serious. *You're* the one who saved me."

"From nasty-assed johns. Yeah, I know. That was our deal."

"No. You saved my life." She swallowed tightly and glanced at Buddy, who looked impatiently at his watch. "I lied to you all those years ago."

"About?"

"My parents didn't kick me out at thirteen because I was running with the wrong crowd." A pained expression marched across her face. "I left because my dad got me pregnant. He'd been sexually abusing me as far back as I could remember."

With shock slamming his system, Beck did his best to keep his expression even. "Why didn't you ever tell me?"

Gloria gaped incredulously.

Beck understood then. "Ah, Messiah City."

"You'd just escaped a whole clan of child molesters. I didn't want you thinking me a victim like the women and girls you'd left behind."

"What happened to your baby?"

"I miscarried ten days after I hitchhiked here."

"I'm sorry." He frowned.

"It was for the best. Truly. I could barely take care of myself."

Beck nodded in understanding, then quirked a brow. "I still don't get how I saved your life."

"The night you ran into me, nearly knocking me off my stilettos?" She weakly smiled. "It was going to be my last."

"Your last night turning tricks?"

"No, my last on earth," she whispered. "I was tired of selling my body. Tired of aching for someone to love me for me, not my pussy or my mouth. When you came barreling around that corner and chased that horrible john away, I knew it was a sign from God or whoever's out there pulling the strings. I had a more important job to do."

"To save me?"

She nodded, a melancholy smile softening her face. "And let you save me right back."

Beck leaned in and pressed a kiss to her forehead as he swallowed back emotion. Then he eased away and smiled. "And now that we've served our purpose and saved one another, I get the honor of placing your big, beautiful heart in the hands of a man who, no doubt, loves your pussy and your mouth, but loves you—the *real* you—even more. Thank you for asking me to walk you down the aisle and give you away."

"Don't make it sound like you're walking out of my life, Kenn—"

"Never," he assured, cutting her off. "I'm simply letting you go to live the happily ever after you've always deserved."

Gloria dabbed another tear from her cheek, then glanced at Heavenly and Seth. "Seriously, it's time for you to start living yours."

"I'm working on that."

As if hearing his heart, Heavenly glanced over her shoulder and flashed him a loving smile.

"Love Me Tender" began blaring from the surround-sound speakers, filling the room. Beck squeezed Gloria's hand one final time, then walked beside her as she floated down the aisle. A finality he hadn't felt when their divorce had become legal wended through his system. This part of his life was over. The only thing ahead of him now was the future. The question was, how did he get it started?

At the altar, Beck kissed her cheek and held her gaze with a warm smile, then placed her hand in Buddy's before melting back to the nearby pew with Heavenly and Seth.

He was already making plans.

CHAPTER ELEVEN

"Dinner by the patio?" Heavenly asked as Seth walked in the door after a long day. She was preparing skewers of chicken-and-veggie kabobs. "Beck is on his way. I thought we might cheer him up. He sounded like he had a lot on his mind."

Seth didn't have to guess what. A handful of days had passed since Gloria and Buddy's wedding, and he was still sorting everything that had happened that weekend.

Things between the three of them were changing. Seth wasn't ready.

Since the Vegas nuptials, Beck's impatience to get on with their future had become almost palpable. It wasn't what the surgeon said. In fact, he'd been surprisingly mute since Seth had confessed the relevant parts of his past a few months back. And Heavenly, bless her, was always sweet and understanding. But he wasn't stupid. He'd seen her wistful tears as Gloria and Buddy exchanged vows. He'd noticed her melancholy after co-hosting Raine's baby shower with Liam's mom and sisters, Rosaleen and Shauna. Though his angel wasn't pushing or complaining, he sensed she was ready to start making their future permanent and expanding their family.

The notion broke him out in a cold, terrified sweat. Well, not actually committing to Heavenly and Beck. No question he wanted to spend the rest of his life with them, despite the fact it might kill his very Catholic mother. He loved his angel, and the life he and Beck had forged with her made him happier than he'd ever been.

Marriage was different. That took place in the Church—something the three of them would never be allowed. Their love was considered a desecration of the union between a man and a woman, sanctified by God. Seth had wrestled with that until he'd made peace with committing that sacrilege.

But having another child scared the absolute fuck out of him.

So where did that leave them?

Seth didn't know…but he either needed to man up and help get Heavenly pregnant or walk away and let Beck start a family alone with her.

Either might kill him.

"Is dinner on the patio all right?" Heavenly set the kabobs down and crossed the room to him, wearing a concerned expression. "We can eat inside if you'd rather."

Seth jerked his attention back to the present. "Outside would be great. It was a pretty day."

She sent him an unsettled smile, as if she sensed his turmoil and wanted to convince herself they were all right more than she believed they were. "Good. I'll set up the table out there."

"Give me a minute to shrug out of this suit, then I'll do it." He leaned down to kiss her softly. When their lips broke apart, he caressed her cheek. "You know I love you."

"I do." But she looked braced for bad news.

"I just wanted to make sure you knew."

Her smile gained a little confidence. "Just like I love you."

"How was your day?" he asked. "Enjoying your last few weeks of quiet before school starts again?"

"Yeah. Raine and I had lunch and ran some errands. Bryn is convinced she's going into labor tomorrow. Liam, too."

"They would know. And that explains why River left work early today. Is she nervous?"

"Very. She's worried she won't be a good mom since she lost hers so young and didn't have a role model." Heavenly sent him another stilted smile. "But I told her she'd have Liam's just a phone call away. Bryn is wonderful."

"Raine will be great. Even if she didn't have Bryn, she'd manage just fine on her own." The rest of Seth's reply caught in his throat.

He'd never stopped to consider that Heavenly might have insecurities about her own mothering skills. Despite not being sure he would ever be ready for more kids, he hated the thought of his angel worrying for an instant. "You know, if you ever have children, you'll be a great mom. The best." He swallowed. "You may not be sure since yours didn't stick around, but I believe that. I was raised by one of the best, so I know you'll be amazing."

She studied him, a thousand questions in her eyes—and he swore he could read every one of them. Didn't he want children? Wouldn't he be giving her any of those children? Why wasn't he ready to try?

Seth had no answers.

"Thank you." Tears pooled in her eyes, and she pasted on a falsely cheerful smile. "Go change and I'll finish prepping dinner."

She turned away from him and focused on the kabobs again. Seth ached to pull her back. It took everything inside him to let her walk away, even across the room. God, they were only ten feet apart, and it felt like a chasm. Like he was already losing her.

A gaping wound opened in his chest at the thought of Heavenly no longer in his life, at not having the right to press his lips to hers as he tumbled her into bed between him and Beck while he shredded every stitch from her body and drove her to screaming pleasure.

But the thought of filling her belly, of creating another vulnerable life that could be viciously snuffed out in a handful of seconds, infected him with bitter fear. He had to get out of here.

Taking the stairs two at a time, Seth disappeared to their bedroom, closing his eyes and pressing his forehead to the cool wall while he tried to breathe past panic.

When he was no longer shaking, he jerked out of his clothes and stared at his suits hanging in a neat row next to Beck's on the *His* side of the closet, taking up more than half the room. Heavenly's things filled the other side, and it seemed so normal, so natural, to have their belongings, their bodies, and their lives entwined this way.

Would he have to walk away from all this?

Cursing, he yanked on swim trunks and a tank, found his flip-flops, then splashed some water on his face. Below, he heard the good doctor swagger in and drop his keys in the dish on the hall table, where all three sets lay together.

The clues had been staring him in the face for months. He'd been playing house. And they had placated him while he'd buried his head in the sand and tried to pretend there was no next step, no tomorrow.

What a fucking idiot he'd been.

"Is Zach coming for dinner?" he heard Heavenly ask.

Beck's brother had become a semi-regular, stopping by two or three times a week to share a meal and conversation with the three of them. Seth had almost gotten used to the somber Beckman brother's presence in the house. But Zach's haunted expressions still sometimes took Seth back to the darkest days of his life. It kept him on edge.

"He said he had something else going on and he'd talk to me tomorrow."

"Oh, okay." Heavenly didn't sound fazed. "Whatever it is, I hope he enjoys it."

"Probably. He seems to be settling into his new life."

"He does."

Seth heard the smile in Heavenly's voice. She cared about everyone around her, and he loved her for it.

A future without her sunshine would be black. It would be worse than losing Autumn.

"Seth?" she called up the stairs.

He dried off his face, then told himself to pull his head out of his ass and act normal. "Yeah?"

"Are the twins coming for dinner? I made plenty."

Taking a deep breath, he made his way down the stairs, well aware that he could no longer stand in place. He had to make a decision soon.

When he reached the lower level, he found Heavenly plating her kabobs and Beck on the patio, just outside the open door, lighting up the grill. "They're working tonight and tomorrow before their epic send-off bash Saturday night, then catching their plane back to New York on Sunday."

Thank fuck he wouldn't have to lie to his brothers about his relationship with Heavenly for much longer.

"So I guess it's just us tonight," she said with a shrug.

"Yep." Beck grinned as he lowered the lid on the grill. "I'm okay with that because I've missed you."

It had been a busy week, and they hadn't spent much time together. Or had Seth been unconsciously avoiding them since the wedding?

"I've missed you." She smiled at the surgeon, then turned to him, her expression wobbling. "Both of you."

He swallowed hard. "I've missed you, angel."

Seth could say that in all honesty. Without her, he felt like a parched man crawling through the desert, a thousand miles from water.

The curl of her lips turned upside down. Concern clouded her face. "Is something wrong?"

Jesus, he couldn't talk about this now. He wasn't ready. But he fucking needed to touch her. He needed to be with them.

He turned to Beck. "How long before we have to put the kabobs on?"

The surgeon seemed to sense he was in a mood. "How long do you need?"

"I-I don't know. A while."

Beck flipped off the grill. "You got it."

Seth came up behind Heavenly and schlepped the tray of kabobs into the refrigerator, then lifted her into his arms, carrying her out to the patio, and setting her between him and Beck, stringing kisses up her neck. "I need you."

Beck answered first. "We're here."

Sending a weighty glance to the surgeon, Seth nodded in thanks but couldn't tame his jumble of words into a coherent sentence. Instead, he clung to the moment, fisting Heavenly's hair in his hands and capturing her mouth, plunging deep as if he could somehow brand himself on her, own her for all time, with a sweep of his tongue.

She responded with a little whimper, opening to him and surging against him as she looped her arms around his neck. Behind her, Beck grabbed the hem of her T-shirt and pulled it up her body. The movement disrupted their kiss for a heartbeat as the doctor whisked it over her head. Seth watched her small waist, lacy bra, and the pale swells of her breasts come into view one stunning inch at a time. Desire flared hot through every vein, sped to every corner of his body. He dragged in a rough breath, then took her face in his hands and seized her lips again.

Beck dragged her shorts down her legs, kneeling behind her until he pulled the garment off, then kissed his way back up her thighs until he reached the lace of her underwear clinging to her pert cheeks. "I can have the rest of her clothes off in ten seconds, but if I keep going, we'll end up fucking her out here."

Reluctantly, Seth dragged himself from her sweet mouth. His unwavering stare drilled down into her wide eyes as he answered. "It's not the first time, and the neighbors can't see. Strip her."

At Heavenly's indrawn breath, Seth lifted her chin, swooped down, and took her mouth once more. Vaguely, he was aware of Beck's lips trailing across her shoulder, teeth nipping into the sensitive curve of her neck, as he unhooked her bra. The lace scraped his skin as the good doctor pulled the undergarment free between them. Then suddenly, her bare breasts pressed against his chest. Her erect nipples only drew up harder when Seth cupped her jaw, forced his way deeper into her mouth, and made love to it like he owned it.

"She's trembling for us," Beck murmured.

Seth felt it, just like he felt her with him kiss for kiss, breath for breath. And she proved she was more than eager when she tugged at his tank, trying hard to lift it up his body and over his head.

It was a distraction. When she diverted her attention from the demand of his kiss to undress him, he missed her lips clinging to his own, the full, lush sweep of her tongue sliding against his. Seth wasn't okay with that.

With an annoyed grunt, he wrenched from her, chest lifting and heaving, as he reached behind him and jerked the tank over his head. With heavy-lidded eyes, Heavenly watched him toss it to the patio with a snarl. His stare a vow to have her, fuck her, pleasure her.

Then his gaze fell to her exposed breasts. "God, I love your tits."

A splash of red flushed her cheeks. He couldn't bring himself to give a fuck that his raspy voice no longer sounded like his own or that he felt like a man possessed. He only cared that she was theirs.

What does that tell you about your feelings?

Seth shelved the voice in his head and lifted his stare from Heavenly's curves to Beck, who lurked at her back, skimming his lips and fingertips across her skin, wringing shivers from her. He hooked his thumbs under the waistband of her panties and eased them down just enough to tease him. Seth felt ready to come out of his skin with impatience. The surgeon had been finding subtle ways to egg him on, pushing every one of his possessive buttons. Trying to force him into making a goddamn decision.

Tonight, Seth felt just reckless enough to do it.

"Take them off," he demanded.

Beck didn't. He nibbled at Heavenly's neck, thumbed her hard nipple, and smiled at her throaty little gasp. "Hmm, you taste good, little girl. I want my mouth on that pussy."

Bastard. "Goddamn it, I need inside her now."

"In a minute." From behind, Beck slid one hand under the waistband of her panties until his fingers disappeared beneath the silk. Her audible gasp whipped through Seth. He fucking got harder. Then the doctor's digits slid down, between her folds. His hand moved rhythmically. Heavenly tossed her head onto Beck's shoulder, arched her back—which thrust her breasts closer to Seth's hungry mouth—and moaned.

He couldn't take it anymore. He shucked his shorts and kicked them aside, leaving himself completely naked. Then he bent and ripped Heavenly's panties down her thighs. The sight of Beck's fingers burrowing in her tender, puffy folds turned him on. He felt like a raging, caged beast, desperate to take her.

As if Beck sensed he was at the end of his rope, the surgeon moved his hand so he no longer shielded her cunt. Instead, he used his fingers to part her folds and reveal all the secrets of her rosy, swollen clit.

Stare glued, Seth fell to his knees.

"That's pretty, isn't it?" Beck taunted.

Seth couldn't answer; he could barely breathe. "Fuck."

"I think you should do that…as soon as I've nibbled on our girl." Before Seth could process those words, Beck lifted Heavenly to the nearby chaise, lit with the rays of the setting sun, and lay back, turning her to face him and positioning her spread legs over his face. Then he lifted his head and fastened his open mouth over her weeping slit, engulfing it.

"Beck!" she wailed, thrusting her fists into his hair, head tossed back.

Seth growled. Watching the surgeon eat at her with savage strokes of his tongue turned Seth on, but he wanted to be inside her sweet, slick pussy right now.

He prowled to the nearby container that held pool noodles and floaties and, with a frustrated yank, tore open the lid. Inside, he found the stash of condoms and lube, fisting one of each as he stomped over to Beck. "I need inside her."

It took the doctor a long moment to lower his mouth from her cunt. When he did, he raised a brow, licking his lips like he had all day, while circling a lazy thumb over her pearl. "I want to wring an orgasm or two out of her first."

Before Beck even finished speaking, Seth shook his head. "I need her like I fucking need to breathe."

Vaguely, he realized he was being a selfish ass and tried to figure out how to backpedal, but Beck looked up at Heavenly, his thumb still tormenting her. "You'll come like a good girl if Seth makes love to you?"

She panted, breaths heavy and uneven, as she gave the surgeon a shaky nod. "Yes. One of you, just please... Do something!"

Seth didn't wait for another invitation. He plucked her off of Beck and set her on unsteady feet, devouring her lips again and absently tossing the lube to the good doctor. That left him holding the condom.

Beck grunted. "Let me get inside her ass, then her pussy is all yours."

"Hurry."

If he was being honest, Seth didn't want to glove up. He didn't want anything between him and Heavenly right now. But he wanted her, wanted to be as deep inside her as possible in a way he couldn't apologize for and couldn't ignore. It was possessive. It was primal. Every instinct told him to forget the condom, bury himself, and spray her with every drop boiling in his balls.

That feeling isn't real, isn't smart, isn't good.

Logic didn't make it go away. Neither did his certainty that Beck was maneuvering him into making this choice.

Seth squeezed the foil packet between his fingers, his head racing, his body buzzing, his need pounding. What the fuck was he going to do?

An instant later, Beck was on his feet, gesturing Seth to lie on the chaise. He flung himself across the padded lounger, his heart thudding furiously as the doctor helped Heavenly perch over him on her hands and knees. Their eyes met, hers dark and dilated with passion. Perspiration dampened the curls around her hairline. He knew the moment Beck applied the lube because she gasped, her intake of air rife with shock. Her next sound told him the surgeon was manipulating her rosette.

"Open up to me."

At his growl, she moaned and closed her eyes, whimpering as he settled behind her and took hold of her hips. "Beck..."

"Bear down. Take my cock, little girl."

Seth watched, keeping a death grip on his desire, as Beck penetrated her. Pleasure transformed her face.

The doctor groaned long and loud as he pulled back, then lunged into her again, the strokes of his hips slow, deep, and deliberate.

"Your turn," he ground out, his voice strained and dark.

Now Seth had to make a fucking decision.

He squeezed his fist tighter, the corner of the foil packet digging into his palm. Open and wear it...or throw caution to the wind and let whatever was going to happen in the future happen?

Above him, Beck continued to ease out and shuttle into Heavenly's backside. Her breathing picked up pace. Her nipples looked like pink confections as they swung in his face. He ached to take them in his mouth while he buried himself in her pussy—and damn the consequences.

But could he live with that?

Seth lay frozen in indecision when he heard a noise he couldn't place. Before he could figure it out, Heavenly gasped and gripped his shoulders, her exhalation a whine of need as she lowered her head and kissed him with a desperate sweep of her tongue.

"Hurry up, man," Beck growled. "If you want our usual finish together, you've got to get inside her now."

"What the hell?" a too-familiar voice called across the backyard.

"Are you fucking kidding me?" said another almost like the first.

The twins. The out-of-place noise he'd heard moments ago had been the slam of the back gate as they'd arrived.

Fuck!

Seth jackknifed up as Beck pulled free from Heavenly, reached for a nearby towel left over from the previous day's swim, and wrapped it around the two of them. As Seth scrambled into his shorts, he started sweating. Mentally, he groped for something to say.

This isn't what it looks like.

Yeah, that would never fly.

Fuck. "Let me explain."

"Oh, we wanna hear this." Jack sounded pissed.

Connor didn't look any less furious. "Tell us how you're not a hypocrite."

As demands went, theirs was valid. As Seth tried to gather his thoughts, Beck cleared his throat. "I'll take Heavenly and, um…"

Seth nodded. "Go inside."

Neither of them should have to defend their relationship to his brothers. That was his cross to bear. And their tenderhearted girl didn't belong in the middle of an argument. Knowing her, she would feel horrible about "causing" family strife.

Which she hadn't.

Heavenly resisted Beck's nudge toward the patio door and sent Seth a glance filled with concern and contrition.

"It's okay, angel," he assured her.

Beck would shelter her from whatever happened next. At least Seth had that assurance.

She nodded reluctantly, and silence prevailed as the two of them gathered more towels and their clothes, then sidled into the house, shutting the door behind them with a deafening click.

Those few seconds of reprieve weren't enough for Seth to get his head together, but one glance told him the twins were ready to rumble.

"How long has this shit been going on?" Jack gestured to the back door where Beck and Heavenly had disappeared inside.

Seth hesitated and tried to think of the right thing to say. But his omissions and half-truths had landed him here. Yeah, he'd meant well when he'd tried to give the twins advice, but clearly they didn't see it that way.

"Since I moved to LA." Well, more or less. There had been six weeks between his impulsive relocation and the night he and Beck had first taken Heavenly to bed in a rush of pent-up desire and passion. But that distinction wasn't important. What they wanted to know was whether he'd ever had a relationship with Heavenly alone. The answer was no.

Connor's eyes bugged out. "You've been lying to everyone for nearly six months? The three of you have been fucking all this time? Wow, hypocritical much?"

His brothers' anger wasn't easy to take, but Seth tried to explain. "Not entirely, no."

Jack snorted. "How do you figure that? Because after your little speech when you caught us with"—he turned to Connor—"what was her name?"

"How the fuck should I remember?" Connor shrugged.

"Emily," Seth supplied.

"That's right," Connor put in.

"Yeah, so after your little speech, you told us it was irresponsible to fuck the same girl, despite the fact we like it and we're goddamn happy doing it." Jack crossed his arms over his chest. "But you're doing it with your pal?"

"What I said was, that neither of you is mature enough to make a lasting relationship with three people work, and I know that because Beck, Heavenly, and I have to work constantly to keep ourselves together. It's not fucking easy. We have to listen and compromise and—"

"We told you we're not interested in anything beyond a few sweaty hours," Jack shot back. "No offense, big brother, but we're twenty-one. Adults. We don't need your sanctimonious ass trying to inform what our dicks do."

Ouch. Then again, he probably deserved that—and more—for not coming clean.

"Pardon me for trying to save you heartache. I know you two don't care about keeping a girl for more than a night yet, but there may come a day when you do. And I'm telling you now, you won't have the maturity or skills to handle it."

"You don't know that," Jack defended.

"I do. Marriage to Autumn taught me a lot about commitment. Beck is divorced now, but he knows a lot about what it takes to make a relationship work, too. We understand the things you should—and shouldn't—do to make love last. But you don't have that experience to fall back on. If you two fall in love with a woman someday, you're likely to run her over or run her off because you don't fucking know how to behave."

"Don't give us that shit," Connor snarled.

"It's not shit. Despite the fact Beck and I have experience and skills, it's still way harder with three people than two." Though they had faced challenges the twins might never—like Heavenly's father dying and Beck's long-lost family returning—his brothers were naive if they thought they wouldn't face adversity. "At the start of the summer, when I told you that you'd need to grow up to make this kind of relationship last, I was being honest. Sex is easy. And between three people who click, it's absolutely off the chain. I admit it."

"Damn straight," they affirmed together.

"But there's more to life than sex, guys. You say you're adults. Then stop acting like teenagers whose sole goal in life is getting ass. You *will* want to settle down one day, and I'm giving you sound advice. You just don't want to hear it. But if you'd stop rebelling and start thinking about your future for a hot second, you'd realize I'm right. And I'm telling you, since Beck, Heavenly, and I moved in almost four months ago, we've had to work hard to stay together. We use all our skills. It doesn't just happen."

"You're living together?" Connor's mouth dropped open wide.

Jack didn't look any less shocked.

Seth shrugged. "Why do you think that fucking expensive apartment was just sitting there vacant when you two rolled into town? The fact is, I was considering breaking the lease before you showed up."

Scowling, Jack sized up the house. "So this is Beck's place? Did he already live here with Heavenly when you moved in?"

"No. We were both single and trying separately to date her. I wasn't lying when I said I'd shared women before. I had, casually. That's why I know that three people trying to make a life together is totally different. But Heavenly needed us both."

Jack snorted. "Yeah, she figured out two cocks are better than one."

Seth slapped him upside the head. "That's not what I mean, dipshit. I'm saying that Beck and I put aside our individual wants to have her for our own because she needed the support and stability we give her together. She was going to school, trying to support herself and her father while he was sick and dying..." He didn't owe the twins his girlfriend's life story, but he wanted them to understand. "She was drowning emotionally and financially, and she didn't know how to ask for help. Beck and I taught her. We each gave her things she needed and—"

"You both top her," Connor observed astutely.

Apparently, what they'd learned at Club Graffiti about the lifestyle had helped them identify the earmarks. "Yeah. And once we figured out how to provide the support she needed while also respecting each other, she flourished."

Jack scratched at his chin. "Okay. I get it. You're not just fucking. Good for you. But Connor and I are still at the hit-it-and-quit-it stage. If we need advice on how to keep a girl for more than a night or two, we'll know who to ask. In the meantime, keep your well-meaning advice to yourself, huh?"

Seth opened his mouth to object, then shut it. At twenty-one, his dad's good buddy had tried to tell him how to live. Granted, Gene had saved his life at sixteen and tried to be a dad after his own had been killed in the line of duty, but he'd been too much of a hothead to listen when the man had insisted that neither he nor Autumn was mature enough to get married. Seth had resented the fuck out of him...but over time, he'd been pissed at himself for not listening. He and Autumn hadn't been ready for that kind of commitment.

The twins weren't, either. If he backed off and let them carry on— and probably fuck up once or twice—maybe they'd come to him for help when they were ready to think about spending more than a night with a woman. "All right."

"Really? You're going to stop lecturing us?" Connor sounded suspicious.

Seth tossed up his hands. "Yep. Not another word."

"Good. If you weren't going to shut up, I would have had to tell Mom the shit you're doing out here in Hollyweird." Jack gave him a cocky grin.

"Nice try. We're already planning to tell her everything after her wedding."

"Seriously?" he scoffed. "Dude... Good luck with that."

Seth knew they were going to need it. "Thanks. But if you two want to be assholes, I can tell Mom about your proclivities, too. And I'm not relying on her to help fund my last year of college, so..."

"Damn it, you always end up getting the last word," Connor groused.

"I'm still better at some things than you. Arguing is one of them." Seth winked.

Weirdly, he was convinced that, as horrible and embarrassing as the twins finding them mid-coitus had been, this conversation was for the best. "You guys want to stay for dinner?"

They both nodded. "That would be great."

"Yeah. Thanks," Jack added.

"Good. Heavenly made plenty. Did you two get off work early?"

Jack and Connor exchanged a guilty glance, then Jack winced. "Not exactly."

Seth raised a brow. "What 'exactly' happened?"

"We got fired." Connor pulled at the back of his neck. "We might have, um...been fucking one of the waitresses in the break room during our lunch hour when our boss walked in."

Seth sighed, but he wasn't surprised his brothers had ignored his advice. "I take it he was pissed?"

They exchanged another glance, then Jack's grimace turned even more guilty. "Well, if you'd seen two dudes going at your barely legal daughter in a semi-public room..."

Pressing his forehead to his palm, Seth shook his head, trying both not to be annoyed and not to laugh. "That would do it."

"Yeah. He told us not to come back," Connor admitted.

"Which is fine by us. That gives us more time to ourselves before we head home. Hey, we're partying on Saturday night with the guys we met this summer. If you and Beck want to come, we're going to take Zach to his first titty bar. He loves tits. Hell, he's a horny bastard in general."

"Yep. When he found his inner freak, he found it hard." Connor frowned. "Wait a minute… Does Zach know about you three?"

"He does. And since you three shared an apartment all summer, I guess he's known for a while that you two like to put a woman between you."

"Yep, and that son of a bitch never said a word—to either of us," Jack grumbled.

Seth had to smile. "I'll be damned. Should have known Beck's brother would be sly. Must run in the family."

Jack laughed. "Probably. Sometimes he's really earnest and do-goody, but he's a decent dude."

"Beck, too."

Jack gaped. "Do you, um…fuck each other?"

"No."

"Not that there's anything wrong with being gay or bi or whatever, if that does it for you." Connor frowned.

"There isn't, but it doesn't," Seth assured. "We're strictly girl-in-between."

"We get that." Curiosity seemed to get the best of him again. "Is it super weird to share a woman with a guy you don't know, like, really, really well?"

Seth pondered that. "No. Once we stopped fighting over Heavenly and got on the same page, it didn't just feel different, it felt right. I think I knew then that, with the two of them is where I belong."

The twins exchanged a befuddled glance, then Jack shrugged. "Well, we're happy for you, bro. Really. You keep doing you."

"Thanks. I guess, then…you two should keep doing you, too."

At least until they ran into problems with a woman they both fell for and needed advice.

"Thanks." Connor smiled. "So…if we're staying for dinner, you got a beer?"

A loud buzzing noise jolted Heavenly out of a sound sleep. She moaned when the electronic whir chimed again.

Beside her, Seth rolled over. "Who the fuck is calling at this hour?" he grumbled as he groped for his device. "Hello?"

Lifting her heavy lids, she saw Seth sitting up—cell phone pressed to his ear—silhouetted by the moonlight spilling through the window, painting his sculpted back and shoulders in a silvery hue.

"Hey, man," Seth greeted, then pinned her with a stunned stare. "They're at the hospital? Now?"

"Who?" She sat up, trying to clear the fog of sleep.

On her other side, Beck bolted upright, scrubbing a hand over his face. "Someone needs me at the hospital?"

"No," Seth assured. "River's calling. Raine is in labor."

Heavenly gasped. "The babies are coming?"

Seth nodded and held up a finger. "Of course, man. Text me your location. I'll throw on some clothes and be there ASAP."

Heavenly grinned at Beck. "The babies are coming."

"They do that, usually after nine months." He smirked.

She playfully swatted his arm as Seth ended the call.

"Sorry, I didn't mean to wake you both," he apologized as he hurried to the dresser and pulled out clothes. "River just got off the phone with Hammer. Raine's water broke half an hour ago, so they rushed her to the hospital. Since River wants to be there for his sister, he asked me to take over his stakeout."

She glanced at the clock. "At two thirty in the morning?"

He nodded. "I'll be back shortly after sunrise. The prick cheating on his wife always leaves his girlfriend's house before then."

"If you know he's there, can't you just—"

"Tell the wife? She knows. But she's paying me for photos of them together. She plans to give them to her lawyer." Seth dragged on a pair of dark jeans. "So far, he's let himself out the door every time. Maybe because his sidepiece can't walk when he's finished with her? I don't know. But we need a damn photo of them, preferably in some compromising position."

As Seth tugged a black T-shirt over his head, Heavenly climbed over Beck. She didn't get far before he cinched his strong hands around her waist and pulled her down on his growing erection. "Where are you going, little girl?"

His deep, raspy invitation had goose bumps erupting across her arms. "Bathroom."

"Ahh." Beck released her with a wolfish grin. "Hurry back."

"So we can go to the hospital?" she asked eagerly, pausing at the bathroom door.

"To sit and wait? We can." Beck shrugged. "But it might take hours. First deliveries usually do."

"I know. I'm just excited. And Raine is understandably nervous."

"She has Liam and Hammer and the best ob-gyn team in LA. She'll be fine."

After taking care of business, Heavenly returned to the bedroom to find her men gone. Masculine voices coming from below told her they were in the kitchen. After sliding on her robe, she padded down the stairs, where Seth was securing the lid of his go mug while Beck popped in a pod to brew his java.

"Any idea how dilated she is?"

"No clue. I didn't ask. Besides, I doubt River knows anything about that stuff," Seth scoffed.

"True. He's more way more focused on orgasms than babies," Beck pointed out.

Like someone else we know.

Heavenly didn't speak her thought aloud. She knew why Seth had avoided even talking about having children. But as Raine's pregnancy had progressed, Heavenly began thinking more about the future and family and all the things she hadn't had since her own childhood. Would it be smarter to wait until she was out of nursing school and a little more established in her career? Yes. But her father's early, untimely death had taught her that no one was guaranteed tomorrow.

Sighing, Heavenly eased in beside Seth. He wrapped an arm around her as she plucked a tea pod from the rack. "Do you want me to pack a snack for you before you leave?"

He flashed her a warm smile. When he looked at her like that, it was impossible to be upset with him about anything, especially not being over the devastating trauma that had him reluctant to start another family. "No, angel. I want you to go back upstairs, climb into bed, and get some sleep."

She shook her head. "I'm too awake and too keyed up about Raine."

"I'll do my best to exhaust you again," Beck drawled with a wicked wink.

"Lucky bastard. Sometimes, owning your own business really blows," Seth grumbled before cupping her nape and claiming her lips until her toes curled. "Try not to have too much fun without me, angel."

She flashed him a shyly vampy grin. "Well, if you get home early enough…"

"If you keep teasing me like that, I'll break down the mistress's door, snap a photo of them in bed together, and haul ass home."

"Sounds like a solid plan to me," Beck quipped.

"Me, too. Unfortunately, breaking and entering will land me in jail and ruin my business." Seth shrugged, then strode toward the garage. "I'll be back as soon as I can."

"Be safe out there," Heavenly called just before the door closed behind him. Then she cupped her mug of tea and found Beck leaning up against the island, watching her with an unreadable stare. "What?"

"Nothing. I was just thinking."

"About?"

"Jack and Connor. Us. Seth. The future." He paused. "Babies."

So she wasn't the only one? "Me, too."

Her uneasy confession lured him closer. In two long strides, Beck stood in front of her, setting his coffee aside and holding her with a piercing stare. He tucked a stray curl behind her ear, grazing her cheek with his warm fingers. Heavenly closed her eyes and savored his touch.

"Feel like curling up on the couch and comparing notes?" he murmured.

After what happened last weekend in Vegas? "I think we should."

With a nod, he slung an arm around her waist and guided her to the family room. Heavenly sat on the couch, tucking her legs beneath her. Beck eased down and cuddled her against his side, surrounding her with his heat and familiar scent.

Beck didn't say anything right away. He seemed to be collecting his thoughts. That suited Heavenly since she was sorting out her own.

"Do you really think Jack and Connor will keep their mouths shut?" She hadn't intended to break the silence, but worry had been plaguing her since the twins had barged into their backyard last night.

"I hope so. But I'm not as convinced as Seth, if that's what you're asking."

"I'm not, either. It makes me nervous."

"Because?"

"We'll be meeting his family in a couple of months. I don't want to walk through the door and already be labeled a whore."

Beck scowled and shook his head. "If that happens, I'll beat the shit out of those bigmouthed bastards, with or without Seth's help."

"You can't go around beating up people who hurt my feelings."

"Want to bet?" He arched a brow. "Anyone who calls you a whore is getting an ass beating. Case closed."

She sent him a faint smile. "Hopefully, it won't come to that. If the twins say anything to Grace about us, Seth will out them, too. But that won't help family harmony."

Beck nodded. "We just have to hope the prospect of losing their college tuition is incentive enough for them to keep quiet. If not, Seth's family will probably shun me, too, for being the interloping deviant who can't keep his cock out of you."

That possibility had crossed Heavenly's mind, too.

"And then what happens?" She blew on her tea, then took another sip. "I worry our relationship will cause a rift between Seth and his family. That would devastate him. They seem really close."

"Yeah. Being estranged from my family is nothing new for me, and I guess that's why it's hard for me to wrap my head around Seth's fear of letting his mom down. But for him, it's clearly enormous."

Heavenly nodded. "I get it. Dad and I were really close. I hated to disappoint him. But then again, we only had each other. It sounds as if Seth is that close to his whole family. I'm still shocked he left them all and moved to LA. Even if my dad had been healthy, I could have never packed my bags and moved across the country without him."

"Seth did that for you, little girl." Beck kissed the tip of her nose. "He'd move across continents to be with you. So would I."

Her heart melted. "You would?"

"Absolutely," he murmured before slanting his lips over hers with a kiss so full of passion, she couldn't help but dissolve against him. Then he eased back and studied her face with a warm gaze.

"What are you thinking?" she whispered.

"You mean besides plucking you off the couch and carrying you back to bed?"

"Besides that." Suddenly Beck sobered, and Heavenly's anxiety surged. "What is it?"

"There's something I've wanted to discuss with you for a while, but there never seemed to be a good time between work, Zach, Gloria's wedding, and Seth's brothers. This summer has been crazy."

"It has, but I always want to hear about whatever is troubling you. Talk to me."

Beck turned serious, resting his elbows on his knees and lowering his head. At the tension in his posture, more trepidation filled Heavenly. She gently stroked his back, both to comfort him and draw on his strength, as she steeled herself for whatever he needed to say.

"Do you still want kids?"

That's what's weighing on him?

"I know you're young," he went on. "You're still going to school and volunteering at the hospital. You've been adjusting to life here with Seth and me. I'm grateful you put off finding a new job this summer so you could help Zach acclimate, so the last thing I want to do is put more pressure on you. But I have to know"—he tensed and pinned her with a solemn stare that broke her heart—"is getting married and having babies still on the table?"

They'd discussed that at the lodge months ago. Everything had been so busy and complicated since. And with Seth's seeming uncertainty about their future, it was no wonder Beck felt unsure.

"Yes. It is as far as I'm concerned." It had been weighing heavily on her mind since Seth had opened up about the tragic deaths of his wife and son. Of course, she could never replace Autumn, and no child she bore would bring back Tristan…but she'd wondered if having a family again would help him heal and feel whole. "I think about it a lot, actually."

Tension left his body with a heavy sigh, then he wrapped her in a tight hug. "Fuck. You have no idea how happy I am to hear that, little girl. I was afraid you'd changed your mind."

"No, I simply haven't been pushing him the way you have, especially about kids."

Beck grimaced. "You've noticed?"

"It's impossible to ignore the push-pull between you two in bed. Even when you both have me mindless and pleading, I still feel it."

"I'm sorry. I'm not trying to make everything awkward, I'm just hoping Seth will put the past behind him and move forward with us, the way we planned before… Well, before."

"You don't think he'll come around on his own?"

"Honestly?" Beck sighed. "I have no clue."

"I think he'll get there. He's doing better. It's slow, but he made peace with Zach. That's a positive step."

"Yeah," Beck conceded. "But that was two months ago. He hasn't made much progress since."

"That's not true. The night before Gloria's wedding he almost…you know, without a condom."

Beck grinned. "I love that we can arouse you into doing some of the dirtiest, sexiest things, but you still blush when you try to talk about them."

She slapped his arm playfully. "Stop it. You know I'm right. Not that Seth forgoing the condom would have mattered that night. I started my period the next day."

"Oh, I remember, damn it. But him *almost* fucking your pretty little pussy bare that night isn't the same as him actually doing it."

"But still… Baby steps."

He shrugged. "So you think we should keep waiting for Seth to work out his fears?"

"I don't think we can force him to move past them. And I'm okay with waiting if that's what he needs."

"How long? Until you get out of school?"

"That would be practical," she pointed out. "It would be harder to study and work with an infant."

"True, but the difficulty wouldn't last forever. The three of us could make it work. It would be worth it."

"It would," she agreed. "But only if Seth is on board. He's not right now. I haven't put a mental deadline on how long I'm willing to wait. I'm not in a huge hurry. Are you?"

"Honestly? Yes. My patience was up at the lodge. Since we'd all agreed that we would let fate decide our future, I prayed we'd get you pregnant that night, but..." Beck sighed.

He was already done waiting? That filled her with panic, but she had to stay calm and try to reason with him. "If I had, Seth probably wouldn't be with us today."

Beck cursed. "I've thought of that, and I'm trying not to be a selfish prick. I'm just tired of my life being on hold. What if it takes him another two years to be ready for kids? Five years? Or more? Once, he suggested we wait a decade. I can't do that, especially since he's running from his demons a lot more than he's fighting them."

"But he *is* fighting. That's something. And I think he'll get there, probably sooner than you imagine..." She did her best to encourage Beck since he'd obviously been gnawing on his frustration in silence for months. "Just...please. Don't give up on us."

"That's the last thing I want," he assured. "And it's not that I don't sympathize with his loss. The enormity of his wife and son being murdered, especially over a case he pursued... I can't even imagine. But Seth can't change any of that now. Beating himself black and blue isn't living. And being afraid of the future won't stop it from coming."

"I know, but we have to keep reassuring him and wait for him to come to terms with his past. What other choice do we have?"

"There are other options...but they come with risks."

His ominous tone sent a chill up her spine. "Risks?"

Beck nodded tightly. "You and I are ready for a family...and it only takes two to tango. We could go upstairs right now and start making babies."

Heavenly wasn't okay with that. "But—"

"But this is an equal partnership," Beck reassured her. "If we did that behind Seth's back, he'd feel betrayed, and rightly so. And he wouldn't stick around."

Her heart splintered at the thought. "I-I could never do that to him."

"No matter how badly you want commitment and children? It's definitely a last resort. But I've started to wonder…at what point does the longing to have a family outweigh the risk of losing him? Would you really wait forever?"

Panic flooded her system, making her stomach knot and her heart ache. He'd asked a question that would kill her to answer. "I don't know. I'm trying not to think of the worst-case scenario. I'd rather believe in the three of us."

"I would, too, but I'm not sure how much longer I can."

Beck had a point. What if Seth decided he never wanted more children? Could she stay with him without ever experiencing the joy of motherhood or raising a family? Did that mean Beck would leave and find another woman to give him the babies he ached for?

She pressed a hand to her trembling mouth to hold in her tears. No, that was her worst nightmare, the one where she'd given her whole heart and been left standing broken and alone and still so very in love with them.

Could she ever truly be happy without either Beck or Seth? Was this the beginning of their end?

No. She couldn't lose them.

They love me…as much as I love them.

She knew that with every cell in her body. They'd rescued her from poverty, given her security, found her dad the medical care he'd needed, saved her from a demeaning job flashing her body to men who saw her as a piece of ass, and flown halfway across the country to help scatter her dad's ashes. They'd helped her see the world and experience new things while lifting her burdens, soothing her worries, and calming her fears. They'd stolen her heart and soul.

Heavenly refused to lose either of them. Somehow, she'd keep them all together.

"I-I don't know how to fix this. All I know is that I want a child with *both* of you." Swiping a tear from her cheek, Heavenly forced the hardest question she'd ever asked off her lips. "How much longer can you wait?"

Pain etched Beck face as he lifted the mug from her hand and cupped her cheeks, forcing her gaze. "I'm not walking out the door tonight, little girl. Hell, I don't ever want to leave. I can't imagine giving up what we have, what we could have in the future. I'm sorry I'm rocking the boat, but I'm not getting any younger. I know what I want, and that's a family with you and Seth. Somehow, someway, we have to help him come to the same conclusion."

"How much longer?" she asked, voice cracking this time.

"Don't cry," Beck whispered as he brushed her tears away with the pads of his thumbs, then pressed a tender kiss to her lips. "I can find a little more patience. If you want to wait until you're done with school, I understand."

But that's only a matter of months.

"What if we can't persuade him to embrace the future by then?"

A sad smile tugged Beck's lips as he lifted her onto his lap and cradled her close to his warm chest. "Then you and I will have some serious soul-searching to do."

"Slow down, little girl," Beck chided as he and Seth hurried to keep up with Heavenly, who power-walked down the hospital hallway. "Raine and the twins aren't going anywhere for a couple of days."

She sent him a self-deprecating smile over her shoulder. "I know, but I can't wait to see them."

Like I can't wait to see our *babies. Hopefully. Someday...*

Since Seth was beside him, Beck kept that thought to himself. In fact, he was surprised Seth had come with them at all.

When Hammer had called just after six this morning, shouting that he and Liam were fathers, Beck had been sure Seth would have zero interest in visiting Raine and the twins, especially after being out half the night completing River's case. But after snapping the prized photo and coming home, he'd consented to accompany them.

Beck was thrilled for the happy new family, especially knowing Raine and the babies were healthy and doing fine. But a part of him was jealous as fuck.

"I was half asleep when I stumbled in this morning," Seth admitted, now freshly showered and holding a cup of coffee as he walked down the hall beside them. "What are the babies' names again?"

"Ciara and Catronia." Heavenly turned with a bright smile. "I think they're Irish or Gaelic. Such pretty, interesting names."

Seth frowned. "But what if they're Hammer's babies?"

"I don't think that matters to him." Beck shrugged. *I sure as fuck wouldn't care in Hammer's shoes.*

As the trio rounded the corner, familiar laughter spilled through the waiting room door. Heavenly raced inside. Beck filed in right behind her, grinning when he saw Hammer and Liam disheveled, bleary-eyed, and looking exhausted as fuck but beaming with pride and joy.

"Hey," Hammer bellowed as he and Liam rushed over and wrapped Beck and Seth in bro-hugs before each kissed Heavenly's cheek.

"How's Raine?" their girl asked anxiously.

"Great," Hammer assured. "Amazing actually."

Liam beamed. "Our wee lass is a superwoman."

"And she only called us motherfuckers twice during delivery." Hammer chuckled.

"But she threatened to cut off our willies more than that," Liam quipped.

Everyone laughed. Beck could definitely picture Raine spitting some choice words during labor.

"Aye, thankfully she only promised to superglue her girl parts together once," Liam's mother, Bryn, added with a wry grin. "But she won't. I suspect you lot have more babies to conceive."

Liam slapped Hammer on the back and sent his friend a knowing grin. "That we do."

"Don't tell Raine that now," Macen warned. "She's liable to kill us."

As more laughter ensued, two women who bore a striking, auburn-haired resemblance to Liam sat across the room, tapping away on their phones.

"Come, you three." Bryn beckoned. "I want to introduce you to my own twin girls. They flew all the way from Ireland to be here for the delivery."

Twins? That explained the double bundle Raine had just delivered.

Beck's hand collided with Seth's as they each slid an arm around Heavenly's waist and nudged her after Bryn.

The PI smiled. "I remember Rosaleen and Shauna. It's been a few years, but..."

"Oh, that's right. You met my whole brood the Christmas we came to visit Liam in New York."

"I did." Seth nodded. "They haven't changed a bit."

"Nay. They're still two peas in a pod."

After exchanging introductions with the pair of fortyish, green-eyed identical twins, Heavenly made some small talk, then excused herself, hurrying back to Hammer and Liam. After a polite murmur, Beck followed, leaving Seth to reminisce with Liam's sisters.

"Can I see Raine and the babies?" Heavenly asked. "Are they up to visitors?"

Hammer nodded. "She's been asking to see you. And if you'll sit with her, that would give us time to run to the cafeteria and grab breakfast."

Heavenly looked elated. "I'd love to."

"Great. You two want to grab a bite with us?" Liam asked him and Seth.

"No more hospital grub for me, thanks," Beck quipped.

Seth hesitated, as if trying to decide whether to take the easy out, then he shook his head. "I already ate. Thanks."

"All right, then." Liam clapped Seth on the back. Giving him silent strength? "The babes are in the nursery. We'll point them out on our way to the elevator. Then you can visit with Raine."

A few feet down the hall, Hammer and Liam paused at a large plate-glass window. Everyone huddled around them...except Seth. He held himself back from the others. Thankfully, Heavenly was too busy smiling wistfully and eyeing the line of pink-and-blue-swaddled babies nestled in clear bassinets to notice.

Hammer raised his arm and held his wristband against the glass. After one of the nurses read his name, she smiled and nodded, then glided two bassinets—each holding a tiny pink-swaddled baby with rosy cheeks and wearing a pink-and-white-striped beanie—in front of the glass.

"Oh, my…" Heavenly pressed a hand to her chest with a quivering exhalation. "They're…beautiful."

The names on the bassinets told Beck which baby was which. Ciara dozed peacefully at the moment. Catronia lay awake, dragging her unfocused stare around the room, as if she was afraid she might miss something exciting.

Hammer and Liam are going to have their hands full…

"We think so," Hammer seconded. "Of course we're biased."

"Congratulations, Daddies." Beck clapped both men on the back. "You two did good."

"Raine did all the hard work." Hammer's voice dripped with pride. "She really was amazing."

"Your girl has always been a lot tougher than she looks," Beck reminded. "After all, she puts up with you two."

"Smart-ass." Hammer laughed.

"Let's go, mate." Liam elbowed Hammer. "My stomach thinks my throat's been cut."

"What else is new?" Hammer scoffed with a grin. "We'll be back in few."

"Did River leave already?" Seth frowned as if he'd just registered the fact Raine's brother wasn't around.

Hammer nodded. "You missed him by ten minutes. He went to grab some shut-eye. I'm sure you'll see him later."

"Whether I want to or not," Cooper teased. "See you all in a few."

"We won't be gone long," Macen assured as he and Liam gathered Bryn and the Irish sisters, then headed out of the maternity ward.

Once they were gone, Seth stepped away from the glass and glanced down the hallway. "I need to hit the head. Did you see a bathroom nearby?"

"Down there, on the left." Beck pointed.

"Be right back." He disappeared down the hall.

Once Seth had gone, Beck tried to shove down his annoyance. Cooper's avoidance of the babies was subtle but still noticeable. Instead, he brought Heavenly against his side before pressing a kiss to her temple. "They're so tiny."

"I know. And so beautiful." She sighed.

Every syllable dripped with longing to bring life into the world, to be the kind of loving mother she hadn't had. It was a kick to Beck's balls. But he also heard more than wistfulness in her tone.

"Heavenly?" He needed to know what she was feeling.

She peered up at him, tears filling her eyes as she nibbled her bottom lip. Then she gave him a subtle nod. "I think...I get it now. Your urgency. It might be smarter to wait...but I don't want to."

His heart skipped, then began thundering in his chest. "You're sure? You want marriage and babies now?"

"Yeah." She gave him a watery grin. "I'm ready. Beyond ready."

A happiness brighter than any he'd ever felt shot through his veins. Beck swept her up in his arms and spun her around in dizzying joy. "Let's start today."

He couldn't wait to get her into bed...naked, panting, and pleading before squeezing his bare cock into her tight pussy.

Yeah, and what about Seth?

Beck didn't have an answer.

"Not in the middle of the hallway." She laughed until he set her on her feet.

"You have a point. Good thing there's a janitor's closet around the corner..." He winked.

"You are *so* bad. Besides, I don't think the three of us will fit." Then she sobered and sent him a regretful stare. "And I don't want to do this without Seth. Somehow, we have to make him see..."

"I know." And he feared that put him back at square one. Sure, Heavenly was more eager now, but until Seth was ready for fatherhood again, nothing would change.

Time for Cooper to decide if he wanted solitude or to share a blissfully complicated life filled with pink-and-blue-swaddled babies, midnight feedings, pacifiers, plushy toys, a minivan, and a white-picket fence.

He sighed. "Got any ideas?"

She shook her head. "You?"

Not really. "Let me work on it some. You do the same. We'll compare notes and see where we go. How's that?"

Heavenly nodded. Her hope had dimmed, but it hadn't died. Beck wouldn't let it. "The best we can do for now."

The squeak of sneakers on the tile floor had them both glancing down the hall to see Seth striding toward them. "I feel better. What did I miss?"

Heavenly glanced at the babies once more, then painted on a smile. "Nothing. You two ready to see Raine?"

Yes, but first…one thing Beck hadn't done was point-blank asked Seth when the hell he'd be ready to think about the future. It was past time for a man-to-man talk.

"Go ahead…make sure she's decent and not sleeping," Beck suggested. "If the coast is clear, Seth and I will join you."

"Are you sure?" she asked.

Seth caught his stare, then nodded as he sidled up to Heavenly and cupped her chin, staring into her eyes as if searching for answers he couldn't find within himself. Then he brushed a feathery kiss across her lips. "Yeah, angel. You go on. We'll be right there."

"Okay." Sending them a last pensive glance, she turned and headed down the hall.

Beck hadn't had time to prepare any words, but he'd try his damnedest to prod Seth down the road toward their shared tomorrow.

Turning back to face the big glass window, he stared at the pink-bundled twins that were now a part of Hammer, Liam, and Raine's forever. "Pretty amazing, huh?"

Seth nodded, easing in beside him. "I forgot how tiny and fragile newborns are."

"Yeah, but they grow up fast. Of course, you know that. You must remember when Jack and Connor were infants, and look at them now. They're adults."

Seth scoffed. "Who still act like kids."

"They'll grow out of it…eventually."

"Will they? Jack and Connor should count their blessings."

"That you didn't rat them out?"

"No, and thank God I didn't or I wouldn't have had any leverage when they found us last night." Seth sighed. "I mean that not all kids actually grow up."

"Oh, I know. I've worked with immature assholes. Kathryn Hitch comes to mind…" he said of the nurse who had once tormented Heavenly during every volunteer shift.

"You're right about her…but that's not what I meant. I was speaking literally, not figuratively. Not every child makes it."

Beck tensed. The conversation had gone from casual to consequential in a heartbeat. He probably shouldn't be surprised Seth had caught on to the fact he'd wanted to talk.

"You're right; not all kids grow up. But babies like those"—Beck nodded toward the glass—"are the future. They're what keeps the generations before us alive and humanity carrying on. You and I are both pragmatic enough to understand that life doesn't come with guarantees. Hell, the three of us might walk out of this hospital and a plane could fall from the sky, ending all our lives. I hope not, but fearing the worst isn't living."

"Aren't you full of sunshine and rainbows today?"

Beck scowled. "I'm not trying to be morose, simply stating a fact."

"Yeah, I get it. So what brought on this philosophical mood?"

"The future," Beck replied, watching Catronia still trying to focus on her new world. "Our future. The one you're dragging your feet on starting."

"I figured that's why you've been pushing me to take Heavenly bareback so often lately."

"Hmm. And I thought I'd been subtle." Beck sent him a crooked grin.

"Oh, you were," Seth drawled derisively. "Like a Mack Truck. Look, I know what you're trying to do and why."

"Enlighten me."

"We both know I'm the one holding up the future with Heavenly we hashed out at the lodge."

"No." Beck shook his head. "We *all* know, especially her. I'm ready. She's ready."

Seth reared back. "She told you that?"

"Yeah."

"She wants to get married and have babies right now?" He still looked skeptical.

Beck nodded. "She said just that while you were in the john."

Seth blew out a breath and started pacing. "And it's my fault since *I'm* the one who can't get over my shit."

"Listen, I'm not assigning blame; I'm telling you how we feel. Besides, you can't be surprised after seeing the longing on Heavenly's face when she looked at those babies." Beck waved a hand at the window.

"Do you honestly think I don't *want* to give her a child?"

"I think a part of you would like to. But the thought of bringing another baby into this world terrifies the fuck out of you."

"It does," Seth barked, then paled as if unable to believe he'd spilled the bald truth.

Sympathy squeezed Beck's heart as he clapped the big guy's shoulder, leaned in, and lowered his voice. "You have to know this time will be different. You won't be the only father, Seth. I'll be here to help raise, love, guide, and most of all, *protect* our children. Trust me. If anyone tries to harm our family, they'll have to get through you *and* me. And so help me God, I will unleash a hailstorm of bullets and die gladly before I'll let anyone harm any kid you and I create with Heavenly."

Seth didn't respond, simply sent Beck a burning stare. Did Seth not believe him? Understand him? Or did he just struggle to have faith?

"That's a promise." Beck gripped Seth's shoulder. "And I never break a promise. I will be there every day, every step, no matter what."

Cooper still didn't speak, merely seemed to absorb his words. Beck had no clue what he was thinking.

"Okay, guys. Raine is dressed and…" Heavenly shuffled into the hall, her words trailing off as she eyed them both curiously. "What's going on?"

"Nothing, angel." Seth approached, cupping her cheek and stroking his wide thumb over her bottom lip. "We were just talking."

"About what?"

"Babies." Beck jerked a thumb toward the glass.

Her eyes widened. Yeah, she understood. "You were? And?"

"Nothing new." But that didn't mean he was giving up.

He shoved his hands in his pockets to keep from beating some sense into Seth's thick skull. It wouldn't do any good. It wouldn't move him to make a decision faster. But at least he'd listened. All Beck could hope now was that Cooper took his words to heart. At the very least, he'd given Seth food for thought.

"Raine, Hammer, and Liam's lives are about to be turned upside down—in a good way." Seth changed the subject, his tone edged with experience.

"Funny you should say that." Heavenly bit her lip. "Raine is really nervous. I tried to reassure her that everything was going to be fine and that her insecurities were just a hormone drop, but I think you two could help cheer her up."

"We'll try," Beck assured. "If we can't convince her she has nothing to worry about—"

"Hammer and Liam will," Seth finished Beck's thought as he banded an arm around Heavenly's waist.

"Thanks," she murmured.

Beck trailed the pair down the hall, eyeing Seth's possessive hold on their girl. The sight was encouraging, but Beck was afraid to read too much into it. Still, he wasn't going to stop encouraging Seth to fully commit to their future. The three of them belonged together. Somehow, he had to convince the stubborn prick that, if he did, life would be perfect.

When they reached Raine's room, Heavenly stepped inside and grinned at her bestie. "I'm back, and I brought a couple of sexy men with me."

"Sexy men?" Raine shook her head. "Send them away. I don't even want to look at a man right now."

Beck wasn't surprised. She looked pasty—a sign she'd lost a lot of blood during delivery—and completely exhausted. But she should be okay in time.

Beck rounded the bed and kissed her cheek. "How are you feeling, princess?"

Seth squeezed her hand. "Hell of a morning, huh?"

She arched her brows at them. "Yeah, it was a hell of a morning after pushing not one but *two*, cantaloupes out of my vajayjay. How do you think I feel?"

Beck slanted her a wry stare. "Probably the same way you look, like shit."

"You did not just say that!" Heavenly gaped at him in rebuke.

"What? She does."

"Your bedside manner sucks," Raine bit out.

Beck ignored her retort. "What's your hemoglobin?"

"I don't know. Ninety-eight point six."

"That's your temperature, princess." Beck sighed. "Where's your doctor?"

"She left to catch the next baby, I guess. This place is like a factory," Raine groused. "If you came to play twenty questions, don't. I'm tired, and I have so many stitches down there"—she pointed to her vagina—"my pussy must look like Frankenstein, not that I can see it around this." She jiggled her post-delivery belly.

"Oh, honey." Heavenly took her hand. "I think you look great. And your daughters are beautiful."

"Your abdomen will tone up, princess, and you'll heal down there in no time."

Raine huffed. "Will I?"

"Yes," Beck promised. "What can I do to help you now? What do you need?"

"Sleep. And for Hammer and Liam to stay off me."

"They have to for at least six weeks." Beck smirked.

"No, I mean forever. The next time those two try seducing me with their monkey bars, I'm telling them my playground is broken."

In unison, he, Seth, and Heavenly all burst out laughing. Raine glowered.

"Ms. Kendall?" a nurse called from the door, wheeling in both bassinets with fussing babies. "Your girls are hungry."

The sight of her daughters was like an instant injection of bliss. The scowl melted from Raine's face and a huge grin took its place. "Aww. There are my sweethearts. Did you miss Mommy? Shh, it's okay. I'm going to feed you and kiss you both back to sleep."

"They're so gorgeous," Heavenly gushed.

"They are," Beck nodded. "You did good, princess."

Suddenly realizing Seth had been nearly mute since they'd entered the room, he peered over his shoulder to find Cooper sitting in a chair, staring at the squalling infants with an inscrutable expression. What was Seth thinking?

While the nurse and Heavenly surrounded Raine with pillows, Beck plopped in the chair beside him. "They're little, but they're loud."

"That they are." Seth nodded.

"But they're miracles."

Cooper didn't refute him, just continued to stare at the babies.

When Raine began unbuttoning her pajama top, Seth stood. "Do you want us to step out of the room while you nurse?"

She scoffed. "It's not the first time you and Beck have seen my tits. You saw them at the club, at the lodge…"

Heavenly blinked, clearly stunned. Beck tried not to grimace. Yeah, they needed to sit her down and explain why they'd seen her best friend naked.

Seth cast Heavenly an uncertain glance, then settled back in his seat. "As long as you're comfortable."

"Unless either of you have a breastfeeding fetish, you're welcome to stay."

"Nope," Seth assured.

"Me, either," Beck added.

"Good to know." Holding her daughters like footballs, Raine, with Heavenly's help, coaxed each to latch on.

Their girl shielded Raine with a baby blanket, then sat and smiled at her bestie.

While she nursed the newborns, they talked—about Jack and Connor leaving in two days and Zach's progress with them. About

River and Dean cohabitating in a bungalow that had become a war zone. About Hammer miraculously *not* passing out during the twins' delivery. And about Liam and his family, who'd flown all the way from Ireland to help Raine with the new babies.

At some point, Raine sighed. "Heavenly, would you mind holding Ciara? She fell asleep while she's supposed to be eating…again. I need to move Catronia to the other side. She's a nursing machine."

"I'd *love* to hold her," Heavenly squealed in delight.

As she took the peaceful infant from Raine's arms, Beck cast a sidelong glance at Seth, who was watching their girl cuddle and coo at the tiny baby. A pained—or was that guilty?—expression skipped across his face.

Yeah, watch her. Watch her real close, then tell me you can't get your shit together.

A few minutes later, Raine settled her hospital gown back in place and regarded them. "Do either of you want to hold Catronia?"

Immediately, Seth gave him a blinding imitation smile. "Go ahead, man. I'm good."

Tamping down his frustration, Beck smiled as he stood and lifted the baby—who weighed next to nothing—off the pillow. "Come here, you pretty little curtain climber. It's time you met your uncle Beck."

Heavenly giggled as she watched him cradle the girl in the crook of his arm. Beck drew Catronia close to his chest, then peered down at her with a grin. She stared up at him with bright, inquisitive eyes.

"You don't know it yet, but you're one lucky little girl," he whispered, slowly strolling around the room. "You've got a mommy and *two* daddies who are going to raise you with more love than you can imagine. Trust me. Your parents are going to spoil you rotten. Anything you want—a pony, a Ferrari—all you'll have to do is bat those baby blues, and your daddies will fall all over themselves to give you your heart's desires."

"That's right," Heavenly assured a sleeping Ciara. "You girls will melt their big, bad hearts."

"When they start asking their daddies for sports cars, I'm throwing both of you under the bus," Raine chided with a mock scowl.

"I'll bet Hammer and Liam would rather deal with them wanting sports cars than boys." Seth chuckled as he stood and bent, peering over Heavenly's shoulder at Ciara.

Beck held his breath as Heavenly sent him a hopeful glance.

"You're right. According to Hammer and Liam, the girls aren't allowed to date until they're thirty-five." Raine shook her head. "Don't worry. Mommy won't let your daddies cloister you away until you're nearly middle-aged."

"Be careful, princess," Beck warned as Heavenly smiled up at Seth. "If Hammer and Liam catch you encouraging the girls to date, your ass will be black and blue for life."

"Good. I can't wait. It's been *forever*," she grumbled.

"Well, you won't have to wait much longer. Once the doctor clears you..." Beck didn't finish. He'd let Hammer and Liam tell her they'd been keeping track of every snarky, sassy remark she'd made while pregnant.

"Would you like to hold her?" Heavenly asked Seth softly.

He tensed. "I-I..."

"She's really good," their girl assured with a hopeful smile. "You'll love her."

With every eye in the room on them, Seth hesitated, his face frozen.

Beck's heart drummed in his chest as he waited, hoping Seth would hold the swaddled pink bundle in his big hands.

Finally, Seth gave their girl a choppy shake of his head. "Y-you keep her. You look happy holding her."

Heavenly whipped her gaze down to the infant, her chin quivering, but not before Beck saw her fat tears and her crushed expression. *Goddamn it.*

Seth must have seen it, too. He cleared his throat. "Sorry." Then he whipped out his phone and headed for the exit, killing all hope that the birth of the twins had helped him turn a corner. "Excuse me."

CHAPTER
TWELVE

September

S eth sat on the roof of Shadows in a white wooden chair, watching the sun sink toward the brilliant orange and yellow horizon. It was a perfect day for a wedding. Beside him, Heavenly nestled five-week-old twins, Ciara and Catronia, in her arms, cooing at them with a sunny smile.

Beneath a towering arch of colorful flowers, Beck stood at the altar, dressed in a sharp black suit. He waited beside Hammer and Liam, who both wore gray tuxedos. They acted like typical grooms, fidgeting and chatting in nervous anticipation.

"Beck looks so handsome," Heavenly whispered, eyeing the surgeon. "I'm really proud of him."

When Hammer, Liam, and Raine had announced their formal handfasting ceremony—the closest possible joining to marriage since they couldn't legally wed—they had asked Beck to officiate. Despite his understandable disdain for organized religion, he hadn't hesitated to hop online and become an ordained minister. The gesture told Seth how much Beck loved his friends.

"He did good. And he cleans up pretty well," Seth teased.

"So do you." Heavenly skimmed an approving gaze down his navy suit.

"Yeah?" he leaned in and growled against her ear. "And you look edible, angel. After this, I want to—"

"Stop whatever you're going to say, mister. Little ears." She giggled.

Scowling, Seth glanced down. Ciara's eyes slid shut. Catronia peered up at him with an curious stare, but still... "They don't understand what I'm saying."

"I do, so you don't even have to finish your sentence. But, um..."

There was a mischievous glint in her eyes. "I have a surprise for you later."

Given her come-hither smile, Seth was game. "Like what?"

"You do know the meaning of the word *surprise*? You'll have to wait."

"You're teasing me. I might punish you for that."

The curl of her lips turned even more sultry. "I'm counting on it."

Seth shifted in his seat. "You're playing with fire, angel."

"And it's so much fun."

He arched a brow at her. "You're spending too much time with Raine."

She laughed, probably because it was true.

Minutes slid by. The grooms adjusted their ties again and watched the door to the roof anxiously—something Beck seemingly ribbed them about. Seth could almost hear the jokes flying now...

Beside him, Heavenly adjusted the babies in her arms, grimacing and repositioning her hold.

"You okay?"

She nodded. "Fine. My hand just fell asleep."

The twins were tiny enough, but they must feel heavy in Heavenly's slender arms, especially since they'd grown so much in the last five weeks. She had volunteered to hold them during the ceremony and was clearly enjoying her duty...but she was struggling. He could help out, lighten her load, just for a few minutes, right? It wouldn't be hard, and it wouldn't hurt him. So...why not?

"I'll take one." Seth reached for Catronia.

She hesitated. "Are you sure?"

"I have done this before," he assured her with a wink.

But as she settled the baby in his arms, his hands began to shake and he broke out in a cold sweat. Seth tried to breathe through it, tucking the pink-cheeked cutie in the crook of his arm and telling himself it was no big deal.

But it was. He was holding a baby again.

Catronia kicked and cooed. Seth tried to block out the gut-punch impact of her baby sounds and scents. They took him out of the moment and back years, to a place he couldn't go anymore, down roads he wasn't ready to travel.

Old feelings—sorrow, guilt, and fury—barraged him. He swallowed tightly, doing his best to shove the emotions aside and focus on the moment. He just had to live through each, one at a time, until the day finally ended. Then all these reminders of his past—and his potential future—would be over.

"I know," she said softly. "Thank you."

He couldn't stand the pity on her face, so he looked away, focusing on the altar and the sunset.

"What time is it?" Heavenly whispered into the silence.

Seth glanced at his watch. "Two minutes since the last time you asked. Don't worry, Raine will be walking down the aisle any second now."

As if his comment had conjured her, the bride appeared at the back of the rooftop, clutching River's arm. Heavenly gasped softly as her gaze fell on her best friend. They joined the other guests and stood, watching the siblings cross the threshold. Raine's dark hair fluttered over her bare shoulders. Her smile shimmered. She looked stunning and full of joy as she walked toward her grooms, her slender legs and bare feet exposed by the slits in her flowing white gown.

"Raine looks so beautiful," Heavenly said, her voice trembling. "She's come so far from that bloody, beaten woman I met in the ER last December."

"She has," Seth whispered, grateful for another topic to focus on. "She's a strong, resilient survivor...like you. You're not the same girl I met that day, either."

"Because you two helped me through everything," she said, giving his arm a tight squeeze while Raine and River strode past them, all smiles.

At the altar, Hammer and Liam were beaming, too. They had forged an unbreakable bond of love with Raine, cemented by the birth of their daughters. At the lodge, when he and Beck had helped the guys break through Raine's walls, Seth had wondered if this day would ever come. Now that the grooms, faces filled with unadulterated love, watched their precious girl glide toward them, their joy was evident.

Seth had never seen Liam this happy. He'd been beside his Irish friend the day he'd married Gwyneth in a somber recitation of vows, as if he'd understood he was shouldering the weight of the world with his I do's. But as River placed his sister's hands in Hammer's and Liam's and the two men settled her between them, Liam looked jubilant.

After working through their considerable issues, the trio now had a shimmering future in front of them.

"Not too late to change your mind, princess." Beck winked.

Everyone took their seats with a laugh, but neither groom looked amused. Liam glared. Hammer growled.

Raine shook her head, her voice unsteady. "It was too late a long time ago."

"Then let's get you married." Beck cleared his throat. "We're here today to witness the joining of three people we all know and admire…"

As Beck led the ceremony, Heavenly nuzzled Ciara's chubby little cheek, then peered up at him and Catronia. "You two okay there?"

His angel worried about him, and he didn't want her to. But the adoration and concern shimmering on her face made his heart skip. He loved her so goddamn much, and he had no clue what he'd done to deserve her, but he was beyond grateful. And not for anything did he want her to know that he was a wreck.

Seth pressed a kiss to her temple. "Fine."

As she watched the ceremony, Ciara in her arms, Seth stole glances at her rapt face. Heavenly would make one hell of a loving mother.

Yeah, and who's going to knock her up?

Quickly, he shuttled the question, but ignoring it didn't erase the longing in her expression. As Raine, Hammer, and Liam committed themselves to one another and their family, tears filled her eyes and rolled down her cheeks.

His angel ached for what those three had. Could he give it to her?

Seth swallowed and tried to imagine would it be like if he, Beck, and Heavenly stood where those three were right now, promising to love, support, encourage, and comfort each other for the rest of their lives. He wanted Heavenly to be theirs. He wanted to put a ring on her finger. But if he did, Beck and Heavenly wouldn't merely have hopes for the future; they would have expectations beyond love and pleasure that Seth wasn't sure he would ever be ready to fulfill.

The trio finished repeating their vows, then a playful smile tugged at Beck's lips. "What these three have worked so hard to put together, let no asshole put asunder. And now—as far as I'm concerned—you're married!"

Seth had to shake his head. He should have expected that, even at the pulpit, Beck would say something irreverent.

What Seth hadn't expected was Liam cupping Raine's chin and commanding her to kneel. Beside him, Hammer raised a demanding brow her way.

"What are they doing?" Heavenly whispered. "Why do they look so…serious?"

From his pocket, Liam pulled a thin band of braided metal with a dangling locket. Seth froze. He knew exactly what they intended.

"They're collaring Raine, too."

Something else Beck and I should discuss.

He glanced up. The doctor's subtle nod confirmed that he agreed.

"I don't know what that means, but the awe on Raine's face tells me it's something special."

"Very," he murmured as Hammer and Liam fastened the locket around her neck with a key. "Beck and I will explain soon."

They would have to teach her so much about the lifestyle before she would truly understand. That was something they could have—and should have—been doing these last few months. Seth knew he'd contributed too much to the list of reasons they hadn't.

With her collar fastened, Hammer and Liam helped Raine to her feet. She glowed not only like a bride but like a woman treasured, owned, and loved. How beautiful would Heavenly look if he and Beck made her theirs permanently? If they gave her the family her heart desired? How happy would she be?

What kind of selfish asshole are you to keep that from her?

"Kiss already," Beck demanded of the trio. "Put an exclamation

THE CONFESSION | 313

point on this marriage/collaring/handfasting shit so we can celebrate."

Another round of laughter went up that quickly morphed into cheers and applause as Hammer and Liam took turns claiming Raine's lips with poignant, passionate kisses. The three turned and each man wrapped an arm around her waist. With triumphant smiles, the grooms escorted their bride down the aisle and headed toward the door leading downstairs.

"That was beautiful." Heavenly sniffled, brushing happy tears from her cheeks. "My heart is just bursting. I'm so happy for them."

"Me, too." As everyone around them migrated to the door, Seth forced a smile and dropped a soft kiss on her lips. The wriggling infant in his arms jolted him from the soft pleasure of her mouth. A cold sweat broke out across his back. "Can I hand you—"

"Hold that thought." Beck barged in beside him. "Mmm, I'll take some sugar, little girl."

Heavenly turned and flashed him a megawatt smile, welcoming the sweep of his lips. "You were amazing up there."

"Thank you." He smiled, then darted several glances between Seth and Catronia, still tucked in his arms. "How you doing there?"

Itching, squirming, dying…

"Fine." He nodded tersely. "Great officiating—except your comedic asides. My advice? Don't quit your day job."

Beck laughed. "Hadn't planned on it. I was just trying to lighten things up. There were way too many teary eyes in the place, including Raine's. I had to do something."

Heavenly raised a guilty hand. "As one of those with teary eyes, thank you."

"You two ready to hit the reception?" Beck asked, jerking his head toward the door.

Their girl nodded. "Yes. I'm dying to see Raine's collar."

"And I need to, um"—*offload this baby*—"hit the can. Can you take her back?" Seth had Catronia halfway in Heavenly's arms before he even finished his sentence.

"Sure." She scooped up the infant, juggling her swaddled form until she comfortably handled both.

Beck arched a brow. "You want me to take her?"

"I'm good," Heavenly assured, sending Seth a worried glance.

He gave her another stilted smile.

"The can is downstairs, by the way," Beck offered, his tone a subtle admonishment.

They both knew Seth knew that.

"Yeah. I forgot."

"Sure." Skepticism laced Beck's tone. Then he gestured toward the exit with a sweep of his arm. "Shall we?"

Heavenly nodded. Seth tried not to scowl as he yanked the door open.

Together, they filed inside, each of them sliding an arm around Heavenly's waist. As they descended the stairs, happy voices and infectious laughter floated up from the dungeon, now a makeshift reception hall. At the bottom, Seth took in the crowd of people gathered around Hammer, Liam, and Raine, offering their congratulations. But what struck him most was Liam's blinding smile. The Irish prick had it all—a supportive co-partner, a beautiful wife, and two sweet daughters. Picture-perfect, at least from the outside. Inside, Seth was as terrified of those things as he was jealous.

"What do you want from the bar?" Beck asked him and Heavenly.

"A glass of white wine would be wonderful. Thank you." She smiled, gently bouncing the babies.

Booze would help take the edge off. "Macallan, neat."

"You got it." The surgeon nodded. "Be right back."

Heavenly turned a wistful stare to the newlyweds, her smile again full of longing. Hell, yearning rolled off her.

Tamping down his guilt, Seth focused on Beck laughing and talking to the people in line as other guests milled around or found a table—anything to avoid looking at Heavenly and facing the indisputable fact that he was the fucking roadblock between her and the future she craved.

"There are my baby girls." Raine rushed toward Heavenly, arms outstretched. "Come see Mommy."

Heavenly placed the twins in Raine's arms one at a time, admiring her bestie's collar. Once again, a wistful smile tugged at his girl's lips.

"They're such angels. Slept through most of the ceremony. Well, Ciara did. Catronia looked around the whole time."

"Because she's so curious." Raine gently peppered their cheeks with kisses.

"Happy, princess?" Beck asked as he handed Seth and Heavenly their drinks.

"Ecstatic." She beamed as Hammer and Liam sauntered up, still grinning like loons.

"Thanks again for officiating." Hammer stuck out his hand.

Beck shook it. "My pleasure."

"Congratulations to you all." Seth raised his glass in the air.

He couldn't remember a time he felt less like celebrating.

"Come here, you cagey prick." Liam wrapped him in a bro-hug before clapping Beck on the back. "We're here today because of you two."

"Oh, I had nothing to do with knocking up the princess. I swear," the doctor teased.

"Not that, you bloody wanker. Hammer and I would have killed you. I'm talking about you two helping us with Raine at the lodge."

Raine groaned. "We don't have to discuss that today, do we?"

"I'm lost. What happened at the lodge?" Heavenly whispered.

"Ancient history. Let's go check out the cake." Raine jerked her head toward the towering confection in the corner.

As the women and babies strolled away, Hammer leaned in and mumbled something to Beck, who nodded.

"We'll be right back," Macen said before the pair strolled toward his office.

"Any idea what they're up to?" Seth asked Liam.

"Not a clue. But I'd be happy for a few minutes alone with you, mate."

Seth tensed. Had Liam sensed his shitty mood? Felt it? He still didn't understand how his buddy's psychic shit worked. "What's up?"

"I'm just curious. Are you any closer than the last time we talked to finding your happiness?"

Seth scowled. "That's more than mere curiosity."

Liam shrugged. "You know I'm not one to beat around the bush."

In other words, was he over Autumn's and Tristan's murders? "I think about it. I'm trying."

"If you want something real and lasting, you'll have to do more than that. You have to grab hold of your loved ones tight and never let go."

I tried that once, remember? It failed spectacularly. "Thanks for the advice. I'll keep that in mind."

"You need to take a leap of faith. And you need to stop making everything between you three so bloody difficult."

"Thanks," he grated out. "Last time I looked, today is about you, Raine, and Hammer."

"It is, but you belong with Heavenly and Beck. You need to stand before an altar, bind hands, and make a lifelong commitment to each other. You won't be happy without them."

"What I need now is to hit the can." Seth turned toward the bathroom—not because he needed to pee. Because he needed to escape.

Liam gripped his arm, eyes narrowed. "You envied me during the ceremony. I felt it."

Seth jerked free and pinched the bridge of his nose. "Leave it alone, Liam."

"No. I want you as fucking happy as I am. You deserve it."

He stared back in stony silence. Why say what he was thinking aloud? Liam probably knew it anyway.

"Why are you still convinced you don't?" Liam frowned.

It was all Seth could do to hold on to his temper. "I said leave it alone."

Liam's expression said that would be a cold day in hell. "I saw you holding my wee Catronia during the ceremony."

"Heavenly's arm was going to sleep."

"If that was the only reason, why did you look as if you were wearing your heart on your face when you held her?"

Suddenly, Seth's suit felt a size too small. He tugged at his tie and felt his composure slipping. "Shut up."

"No. You know what you need to do, mate. You should start by being honest with them, because I don't think you have been. What are you waiting for, a damn anvil to fall on your head? If that's what it's going to take for you to risk your heart again, I'll drop the bugger on you myself."

Liam was using his "gift" to dissect his soul, and Seth had had enough. "I already have a headache, thanks."

"Tell me, what would you do if Beck got Heavenly pregnant? Would you love and care for the bairn as your own? Help raise and love the child? Or pretend it didn't exist?"

"What kind of question is that?" Seth bristled.

"One you need to ask yourself, if you haven't already."

"That's not a news flash. I know."

"Then get busy. Because if you're still worried about history repeating itself, think about last Christmas in New York. Remember your misery? If you give up again, you won't be merely leaving the door open for Beck to ask Heavenly on dates. This time, friend, he'll walk her down the aisle, put a ring on her finger, and claim her for himself. There won't be any more second chances. He will love her for the rest of his life and give her all the babies she wants. Can you handle not being a part of that picture? Do you want to be alone, like Pike over there?" He gestured across the room.

Against a wall, the tatted dungeon monitor stood by himself, club soda in hand. He looked lonely.

"It's not that simple," Seth growled out. "And you damn well know it."

"Bollocks. Your heart knows what it wants. It was written all over your face up on the roof. It's your fear that won't get out of the way." Liam sent him a sympathetic smile. "Believe me, I know. I had them, too. You saw what I went through with Raine. Where would I be today if I'd tucked tail and left?"

He'd be alone and miserable, just like Pike.

"You know what I'm saying." Liam clapped his shoulder. "I'm not trying to beat you over the head. I just hate to see you ache for something so fiercely yet be too afraid to go after it, like you do everything else."

"Liam?" Raine called, bustling toward them, waving a cell phone in the air. "Your parents FaceTimed to congratulate us. They want to chat."

"Thank you, love." Liam's face glowed with happiness as he took the phone and leaned into his ear. "Happiness is only as elusive as you allow it to be. Think about it."

Liam's words seared Seth's brain when the Irishman snaked an arm around his wife, smiled into the camera, and strode away.

Seth let out a tense breath. First Beck had pushed, then Liam. Hopefully, all his well-meaning friends were done climbing up his ass for the night.

He turned to find Beck, standing at the end of the hall that led to the private rooms, now heading his way.

Beck frowned. "You good? You look pissed."

He was, goddamn it. "Headache. What did Hammer want?"

"To give me the keys and security codes for the club. I'm the contact person in case anything happens while those three are on their honeymoon."

Seth frowned. "I didn't think they were taking one right away."

Beck lowered his voice. "It's a surprise for Raine. They're taking her to Paris."

"Nice."

"Hammer also asked to see you in his office."

"What for?"

"He didn't say." Beck shrugged. "Where did Heavenly go?"

"She was with Raine, but..." Seth scanned the dungeon, then pointed toward the bar. "She's over there, with Zach."

Beck nodded. "I'll go see what they're talking about."

"I'll join you two when I'm done with Hammer."

At Beck's thumbs-up, Seth wound his way through clusters of people laughing and chatting until he reached Hammer's door and tapped on it. "Everyone decent?"

"Yep. I'm not getting naked for you, pal."

Seth stepped in. "Thank god."

Hammer wore a wide smile as he rounded the desk and gave Seth a hearty slap on the back. "Thanks for popping in. I'm trying to get everything tied up before we leave."

"I heard you're honeymooning in Paris. Congrats."

He grinned and shrugged. "Raine has always wanted to go. What can you do? Happy wife, happy life."

"That sounds amazing."

"We're pretty fucking happy, I'll admit." Hammer's grin became a self-deprecating chuckle. "I need a favor."

"Anything."

"Beck agreed to be point man for the club. I was hoping you'd do the same for the house. Three of Liam's sisters will be there watching the twins, but—"

"Absolutely." Seth nodded. "Happy to."

"Thanks, man." Hammer's smile was so wide now, it threatened to split his face.

Seth had seen Macen at his best and worst, but he didn't remember ever seeing him loopy, flustered, and not in total control. Was that what happiness had done to him?

"If Caitlyn, Meg, or Aisling need anything, I'll take care of it," Seth vowed. "You focus on your time with Raine and Liam."

"I will. And I'll breathe a lot easier knowing you and Beck are looking after everything." He handed Seth a ring of keys and an envelope. "These are for the house, garage, and cabana. Raine wrote out a list of phone numbers for Liam's sisters. I think she also jotted down everyone from the pediatrician to the gardener, so…"

For the first time since he'd arrived, Seth genuinely smiled. "She's covering all the bases."

"She is," Hammer confirmed with a sanguine shrug, then frowned. "How are you doing?"

"Fine."

"No, I'm serious. You doing better?" Hammer's stare delved deeper than Seth wanted. "You know there are no secrets between Liam and me, man. He's…concerned about you."

Are you fucking kidding me? Now Hammer is going to crawl up my ass, too?

"I said I'm fine," Seth bit out.

Hammer scowled. "And I'm a Boy Scout. Listen, you helped Liam and me with Raine. Let us help you."

"Oh, Liam already tried, thanks. Anything else?"

"How about you fucking listen? I get you, man. I really do. Juliet was pregnant when she killed herself. Besides the coroner and Liam, I've told almost no one…until now."

Shock blasted at Seth's fury. He slumped down into the nearest chair. "Jesus, Hammer… How did you deal—"

"With it? I didn't. I ran away, clear across the country to escape the memories, just like you."

Seth shook his head. "I wasn't running. I came to help Liam. I moved here for Heavenly."

"And you started a new life, like me." Hammer's smile was acidic as he perched on the edge of the desk. "You told yourself you were really moving on, didn't you? Yeah, I did the same. It took a while for me to realize that changing scenery didn't do a damn thing to erase my loss. It took me even longer to figure out that you can either learn from your mistakes or let them eat you alive."

"Our situations aren't the same." Seth scrubbed a hand through his hair. "I wasn't there to protect my wife and child."

"I wasn't there to protect mine. And like you, the signs were there. I just didn't see them."

"Hammer, I don't—"

"Want to deal with it? I know. But tell me what will convince you to. Are you waiting for someone who will love you more?"

"No." Heavenly seemed to love him unconditionally, though god knew why…

"Someone who understands you better?"

"No." Beck and Heavenly understood him too damn well, some-times better than he understood himself.

"Someone you can truly be yourself around?"

"No." They accepted him—warts, flaws, and foibles—and still wanted him.

"Then what the fuck are you waiting for?"

"I don't know." *Someone to forgive me.*

Hammer shook his head. "Figure it out fast. Because I'm going to tell you, if you keep waiting, they'll move on. Raine and Liam almost did without me. If I hadn't pulled my head out of my ass, I wouldn't be celebrating today. And I wouldn't be having a son."

Seth froze. "A son?"

Somehow, Hammer's smile turned even brighter. "Yeah. Raine just told me. We probably should have waited at least six weeks, but… yeah. She's pregnant again, and Liam says it's my son."

Hammer was having a boy?

The news was a sucker punch. It left him reeling. Struggling to breathe. Bleeding.

Congratulations, Mr. Cooper. It's a boy!

The September day that had marked the birth of his son had been one of the happiest of his life. All too soon, it had become a scar on his soul.

His eyes stung. Seth swallowed. "That's great. I'm happy for you."

"You don't have to bullshit me when I can see you're struggling. I understand." Hammer cupped his shoulder.

Seth jerked away. "I told you, I'm fine."

Hammer held his stare for an uncomfortable moment, dissecting him without a word. Then he sighed. "Whatever you say. If you decide to be honest, you know where to find me."

"Macen?" River called, knocking on the door.

Seth launched from his chair and yanked it open. "What?"

River recoiled. "Whoa, boss. Just came to tell my brother-in-law that the caterers are serving dinner and my sister wants him at the head table pronto." He sent Hammer a grin. "It's another photo op, too. I know how much you love those."

Macen groaned. "Be right there. Fucking photographer…"

"Better you than me."

"You'll get your turn someday, you bastard."

River's grin turned cheesy. "But not today…"

Hammer flipped him the bird, which made River smile even more.

Then he was gone, and Macen turned the weight of his gaze back on Seth. "Anything you want to say?"

"No."

He sighed and rose. "Then let's go."

Seth couldn't get out of his office fast enough. He pocketed the keys and envelope Hammer had given him, donned a plastic smile, and rejoined the party.

Heavenly smiled when she caught sight of him and rushed over. "They're about to serve dinner."

"So I heard." He dragged a knuckle down her soft cheek because he couldn't help himself. What would he do if he couldn't touch her this way anymore? Even the thought nearly destroyed him. "Guess we'd better find a table."

"Beck already snagged one. Over there." She pointed somewhere near the happy trio.

Beck waved.

"Let's go." Seth took her hand and led her across the room, trying to shove down his anger and compartmentalize his fear. Instead, he focused on Heavenly, on her love and warmth, her vivacity and charm. By the time they reached their seats, he was almost calm.

Heavenly sat beside Beck, who was grinning and talking to Zach and Liam's sisters. Seth flanked her and half listened to the conversation about the ladies' long flight from Ireland.

"I wish Maeve could have come with us," Aisling said. "But she recently gave birth to a new bairn—"

"A boy this time," Meg exclaimed. "She couldn't bear to leave him—"

"Even for her baby brother's celebration, the silly twit." Caitlyn rolled her eyes.

Everyone else at the table spent the meal laughing and sharing stories. Seth watched for long minutes, smiling and nodding when the conversation called for it. Mostly, Liam's and Hammer's words dive-bombed his brain.

"You should have seen the look on her face when we found her at the zoo," Beck chuckled as he told them all about their elaborate version of hide-and-seek with Heavenly.

"How did you find her so quickly?" Aisling asked.

"I'm a private investigator," Seth replied. "If I couldn't find her, I wouldn't be very good at my job." Of course, the Tiffany necklace he'd given Heavenly with the embedded GPS chip helped, too.

Beck shot him a knowing smirk.

"Clearly, a bloody good one." Liam's sister looked impressed.

"He is." Heavenly smiled, toying with said necklace.

Thank god she never took it off.

"He's good at everything, isn't he, little girl?" Beck drawled.

A blush stained her cheeks. Seth fought the urge to press his lips to hers, but he would only want more. For now, he lowered his hand beneath the table and stroked her thigh, trying not to think about anything except how good she felt.

"You both are." She smiled shyly as his hand collided with Beck's under her skirt.

"Great minds." Beck smirked before taking a sip of water.

"Come on, girls," Meg prodded. "We promised Da we'd take photos. If we don't send some by morning, he'll get his knickers in a twist."

"That he will." Aisling pushed her plate away and rose, tugging her cell phone from her clutch, nodding as the others followed suit. "We'll be back."

As the sisters began happily snapping photos of the decorations and people, Zach shook his head.

"What's wrong?" Beck asked his brother. "Liam's sisters too much for you?"

"They're...talkative. They pick up where the last one leaves off. It's..."

"Exhausting?" Seth drawled.

"Just...different, like everything today."

"You mean the handfasting ceremony?" Beck asked.

"Yes, but I'm more surprised you officiated it."

"I did it for them," Beck said, nodding toward Hammer, Liam, and Raine. "They're some of my best friends. They deserve happiness."

"I gathered. It's just...I've never heard anyone curse at the pulpit before."

Heavenly covered her mouth to hide her giggle. Beck laughed, long and hard. Seth choked out an appropriate chortle. Would this night ever fucking end? He just wanted to go home, undress their girl with Beck, lose himself inside her, and stop thinking about this maudlin shit.

If you do, how will that change tomorrow?

The deejay started up a new song, a slow ballad. Beck held out his hand to Heavenly. "How about a dance?"

She took it with a smile. "That's so romantic. I'd love to."

He helped her to her feet and winked. "It also gives me a chance to rub up against you."

Her smile widened. "That works for me, too."

He led her to the middle of the floor and turned her into his arms. Seth looked on, both resentful that he wasn't holding her and grateful to have a few moments alone.

"I envy them," Zach said.

Seth tugged his attention back across the table. He'd been so focused on Beck and Heavenly, he'd forgotten the guy still sat three chairs away. "Who?"

"Liam, Raine, and Hammer." He nodded at the trio across the room, approaching their white confection of a wedding cake.

I envy them, too.

Those three had come through the worst in life and emerged stronger, more committed, and irrevocably in love.

He studied Zach, who didn't seem like a threesome kind of guy. "Because…?"

"They have family, purpose, a sense of belonging. I'd give anything to have all that again." Zach sighed.

Seth dissected his words, then nodded slowly. When he'd lost Autumn and Tristan, he'd still had his mom and four brothers to fall back on, not to mention good friends like Liam and Hammer. Who had Zach had, except the brother he hadn't seen in a decade and a half?

"After the kind of loss you've endured, it takes time to find yourself. Believe me, I know. You'll get there," Seth assured. "Hell, you might even find love again, too. At the very least, you should have more privacy for romance now that my brothers are back in New York."

"They were a lot of fun and a good distraction when I needed one. But the past few weeks have been blessedly quiet. And I've learned a few things on my own."

"Yeah?"

Zach nodded, his stare direct and disparaging. "I've figured out how to spot a fool."

Seth bristled. "Are you calling me a fool?"

"I am."

What the fuck was up with everyone tonight? This was supposed to be a happy occasion. Or had everyone gotten the *fuck up Seth's evening* memo? "You know I could kill you with one punch, right?"

"Probably," Zach conceded with a shrug. "But that wouldn't change what you are."

"Look, you and I made our peace. I apologized for the way I behaved when we first met. Why the fuck are you piling on me now?"

Zach leaned across the table. "Because you lost the people most precious and you didn't learn anything from it. In the weeks of solitude since your brothers left, I've been so lonely. Sure, I can find company for a night, but it's meaningless. I'd give *anything* to spend five minutes with someone who truly loves me. You've got two who would walk through fire for you—without question. Without blinking." He glanced at Beck and Heavenly. "Yet you sit here on the sidelines, watching, removed, because you're too afraid to embrace a future with them."

Seth gripped the table to stop himself from laying Zach out in a single punch. "Who the fuck told you that?"

"I overheard Beck and Heavenly talking after dinner last week. They want kids. You don't."

That made his blood boil. It didn't matter if it was true. "Do you always eavesdrop on people's conversations?"

"No. I'm simply a concerned brother, trying to navigate the same road you've been walking for years. I'm worried Beck will miss his chance at happiness because you're too scared to accept the unconditional love he and Heavenly are dying to give you. I want to shake you, tell you to pull yourself together and stop being afraid of losing everything again."

Seth wanted to argue Zach's observation, but he couldn't. "How about you mind your own fucking business?"

"Beck is my fucking business," Zach shot back, then shook his head. "I can't believe you told me that if I had any questions about grieving and healing, I should come to you." He scoffed. "At least I've already figured out what's important. If I ever have a chance at love and happiness again, I won't waste a second on fear."

With that, Zach rose and found his way to a couple of the only other people he knew at the party, Dean and Jericho.

Seth stood, chest heaving as he tried to bring his temper back under control. It was too fucking loud here. Too fucking happy.

He had to get out.

Before he could fish the keys of his SUV out of his pocket, slap them in Beck's hand, and call an Uber, Heavenly and the surgeon came off the dance floor, hand in hand, all smiles.

Their girl sidled up to him, wrapping her hands around his arm and her warmth around his cold heart. "You want to dance?"

Beck saved him from answering. "Hang on a second. They're cutting the cake."

And Seth would have to walk right past the celebrating trio to get out the fucking door. He was trapped in this loud, crowded room. It felt like the walls were closing in, the ceiling caving in. It was claustrophobic. He couldn't breathe. He could only watch happy people feed each other cake, share kisses, and talk about their amazing future.

He was going to lose his shit.

Thankfully, they wrapped up the festivities shortly after that. Raine tossed her bouquet. Of course Heavenly caught it, then looked at him with adoration and hope in her eyes. Then the love-drunk trio left.

That was his cue.

"Take these, man." He handed his keys to Beck. "You and Heavenly stay. I've got to get out of here. Headache."

Beck slanted him an unreadable stare. "We'll go with you."

Last fucking thing he wanted. "Stay. Have fun. I know Heavenly has been looking forward to this."

"Now that Raine is gone, I'm sure she'll be happy to leave."

"No, really. I don't want to be a buzzkill. Stay. I insist."

Beck grabbed Heavenly's hand, and together, they closed in. "So do we. Let's go."

S eth sulked in the backseat of his own fucking SUV, fuming as Beck drove them home because, according to the surgeon, he was too angry to drive.

Screw him.

They'd slipped out of the reception after Raine, Liam, and Hammer had left to start their new life together and the vanillas had begun to call it a night. It wouldn't be long before the reception hall reverted to a dungeon for the club members who wanted to play. Heavenly wasn't ready for that. He and Beck both agreed, so whisking their girl away had been the right call.

While Seth appreciated that fact, he still broiled with rage.

Goddamn Beck. He'd opened his big mouth and started this shit. Now all their friends were up his ass, questioning his decisions. They completely misunderstood him. He was in favor of marriage. In fact, he couldn't imagine life without Heavenly, and he looked forward to slipping a ring on her finger to prove it. But babies? The good doctor was just itching to force fatherhood down his throat. Seth didn't fucking appreciate it.

But the car wasn't the place to argue, and Heavenly didn't need to hear this confrontation.

It was going to be ugly.

Beside him, she sat, silent, hands folded in her lap. He hadn't expected her to slide into the back beside him as Beck pulled away from the party. Why had she?

Heavenly and Beck made eye contact in the rearview mirror. He'd bet the two of them had cooked up some new scheme to bring him around to the idea of knocking her up. That fit since Beck had seemingly convinced her she needed babies right this goddamn minute.

"Seth?" Heavenly wrapped a soft hand around his arm. Her big blue eyes asked if he was all right.

He wished she wouldn't touch him like that. He didn't want her pity. He'd ten times rather she pull up her pretty dress and offer him her pussy. He'd tucked a condom in his pocket, just in case. But that wasn't what she sought, so he braced against his racing heart and his rush of lust. "I'm fine."

In the rearview mirror, Beck flashed him a dubious scowl.

Yeah? Fuck you, too.

She leaned closer. Her tits pressed against his arm, inciting another surge of desire. Seth gritted his teeth and closed his eyes. Why was it that, no matter what he was doing or how he was feeling, he always fucking wanted her? Love. Yeah, he could pin a bunch of the blame on that. But the need—primal, feral, uncontrollable—stemmed from something else he couldn't put into words.

"Are you sure?" she asked.

He didn't want to lie to her again, so he sent her a tight smile, then focused out the window at the passing So Cal night.

Beside him, he could all but feel her concern. Her goddamn compassion wrapped around him, strangling more than comforting him.

"Talk to me, Seth," she urged softly. "You're not okay."

He swallowed back his encroaching temper. "Don't worry. Just… don't."

She pulled back, withdrawing her hand and retreating to the opposite side of the backseat. Seth cursed under his breath.

"Sorry. It's not you." He squeezed her hand, then released it. "I'm just not in a good mood."

"I can make you some fresh coffee when we get home. Or a cup of soup, if you're feeling under the weather."

Bless her for trying, but… "No, angel. I just need"—*a hard fuck*—"a good night's sleep."

She scooted closer again. The love and welcome in her eyes were a gut punch of temptation.

"If you want, I'll tuck you in." With a lingering glance, she kissed his shoulder. Even through his dress shirt, her lips seared his skin.

Seth swallowed. He shouldn't take advantage of her kindness. He shouldn't risk her thinking he intended to give her the children Beck had convinced her to crave. But he needed her too much to turn her down. "I'd love that."

Beck cleared his throat. "After you and I…chat."

Of course the bastard had something to say. He meant to protect Heavenly, and a part of Seth appreciated that. The other part wanted to tell Beck to fuck right off because the doctor wasn't anyone's daddy, least of all his.

He pulled his phone from his pocket and pretended to scan it. "On second thought, I have to go out for a while. I should check on a case."

In the mirror, the surgeon glared at him, jaw grinding, but said nothing.

The rest of the ride home was silent. Undercurrents of tension—Heavenly's worry and Beck's reproval—swirled inside the cab, mixing with his own seething fury, as if someone had turned up the heat under his temper, nearly bringing it to a boil.

Finally, Beck parked in the garage. Seth was out before the doctor even cut off the engine and darted into the house. The smart solution would be to change out of this monkey suit, grab his car keys, and fucking leave before he said or did something he'd regret. If Beck got up in his face again, Seth doubted he could be responsible for his actions, and Heavenly didn't need to see the angry side of him—ever.

As the door slammed behind him, he heard Beck on his tail. "Where the hell are you going?"

Seth didn't even glance over his shoulder. "I told you. Work."

"Wait," Heavenly called from the door. "My surprise. I want to show you before you go."

He gritted his teeth, grasping for patience. But he didn't want to crush her. None of this was her fault. He nodded. "Sure."

Her smile brightened the room and almost made him forget how fucking close his cool was to detonating. "I'll be back in five minutes. Don't go anywhere."

When he nodded, she dashed upstairs, leaving him alone with Beck. *This ought to be fun.*

Once he heard the door to their bathroom shut, Beck got in his face. "What the fuck is wrong with you?"

"You and your big mouth. Did *everyone* at that wedding need to know our problems? After you disappeared to have your little meeting with Hammer, Liam was all up in my business about the future—your favorite fucking subject. Not ten minutes later, Hammer beat the same drum. He thought he could commiserate with me because Juliet died pregnant. Then he wanted to rub my face in his happiness by telling me Raine is expecting his son." Seth snorted. "That put me in a great mood. And as if that wasn't fucking enough, your brother hopped on the *let's berate Seth* bandwagon because he overheard you and Heavenly talking about the fact I don't want to indiscriminately knock her up and add to the world's overpopulation. So how about you just shut the fuck up and let me cool off for a bit, huh?"

Beck reared back, then growled like he was ready to throw down.

Good. Bring it on.

"First of all, motherfucker, I didn't say shit to Hammer. Maybe your old pal Liam did. But I did not spew one fucking word. Second, I never meant for Zach to hear my personal conversation with Heavenly. A thousand fucking apologies. But let's be real, you don't give two shits about the world's overpopulation crisis. What pissed you off is that everyone wants you to face your problems, so you've made me the scapegoat for your fears. And that's bullshit. It's time for you to pull your head out of your ass."

"Oh, that's real fucking nice. All of you sound like, 'Hey, I know you suffered a horrific loss and that your whole fucking world fell out from under you, but would you do me a favor and get the fuck over it? Thanks,'" Seth mimicked. "Yeah, let me get right on that shit."

"Maybe you should. Everyone is only 'up in your business' because they fucking care. And what do you do? Growl and snap before you bury your head in the proverbial sand. That's not going to solve a damn thing. How long are you going to keep clutching the past in your tight fist? Long enough to let the future slide through your fingers, I guess. You're *thisclose* to happiness, man. But it's all about to get away from you because you're mourning a wife you didn't love as much as you love Heavenly. Is it guilt holding you back? I get that would be hard. It would be a mind fuck, for sure. But don't take it out on Heavenly."

"That's not the problem. Before we ever took her together, I accepted how crazy my feelings for her are. Hell, this relationship will horrify my family, but I love her enough to risk alienating my mother for the rest of my life. The problem is my job. It's not all cheating spouses and employee background checks. It can be fucking dangerous. Maybe you don't get that because you work in a sterile environment. Maybe the smell of rubbing alcohol and disinfectant has gone to your brain. But you snap your fingers in the OR and people obey. You play God. And good for you. It doesn't work like that in the real world. Bad shit happens every day. No one controls the violent chaos. I know firsthand it can be deadly to the people in my life."

"We're willing to accept that risk. So what's your next excuse? The truth is, you don't want to suffer loss again, so you've given up on happiness, on the future. Screw enjoying whatever time we could have together, whether that's five minutes or five decades." Beck marched closer, clearly on a righteous rampage. "Look, what you went through is something I'd never wish on my worst enemy. I completely understand that it gutted your life and that you feel responsible. And I'm so fucking sorry. But neither my regret nor your guilt will change a damn thing. Only you can decide to move on. But you're too busy feeling sorry for yourself to even try."

Seth's temper flared hotter. "That's bullshit! I don't—"

"Go to therapy or look for ways to manage your emotions? Oh, I know. You just keep living in the moment without any thought to either dealing with your past or working toward your future."

"You don't know what the fuck you're talking about. Therapy is useless and—"

"Is it? How do you know? Are you actually trying to process your past? Have you ever?"

"Of course." What the fuck did Beck think, that he'd simply been sitting around with his thumb up his ass? "I'm sorry I can't just snap my fingers and be all right for you."

Beck cocked his head like he was dissecting an insect pinned to a board. "Have you ever told anyone everything?"

What was he getting at? "Of course. The police know. My dad's former partner, Gene, knows. You and Heavenly know."

"But we don't, not everything. We know *how* you wound up in Silas Nichols's dirty apartment in South Bronx. But we don't know *why*. There have been holes in your story from the very beginning, and I want some fucking answers. Why were you obsessed with the cold case that put you on his path? And who did you owe favors to in order to learn his identity?"

Seth went cold. He should have guessed Beck would demand all the details, especially the dirty ones. He'd been lucky to put the son of a bitch off for the past few months.

Time was up.

Pacing, Seth scrubbed a hand down his face. He didn't want to carve open his chest and spill more truth, but the asshole would only keep dogging him. Fine. He'd unload this guilt fest. Besides, if he was going to put off having kids—probably forever—he should explain his reasons.

Swallowing, Seth paced into the kitchen, vaguely aware of Beck following. With his gut in knots, he stared out at the dark patio and the shimmering pool beyond. "The cold case I was investigating when Autumn and Tristan were killed? It was my father's murder." He sighed. "I've never told anyone that before now, not even my mother."

"Holy shit." Beck sounded shaken.

Seth didn't dare turn around and look at the surgeon. Instead, he cleared his tightening throat and went on. "The official report concluded that he was in the middle of a drug bust gone wrong. And the whispers afterward were that he was on the take. Bullshit. My dad would *never* have sold out. He lived by a code. He always did what was right. Those rumors? No. Fuck no. Half the reason I joined the force was to prove that and figure out exactly how my father died. I had to know who lured him to the scene and why. The other half was to make him proud. I managed the first, but the second... I failed in every way."

"No wonder that cold case was so personal for you." Beck dropped a hand on his shoulder. "I'm not surprised you went to such lengths to clear his name. I can't wrap my head around doing the same, but your father was a hero. Mine twisted the teachings of the Bible into a pretext for molesting little girls. But you and your dad were tight, right? I'm sure he's proud you avenged him by offing Silas."

Seth scoffed. "No, he's turning over in his grave. After I lost my wife and son and turned in my badge, I didn't just go dark, I *became* the dark. For over a year, I haunted every bar, brothel, crack den, and mob hangout. I got in bed with pimps, drug dealers, and mobsters until someone finally gave me Silas's name."

"In bed...how?"

Seth hesitated, then shrugged. Might as well puke up all the ugly shit. "I was their hitman. I killed other criminals for intel. And I slept just fine at night."

Behind him, Heavenly gasped. Seth turned to find her on the stairs, wide-eyed, looking pale and shell-shocked. She'd obviously been standing there long enough to overhear things he'd never intended to tell her, things her tender heart probably couldn't grasp...or forgive.

Fuck.

Then her "surprise" registered. The overhead light beamed down on the frilly pink confection she wore. It was so sheer he saw every inch of her body. Tiny bows held together fabric slitted open across her breasts, playing peekaboo with her tempting pink nipples. The baby doll floated around her thighs, barely concealing her pussy.

Everything about her called to him. Lust hit his system like a battering ram. He needed her to erase the darkness inside him. She would give him light again.

He charged past Beck, bumping the surgeon's shoulder, and rushed toward her. "Angel..."

"Oh, my gosh. Seth..." Her eyes softened. She opened her arms to him. "I had no idea..."

Later, he'd unpack how it was fucking possible she wasn't horrified and repelled. Even if she only gave him a pity fuck now, he needed her.

The instant he reached Heavenly, he cinched a hand in her hair and banded his arm around her waist. As his mouth crashed over hers, he surged deep, lifted her off her feet, and took her down to the stairs, hovering above her. He tore away from their kiss, panting, and tugged at the bow tied across her left breast. "I need this. I need you."

Seth didn't wait for her response. His animal urge to possess every part of her drove him. He swooped down and inhaled her nipple into his mouth, against the roof, and sucked as if his life depended on it. He circled it with his tongue. He raked it with his teeth. He tugged it until she gasped. He drank in her cries.

Jesus, she was the balm that took the edge off his pain. She was perfect. He just needed more.

Seth plucked at the other bow across her breast and drew her untended nipple onto his tongue as he encircled her hips and filled his palms with her bare, lush ass, fitting her against his near-bursting cock. Yes, as soon as he was inside her, balls deep, she would erase everything but pleasure. He would be perfect, too.

"I can feel the heat of your pussy," he muttered thickly against her nipple. "I'm going to fuck you so hard. Drown in you. Disappear inside you…"

"Wait!"

It took Seth a moment to register the fact that the hands she'd laid on his chest weren't caressing him but pushing him away.

No. He clutched her tighter, grinding against her cunt, his mouth seeking hers again.

She turned her head before he could fuse their lips together. "Seth, stop!"

Suddenly, he was hauled back by a fist in the collar of his dress shirt and spun away from Heavenly. Beck glowered in his face. He looked beyond pissed.

That made two of them.

"What the fuck are you doing? She said stop!" Beck shoved him and sent him stumbling back, then he stood protectively between him and Heavenly. "You don't get to fuck her on the goddamn stairs. You don't touch her at all until you get yourself under control."

"She's my woman, too. Get. The fuck. Out of my way."

Beck bared his teeth. "Heavenly, go upstairs. Lock the bedroom door. Don't open it until I come for you."

Seriously? "You don't fucking own her."

"I don't, but I'll protect her with everything I've got. She said no. Touch her, and I'll kill you."

Seth's laugh turned ugly. "You can try."

"Stop it!" Heavenly retied the bows across her breasts with shaking fingers and scrambled to her feet. "Both of you."

Beck shucked off his suit coat and handed it to her. "Cover up."

To hide what Seth needed to see—to possess—for his sanity? Fuck that.

She shook her head. "He's already seen it all. You both have. My nipples aren't the issue. Our lack of communication is. From the start, we've hidden the messy parts of our lives from each other. That's never ended well, but we keep making the same mistakes. We're not learning."

"I'm coming clean," Seth growled. "I'm telling you everything."

"Only because we pushed you." She slanted him a disillusioned stare. "You were the one who said, 'People can't be in relationships with partners who aren't honest. Without that, what do we really share? And why should we go on?'"

"Don't throw my words back in my face," he snarled. "We're talking about two very different things. Beck and I could help you with your problems. You—"

"Can't help with yours? How do you know? You never let us try. Instead, you kept important details about Autumn's and Tristan's deaths from us, the killings you committed to clear your dad's name, and God knows what else. You shouldered every bit of pain and convinced your-self that you failed your father, your wife, your son—heck, your whole family—like that's some unforgivable sin." She brushed past Beck and moved to take his hands. "It's not. We're all human, and sometimes we fail. All we can do is our best, learn from our mistakes, strive to do better, and lean on those who love us. You're not doing that. I'm not sure you ever will. Which means that, aside from my pussy, I'm useless to you." Tears filled her eyes. "And that breaks my heart."

The big, fat drops rolling down her face were like a knife in Seth's chest. "That's not true. You're everything to me. I love you."

"No." She shook her head, tears flowing freely. "You love using my body to escape your problems. I'm not a Band-Aid; I'm a flesh-and-blood woman." She beat her fist to her chest. "I've given you every part of me, and you keep hiding behind your pain. It's ripping me apart. I can't do it anymore."

Icy panic flooded every limb and flared down his nerve endings. He grabbed her shoulders. "I'm sorry. I won't hurt you again, I swear."

She sniffled and jerked free. "You will if I let you."

Jesus, now she was twisting the knife. "Heavenly—"

"Are you ready to truly commit to a future with us? Because I don't think you are."

"Angel, don't do this. Try to understand." He clenched his fists. "It's not that easy. It's—"

"It can be, but you keep using your past as an excuse. Be honest, you never planned on making a family with Beck and me, did you?"

He grappled for a reply. "Having kids isn't the only path to fulfillment. Aren't you happy with our lives? With us?"

Her tight smile was filled with a bitter pain, and he hated like hell that he'd put it on her face. "So that's a no to kids. You wanted the sex to numb your failures, but not the commitment. Not the future. I'm sorry, Seth. I won't sacrifice having a family because you're too scared to make one." She swiped at the tears spilling down her cheeks. "Unless you're willing to reconsider, I don't know how much more we have to say."

Then Heavenly did something Seth never thought he'd see. She turned her back on him, climbed the stairs, and slammed their bedroom door between them.

He gaped, fear and an impending sense of doom breaking his heart. "No. That can't be it. It can't."

"She only said what needed to be said," Beck pointed out. "What we've both been feeling. Hurts like a bitch, doesn't it? The truth usually does..."

"Listen, man. I just need more time."

"You've had eight years. If you were actually trying to help yourself, we'd gladly give you all you needed. But you're not. Heavenly and I have waited for months." Beck shook his head. "We're done. We're starting our future tonight. Fair warning, I'm heading upstairs to comfort her. If she wants me, I won't be gloving up, not tonight, probably not ever again."

Rage jolted Seth. He felt like his head was going to explode. "You're going to get her pregnant."

"God, I hope so. You can be a part of that, but you've got to decide if your past is more important than your future. If it is, well..." Beck shrugged. "You know the way out."

Then he turned and followed Heavenly up the stairs, never looking back.

THE END...
FOR NOW

We cordially invite you to join Beck, Heavenly, and Seth for the epic conclusion (we mean it this time!) of the Heavenly Rising saga, The Commitment!

THE COMMITMENT
The Unbroken Series: Heavenly Rising (Book 4)
by Shayla Black and Jenna Jacob
July 25, 2023
(will be available in eBook, print, and audio)

THE COMMITMENT
The Unbroken Series: Heavenly Rising (Book 4)
by Shayla Black and Jenna Jacob
COMING SOON!
(will be available in eBook, print, and audio)

If you want more of juicy, filthy, adult-soap goodness, don't miss the twists, turns, and thrilling conclusion in The Unbroken Series: Heavenly Rising saga, The Commitment.

THANK YOU

Thank you for reading The Confession! If you enjoyed it, please review and recommend it to your reader friends. That means the world to us!

If you'd like an easy way to keep up with the latest news, releases, and sales from Shayla and/or Jenna, subscribe to our newsletters for announcements about new and upcoming titles, series' previews, exclusive excerpts, teasers, random stuff about author life, and more!

Shayla's VIP Reader Newsletter or www.shaylablack.com

Jenna's Reader Newsletter or www.jennajacob.com

ABOUT SHAYLA BLACK

LET'S GET TO KNOW EACH OTHER!

Shayla Black is the *New York Times* and *USA Today* bestselling author of more than eighty contemporary, erotic, paranormal, and historical romances. Her books have sold millions of copies and been published in a dozen languages.

As an only child, Shayla occupied herself by daydreaming, much to the chagrin of her teachers. In college, she found her love for reading and started pursuing a publishing career. Though she graduated with a degree in Marketing/Advertising and embarked on a stint in corporate America, her heart was with her stories and characters, so she left her pantyhose and power suits behind.

Shayla currently lives in North Texas with her wonderfully supportive husband, her daughter, and two spoiled tabbies. In her "free" time, she enjoys reality TV, gaming, and listening to an eclectic blend of music.

TELL ME MORE ABOUT YOU.

Connect with me via the links below. You can also become one of my Facebook Book Beauties and enjoy live, interactive #WineWednesday video chats full of fun, book chatter, and more! See you soon!

Website: http://shaylablack.com
VIP Reader Newsletter: http://shayla.link/nwsltr
Shayla Store: https://www.shaylablack.com/bookstore/

Facebook Book Beauties Chat Group: http://shayla.link/FBChat

facebook.com/ShaylaBlackAuthor
instagram.com/shaylablack
tiktok.com/@shayla_black
twitter.com/ShaylaBlackAuth
bookbub.com/authors/shayla-black
pinterest.com/shaylablacksb

OTHER BOOKS BY SHAYLA BLACK

CONTEMPORARY ROMANCE

WICKED & DEVOTED

Romantic Suspense

Wicked as Sin (One-Mile & Brea, part 1)

Wicked Ever After (One-Mile & Brea, part 2)

Wicked as Lies (Zyron & Tessa, part 1)

Wicked and True (Zyron & Tessa, part 2)

Wicked as Seduction (Trees & Laila, part 1)

Wicked and Forever (Trees & Laila, part 2)

Coming Soon:

Wicked as Secrets (Matt & Madison, part 1) (April 11, 2023)

REED FAMILY RECKONING

Angsty, emotional contemporary romance

SIBLINGS

More Than Want You (Maxon & Keeley)

More Than Need You (Griff & Britta)

More Than Love You (Harlow & Noah)

BASTARDS

More Than Crave You (Evan & Nia)

More Than Tempt You (Bethany & Clint)

Coming Soon:

More Than Desire You (Xavian & Corinne) (November 1, 2022)

FRIENDS

More Than Dare You (Trace & Masey)

More Than Hate You (Sebastian & Sloan)

1001 DARK NIGHTS

More Than Pleasure You (Stephen & Skye)

More Than Protect You (Tanner & Amanda)

More Than Possess You (A Hope Series crossover) (Echo & Hayes)

FORBIDDEN CONFESSIONS (Sexy Shorts)

Sexy Bedtime Stories

FIRST TIME

Seducing the Innocent (Kayla & Oliver)

Seducing the Bride (Perrie & Hayden)

Seducing the Stranger (Calla & Quint)

Seducing the Enemy (Whitney & Jett)

PROTECTORS

Seduced by the Bodyguard (Sophie & Rand)

Seduced by the Spy (Vanessa & Rush)

Seduced by the Assassin (Havana & Ransom)

Seduced by the Mafia Boss (Kristi & Ridge)

FILTHY RICH BOSSES

Tempted by the Billionaire (Savannah & Chad)

Coming Soon:

Tempted by the Executives (January 24, 2023)

THE WICKED LOVERS (Complete Series)

Steamy Romantic Suspense

Wicked Ties (Morgan & Jack)

Decadent (Kimber & Deke)

Delicious (Alyssa & Luc)

Surrender to Me (Kata & Hunter)

Belong to Me (Tara & Logan)

Wicked to Love (Emberlin & Brandon)

Mine to Hold (Delaney & Tyler)

Wicked All the Way (Carlotta & Caleb)

Ours to Love (London, Javier, & Xander)

Wicked All Night (Rachel & Decker)

Forever Wicked (Gia & Jason)

Theirs to Cherish (Callie, Thorpe, & Sean)

His to Take (Bailey & Joaquin)

Pure Wicked (Bristol & Jesse)

Wicked for You (Mystery & Axel)

Falling in Deeper (Lily & Stone

Dirty Wicked (Sasha & Nick)

A Very Wicked Christmas (Morgan & Jack)

Holding on Tighter (Jolie & Heath)

Devoted to Wicked (A Devoted Lovers crossover) (Karis & Cage)

THE DEVOTED LOVERS (COMPLETE SERIES)
Steamy Romantic Suspense

Devoted to Pleasure (Shealyn & Cutter)

Devoted to Wicked (A Wicked Lovers crossover) (Karis & Cage)

Devoted to Love (Magnolia & Josiah)

THE UNBROKEN SERIES
(co-authored with Jenna Jacob)
Raine Falling Saga (COMPLETE)

The Broken (Prequel)

The Betrayal

The Break

The Brink

The Bond

Heavenly Rising Saga

The Choice

The Chase

The Confession

Coming Soon:

The Commitment (July 25, 2023)

THE PERFECT GENTLEMEN (Complete Series)

(co-authored with Lexi Blake)

Steamy Romantic Suspense

Scandal Never Sleeps

Seduction in Session

Big Easy Temptation

Smoke and Sin

At the Pleasure of the President

MASTERS OF MÉNAGE (Complete Series)

(co-authored with Lexi Blake)

Steamy Contemporary Romance

Their Virgin Captive

Their Virgin's Secret

Their Virgin Concubine

Their Virgin Princess

Their Virgin Hostage

Their Virgin Secretary

Their Virgin Mistress

STANDALONE TITLES

Naughty Little Secret

Watch Me

Dirty & Dangerous

Her Fantasy Men

A Perfect Match

THE HOPE SERIES (Complete Series)

Steamy Contemporary Romance

Misadventures of a Backup Bride (Ella & Carson)

Misadventures with My Ex (Eryn & West)

More Than Possess You (Echo & Hayes) (A Reed Family Reckoning crossover)

SEXY CAPERS (Complete Series)

Bound and Determined (Kerry & Rafael)

Strip Search (Nicola & Mark)

Arresting Desire (Lucia & Jon)

HISTORICAL ROMANCE
STANDALONES

The Lady and the Dragon

One Wicked Night

STRICTLY SERIES (Complete Duet)

Victorian Historical Romance

Strictly Seduction (Madeline & Brock)

Strictly Forbidden (Kira & Gavin)

BROTHERS IN ARMS (Complete Trilogy)

Medieval Historical Romance

His Lady Bride (Gwenyth & Aric)

His Stolen Bride (Averyl & Drake)

His Rebel Bride (Maeve & Kieran)

BOXSETS/COLLECTIONS

Wicked and Worshipped (One-Mile and Brea duet)

Wicked and Forbidden (Zyron and Tessa duet)

More Than Promises (Reed Family Reckoning: Siblings)

Forbidden Confessions: First Time

Forbidden Confessions: Protectors

First Glance (A trio of series starters)

Unbroken: Raine Falling Complete Series

Unbroken: Raine Falling, Volume One

Unbroken: Raine Falling, Volume Two

The Strictly Duet (Victorian historical romance)

ABOUT JENNA JACOB

USA Today Bestselling author Jenna Jacob paints a canvas of passion, romance, and humor as her alpha men and the feisty women who love them unravel their souls, heal their scars, and find a happy-ever-after kind of love. Heart-tugging, captivating, and steamy, her words will leave you breathless and craving more.

A mom of four grown children, Jenna, her husband Sean and their furry babies reside in Kansas. Though she spent over thirty years in accounting, Jenna isn't your typical bean counter. She's brassy, sassy, and loves to laugh, but is humbly thrilled to be living her dream as a full-time author. When she's not slamming coffee while pounding out emotional stories, you can find her reading, listening to music, cooking, camping, or enjoying the open road on the back of a Harley.

CONTACT JENNA:

Website: www.jennajacob.com
E Mail: jenna@jennajacob.com
Facebook Page: https://www.facebook.com/authorjennajacob
Jenna's Jezebels Party Page: https://www.facebook.com/groups/jennajacobsjezebels
Instagram: https://www.instagram.com/jenna_jacob_author/
TikTok: https://vm.tiktok.com/ZMR8v5QWA/
BookBub: https://www.bookbub.com/authors/jenna-jacob
Amazon Author page: http://amzn.to/2Bmp0wP
Newsletter: http://bit.ly/JennaJacobNewsletter
Goodreads: http://bit.ly/2lZagNE

OTHER BOOKS BY JENNA JACOB

BAD BOYS OF ROCK (COMPLETE SERIES)

Rock Me (Prequel)

Rock Me Longer

Rock Me Harder

Rock Me Slower

Rock Me Faster

Rock Me Deeper

COWBOYS OF HAVEN

The Cowboy's Second Chance at Love

The Cowboy's Thirty-Day Fling

The Cowboy's Cougar

The Cowboy's Surprise Vegas Baby

THE BRIDES OF HAVEN

The Cowboy's Baby Bargain

The Cowboy's Virgin Baby Momma

Coming Soon:

The Cowboy's Million Dollar Baby Bride (January 24, 2023)

THE DOMS OF GENESIS

Embracing My Submission

Masters of My Desire

Master of My Mind

Saving My Submission

Seduced By My Doms

Lured By My Master

Sin City Submission

Bound To My Surrender

Resisting My Submission

Craving His Command

Seeking My Destiny

Tempting My Billionaire Daddy

PASSIONATE HEARTS

Small Town Second Chance

STANDALONE TITLES

Innocence Uncaged

UNBROKEN: RAINE FALLING

(Co-authored with Shayla Black)

The Broken (Prequel)

The Betrayal

The Break

The Brink

The Bond

UNBROKEN: HEAVENLY RISING

(Co-authored with Shayla Black)

The Choice

The Chase

The Confession

Coming Soon:

The Commitment (July 25, 2023)

BOXSETS/COLLECTIONS

Bad Boys of Rock Boxset

Unbroken: Raine Falling Complete Series

Unbroken: Raine Falling Volume One

Unbroken: Raine Falling Volume Two

Printed in Great Britain
by Amazon

83889707R10203